HE   ES

THE NEXT BEST THING

Kristan Higgins

CHIVERS

British Library Cataloguing in Publication Data available

This Large Print edition published by AudioGO Ltd, Bath, 2012.
Published by arrangement with Harlequin Enterprises Ltd

U.K. Hardcover   ISBN   978 1 4458 3033 9
U.K. Softcover   ISBN   978 1 4458 3034 6

Printed and bound in Great Britain by
MPG Books Group Limited

This book is dedicated—finally!—
to my patient, funny, generous
and lovely mother,
Noël Kristan Higgins. Thank you, Mom,
for everything. I love you so.

ACKNOWLEDGMENTS

To Maria Carvainis, my dear friend and agent—humble and profound. Thanks for all you do for me.

At HQN Books, many thanks to the brilliant Keyren Gerlach, whose insightful comments and belief in this book helped it shine, and to Tracy Farrell and the rest of the wonderfully encouraging team for their faith and support.

Thanks to my oldest and very dear friend, Catherine Arendt, and her family, who advised me on the vocabulary of Rhode Island. Stuffies, bubbla, no sir! The coffee milk's on me next time.

Mark Rosenberg, Marc Gadoury and Kate Corridan of the Apple Barrel at Lyman Orchards in Middlefield, Connecticut, are responsible for the best baked goods in New England. Thanks to them for letting me watch, ask questions and generally get in the way as they baked the morning bread and goodies for the lucky patrons of Lyman's.

I am grateful to Cassy Pickard for cheerfully supplying me with Italian curses, as well as for reading the first draft, and to Toni Andrews, who knows more about plotting than just about anyone. My friends at CTRWA have been wonderfully supportive and enthusiastic about this project, and I'm very lucky to have them as a sounding board.

Last on this list but first in my heart, thanks to the three loves of my life—my wonderful husband and the two best kids in the world.

CHAPTER ONE

'You have a whisker.'

Though I hear the loudly whispered comment, it doesn't quite register, as I am rapt with adoration, staring at the wonder that is my hour-old niece. Her face still glows red from the effort of being born, her dark blue eyes are as wide and calm as a tortoise's. I probably shouldn't tell my sister that her baby reminds me of a reptile. Well. The baby is astonishingly beautiful. Miraculous.

'She's amazing,' I murmur. Corinne beams, then shifts the baby the slightest bit away from me. 'Can I hold her, Cory?' My two aunts mutter darkly—only Mom has held the baby so far, and clearly, I'm breaking rank.

My sister hesitates. 'Um . . . well . . .'

'Let her, Cory,' Chris encourages, and my sister reluctantly hands over the little bundle.

She's warm and precious, and my eyes fill with tears. 'Hi there,' I whisper. 'I'm your auntie.' I can't believe how much I love this baby . . . she's fifty-five minutes old, and I'm ready to throw myself in front of a bus for her, should the need arise.

'Pssst. Lucy.' It's Iris's voice again. 'Lucy. You have a whisker.' My seventy-six-year-old aunt taps her upper lip. 'Right there. Plus, you're holding her wrong. Give her to me.'

'Oh, gee, I don't know about that,' Corinne protests, but Iris deftly takes the baby from me. My arms feel lonely without the sweet weight of my niece. 'Whisker,' Iris says, jerking her chin at me.

Almost against my will, my finger goes to my upper lip . . . gah! Something thick and almost sharp, like a piece of barbed wire, is embedded in my skin. A whisker! Iris is right. I have a whisker.

My tiny aunt Rose sidles up to me. 'Let's take a look here,' she says in her little-girl voice, studying my lip. Then, before I know it, she seizes the offending hair and yanks.

'Youch! Rose! That hurt!' I press a finger against the now smarting hair follicle.

'Don't worry, honey, I got it. You must be coming into the Change.' She gives me a conspiratorial smile, then holds my whisker up to the light.

'I'm thirty years old, Rose,' I protest weakly. 'And come on, stop looking at it.' I brush the whisker from her fingers. The whisker was a fluke. I'm not menopausal. I can't be. Could I? Granted, I'm feeling a bit . . . mature today, given that my younger sister has had a baby before I did . . .

Rose scrutinizes my face for another hair. 'It can happen. Your second cousin Ilona was thirty-five. I don't think you're too young. A mustache is usually the first sign.'

'Electrolysis,' my mother recommends as

she tucks the blankets around Corinne's feet. 'Grinelda does it. I'll have her look at you next time she comes in for a reading.'

'Your psychic also does electrolysis?' Christopher asks.

'She's a medium. And yes, Grinelda is a very talented woman,' Iris says, smiling down at Emma.

'Don't I get a turn to hold that child? I seem to remember I'm also her great-aunt,' Rose peeps. 'And personally, I bleach. Once I shaved, and three days later, I looked like Uncle Zoltan after a bender.' She accepts my niece from Iris and her wrinkled, sweet face morphs into a smile.

'Oh, shaving. Never shave, Lucy,' Iris says. 'You get stubbly.'

'Um . . . okay,' I say, shooting a glance at my sister. Surely this is not normal conversation in a labor and delivery room. 'So how are you feeling now, Corinne?'

'I'm wonderful,' she says. 'Can I please hold my daughter again?'

'I just got her!' Rose protests.

'Hand her over,' Christopher orders. With a martyred sigh, Rose obeys.

My sister gazes down at the baby, then looks up at her husband. 'Do you think we should put some Purell on her?' she asks, her brow wrinkling in worry.

'Nah,' Chris answers. 'You girls scrubbed in, right?'

3

'Absolutely. Don't want Emma to catch the polio,' Iris says, not a trace of sarcasm in her voice. I suppress a smile.

'Chris, honey, how are *you* feeling, sweetie?' Corinne asks her husband.

'A lot better than you, honey. I didn't just give birth, after all.'

Corinne waves away his protest. 'Lucy, he was so wonderful. Really. You should've seen him! So calm, so helpful. He was amazing.'

'I didn't do a thing, Lucy,' my brother-in-law assures me. He reaches out to touch the baby's cheek. 'Your sister . . . she's incredible.' The new parents gaze at each other with sappy adoration, and I feel the familiar, wistful lump in my throat.

Jimmy and I might've looked at each other like that.

'Hello! I'm Tania, your lactation coach!' A booming voice makes us all jump. 'Well, well! Quite a turnout, I see! Do you want an audience, Mother?'

'Corinne, we'll go,' I say, though it's quite possible that my mother and aunts would like to stay and offer a running commentary. 'We'll see you later. I'm so proud of you.' I kiss my sister, touch the baby's cheek once more and try not to notice as Corinne wipes her baby's face. 'Bye, Emma,' I whisper, my eyes filling yet again. 'I love you, honey.' My niece. I have a niece! Visions of tea parties and jump rope fill my head.

My sister smiles at me. 'See you later, Lucy. Love you.' She risks a pat to my arm with one hand, already instinctively adept at handling the baby.

'Let's take a look at those nipples,' Tania the lactation coach barks. 'Husband, take the baby, won't you? I need to see your wife's breasts.'

Like a well-trained border collie, I herd Mom, Rose and Iris out of the room. In the hallway, I notice something. My mother, aunts and I all seem to be wearing black today. My step falters. Mom is clad in a chic black wraparound sweater, something that wouldn't look out of place on Audrey Hepburn; Iris wears a shapeless black turtleneck and Rose a black cardigan over a white shirt. My T-shirt of the day happens to be black—I get up at 4:00 a.m. and don't spend a lot of time on clothing choices . . . this one just happened to be on the top of the pile.

By an ironic and unfortunate twist of fate, my mother, Iris and Rose bear the maiden name Black, translated from Fekete when my grandfather immigrated from Hungary. By an even more ironic and unfortunate twist of fate, all three were widowed before the age of fifty, so it's only natural that they're called the Black Widows. And on this happiest of days, somehow we're all wearing black. It dawns on me that today I, also widowed young, am more like a Black Widow than like my radiant sister.

5

That today I found my first whisker and was advised on facial hair management.

That I'm a long way off from having a baby of my own, a thought that's been on my mind more and more recently. It's been five years since Jimmy died, after all. Five and a half. Five years, four months, two weeks and three days, to be precise.

These thoughts override the chatter of my aunts and mother as we drive over the short bridge to Mackerly, back to the bakery where the four of us work.

'We're going to the cemetery,' Mom announces as they pile out of the car, first Iris, then Rose, then my mother. 'I have to tell your father about the baby.'

'Okay,' I say, forcing a smile. 'See you in a while, then.'

'You sure you don't want to come?' Rose asks. All three of them tilt their heads looking at me.

'Oh, gosh, I don't think so.'

'You know she's got a thing about that,' Mom says patiently. 'Let's go. See you later, hon.'

'Yup. Have fun.' They will, I know. I watch as they walk down the street toward the cemetery where their husbands—and mine—are buried.

The sun shines, the birds sing, my niece is healthy. It's a happy, happy day, whisker or no whisker. Widowed or not. 'A happy day,' I say aloud, heading inside.

The warm, timeless smell of Bunny's Hungarian Bakery wraps around me like a security blanket, sugar and yeast and steam, and I inhale deeply. Jorge is cleaning up in back. He looks up as I come in. 'She's gorgeous,' I say. He nods, smiles, then goes back to scraping dough from the counters.

Jorge doesn't speak. He's worked at Bunny's for years. Somewhere between fifty and seventy, bald, with beautiful light brown skin and a tattoo on his arm depicting Jesus' agony on the cross, Jorge helps with cleanup and bread delivery, as Bunny's supplies bread—*my* bread, the best bread in the state—to several Rhode Island restaurants.

'I'll deliver to Gianni's tonight, Jorge,' I say as he starts loading up the bread. He nods, heads for the back door and stands for a second, his way of saying goodbye. 'Have a great afternoon,' I say. He smiles, flashing his gold tooth, then leaves.

The freezer hums, the malfunctioning fluorescent light over the work area buzzes, the cooling ovens tick. Otherwise, there's just the sound of my own breathing.

Bunny's has been in my family for fifty-seven years. Founded by my grandmother just after my grandfather died at the age of forty-eight, it has been run by women ever since. Men don't tend to fare that well in my family, as you might have noticed. After my own

7

father died when I was eight, Mom started working at Bunny's, too, alongside Iris and Rose. And after Jimmy's car accident, I came on board as well.

I love the bakery, and the bread I create is proof of a beneficent God, but it's fair to say that if circumstances were different, I wouldn't work here. Bread, while deeply rewarding, is not my true passion. I was trained to be a pastry chef at the great Johnson & Wales Culinary Institute in Providence, just about a half hour from Mackerly, a tiny island south of Newport. Upon graduation, I snagged a job at one of the posher hotels in the area. But after Jimmy died, I couldn't keep it up. The pressure, the noise, the hours . . . the people. And so I joined the Black Widows at Bunny's. Unfortunately for me, the division of labor had been decided years ago—Rose on cakes and cookies, Iris on danishes and doughnuts, Mom on management. That left bread.

Bread-baking is a Zenlike art, not fully grasped by much of the world, and an art that I've come to love. I arrive at four-thirty each day to mix the dough, measure it out, let it rise and get it in the oven, head home for a nap around ten, then return in the afternoon to bake the loaves we supply to the restaurants. Most days, I'm home by four. It's a schedule suited to the erratic sleep patterns that came home to roost when my husband died.

I find that I'm feeling for another whisker.

If there was one, after all, there might be others. Nope. I seem to be smooth, but I check the mirror in the bathroom just in case. No more whiskers, thank God. I look normal enough . . . strawberry-blond hair pulled into a ponytail, light brown eyes—whiskey eyes, Jimmy used to call them—a few freckles. It's a friendly face. I think I'd make someone a very cute mom.

I've always wanted a family, a few kids. Despite one errant whisker, most of the evidence still indicates that I'm still young. Or not. What if Aunt Rose is right, and menopause is lurking in the shadows, waiting to pounce? One whisker today—a few months from now, I may need to start shaving. My voice may change. I'll dry up like a loaf of bread left to rise too long in a warm oven; that which was once light and full of promise, left alone too long, now a hard, tasteless lump. That whisker was a warning. Crikey! A whisker!

I risk a quick squeeze to my breasts. Phew. The girls seem to be in good shape, no drooping or sagging yet. I'm still young. Fairly ripe. But yes, perhaps my shelf life isn't as long as I like to pretend it is. Dang whisker.

Jimmy would want me to move on, to be happy. Of course he would. 'What do you think, Jimmy?' I say out loud, my voice echoing off the industrial-size Hobart mixer, the walk-in oven. 'I think it's time for me to start dating. Okay with you, honey?'

I wait for an answer. Since his death, there have been signs. At least I think so. In the first year or so after his death, dimes would turn up in odd places, for example. Sometimes I'd catch a whiff of his smell—garlic, red wine and rosemary . . . he was head chef at Gianni's, the restaurant owned by his parents. Once in a while, I dream about him. But today, on the issue of my love life, there's nothing.

The back door opens, and my aunts and mom come in. 'The cemetery was beautiful!' Iris announces. 'Beautiful! Although if I catch those mowers cutting it so close to my Pete's grave, I will strangle them with my bare hands.'

'I know it. I told the committee the same thing,' Rose cheeps. 'Last year, they mowed right over the geraniums I planted for Larry. I thought I'd cry!'

'You did cry,' Iris reminds her.

Mom comes over to me in a cloud of Chanel No. 5. 'That baby sure is beautiful, isn't she?' she says, smiling.

I grin up at her. 'She sure is. Congratulations, Grammy.'

'Mmm. Grammy. I like the sound of that,' she says smugly.

Iris nods in agreement—she's already a grandmother, courtesy of the two kids her son, Neddy, and his ex-wife produced. Rose, meanwhile, pouts.

'It's not fair,' she says. 'You're so much younger, Daisy. I should've been a grandmother first.' Rose and Iris are well into their seventies; my mother is sixty-five, and Rose's only son has failed to reproduce (which is probably a good thing, given Stevie's propensity for stupid acts).

'Oh, Stevie will get some girl pregnant, don't worry,' my mom says mildly. 'I wonder, though, if he manages to find someone who'd marry him, if she'd die young, too.' Then, aware perhaps that this is a sensitive subject, the Black Widows turn as one to look at me.

You see, in my generation, the Black Widow curse has only struck me (so far). My sister lives in constant fear that Chris will die young, but so far, so good. Iris's daughter, Anne, is gay, and for some reason, the Black Widows are confident that Laura, Anne's partner of fifteen years, will be spared due to sexual orientation. Neddy's ex-wife is also deemed safe. Both Ned and Stevie are healthy, though Stevie's on the dim side (he once ate poison ivy on a dare. When he was twenty-two). The biological men in our family are spared . . . it's just the husbands who seem to meet an early death. My grandfather, my great-uncles, my own dad, my aunts' husbands . . . all died young.

Also, no Black Widow has ever remarried. The late husbands became saints, the wives

11

became proud widows. The idea of finding another man is traditionally scoffed at, as in, 'Bah! What do I need a man for? I already had my Larry/Pete/Robbie. He was the Love of My Life.'

Back before I was a widow, I thought that maybe the Black Widows almost *liked* being alone. That they were independent women, proud of how they'd coped. Maybe their disdain of remarrying was more a statement about their own security, independence, power, even. When I became a widow myself, I understood. It's fairly impossible to imagine falling in love again when your husband's life ends decades before you expect it.

The back door opens again. 'Friday night happy hour has arrived!' calls a familiar voice.

'Ethan!' the Black Widows chorus, flattered and feigning surprise over his arrival.

'I hear from my sources that it's a girl,' he says. 'Congratulations, ladies.'

Ethan Mirabelli, my late husband's younger brother, comes in through the back door, an insulated bag in hand. He kisses each Black Widow, with an extra-long hug and some murmured words for my mother, who beams and pats him on the cheek. Then Ethan glances at me. 'Hey, Luce. Congratulations on being an auntie again.'

'Thanks, Ethan,' I answer, smiling. 'I guess it's not quite a cousin for Nicky, but close enough, right?' Nicky is Ethan's son. Then I

12

wince, realizing I may have just hit a sore spot. Nicky's cousins would have to have been Jimmy's kids . . . Jimmy's and mine.

'Absolutely,' he answers, letting me off the hook.

'And how is Nicky?' asks Aunt Iris.

'He's handsome, brilliant and has a way with the ladies. The apple doesn't fall far from the tree.' Nicky is four, but everything Ethan says is true. My brother-in-law smiles at me, then unpacks his bag, something he found God knows where—a minibar, complete with martini shaker, small knife, shot glass and a few bottles of alcohol. 'I thought French martinis today, girls,' he says, pouring the vodka. 'They're pink, in honor of the baby. I can only hope she's as gorgeous as the rest of the Black women.'

As expected, the Black Widows coo and giggle in response. Ethan has them wrapped around his little finger.

'Is it too early for drinking?' Rose asks in her sweet voice, glancing at the clock and holding out her glass. Four-thirty. No earlier than any Friday.

'You don't have to have one,' Ethan says, just as he's about to pour the martini into her glass.

'Don't be fresh,' Rose says, swatting his hand. 'Fill 'er up.' He grins and obeys. 'Ethan,' Rose continues, 'what I want to know is, how could you get that nice girl pregnant?'

13

Ethan lifts an eyebrow in his trademark bad-boy look. 'Want to step into the office? I'll be happy to show you.'

Aunt Rose whoops with mock horror and sincere appreciation. 'What I mean is, why didn't you marry her? That nice Parker?' Like they haven't heard this a million times.

Ethan winks at me. 'I asked, if you remember. She wouldn't have me. She knew I was secretly in love with the Black Widows and my heart would never be hers.' He turns to me. 'Here you go, Lucy.'

'Thanks, Eth,' I say.

Friday afternoon cocktail hour is a tradition here at the bakery. Ethan, who travels throughout the country for his work, comes home to Mackerly each weekend to see his son . . . and to check on me, I admit. Since Jimmy died, Ethan's been very loyal. A great friend. But he starts most weekends off by coming to the bakery for happy hour and flirting with my mother and aunts, and they think he pretty much walks on water.

'So how's the baby?' Ethan asks the Black Widows, then sits back and grins as they regale him with her loveliness.

I take a token sip from my glass, listening and smiling. Though they've all been widows most of their lives, the Black Widows are more full of life than most people I know.

Then I glance at my watch and set my drink aside. 'I have to make the bread run to

Gianni's, guys. Ethan, want to come?'

'Hell, no,' he answers with great cheer. 'Why on earth would I visit my parents when I can drink with these Hungarian beauties instead?'

More tuts, more feigned disapproval at Ethan's casual dismissal of his parents, more deep appreciation and secret consent from the Black Widows.

'Does being a gigolo pay well?' I ask.

Ethan laughs. 'Maybe I'll see you later, Luce.' We both live in the Boatworks, an old sailboat factory turned condominiums.

I go in the back and load up the bread for Gianni's delivery. Much of it is still warm. My breathing slows, my movements gentle and efficient with practice as I bag each loaf, setting it in the large bakery box. The scent of fresh bread is what heaven must smell like, comforting and homey. When the box is full, I heft it up, push open the back door and head outside to the street and bright sunshine.

To my consternation, Starbucks, which is located just around the corner from Bunny's, is full, even at this hour. Bunny's could use some of those customers, I think. For years, I've been urging the Black Widows, each of whom owns thirty percent of the bakery, to shift our emphasis from bakery to café. Of course, that would mean changing, and the Black Widows don't like change. I own ten percent of the bakery, so I could never outvote

15

them. I can't even filibuster.

Around the corner from Starbucks is Gianni's Ristorante Italiano, owned by Gianni and Marie, my in-laws. 'Lucy!' they cry in delight as I struggle through the back door.

'Hi, Marie, hi, Gianni,' I say, stopping to receive my kisses. Paolo, the sous chef and a vague relation from Rome, takes the loaves from me, as Micki, a prep chef, calls out a hello as she chops garlic and parsley. Kelly, a longtime waitress who went to school with me, waves as she talks on the phone.

'How are you? The baby? Everyone healthy, please God?' Marie asks. I'd called them before going to the hospital—we're very close.

'She's so beautiful,' I tell them, beaming. 'My sister was a champ, too. Seventeen hours.'

'Any tearing?' Marie asks, causing Gianni to wince.

'Um, we didn't cover that just yet,' I murmur.

'We'll send some food,' Gianni says. 'A new baby's such a blessing.'

For a second, we fall silent. My eyes go to the shrine above the twelve-burner stove. Two candles, the red bandana Jimmy always wore while cooking and a photo of him taken on our wedding day. His broad, genial face grins at me, those amazing eyes sparkling. He favored the northern Italian side of the family . . . . curly, dirty blond hair, eyes like the

16

Mediterranean Sea and a smile that could power a small town. A big man, broad-shouldered and tall with a booming laugh, he made me feel protected and safe and utterly, completely loved.

Dang it. My eyes seem to be filling with tears. Well. The Mirabellis don't mind. Marie strokes my arm, her dark eyes filling, too, and Gianni pats my shoulder with a beefy hand.

'Is Ethan coming home this weekend, do you know?' Marie asks me, wiping her eyes.

I hesitate. 'Um, I think so.' Knowing their son was down the street with my family would only hurt them.

'That job of his,' Gianni mutters. 'Foolishness. Ah!' He flaps his hands in disgust while I suppress a grin.

Though Ethan once studied to be a chef at the same school I myself attended, he dropped out just before his senior year to work for a large food corporation. A company most famous for making *Instead*, a hugely popular drink that contains all the nutrition of a well-balanced meal without the inconvenience of actually having to eat. I think my in-laws would've preferred it if Ethan had become a drug dealer or porn star, frankly. After all, his company's mission is basically to discourage sit-down dining, and they own a restaurant.

My eyes go back to Jimmy's picture. Now is not the time to tell the Mirabellis about my

17

decision to get back on the horse. It can wait. Why ruin their weekend? Because while they wouldn't begrudge me the comfort of husband and children, I know it won't be easy to hear. Besides, I have some housekeeping to take care of first.

Around nine that night, I'm playing a lively game of Scrabble with my computer, seventeen pounds of purring pet on my lap— my cat, Fat Mikey. A knock sounds on the door. 'Come on in,' I call, knowing who it is.

'Hey, Lucy,' Ethan says, opening the door. I rarely bother locking up—the building has a coded security system in the lobby, and Mackerly's crime rate is practically nonexistent.

'Hi, Eth. How's it going?' I tear myself away from the computer . . . I was just about to play *zenith*, which would totally slay Maven, my archenemy computer foe, but humans come first. Or they should. I play the word discreetly, then close the lid of my computer. Take that, Maven!

'Everything's great.' Ethan, who has logged many hours in my apartment over the past five years, makes himself at home by opening the fridge. 'Can I have one of these?' he calls.

I swallow. 'Sure. I made them for you.' Earlier in the evening, I did what I often do— created a fabulous dessert. Inside the fridge are six ramekins of pineapple mango mousse, each one topped with a raspberry glaze. I

18

figured Ethan will eat at least three, and I need to be on his good side.

'You want one?' he calls. I can tell he's already eating.

'No, thanks. They're all yours.' I don't eat my own desserts. Haven't in years.

'This is fantastic,' he says, coming into the living room.

'Glad you like it,' I say, not meeting his eyes.

'Hey, thanks for e-mailing those pictures of Nick,' he says, already scraping the ramekin clean.

'Oh, you're welcome. He sure looked cute.' Ethan and I grin at each other in a moment of mutual Nick adoration. On Wednesday, the nursery school put on a play about the life cycle of the butterfly. Nicky was a milkweed seed. It's become my habit to photograph Nicky and e-mail pictures to Ethan while he's traveling, since Parker, Nick's mother, never seems to remember her camera.

'Um, listen, Ethan, we need to talk,' I say, cringing a little.

'Sure. Let me grab another one of these. They're incredible.' He goes back into the kitchen, and I hear the fridge open again. 'Actually I have something to tell you, too.' He returns to the living room 'But ladies first.' Sitting in the easy chair, he smiles at me.

Ethan looks nothing like his brother, which is both a comfort and a sorrow. Unlike Jimmy,

19

Ethan is a bit . . . well, average. Nice-looking, but kind of unremarkable. Medium brown eyes, somewhat disheveled brown hair, average height, average weight. Kind of a vanilla type of guy. He has a neat little beard, the kind so many baseball players favor— three days of stubble, basically, which gives him an attractive edginess, but he's . . . well, he's Ethan. He looks a bit like an elf in some ways—not the squeaky North Pole elves, but like a cool elf, a Tolkien elf, mischievous eyebrows and sly grin.

He regards me patiently. I swallow. Swallow again. It's a nervous habit of mine. Fat Mikey jumps into Ethan's lap and head butts him until Ethan obliges the bossy animal by scratching his chin. Ethan rescued him from the pound a few years back, saying no one would take the ugly beast, and gave him to me. Fat Mikey has never forgotten just who sprung him from prison, and now favors Ethan with a rusty purr.

I clear my throat. 'Well, listen. You know, ever since Jimmy died, you've been, just . . . well. Incredible. Such a good friend, Ethan.' It's true. I don't have the words to voice my gratitude.

His mouth pulls up on one side. 'Well. You've been great, too.'

I force a smile. 'Right. Um . . . well, here's the thing, Ethan. You know that Corinne had a baby, of course. And it got me thinking that,

20

well . . .' I clear my throat. 'Well, I'd like to have a baby, too.' Gah! This isn't coming out the way I want it to.

His right eyebrow raises. 'Really.'

'Yeah. I've always wanted kids. You know. So, um . . .' Why am I so nervous? It's just Ethan. He'll understand. 'So I guess I'm ready to . . . start dating. I want to get married again. Have a family.'

Ethan leans forward, causing Fat Mikey to jump off his lap. 'I see,' he says.

I look at the floor for a second. 'Right.' Risking a peek at Ethan, I add, 'So we should probably stop sleeping together.'

CHAPTER TWO

Ethan blinks. His expression doesn't change. 'Okay,' he says after a beat.

I open my mouth to brook his argument, then realize he hasn't made one. 'Okay. Great,' I mumble.

Ethan sits back and looks toward the kitchen. 'So seeing your new niece really got to you, huh?'

'Yes. I guess so. I mean, I've always wanted . . . well, you know. Husband, kids, all that. I've been thinking about it lately, and then today—' I opt not to describe my whisker. 'I guess it's time.'

21

'So is this theoretical, or do you have someone in mind?' he asks. Fat Mikey lets out a squeaky meow, then lifts his leg and starts licking.

I clear my throat. 'It's theoretical. I just . . . I just figured we should make a clean break of it first, you know? Can't have a friend with privileges if I'm trying to find a husband.' A nervous bleat of laughter bursts from my throat.

Ethan starts to say something, then seems to change his mind. 'Sure. Most boyfriends wouldn't like to find out that you've got a standing arrangement with someone else.' His tone is mild.

'Right,' I say after a pause.

'Is that door still sticking?' He nods to the slider, which leads to the tiny balcony.

'Don't worry about it,' I mutter. My face feels hot.

'Oh, hell, Luce, don't worry. I'll fix it. You're still my sister-in-law.' For a second, he just stares at the glass door.

'Are you mad?' I whisper.

'Nah.' He stands up, then comes over to me and drops a kiss on the top of my head. 'I will, of course, miss the smokin' sex, but you're probably right. I'll drop in tomorrow to fix the door.'

That's it? 'Okay. Um, thanks, Ethan.'

And with that, he's gone, and I have to say, it feels odd. Empty and quiet.

I'd thought he might have been a little more . . . well . . . I don't know what. After all, we've been sleeping together for two years. Granted, he travels all week, and on the weekends when he had Nicky, obviously we didn't do anything, but still. I guess I didn't expect him to be so . . . blasé.

'What are we complaining about?' I ask myself out loud. 'It couldn't have gone any better.' Fat Mikey rubs against my ankles as if in agreement, and I reach down to pet his silky fur.

The evening stretches in front of me. I have seven hours until I head for the bakery. A normal person would go to bed, but my schedule is erratic at best. Another thing Ethan and I have in common: the man only sleeps four or five hours a night. I wonder if we'll still play Scrabble or Guitar Hero late at night, now that we're not . . . well, we were never really a *couple*. Just friends, and sort of relatives, linked forever by Jimmy. And lovers, though my mind bounces away from that word. *Friends with privileges* sounds much more benign.

In the first year after Jimmy died, Ethan had been one of the few people whose company I could stand. My friends—well, it was hard for both them and me. I'd married and buried a husband when most of my peers weren't even thinking about a serious relationship. A lot of them just sort of . . .

23

faded away, not knowing what to say or do for a woman widowed at twenty-four after eight months and six days of marriage.

Corinne ached for me, but seeing her eyes well up every time she saw me didn't do much for my emotional state. My mom had a grim resignation to Jimmy's death, almost a *been there, done that, own that crappy T-shirt* attitude as she patted my hand and shook her head. My aunts, forget it. To them, it was my destiny . . . *Poor Lucy, well, at least she got it over with.* Not that they were heartless enough to say that, but there was sort of a maudlin welcome feeling when I was around them, as if my widowhood was simply a fact of life. As for Gianni and Marie, I could hardly bear to be around them. Jimmy was their firstborn son, the chef in their restaurant, the heir apparent, the crown prince, and of course, the Mirabellis were absolutely ruined. Though we saw each other often, it was agony for all three of us.

But Ethan . . . maybe because we were almost the same age, maybe because we'd been pals at Johnson & Wales before he fixed me up with Jimmy, but whatever the reason, he was the only one who didn't make me feel worse.

In those first few black months, Ethan was a rock. He found this very apartment, right below his. He bought me a PlayStation and we spent far too many hours racing cars and shooting each other on the screen. He cooked for me, knowing I'd eat Sno-Balls and Ring Dings if left to my own devices, coming down with a pan of eggplant parmigiana, chicken marsala, meat loaf. We'd watch movies, and he didn't care if I'd forgotten to shower for the past couple of days. If I cried in front of him, Ethan would patiently take me in his arms, stroke my hair and tell me that someday, we were both going to be okay and if I didn't stop blubbering on his shirt, he was going to fit me with a shock collar and start using it.

Then he'd head out for another week of traveling and schmoozing, which seemed to be what he was paid so handsomely to do. He'd e-mail me dirty jokes, bring me tacky little souvenirs from whatever city he was in, send pictures of himself doing those stupid daredevil things he did—helicopter skiing in Utah, sail-surfing in Costa Rica. It was part of Ethan's job to show the demographic of *Instead*'s consumers that eating a real meal was a waste of time when such fun awaited them. Which was ironic, given that Ethan loved to both eat and cook.

After the first six months or so, when I wasn't quite so soggy, Ethan backed off a little, started doing the things normal guys do. For about two months, he dated Parker Welles, one of the rich summer folks, and to me, they seemed quite nice together. I liked

Parker, who was irreverent and blunt, and assumed Ethan had found his match, so I was quite surprised when Ethan told me they'd broken up amicably. Then Parker found out she was pregnant, informed Ethan and politely declined his marriage proposal. She stayed in Mackerly, living in her father's sprawling mansion out on Ocean View Avenue, where all the rich folks live, and gave birth to Nick. Why she passed on Ethan is a mystery—she's told me time and again she thinks he's a great guy, just not the one for her.

After Nicky came into the world, Ethan and I found ourselves hanging out once more. I guess the privileges part was bound to happen eventually, though neither of us planned on it. In fact, you could say that I was stunned the first time he—well. More on that later. I should think about something other than Ethan.

Looking around my apartment, I sigh. It's a nice place—two bedrooms, a living room, big sunny kitchen with ample counter space for baking. Prints hang on the walls as well as a large photo of Jimmy and me on our wedding day. The furniture is comfortable, the TV state-of-the-art. My balcony overlooks a salt marsh. Jimmy and I were in the process of moving into a house when he died. Obviously I hadn't wanted to live there without him, so I sold it and moved here, Ethan's proximity a great comfort.

I had imagined that Ethan and I would spend more than ten minutes breaking up, and I find myself at a bit of a loss for what to do. It's nine-thirty on a Friday night. Some nights, Ash, the Goth teen who lives down the hall, comes over to play video games or catch a movie, but there's a high school dance tonight, and her mother forced her to go. I could go over the syllabus for the pastry class I teach at the community college, but I'd just be gilding the lily, since I planned that out last week. My gaze goes to the TV.

'Fat Mikey, would you like to see a pretty wedding?' I ask my cat, hefting him up for a nuzzle, which he tolerates gamely. 'You would? Good boy.'

The DVD is already in. I know, I know, I shouldn't watch it so much. But I do. Now, though, if I really am moving on, if I'm going to find someone else, I really do need to stop. I pause, think about scrubbing the kitchen floor instead, decide against it and hit Play.

I fast-forward through me getting ready, watching in amusement the jerky, sped-up movements of Corinne pinning the veil into my hair, my mother dabbing her eyes.

Bingo. Jimmy and Ethan standing on the altar of St. Bonaventure's. Ethan, the best man, is cracking a joke, no doubt, because the brothers are laughing. And then Jimmy looks up and sees me coming down the aisle. His

27

smile fades, his wide, generous mouth drops open a little and he looks almost shocked with love. Love for me.

I hit Pause, and Jimmy's face freezes on the television screen. His eyes were so lovely, his lashes long and ridiculously pretty. A muscular physique despite cooking and eating all day, the longish blond hair that curled in the humidity, the way his eyes would half close when he looked at me . . .

I swallow, feeling that old, familiar tightness in my throat, as if there's a pebble lodged in there. It started after Jimmy died—I'd actually asked my cousin Anne, who's a doctor, to see if I had a tumor in there, but she said it was just a classic symptom of anxiety. And now it's back, I suppose, because I'm about to, er . . . move on. Or something.

The last part of becoming fully alive again—because when Jimmy died, he took a huge part of me with him—would be to find someone new. I want to get married and have babies. I really do. I grew up without a dad, and I wouldn't willingly take on single motherhood. And though I'll always miss Jimmy, it's time to move on. Finding another husband . . . it's a good idea. Sure it is.

It's just that I'll never love anyone the way I loved Jimmy. That's the truth. And given how I was ripped apart when he died, it's probably a good thing. I never want to feel anything like that again. Ever.

CHAPTER THREE

On Wednesday, I ride my bike around Ellington Park. It's a gorgeous day in early September, the breeze off the ocean spicing the salty air with a hint of autumn leaves, just beginning to turn at the tips. My spirits are bright as I pedal along the park. One would be hard-pressed to feel glum on such a sparkling day as this.

Mackerly, Rhode Island, is as charming and tiny a town as they come in New England. Roughly two hundred yards off mainland Rhode Island, we boast two thousand year-rounders, five hundred more summer folk and a lot of pretty views of the ocean. A tidal river bisects the island, and all traffic, foot and otherwise, must cross that river.

James Mackerly, a Mayflower descendant, planned our fair town around a massive chunk of land—Ellington Park, named after his mother's family. On the far end of the park is the town green, notable for a flagpole, a memorial to the Mackerly natives who died in foreign wars and a statue of our founding father. The green bleeds south into Memorial Cemetery, which in turn leads to the park proper—gravel paths, flowering trees, the aforementioned tidal river, a playground, soccer field and baseball diamond. The park is dotted with elm and maple trees and enclosed by a beautiful brownstone wall. Farther up Narragansett Bay are Jamestown and Newport, and so Mackerly, being a little too tiny, is often overlooked by tourists. Which is fine with most of us.

The Boatworks, where Ethan and I both live, is directly across from the south entrance of the park. Bunny's is across from the north entrance, in view of the town green and the statue of James Mackerly sitting astride Trigger (well, the horse's name wasn't known, but we all call him Trigger). If I were a normal person, I'd head over the little arched footbridge, enjoy the gorgeous paths through the park, walk through the cemetery and emerge onto the green in front of the bakery and all the other little stores in the tiny downtown—Zippy's Sports Memorabilia the building right next to and owned by Bunny's, Lenny's Bar, Starbucks and Gianni's Ristorante Italiano. If I went that way, my route to work would only be a half mile. But I'm not normal, and so each day, I circumnavigate the park, stretching a half-mile route to three miles, heading west down Park Street so I can cross the river on Bridge Street, then turn again onto Main.

I don't like the cemetery. I love the park, but I can't go into the cemetery. Instead I ride around it. Every day, which is a great excuse for exercise.

I duck to avoid smacking my head on a low-hanging branch as I cruise along the cemetery wall. Underneath a generous chestnut tree and very close to the street is my father's grave. *Robert Stephen Lang, age 42, Beloved Husband and Father.* 'Hi, Daddy,' I call as I pass.

Even before my dad died, and long before Jimmy, I'd hated the cemetery, and for good reason. When I was four, Iris's husband, Uncle Pete died (esophageal cancer after a lifetime of Camels Unfiltered). I hadn't been allowed to see him in the hospital—the hospice ward is no place for a kid—and so I didn't realize how thin and wasted he'd become. The casket was closed at the wake, and pictures of a younger, healthier Pete had adorned the funeral home.

At any rate, we all went to the cemetery, the men somber in their suits, black umbrellas provided by the funeral home hovering above the mourners. It had been a wet spring, and the ground was soft, saturated with rain. Our heels sank into the earth, and rainwater seeped into our shoes. I was sad, of course . . . all those grown-ups crying quite unnerved four-year-old me. I was about to become considerably more upset.

Cousin Stevie, future eater of poison ivy, was eight at the time. We all stood around the grave as the priest began the traditional funeral prayers. Stevie was bored . . . his own

31

dad was still alive (to die three years later in a railroad accident). Everything was boring to Stevie at that age. He'd been good until now, thanks to Rose's threats of his own imminent death if he didn't behave, but he couldn't hold out any longer.

As I said, it had been a rainy spring. The night before had seen a nor'easter that dumped an additional two inches into the earth, I found out later at the many retellings of this awful tale. All I knew was that it was muddy, my mother was crying and Stevie was more fun to look at than my sad mommy.

And Stevie was bored. So, being Stevie, he started doing something. Something ill-advised. Something stupid, one might say. He dug his toe into the muddy earth, and a clump of soil fell into the grave, landing with a wet splat. Stevie was fascinated. Could he get another clot of earth to fall? Without his mother noticing? He could. How about another? Yes, another. Bigger this time. *Splat*. What a neat sound.

The adults were droning their way through the Lord's Prayer. Stevie looked up, saw that I was watching and decided to show off for his little cousin. He dug his toe in up to his ankle, wriggled it, and suddenly, the earth under Stevie crumpled away in a mud slide into the grave. Stevie staggered back, arms flailing, fell against the casket, causing it to slide just an inch or two toward the compromised edge of the grave. Then, in slow motion, Uncle Pete's casket slid slowly, then listed into the yawning earth. One corner hit the other side of the grave. The casket tipped . . . and opened.

Uncle Pete's body—oh, gosh, it's hard just to remember this story—Uncle Pete's decimated body tipped out, fell almost all the way out of the casket and dangled there for a second before falling with a horrifying squelch into the sodden grave.

The screams that followed still echo in my mind. Aunt Rose shrieking. Uncle Larry, knowing instinctively that his son had caused this, repeatedly smacking Stevie on the bottom as Stevie wailed. Iris fainting. Neddy and Anne screaming and sobbing. My father hauled my pregnant and awkward mother away from the terrible sight. As for me, I stood frozen, staring down at that thing that didn't even look like Uncle Pete, facedown in the muck.

Four years later, dehydrated from crying and terrified that he would meet a fate similar to Uncle Pete's, I'd fainted at the cemetery during my own dad's funeral and, according to family legend, nearly fell into the grave myself.

So. I'd say I have just cause to be phobic about cemeteries. The only thing I remember about Jimmy's graveside service was that I was shaking so hard that I wouldn't have been able to stand were it not for Ethan's arm around me.

The truth is, not all cemeteries freak me out. In grammar school I went on a field trip to a Colonial cemetery not far from Mackerly, and I did just fine. Once, Jimmy and I spent the weekend in Orleans on Cape Cod and found a beautiful cemetery with wide expanses of shade, and we actually had a picnic amid the granite stones and sad stories from long ago. But this one, where so many of my menfolk lie . . . this one I just can't go in. Aside from the funeral, I've never been to Jimmy's grave. I'm not proud of this. It makes me feel like a bad widow, but I just can't seem to walk down that path, go through those gates.

It's okay, I rationalize. I get my cardio workout this way. I reach the intersection of Bridge and Main Streets, ring my bicycle bell and then cross, cruising into the bakery parking lot. My sister's car is here. Oh, goody!

Jorge comes out as I head in. 'Did you see the baby?' I ask. He grins and nods. 'Isn't she pretty?'

He nods again, his dark eyes crinkling.

'See you later, Jorge.' He'll be back for the afternoon deliveries.

'Hi, Cory!' I say, gently twisting past the Black Widows to see the baby. 'Oh. Oh, wow. Oh, Corinne.' I saw Emma yesterday at my sister's house, but the thrill has yet to fade. The baby is sleeping in my sister's arms, pink

34

and white skin, eyelids so new and transparent I can see the veins. Her lips purse adorably as she sucks in her sleep.

'She has eyelashes!' I exclaim softly.

'Not so close, Lucy,' Corinne murmurs, fishing a travel bottle of Purell out of her pocket. 'You have germs.'

I glance at my sister. Her eyes are wet. 'You okay, Cor?' I ask.

'I'm great,' she whispers. 'It's Chris I'm worried about. He woke up twice last night when the baby cried. He needs his sleep.'

'Well, so do you,' I point out, obediently slathering my hands.

'He needs it more.' Corinne tucks the blanket more firmly around Emma. 'He can't get worn-out. He might get sick.'

My aunt Iris bustles over, wearing her customary man's flannel shirt. She holds her hands out for inspection. 'Completely sterilized, Corinne, honey. Let me hold the baby. You sit.'

'*I'll* hold the baby,' my mother states, gliding over like a queen. Today she's wearing red patent-leather shoes with three-inch heels and a red and white silk dress (Mom doesn't do any baking—strictly management). She sets down a cup of coffee and some cookies for Corinne and holds out her arms. Corinne, looking tense, reluctantly passes the baby to our mom.

Mom's face softens with love as she gazes at

her only grandchild. 'Oh, you are just perfect. Yes, you are. Lucy, take care of Mr. Dombrowski.'

'Hi, Mr. D.,' I say to the ninety-seven-year-old man who comes in to the bakery every afternoon.

'Good day, my dear,' he murmurs, peering at our display case. 'Now, that one's interesting. What would you call that?'

'That's a cherry tart,' I say, suppressing a little shudder. Iris makes those by glopping a spoonful of canned cherry filling onto some frozen pastry. Not quite what I would do. No, I'd go for some of those beautiful Paonia cherries from Colorado—there's a market in Providence that has them flown in. A little lemon curd, some heavy cream, cinnamon, maybe a splash of balsamic vinegar to break up the sweetness, though maybe with the lemon, I wouldn't need—

'And this? What's this, dear?'

'That one's apricot.' Also from a can, but I don't mention that. It's odd—my aunts are incredible bakers, but they save those efforts for our family gatherings. For the non-Hungarian, not-related-by-blood population, canned is plenty good enough. Frozen (and refrozen, and re-refrozen) is just fine for the masses, who wouldn't know good *barak zserbo* if it bit them.

Mr. Dombrowski shuffles along the case, surveying every single thing we have in there.

36

He never buys anything other than a cheese danish, but the sweet old man doesn't have a lot to do. Coming in to buy his danish—half of which he'll eat with his tea, half with tomorrow's breakfast—gives a little structure to his day. He creeps along, murmuring, asking questions as if he's about to decide just how to split up Germany after World War II. I well understand the division of hours. Mr. D.'s alone, too.

As I ring up Mr. D's meager sale, Corinne picks up the phone and punches a number. 'Chris? Hi, honey, how are you? How are you feeling? You okay?' She pauses. 'I know. I just thought you might be a little tired. Oh, I'm fine, of course! I'm great. Oh, she's fine! Wonderful! She's perfect! She is. I love you, too. So much. You're a wonderful father, you know that? I love you! Bye! Love you! Call you later!'

As I mentioned, Corinne lives in terror that her seemingly healthy husband is on the brink of death. Growing up, Corinne and I didn't give much thought to what seemed to be a family curse. Sure, Mom and the aunts were widows . . . unlucky, sure, but that didn't have anything to do with *us*. Still, when I met Jimmy, it crossed my mind that I had the smarts to fall in love with a strapping man, six foot two of burly machismo and low cholesterol (yes, I insisted on a physical when we got our blood tests done). And maybe

37

taking out a hefty life insurance policy on your fiancé isn't what most brides have on their lists, but it was a move that turned out to be horribly prescient.

Anyway, when Jimmy died, it kind of cemented the idea in Corinne's brain that she, too, was destined to be widowed young. She managed to marry Christopher, though he had to ask her seven times before she caved. She cooks him low-fat, low-salt food, sits next to their elliptical with a stopwatch every day to make sure he gets his forty-five minutes of cardio and tends to hyperventilate if he orders bacon when they go out for breakfast. She calls him about ten times a day to ensure that he's still breathing and remind him of her lasting and abiding love. In any other family, Corinne would be gently urged to take medication or see a counselor. In ours, well, we just think Corinne is smart.

'So what's new with you, Lucy?' my sister asks, frowning. Her eyes are on her baby, her fists clenched, mentally counting the seconds before she can get Emma back.

I take a deep breath. Time to face the music, now that I've had a few days to think on it. 'Well, I think I'm ready to start dating again,' I say loudly, then swallow—there's that pebble feeling—and brace myself.

My announcement falls like an undercooked angel food cake. Iris's and Rose's eyes are wide with shock, their mouths

38

hanging open. Mom gives me a puzzled glance, then looks back at her grandchild.

But Corinne claps her hands together. 'Oh, Lucy! That's wonderful!' Tears leap into her eyes, spilling out. 'That's . . . it's . . . Oh, honey, I hope you'll find someone wonderful and perfect like Chris and be just as happy as I am!' With that, she bursts into sobs and races into the bathroom.

'The hormones,' Iris murmurs, looking after her.

'I cried for weeks after Stevie was born,' Rose seconds. 'Of course, he was ten pounds, six ounces, the little devil. I was stitched up worse than a quilt.'

'I bled for months. The doctors, they lie,' Iris adds. 'And my *kebels,* hard as rocks. I couldn't sleep on my stomach for weeks.' It is tradition to refer to girl parts in Hungarian, for some reason.

My reprieve is short-lived. The Black Widows turn to me. 'You really want another husband?' Iris demands.

'Oh, Lucy, are you sure?' Rose cheeps, wringing her hands.

'Um . . . I think so,' I answer.

'Well, good for you,' Mom says with brisk insincerity.

'After my Larry died, I never wanted another man,' Rose declares in a singsong voice.

'Me, neither,' Iris huffs. 'No one could fill

39

Pete's shoes. He was the Love of My Life. I couldn't imagine being with someone else.' She glances at me. 'Not that there's anything wrong with *you* wanting someone else, honey,' she adds belatedly.

The bell over the front door opens, and in comes Captain Bob, an old friend of my father's. Bob owns a forty-foot boat in which he takes groups for a one-hour cruise around Mackerly, complete with colorful narrative and irregular history. I know, because I often pilot his boat as a part-time job.

'Hello there, Daisy. A beautiful day, isn't it?' His ruddy face, the result of too much sun and Irish coffee, flushes redder still. He's been in love with my mother for decades. 'And who've you got there?' Captain Bob adds, his voice softening. He takes another step toward Mom.

Mom turns away. 'My granddaughter. Don't breathe on her. She's only five days old.'

'Of course. She's beautiful,' Bob says, looking at the floor.

'What can I get you, Captain Bob?' I ask. *Other than a date with my mom.*

'Oh, I'll have a cheese danish, if that's okay,' he says with a grateful smile.

'Of course it's okay.' I smile while fetching his order. The poor guy comes in every day to stare at my mother, who takes great delight in snubbing him. Perhaps this should be my first

40

lesson in dating—treat men badly, and they'll love you forever. Then again, I never had to treat Jimmy badly. Just one look, as the song says. That's all it took.

My sister emerges from the bathroom, her eyes red. 'I need to feed her,' she announces. 'My boobs are about to explode. Oh, hi, Captain Bob.'

Bob flinches and murmurs congratulations, then takes his danish and change.

'Is nursing hygienic?' Rose wonders.

'Of course it is. Best thing for the baby.' Iris turns to Captain Bob. 'My daughter's a lesbian doctor. An obstetrician. She says nursing's best.' It is true that my cousin Anne is a lesbian and an obstetrician . . . not a doctor to lesbians (or not solely lesbians) as Iris's description always causes me to think. Bob murmurs something, then slinks out the door with another look of longing for my mother, which she pretends to ignore.

'I never nursed,' Rose muses. 'In my day, only the hippies nursed. They don't bathe every day, you know. The hippies.'

Corinne takes the baby to the only table in Bunny's—the Black Widows don't encourage people to linger. 'This is not the Starbucks,' they like to announce. 'We don't ship food in from a truck. Get your fancy-shmancy coffee somewhere else. This is a *bakery*.' My aunts are one of the many reasons the Starbucks down the street does such a brisk business.

41

Corinne lifts up her shirt discreetly, fumbles at her bra, then moves the baby into position. She winces, gasps and then, seeing me watch, immediately slaps a smile on her face.

'Does it hurt?' I ask.

'Oh, no,' she lies. 'It's . . . a little . . . it's fine. I'll get used to it.' Sweat breaks out on her forehead, and her eyelids flutter in pain, but that smile doesn't drop.

The bell rings again, announcing another visitor. Two, in this case. Parker and Nicky.

'Nicky!' the Black Widows cry, falling on the lad like vultures on fresh roadkill. The boy is kissed and hugged and worshipped. He grins at me, and I wave, my heart swelling with love. He is a beautiful boy, the image of Ethan.

'Is there frosting?' he asks, and my mother and aunts lead him to the back to sugar him up.

'Frosting's not good for him, Parker,' my sister points out, wiping the nursing-induced sweat from her forehead. 'It's all sugar. You shouldn't let them give Nicky sugar.'

'Well, given that *my* aunts taught me how to throw up after meals,' Parker replies calmly, 'a little frosting therapy seems pretty benign.' She smiles at me. 'Hi, Luce.'

'Hi, Parker,' I return, smiling back.

Maybe it's because she was the first friend I made after being widowed, one of the few people in town who hadn't known me before, maybe it's because I generously ignore the fact that she's tall, slim, gorgeous and rich, but Parker and I are friends. The first thing she ever said to me upon learning that I was Ethan's brother's widow, was 'Jesus! That just sucks!' No platitudes, no awkward expressions of sympathy. I found that quite refreshing. I was rather flattered when she called me after her breakup with Ethan, and even more when she included me on the details of her pregnancy. At the time, everyone else was still doing the kid-gloves thing. *Don't mention babies . . . she's a widow. Don't talk about your love life . . . she's a widow.* To Parker, I was just me—a widow, yes, but a person first. You'd be surprised how rare that take on things can be.

'So this is the baby,' Parker says now, leaning over to gaze on Emma, who is glugging away like a frat boy at a kegger. 'Wow. She really is beautiful, Corinne.'

'Thanks,' Corinne says, shifting the baby away so as to avoid any ebola or tuberculosis Parker may be carrying. 'Lucy, can you just reach into my bag and dial Chris's number? I just want to check in.'

'You just called him,' I remind her.

'I know,' she says, a tear slipping down her cheek.

'You okay, honey?' I ask. 'Is this just hormonal?'

'I'm wonderful,' she says, smiling through her tears.

I do as instructed. Corinne takes the phone and stands, the baby still firmly attached, and wanders into the corner to talk with her husband once more.

'Your sister has issues,' Parker states, glancing into the kitchen to ensure that her son is eating enough frosting. She takes Corinne's seat and smiles.

'True enough. How was your weekend?'

'It was great. Ethan came over, and we all watched *Tarzan,* and then he rigged up a rope in the dining room so Nicky could swing around like the Ape Man. Wait till my dad sees that.' She smiles fondly. The dining room at Grayhurst (yes, the house has a name, which I always thought was so cool) probably could seat a couple dozen.

'Sounds fun.' I pause. 'Um, so, guess what? I'm going to start dating again.'

'Oh, yeah? You and Ethan gonna be a real couple?'

Parker knows about Ethan and me and our, er, arrangement. I told her one night, over too many mojitos and not enough food. Parker never seemed to have a problem with it. It was long after they'd broken up, after all.

'No. Not Ethan. He's just . . . no.'

'He's just what?' Parker asks, picking up one of Corinne's ignored cookies and taking a bite. 'He's great in bed, as I dimly recall. Of course, it was almost five years ago, and we were only together a little while, but I

44

remember this thing he did—'

'Shh!' I glance around, praying that the Black Widows haven't overheard. 'Please, Parker!'

'What?'

'What? Well, Ethan's my brother-in-law,' I whisper. 'And just for the record—again—no one else knows that we've been . . . um . . . intimate. I'd like to keep it that way, okay?'

'Well, aside from him being Jimmy's brother, why?' Parker says in a lower voice. 'He's a great dad, which I'm sure is number one on your list of priorities.'

I blink. 'How did you know there was a list?'

'Please. Of course there's a list. Probably a color-coded list.'

There is a list, of course, and yes, Strong Fatherhood Potential is indeed in the top three (in red, for nonnegotiable). I bite my lip. 'Well, Ethan's not, um . . . the right type.'

'Except in bed?' Parker suggests with an evil smile.

'Shh, Parker! Come on!' She chuckles, and I sigh. 'He's just not . . . well, first of all, I want a husband who's not going to die anytime soon. And Ethan's always jumping out of things and driving a motorcycle and stuff like that.'

'He wears a helmet,' Parker says.

'Not good enough.'

'So is immortality also on the list, then?'

45

She raises a perfectly shaped eyebrow.

'Of course not. I'm not unrealistic. But yes, Low Risk for Early Death is on the list.' Number one in fact.' Parker grins, and I continue. 'The fact remains that Ethan, while a great guy, is just not for me, okay? And you know exactly what I'm talking about, because you've told me the same thing, even though you'd make a beautiful family and could have more little Nickys running around.'

Parker smiles. 'Did you know he moved back to Mackerly?'

I pause. 'Ethan?'

'Yes, dummy.'

'What do you mean?'

Parker takes another bite of cookie. 'He took a job with International Food's headquarters in Providence so he could be closer to Nick. Around all the time, not just on weekends.'

'Oh,' I say, mildly hurt that I don't know this already. Right . . . he mentioned something Friday night about having something to tell me, but must've forgotten. 'Wow. That's big news.'

'Mmm. Anyway. He'll be back permanently as of this weekend.'

'Well. That's good.' I pause. 'Good for Nicky, certainly.'

'Mommy! I ate blue frosting!' Speaking of Nick, the little guy charges out of the kitchen, the lower half of his face stained with blue

46

from the hideous fondant Rose uses to frost her cakes (I'd only use butter cream, but Rose is the cake decorator at Bunny's, no matter how superior my frosting might be).

'That's great, buddy!' Parker says. 'Give me a blue kiss, okay?' She leans over and puckers, and Nicky laughingly obeys.

'Want one, Aunt Wucy?' he asks. Though he's lately mastered his L sound, he still calls me 'Wucy,' which I find utterly irresistible.

'I sure do, honey,' I answer. He climbs onto my lap and obliges, and I breathe in his smell, salt and shampoo and sugar, and hug him tight for a second, relishing his perfect little form, before he wriggles down to play with his Matchbox cars.

'I gotta get going. Books to write.' She sighs dramatically.

Parker is the author of a successful children's series—The Holy Rollers, child-angels who come down from heaven, don roller-skates and help mortal kids make good choices. Parker hates the Holy Rollers with a mighty passion and wrote the first one as a farce . . . stories so sticky-sweet that they made her teeth ache. However, her sarcasm was lost on an old Harvard chum who ran the children's division of a huge publishing company, and The Holy Rollers are now published in fourteen languages.

'What's this one about?' I ask, grinning.

She smiles. *'The Holy Rollers and the Big*

Mean Bully, in which the God Squad descends to beat the shit out of Jason, the seventh-grade thug who steals lunch money.'

'Beat the shit out of Jason!' Nicky echoes, zipping his car along the window.

'Oops. Don't tell Daddy I said that, okay?' Parker asks her son, who agrees amiably.

'Want me to keep an eye out?' Parker asks, scooping up Nicky's little cars into her buttery leather pocketbook.

'For what?' I ask.

'For your new husband?'

'Oh. Sure. I guess,' I say.

'Now there's a can-do attitude!' she says with a wink, then takes my nephew by the hand and breezes out, her blond hair fluttering in the wind.

CHAPTER FOUR

Ethan was two years behind me at Johnson & Wales. I didn't know him until my junior year—while I'd grown up in Mackerly, the Mirabelli family had moved to town and opened Gianni's my second year of college. They heralded from Federal Hill, the Italian section of Providence, and their restaurant was an instant success. I'd eaten there a time or two, but I hadn't met any of the family until Ethan approached me one day as I was

48

lounging on the grass at school, sketching out my final project for Advanced Cake Decorating.

'Aren't you one of those bakery babes from Mackerly?' he asked. I grinned and affirmed that indeed I was.

'I'm Ethan Mirabelli,' he said. 'My family owns Gianni's. Do you know it?'

'I sure do,' I said. 'Best food this side of Providence.' I shaded my eyes and took a better look at young Ethan Mirabelli. Fairly cute. Lively brown eyes, mischievous smile, the kind that curled up at the corners in a most adorable way. 'Do you work there?'

'Not yet. My brother and dad are the chefs now, but maybe someday. What about you? Are you in the chef program, too?' he asked, sitting on the grass next to me.

'Pastry chef. I'm a sucker for dessert,' I answered.

'She loves sweet things,' Ethan murmured, lifting an eyebrow and giving me a sidelong glance. Flirt. I grinned again. 'You'll have to come in and try my mom's tiramisu,' he said. 'It's the best in four states. Including New York.'

Ethan and I became instant pals. We hung out together, met for lunch a couple times a week, sat together on the old couches at the Cable Car theater and watched foreign movies, snickering inappropriately at the love scenes. 'Sex in German,' Ethan murmured.

49

'How awful.' The couple next to us glared, then muttered to each other—in German—sending us into gales of silent, wheezing laughter.

We didn't date, but we were compadres. He was a sophomore, I was a senior, and we were at the age where that still sort of mattered . . . my almost twenty-two felt much older than his still nineteen. He couldn't go out for a beer—not legally, anyway—and I was interviewing with hotels and restaurants while he was years away from graduation. And though he was pretty cute and very fun, it wasn't, as we girls liked to say, *that way*. We never held hands or kissed or anything. We were just friends.

A few months after we met, Ethan and I shared the short ride home to Mackerly, and he brought me to Gianni's.

'Hey, guys,' he called as we went into the kitchen.

'Hey, college boy, nice of you to drop by and visit the working class,' came a voice, and Jimmy turned around, and that was that.

His eyes got me first . . . blue-green, ridiculously pretty. The rest of his face was awfully nice, too. Gorgeous cheekbones, generous lips, a little smile tugging at one corner. Time seemed to stop; I noticed everything . . . the golden hair on his muscular forearms, a healing burn on the inside of one wrist. The pulse in his neck, which was tan and smooth and seemed to urge me to bury my

50

face there. Jimmy Mirabelli was tall and strong and smiling, and I didn't realize I was staring at him—and he at me—until Ethan cleared his throat.

'This is my brother, Jimmy,' Ethan said. 'Jim, this is Lucy Lang. Her family owns Bunny's Bakery.'

Jimmy took a few steps over, and rather than offer me his hand, he just looked at me, and that little crooked grin grew into a slow smile that spread across his face. 'Hi, Lucy Lang,' he murmured as I blushed. Ethan said something, but I didn't hear. For the first time in my young life, I'd been hit hard with lust. Sure, I'd had a couple of boyfriends here and there, but this . . . this was indeed *that way*. A warm squeeze wrapped around my stomach, my mouth went dry, my cheeks burned. Then Jimmy Mirabelli did take my hand, and I almost swooned.

Hours after I left the restaurant, Jimmy called the bakery and asked me out. I said yes. Of course I did. And when Ethan and I drove back to school that Sunday night, I thanked him for introducing me to his brother. 'He's a great guy,' Ethan said mildly, then listened as I gushed some more.

Jimmy Mirabelli was, I quickly learned, the missing link in my life—a man.

It hadn't been easy for Mom, raising Corinne and me alone. She'd done her best— we had enough money, with Dad's life insurance policy and Mom's small but regular income from the bakery. Mom wasn't a bad mother, but she was a little distant, not the type to ask where we were going or with whom—she said she trusted us to make smart decisions, and then she'd turn back to her crossword puzzle or true-crime novel, her parenting done for the night.

I grew up in a constant state of father-envy. I adored my friends' dads . . . the approval, the affection, the strictness, the rules. I remember Debbie Keating, my BFF from grade school, getting absolutely chewed out for wearing a trashy tank top and blue eye shadow to our seventh-grade dance. Boy, did I ever want a dad to make sure *I* wasn't trashy! To protect me and adore me the way only Dad could. My small and precious cache of memories told me my dad had been a very good father, and a good father loves his daughter like no one else. He adores her, protects her, bails her out when she gets in trouble, defends her from her mother's chastisement. He urges her to be whatever she wants (president, astronaut, princess), and later in life, advises on which boy is good enough for her (none) and when she can start dating (never).

But, given the Black Widow curse, men were scarce in my life. I had no uncles, no grandfathers, no brothers . . . my closest male relation was Stevie, and you already know about him. Corinne and I used to try to summon our father, sitting in the closet where my mom still kept a few of his clothes, holding a coat or a sweater against our faces, chanting, 'Daddy, Daddy, talk to us, Daddy.'

Mom never even considered dating, but I enjoyed picturing her with another guy, marrying him, some gentle, kind soul who would love Corinne and me as his own and indulge us in ways our mother didn't. One summer, I waitressed at a nice restaurant in Newport, and Joe Torre, then manager of the New York Yankees, came in for dinner with his wife. Though Rhode Island is part of Red Sox nation and we're raised to hate all things New York, I thought Mr. Torre was a very nice man. Dinner cost $112 that night; he left $500 and a signed napkin that said 'The service was very special. Thank you so much. Joe Torre.' Whenever I pictured a stepfather, it was always Joe Torre's dolorous, bulldog face that came to mind.

It was fair to say that I was hungry for men . . . not in the sexual way necessarily, but in the way a vegetarian yearns for a steak when the scent of roasting meat is in the air. The way a Midwesterner can yearn for the ocean, even if they've only seen it once. When a man came into the bakery, I hustled to be the one waiting on him, regardless of his age, and soaked up all that fascinating masculinity— how he moved, spoke, stood. How his eyes crinkled when he smiled at me, how decisively he'd ask for whatever it was he wanted. The blunt fingers, the hair on the back of the hands, the shadow of beard.

At the time I met Jimmy, Ethan was probably my closest male friend, but he was all fun, no gravitas. A boy, in other words, not a man. Not then.

Jimmy . . . he was a man. Strong, solid, tall, three years older than I was, he was so commanding and capable. He'd never worked anywhere but in a kitchen, and he knew what he was doing. Quick, sure movements, the ability to make a decision in a heartbeat, confident and secure and talented, he was dazzling.

I started coming home from school more and more, because Jimmy's job didn't give him much wiggle room on the weekends. Gianni worked in the kitchen alongside his son, yelling at the sous chef and prep chefs, and whenever he saw me, he'd give me a kiss on the cheek and call me Jimmy's Girl. Marie, who served as hostess of the patrons and terror of the waitstaff, would seat me at the family table, urging me to eat more so I wouldn't be 'so thin.' She'd grill me about if I wanted children (yes), how many did I think I wanted (three or four) and did I ever want to move away from the area (absolutely not). Then she'd smile and, I imagined, do the math as to how much longer she'd have to wait for a grandchild.

And then Jimmy would come out of the kitchen, schmooze a little with the diners, always hearty and friendly. His eyes would seek me out, and he'd look at me a beat too long, letting me know I was the one he wanted to be with. He'd walk past, back to the kitchen, stopping for a kiss, squeezing me on the shoulder with his strong hands, leaving me in a wake of garlic and lust.

Being with him was being with a local celebrity—someone who was better looking than first remembered, who smelled better, who, when he wrapped his arms around me and lifted me off my feet, made me dizzy with love. Everyone knew Jimmy, despite the fact that he'd just moved to town a year or so before, and he remembered everyone's names, sent over complimentary appetizers, asked after children. Everyone adored him.

He was a wonderful boyfriend, bringing me flowers, hiding notes in my dorm room on the rare occasions he made it to Providence, calling a couple of times a day. He constantly told me I was beautiful, and with him, I felt it like never before. He'd gaze at me as we lay in the grass in Ellington Park as the tidal river flowed past, the smell of brine and flowers mingling as the sun beat down on us, and he'd forget what he was saying, breaking off midsentence to reach out and touch my face with his fingertips or kiss my hand, or even better, lay his head in my lap and say, 'This is

55

all I'll ever need. This and a little food.'

It was Jimmy who gave Bunny's a boost when he suggested that Gianni's buy their bread from us. He recommended us to other restaurants, too, and that side of the business mushroomed. My mother and aunts thought he just about walked on water because of it. 'That Jimmy,' they'd say, shaking their heads, their dormant love of men peeking through the snows of their widowhood. 'He's something, that Jimmy. He's a keeper, Lucy.'

They didn't have to tell me.

Jimmy waited till I was done with college to propose. He asked me to have a late dinner with him at Gianni's one night, after everyone else had left. It was something we did once in a while, the restaurant only lit by a few candles. I still remember the taste of everything he made that night . . . the sweetness of the tomatoes, the yeasty tug of the bread, the smooth vodka sauce on the perfectly cooked pasta, the tender, buttery chicken.

When it came time for dessert, Jimmy went into the kitchen and returned with two dishes of Marie's famous tiramisu, a cool, rich combination of chocolate cream, sponge cake and coffee liqueur topped with the creamy mascarpone. He set my dish down in front of me. I glanced down, saw the engagement ring perched on top of the cream. Without missing a beat, I picked it up, licked it off and put it on my finger as Jimmy laughed, low and dirty. Then I looked into Jimmy's confident, smiling, utterly handsome face and knew I'd spend the rest of my life crazy in love with this guy.

Obviously things didn't turn out quite that way.

When we'd been married for eight months, Jimmy drove down to New York for a chef supply show. He'd gotten up at 5:00 a.m. to get there early, spent the whole day learning about new oven technologies, hearing how remodeling a restaurant kitchen could save time and money, looking at hundreds of new or redesigned tools for the chef. Then he and a bunch of other chefs headed out for dinner.

It was past midnight when he called me from outside New Haven, nearly two hours from Mackerly.

'You didn't have too much to drink, did you?' I asked, cuddled up in our bed. I'd been waiting up for him, and in truth was disappointed that he was still so far away.

'No, baby. One glass of wine at about five, that's it. You know me.'

I smiled, mollified. 'Well, you're not too tired, are you?'

'I'm a little beat,' he admitted, 'but not too bad. I miss you. I just want to get home and see your beautiful face and smell your hair and get laid.'

I laughed. 'Now that's funny,' I said, 'because I just want to see *your* beautiful face

57

and get laid, too.'

I didn't say, *Jimmy, at least pull over and take a nap.* I didn't say, *Baby, we have our whole lives together. Get a motel room and go to sleep.* Instead, I said, 'I love you, honey. Can't wait to see you.' And he said the same thing, and that was the last thing he ever did say.

About a hundred minutes after we hung up, Jimmy fell asleep at the wheel, crashed into an oak tree six miles from home and died instantly, and the rest of my life was rewritten.

*   *   *

'How's the cake?' I ask Ash, my seventeen-year-old Goth neighbor from down the hall.

'It's fantastic. You sure you don't want any?'

'I'm sure. I taught this one in class, remember? You can make it yourself.' Ash, who doesn't have a lot of friends her own age, helps out at my six-week pastry class from time to time.

'Why bake for myself when I, like, have my own bakery right down the hall?' She takes another huge bite. 'Anyway, stop stalling, Lucy. Get this done.'

Feeling the need for a little company, I'd bribed Ash with bittersweet chocolate cake and the latest James Bond DVD. Tonight, I'm registering on a dating Web site, and while it seems like the perfect way for me to find someone, my stomach jumps nonetheless. I drain my wineglass, then drop a kiss on Fat Mikey's head. He blinks fondly at me, then, fickle as only a cat can be, pricks my knee with his claws and jumps down.

'Lucy, I'm, like, aging rapidly here,' Ash reminds me. 'I do have school tomorrow, and my stupid mother wants me home at like, eleven.'

'Sorry, sorry,' I mutter. I need to do this. Aside from hitting a sperm bank, this is the way to get what I want. Find a husband. I glance at my young friend, who could also do with a boyfriend. As always, her hair is Magic-Marker black, her eyes ringed with eyeliner, her eyebrows painfully overplucked. Because she's been eating, some of her black lipstick has been dislodged, revealing a Cupid's bow mouth in the prettiest imaginable shade of pink.

'What are you staring at?' she asks. 'Get your butt in gear. The movie's two hours long.'

I obey, entering my pertinent information, then click to the next screen and begin the questionnaire.

'Heard from Ethan lately?' Ash asks with careful nonchalance. She's had a crush on him for years.

'Um, not really. I saw him on the water today, though,' I say, looking at her again. 'He was sailing.' The truth is, I haven't really talked to Ethan since that night.

'So cool.' She blushes, then picks at the sole of her engineer boot to hide her love.

I hide a smile and look back at the computer. I'm only halfway done. It's really too bad that I don't live in a society of arranged marriages. The Black Widows could pick someone out for me . . . a nice enough man who didn't have expectations of romantic love. That being fond of each other would be sufficient . . . he'd take care of me, I'd take care of him, we'd be the parents of the same children, rather than two people crazy in love.

Fat Mikey heads over to the slider to gaze into the night. If I open the door, he'll take the fire escape down to the street, then kill something and bring it back to me. His way of showing love, his soul as romantic as Tony Soprano's. 'Not tonight, buddy,' I tell him, clicking 'maple' for the *If you were a tree* question. Finally I get to the screen that offers the available men in a twenty-mile radius. 'And here they are,' I say. Ash lurches off the couch and peers over my shoulder.

'Hey, there's Paulie Smith,' she says. Paulie and I play in the baseball league.

'I wonder if his wife knows he's looking,' I murmur, clicking on the next choice. 'Oh, it's Captain Bob. Nice that he's at least trying to score with someone other than my mom.'

'Totally gross,' Ash mutters. 'Hey, look at this one.' She taps the screen with her stubby black nail. 'He's cute.'

60

I look. Soxfan212. Nice eyes, lawyer, single, no kids.

'Oops,' Ash says at the next bullet point. 'That's a deal breaker, isn't it?'

Soxfan212 likes to sail. Immediately, I picture him clinging to an overturned boat in high seas, rain pelting down, sharks circling, the rescue helicopter waving regretfully as they fly off, unable to make the save.

'Sorry, Soxfan,' I say.

This afternoon, the same images of death and drowning were strong in my mind when I saw Ethan as I was piloting for Captain Bob. The wind was much too fierce in my opinion, and Ethan's sailboat, a two-masted sixteen-footer, sliced through the water, tilting with speed, sails taut. Ethan waved, grinning, and it was all I could do not to radio the Coast Guard so they could tell Ethan to slow down. He's a good sailor—won a few races and whatnot—but it just seems crazy, going out in the ocean over your head, alone, on a boat, in the wind. Though I guess that *is* the point of sailing.

'Okay, let's move on,' Ash says firmly. 'Here. Type in your little message.'

'Right.' I type dutifully. *Thirty years old, no kids, widowed five years ago. Seeking long-term relationship, hoping to meet someone I won't love a whole heck of a lot but won't hate, either. Good teeth a plus.*

'What do you think?' I ask my friend. 'Will

61

they be lining up for me?' Ash just shakes her head. Fat Mikey rolls his eyes (I swear), then begins licking his privates.

'You have three minutes,' Ash says, 'and I'm starting the movie. And you can't watch it if you don't finish this.'

'Yes, Mother,' I say. I call to mind my tiny niece, the indescribable look on my sister's face when she looks at her child, the wonder and pride and protectiveness. I remember Nicky's wriggly hugs, how he danced in excitement yesterday when telling me about finding a woolly bear caterpillar. I look at Ash, the nicest kid I know, though she tries desperately to hide it in her hideous clothes and makeup.

And so I delete what I've written and type something a bit more palatable.

'Good for you, Lucy,' Ash affirms. 'Now grab a Twinkie and come watch the wonder that is Daniel Craig.'

CHAPTER FIVE

'So? You want to date her? She's perfectly nice. A widow. Sure, she was sad when her husband, bless his heart, crashed into that tree, but none of the Prozac, you know what I'm saying? And as you can see, she has a nice figure.'

Aunt Iris has just dragged me from the kitchen, where I was taking out fifteen loaves of rye. A man in his forties, short, plump, balding, stands in front of the counter, frozen in terror. Was I wishing that the Black Widows would fix me up? I take it back.

'Sorry about this,' I said. 'Can I help you?'

'Um . . . I just . . . I wanted a danish.'

'And you got a danish,' Iris says pointedly. She jerks her head toward me. 'So what do you think?'

'I need some change,' the man whispers to me.

'Sure.' I snatch the twenty from where it's being held hostage in Iris's hand and hit a key on the cash register. 'Just one danish? Anything else?'

'Nothing else! Uh, I mean, no thanks.' He looks warily at Iris, then back at me. 'I'm sorry.'

Iris bristles, swelling like an indignant and regal toad. 'Oh, she's not good enough for you, is that it? Why? What's special about you, huh, mister?' She grabs me by my shoulders, gives a brisk shake. 'Look at those hips. She was born to have children, and none of this epidural crap. Ask my daughter. She's a lesbian doctor.' Aunt Iris releases me, folds her arms and stares the man down. 'I had two children, not a drop of painkiller for me. Did it hurt? Of course it did. It was *childbirth*, for heaven's sake. I made do. I bore it. The

63

tearing . . . not so bad. It didn't kill me.'

I hand the man his change. 'Have a nice day. Come again.'

The man *won't* be coming again, I assure you. He scuttles out the door. I'd be willing to bet he never comes to the *island* again.

'Iris, maybe you could . . . tone it down a little?' I suggest.

'What?' Iris asks, wounded. She snatches up a rag and starts polishing the immaculate counter. 'Tone what down?'

'Well, parading me out here like a farm animal at an auction.'

'You said you wanted to date someone, so I'm helping, that's all.'

'That was more along the lines of pimping, with a crash course in obstetrics thrown in.'

'So fussy! I thought beggars couldn't be choosers,' she huffs.

'I'm not a beggar! I just . . . I can meet someone on my own. You're so nice to try, but please don't harass the customers. Business is bad enough.'

'Business is fine,' she snorts. 'Listen to her. Business is bad. Fifty-seven years of bad business, huh? Put you through your fancy-shmancy baking college, didn't it? Hmm?'

'Yes, Aunt Iris. It did,' I admit. 'It's just that we could do a lot more if we put in some tables, offered coffees and—'

Iris's magnificent eye roll is interrupted as the bell rings. My aunt's usually stern face morphs into sycophantic adoration. 'Oh, Grinelda! Hello, hello! Come in, dear! So nice of you to visit us.'

I stifle a sigh.

Grinelda is a frequent visitor to Bunny's. She is a self-proclaimed gypsy, and my aunts and mother revere her. Gypsies have a special place in the hearts of Hungarians, and the Black Widows, devout Catholics all, view Grinelda as second only to the Book of the Apocalypse in terms of prophetic abilities. Like Madonna or Cher, Grinelda has no last name, which means she must be paid in cash. Also like the aforementioned pop stars, Grinelda likes to dress up. Today's ensemble is sort of 'attention deficit disorder meets kindergartner on sugar high.' Long, shiny purple skirt riding higher in the back than in the front, as it must make the long journey over Grinelda's impressive rump. Red blouse with a piece of duct tape running up one shoulder seam, pilling black shawl, a sliding jingle of cheap bracelets and punishing, clip-on earrings.

Her voice rusted by fifty years of small brown cigars, Grinelda now croaks out a greeting. 'Daisy, Iris, Rose . . . your loved ones await a word.'

'Lucy, honey, don't just sit there like a lump, get her something to eat!' Aunt Rose trills, bursting from the back of the kitchen from where she was slathering a wedding cake

65

in her special blend of Crisco and confectioner's sugar. 'Go!' She yanks off her apron and smoothes her hair.

I do as I'm told, heaping ten of Bunny's most garish and colorful cookies on a plate and stirring three teaspoons of sugar into a large mug of 'staff-only' coffee.

My mother emerges from her office, applying another coat of lipstick as she does. 'Oh, good, she's here. Lucy, do you want a reading, too? Electrolysis, maybe?'

'No, thanks,' I say, ignoring the mustache crack. 'Mom, Grinelda's about as a psychic as a fern. And a hundred bucks a pop? I just don't think you should—'

'Shh! She'll hear you, honey. Quiet down and go in the back if you're such a cynic. Go! Shoo!' Mom takes the plate of cookies from me, and approaches Grinelda with the reverence of a Wise Man nearing baby Jesus. 'Grinelda! Welcome!'

I've always found it odd that Mom is as sold as her sisters on Grinelda, since she seems so much more sophisticated, but I guess we all have our weak spots. And though I am indeed cynical about Grinelda's abilities, I peek from the kitchen. Grinelda may be a fraud, but she's still fun to watch.

'Daisy, my dear,' the gypsy croaks, cutting her crepey eyes to me, 'it's so good to see you. I'm feeling a bit tired today, but I'll do my best.'

66

The three sisters cluck and fuss around Grinelda, who doesn't waste time, shoving two cookies into her mouth at once. Through a spray of crumbs, she says, 'I'm getting a letter . . . someone's coming.' My aunts and mother clutch hands, crowding around the little table. 'The letter is . . . L. Yes. It's a man whose name begins with L. Does one of you know a man whose name begins with L?'

'Doesn't everyone know a man whose name begins with L?' I ask sweetly. I am ignored.

'Larry,' Aunt Rose breathes. 'My Larry.' As if Grinelda didn't know Rose's husband's name. She's been bilking the Black Widows for years.

'Larry . . . he wants you to know something . . . he's still with you. True love never dies. And whenever you see a yellow flower next to a red flower, it's a sign from him, a sign that he loves you.'

The fact that Grinelda walks through Ellington Park to get here, and that the park is planted with dozens and dozens of red and yellow chrysanthemums currently in robust bloom and easily visible from this very shop, is lost on little Rose. She clutches her hand to her ample bosom. 'Oh, a sign! Larry, honey, I love you, too, sweetheart!'

Well, I can't help it. My throat feels a little tight. Sure, Grinelda's full of garbage, but the expression on Rose's face is probably worth the hundred bucks she just shelled out.

67

'The man is fading . . . and now there's someone else. Another man . . . tall. Limping. Name starts with a P.'

'Pete! My Pete!' Iris trumpets. 'He walked with a limp! Shot in the leg by his idiot brother!'

Grinelda lights a cheroot and sucks on it, nodding wisely, then exhaling a bluish stream of smoke. 'Yep. Limping.'

While I don't believe Grinelda can see the dead, I do believe that those who have died visit us. There are those rogue dimes, for example, found in unusual spots . . . the exact middle of the kitchen counter, or in my sock drawer. Occasionally I'll dream that Jimmy's back on earth for a chat. He always looks gorgeous in those dreams, and is always just checking in. The widows group I'd belonged to assured me that this kind of thing was a fairly common experience.

So it's not that I don't believe. I just don't believe Grinelda.

My latest batch of bread has twenty minutes to go before it'll be done. A little air would be nice, so I head out for a stroll down Main Street. The trees have lost their deep green summer lushness, and the sunlight has a mellow, golden softness to it. An elderly couple walks slowly across the green, him with a cane, her clinging to his arm. Beautiful. They head into the cemetery, and I look away.

The dark, rich scent of roasting coffee wafts

68

out from Starbucks. I could really use a strong cuppa joe . . . I was up till 2:00 a.m. this morning watching *The Hunt for Red October*, and my tired brain yearns for a caffeine fix. I can't go in, of course. Starbucks is my competitor, and it's run by the meanest girl in Mackerly—Doral-Anne Driscoll.

Well, she's not the meanest girl anymore. That's not fair. She's the meanest *woman*. I've known her all my life, and she basically lived the cliché of Tough Townie . . . multiple piercings in her ears, eyebrows, nose and tongue, jeans so tight you could count her pocket change, a surly sneer perpetually spreading across her thin and usually cursing mouth. Tattooed by the time she was fourteen, smoking, drinking, sleeping around . . . the woiks, as Bugs Bunny would say. And then there was the utter contempt she had for me, a rather meek and shy child who lived to please teachers and sang in St. Bonaventure's choir.

Unlike most of my graduating class, Doral-Anne never left Mackerly. She sneered and spat with what we all knew was just envy whenever college was mentioned. She waited tables at a diner in Kingstown, and when Gianni's opened in Mackerly, she got a job there.

Well before I met Ethan or Jimmy, Doral-Anne was talking about Gianni's. Every time I ran into her when home for the weekend, she'd bring it up. How great it was working there. How much money she made. How fantastic the owners were. College—especially *my* college—was for pussies. *She* was in the restaurant business. Probably Gianni's was going to train her to be manager.

In my 'try to be nice to everyone' way, I'd tell her that sounded great, which seemed to make her nastier than ever. ' "That sounds great," ' she'd mimic. 'Lang, you're such a stupid little goody-good.'

When I met Jimmy, Doral-Anne was still a waitress, no management position in sight. She didn't dare take potshots at me at Gianni's, not when the chef himself was in love with me, not when the owners treated me like gold, and man, did she hate it. Narrowed eyes every time I came in. Jerky, hard movements. Overly loud laughter to show how much fun she was having.

A month after Ethan introduced Jimmy and me, Doral-Anne got caught stealing and was fired. And because I'd seen her in action there, heard her claims of being groomed for manager and because I now held a place of honor in the Mirabelli family, she hated me all the more.

Doral-Anne's hostility toward me didn't waver after I became a widow. Once, four or five months after Jimmy died, I saw her at the gas station; she was obviously pregnant. I'd heard through the gossip that floated into the

70

bakery that the father was some biker dude who'd passed through town.

'Congratulations, Doral-Anne,' I said dutifully.

She turned to me, eyes narrowed with malicious glee, she stuck out her pregnant belly, rubbed it with both hands and said, 'Yeah. Nothing like a baby. I'm so happy. Bet you wish you could have one, too, huh? Too bad Jimmy didn't get you pregnant before he died.'

Wordlessly I'd stopped pumping, though my tank was far from full, got into my car and drove home, my hands shaking, my stomach ice-cold.

Doral-Anne had her baby—Leo—and a couple of years later, popped out another one. Kate. Rumor had it the father was Cutty, the married owner of Cutty's Bait & Boat Rental, and though Cutty's wife left him, he never publicly acknowledged paternity. Doral-Anne bounced from waitressing job to waitressing job. Then a year ago, Starbucks opened in our tiny little town, and Doral-Anne was hired as manager. From the way she acts, Starbucks has found the cure for cancer, AIDS and the common cold.

Speak of the devil. Doral-Anne appears in the doorway, broom in hand. Seeing me standing across the street, she shoves the broom behind her, the ropy muscles of her thin arms snaking and lean. 'What's up,

71

Lang?' she calls, the edge in her voice carrying easily across the quiet street.

'Hi, Doral-Anne,' I answer. 'How's it going?' Then I bite my tongue, wishing I hadn't asked.

'It's great! Business is booming. I guess you know that, since so many of your customers come here now. Guess your fancy cooking school didn't help so much after all. Welp, see ya!' She flips back her lank, overly long bangs and goes back inside.

Gritting my teeth, I chastise myself for giving her the opening. I need to get back to the bakery, anyway. My internal timer says there are only five minutes till perfection.

As always, the smell of bread comforts me, not that Doral-Anne did any real damage . . . she's nasty, that's all. The comforting murmur of the Black Widows communing with the dead floats into the kitchen, though I can't make out actual words. I open the oven door. Ah. Five dozen loaves of Italian, baked to hot, golden perfection. 'Hello, little ones,' I say. Flipping them off the sheets so they won't overcook on the bottom, I leave them to cool, then head for the proofer, the glass warming cupboard where the loaves rise before going into the oven. This batch contains a dozen loaves of pumpernickel for a German restaurant in Providence, some sourdough for a fusion place, and three dozen loaves of French for the local customers who just love my bread (as well they should). I set the temperature a little higher, since our oven tends to lose oomph around this time of day, then take a warm loaf of Italian and just hold it, savoring the warmth, the rub of the cornmeal that coats the bottom, the crisp and flaky crust.

It occurs to me that I'm cradling the warm loaf as one would hold an infant. Really need to get cracking on that new husband. eCommitment has yielded nothing so far, so I may need to try another venue. But first, lunch. I'm starving.

Putting the loaf gently in the slicer, I press the button, still as charmed by the machine as I was as a child, then open the fridge to see what offerings it holds. Tuna salad, no celery . . . perfect. I pop two slices of the fresh bread into the toaster, then open a bottle of coffee milk and wait.

While I love the bakery and love working with my aunts, I can't help wishing Bunny's was different. More tables, more refined pastries than just danish and doughnuts. If we sold biscotti, for example. ('Biscotti? That's Italian,' my aunts said the last time I broached the subject. 'We're not the Italians.') If we sold cakes by the slice—not Rose's wedding cakes, but the kind that people might actually like to eat. Coconut lime, for example. Sour cream pecan. Chocolate with mocha frosting and a hazelnut filling. If we sold coffee and

73

cappuccino, even, heaven protect us, lattes.

'Lucy, honey, can you get Grinelda some more coffee?' Aunt Rose calls.

'Sure,' I answer. My toast is still browning. I grab the pot and sugar bowl and, heading into the front, note that my mother is wiping her eyes. 'How's Dad?' I can't help asking.

'He thinks Emma is just beautiful,' Mom answers. 'It's amazing, Grinelda. You have such a gift.'

'Such a gift,' I murmur with a dubious glance at the gypsy, who is chewing on another cookie. An eleven-by-seventeen-inch piece of paper is taped to Bunny's front door . . . the door through which Grinelda entered. Daisy Is A Grandmother!!! the sign says, right above the picture of my niece. *Emma Jane Duvall, September 8, 7 lbs. 3 oz.*

The readings are over. My aunts wander back to the kitchen to get a box for Grinelda's loot as my mother fills the medium in on Corinne's nursing issues. As I pour Grinelda some more coffee, she cuts her pale blue eyes to me.

'I have a message for you, too,' she says, a chunk of sugar cookie falling from her mouth onto her sequined lap.

'That's okay, Grinelda. I'm fine,' I answer.

'He wants you to check the toast. Your husband.' She pops the fallen cookie bit back into her mouth and regards me impassively. My mother quivers with attention.

'Lucy! Your toast is about to burn back here, honey!' Iris calls.

Mom's eyes nearly pop out of her head. 'Oh. My. God!'

'Thanks, Iris,' I call.

'What else?' my mother breathes, reaching out to clutch Grinelda's age-spotted hand.

'Check the toast. That's his message,' she says, taking a slurp of coffee.

'Got it. Thanks.' I look up at the ceiling. 'Thanks, Jimmy! My sandwich would've been ruined without your divine intervention.'

'A cynic. That's what she is,' Rose says, hurrying to pat Grinelda's shoulder. 'She'll come around.' Rose looks outside. Across the street, the chrysanthemums planted around the statue of James Mackerly glow with good health. 'Oh, my word,' she whispers. 'Yellow flowers next to red! Oh, Larry!'

*   *   *

I race for second, slide at the last second, and bang! I'm in.

'Safe!' calls Sal, the umpire at second.

My teammates cheer. 'Of course I'm safe, Ethan,' I say to my brother-in-law, who missed the tag. 'You're no match for my incredible speed.'

'Apparently not,' he murmurs, a smile curling up the corners of his mouth. Something tugs in my stomach, and I look over at third base. May need to steal that, too.

'Nice try, Ethan!' Ash calls from the stands.

'Thanks, Ash!' he says, tossing her a little salute. She blushes so fiercely we can practically feel the heat. Poor Ash . . . she really needs friends her own age.

Just about every able-bodied adult under the age of seventy plays on the Mackerly Softball League, and every one of the six downtown businesses sponsors a team. So does International Food Products, Ethan's company, the team Bunny's Bakery is playing tonight.

Not only am I the organizer of our little baseball club, spending hours and hours each winter on team assignments, scheduling, equipment maintenance and so on, but I'm one of the league's best players, I'm proud to say. My batting average this year is .513. (Crazy, I know!). As pitcher, I lead the league in strikeouts, and I have more stolen bases than all my teammates combined. It's fair to say I absolutely love playing softball.

Ellen Ripling is up and takes a strike. She hasn't been on base since June 22, and given that it's now mid-September, my hopes are not high that she'll get me to third. However, it's 4-1 Bunny's, and it's the bottom of the eighth. I watch and bide my time. Ball two. I glance at Ethan, who's smart enough to stand close to the base in case I bolt. 'How's your new job?' I ask. Aside from a few chance meetings in the lobby of our building, Ethan and I haven't really talked since he moved back to Mackerly permanently.

'It's okay,' he says. 'Lots of meetings.'

'You haven't really told me about it,' I prod.

'Mmm. Well, I've been busy. Settling in, all that crap.'

I take another look at Ethan. His brown eyes flick to me, and he smiles automatically, that elvish smile that curls so appealingly at the corners. 'Want to come over later?' I ask. 'Tell me about it?'

His gaze flicks back to the batter as Ellen strikes out. Inning over. 'Not sure about that,' he says.

Charley Spirito, Bunny's right-fielder, ambles over as Ethan and I make our way off the infield. 'Hey, Luce,' he says, 'what's this I hear about you looking for a man? Your aunts were saying you're gettin' back in the game. True?'

I wince. My aunts may not fully approve of my efforts to remarry, but that hasn't kept them from advertising my wares to every male who comes in the bakery. Iris's method of not handing over change until I have been viewed has caught on. This morning, Rose presented me to Al Sykes and asked him if he wanted to date me. Given that he was my social studies teacher in sixth grade and roughly forty years my senior, I was grateful when he declined.

'So?' Charley prods.

77

'It's true,' I admit. 'Why? You know any men?'

He grins, hitches up his pants and looks at my chest. 'I'm a man, Luce. You wanna go out with me? I could show you a good time, you know what I'm saying?'

Ethan cuts him a glance but says nothing.

A Del's Lemonade truck pulls into the parking lot, and I find myself wishing I was sipping a frozen drink—or driving the truck—or lying underneath its wheels—rather than talking about my love life on the infield. I've known Charley my whole life. The idea of kissing him . . . getting naked with him . . . I suppress a shudder.

'Then again, a date with you is basically signing my own death warrant, right, Luce?' Charley says, apparently irked at my hesitation. 'I mean, who'd want to do a Black Widow?'

My mouth falls open in surprise, but before I can do anything, Charley is lying on the field, clutching his face.

'Fuck, Ethan! You hit me!'

'Get up,' Ethan growls.

'Ethan,' I say, putting my hand on his arm. He shakes it off.

'Get up.' He stands over Charley, waiting.

I grab Ethan's arm a little harder this time. 'Ethan, he's not gonna fight you. You know that. Leave him alone.' Charley, whose eye is rapidly swelling, shoots me a watery and

78

grateful glance. Ethan did some boxing for a while, one of his many hobbies that involve physical harm to his person. Charley, though he's the middle school gym teacher and seems as physically fit as the next guy, would be an idiot to fight Ethan Mirabelli. And though it could be said that Charley is indeed an idiot, he's not that dumb.

'Lucy, I'm sorry for what I said,' Charley announces loudly enough for all to hear. 'I'm a fuck-up, and that was a shitty thing to say. Okay?'

'Thank you for the beautiful apology, Charley,' I say just as loudly, turning to Ethan. His jaw is tight, his eyes hot. 'Good enough, Ethan?'

'Good enough,' he mutters, then goes to his dugout.

Paulie Smith is our closer and makes short work of International's final three batters. I wonder if he has a date . . . but no, there's his wife. My teammates and I touch knuckles and pack up our gear, exchanging insults and compliments in our dugout.

'You coming to Lenny's, Lucy?' Carly Espinosa, our catcher, asks, slinging her bag over her shoulder, then wincing as it hits her in the leg.

'Um, no, I have something I need to do,' I say.

'See you around, then,' she answers, sauntering after the rest of the team as they

79

head toward the park.

I walk over to the other dugout, where Ethan stuffs his gear into his bag with considerable force. His temper, though rarely unsheathed, takes a while to fade.

'You okay?' I ask.

'Sure,' he says, not meeting my eyes.

I sit on the bench next to him. 'Charley's a dope, that's all,' I say.

'Yup.' He shoves his glove into the bag, then sits for a second, staring at the concrete floor of the dugout. 'So what kind of guy are you looking for, anyway, Lucy?' he asks.

I take a quick breath. 'I don't know. Someone decent. Someone who'd be good to me.' *Someone who won't die young.* 'You want to grab dinner, Ethan? I'm heading over to see your folks.'

'Have you told them about your plan yet?' he asks knowingly. I haven't, and a little moral support would be appreciated.

'Um, no, not yet. I figured I would tonight.' *Please come.*

Ethan tightens the drawstring on his bag and gives me a sidelong glance. 'Sorry. I'm having dinner with Parker and Nicky.' He reaches out, ruffles my hair and is gone, leaving me to sit in the dugout alone. He stops and says something to Ash, who is lingering, hoping for just this interaction.

'Have fun,' I call belatedly. Dinner with the nuclear family. How nice.

80

I wonder for a minute if, now that he's in Mackerly all the time now, Parker and he will get together. If their fondness for each other will blossom into something deeper. If they'll end up married after all this time. I kind of hope so. They're both great people, and they already have Nicky, who's about as wonderful a child as a child can be. Ethan says something to Ash, earning a smile, then continues toward home.

My sentiments about Ethan and Parker are echoed by my mother-in-law an hour later as we sit in the owners' booth at Gianni's.

'That Ethan,' Marie begins, her traditional opening when talking about her younger son. 'He's working in Providence at that horrible company, he's here, he makes a decent living. He should marry that Parker. Be a father to Nicky.'

'He *is* a father to Nicky,' I say mildly, looking at the mural of Venice above our table. 'A wonderful father.'

'A full-time father,' Gianni corrects. 'Thank you, sweetheart,' he adds as Kelly serves our dinner. 'Oh, for Christ's sake, where's the parsley? Ivan, for the love of God!' Gianni lurches up from the table to go yell at his latest chef, which has happened roughly every six minutes since I've been here, and probably happens more often when I'm not.

My father-in-law had bypass surgery last year, and he just can't take the stress of running the kitchen himself. That being said, he goes through chefs like tissues. No one, of course, was as good as Jimmy. No one knew the family recipes, the traditions. No one could ever fill Jimmy's shoes, either as a son or a chef. And so Gianni suffers, his knees increasingly stiff, his temper increasingly short.

'Eat, sweetheart. You're too thin.' Marie, who is wider than she is tall, spears a tortellini from her own plate and holds it out for me. I eat it obediently, smiling. Marie always loved two things about me—I adored her son, and I ate well. I'm not thin, let me assure you, but to an Italian family who owns a restaurant, I look like I just staggered back from forty days in the desert.

Gianni returns from the kitchen, his face flushed, blood pressure up, no doubt, and sits heavily. 'Eat, sweetheart,' he urges me, shoving my plate closer.

'It's wonderful,' I say, and it is . . . eggplant rolatini, one of my favorites. The sauce is a little too acidic, granted, not like when Ethan made it last month at his place. For a vice president of a company whose sole purpose is to get people to avoid eating, Ethan is a fantastic cook. I wonder if he has to hide this fact from his bosses.

'It's not as good as Jimmy's,' Marie declares, putting her fork down with an abrupt clatter.

82

'Of course not,' I murmur, patting her hand and swallowing. *Now or never.* 'Listen, speaking of Jimmy . . .' My in-laws regard me somberly from across the table, waiting. 'Well,' I begin, 'um . . . you know that my sister had a baby, of course.'

'Did she get our eggplant?' Gianni asks.

'Oh, yes, she did. And it was wonderful. She was so grateful.'

'She called, dummy, remember? You talked to her yesterday.' Marie elbows her husband in the side.

'Anyway,' I attempt.

'She's nursing, I hear,' Marie interrupts.

'Um, yes. Anyway—'

'Should I send veal next time? You know what they say about new mothers and red meat,' Gianni says thoughtfully.

'Actually . . . well, Corinne doesn't eat veal. But getting back to—'

'Not eat veal? But why?' Marie frowns.

Rather than launch into the story of Halo, a calf whose birth Corinne witnessed during a field trip in third grade and her resultant 'no-beef' policy, I sit back and fold my hands on the table. 'I need to tell you something,' I say firmly. My mother-in-law takes Gianni's arm protectively. 'I've been thinking a lot lately about Jimmy,' I say more quietly. 'And I think I'm ready to . . . maybe . . . start dating.'

They don't move a muscle.

I take a deep breath. 'I want to get married

83

again. Have kids. There will never be another Jimmy . . . he'll always be my first love.' I swallow. 'But I don't want to grow old alone, either.'

'Of course not,' Gianni says, rubbing his chest, Italian sign language for *Look what you've done to me.* 'You should be happy.'

'Of course,' Marie says, knotting her napkin in her hands. Then she bursts into tears. Gianni puts his arm around her, murmurs in Italian, and they're so dang loving and so *joined* that I start crying, too.

'You deserve happiness,' Marie sobs.

'You're a wonderful girl. You'll always be like a daughter to us,' Gianni says, wiping his eyes.

'And you'll always be my family,' I hiccup. 'I love you both so much.'

Then we clutch hands and indulge in a good old-fashioned crying jag.

CHAPTER SIX

'Trust me, it works wonders.' Parker surveys me through narrowed green eyes.

'You can't be more than a size six,' I say, looking at the . . . thing . . . in Parker's hand. 'I'll never trust you.'

We're in my room, and to my chagrin, I seem to have put on a few pounds recently.

84

Too many Twinkies, too many Ho Hos, my substitute for the desserts I bake myself, which I can't seem to eat. Corinne, nursing Emma, watches as Parker turns back to my closet, which is one of those fabulous California thingies—shelves, drawers, racks. The woiks.

'Why haven't I ever seen you in any of this stuff?' Parker asks, taking out a pair stiletto heels. Oh, I remember those! My first pair of Stuart Weitzman shoes. So pretty. 'Do you ever wear these?'

'Well . . . I'm a baker,' I say. 'Those bad boys would kill me. But I like them, sure. I'm a woman, after all.'

'These all have tags on them!' Parker exclaims, falling upon my sweater section.

'Right,' I murmur.

'You shouldn't spend money if you aren't going to wear them,' Corinne lectures.

'Well, I don't want to be like Mom,' I say in my own defense. My mother, after all, dresses more like Coco Chanel than a woman who works in a tiny bakery. But yes, I have a secret weakness for clothes, and looking in my closet, I see Corinne's point. Clothes, shoes, belts and scarves bulge out toward the room as if imploring me to wear them. So many pretty colors, so much gorgeous fabric—the seductive smoothness of leather, the shimmering silk, the soft comfort of cashmere. Most of that stuff has never been worn.

85

Which, yes, seems pretty dumb.

'Is this La Perla?' Parker demands, yanking a bra out of a drawer.

'Isn't it the prettiest?' I ask.

Parker, whose trust fund could erase the government deficit, glances at the price tag and her eyes widen, and a faint tingle of panic runs through my joints. Okay. Maybe I have a little indulgence issue. Maybe I shouldn't be spending Jimmy's life insurance on, er, underwear. But hey! I'm a tragic widow. I deserve pretty underwear. And Nordstrom's in Providence is so lovely, so soothing. The clerks are always delighted to see me.

Parker gently (reverently?) replaces the La Perla bra. 'Okay, we'll discuss this later. For now, try this. Trust me, it'll work.'

'I don't want to put it on. I'm scared,' I answer, grinning at my sister, who's trying to detach her little parasite by sticking a finger in Emma's mouth. She yanks up her shirt, exposing the unoccupied breast, and Parker and I flinch simultaneously. The . . . er . . . breast looks more like a missile than a mammary gland—rock-hard, the skin taut, white and veined. What really gets me is . . . poor Corinne . . . the cracked, engorged nipple, which looks from here to be the size of a dessert plate.

'How the hell did it crack? It can't be good for you, bleeding nipples,' Parker says, reading my mind. 'Let alone Emma. What if she

86

drinks blood, like some little vampire baby?'

'It's fine,' Corinne says, though her forehead is dotted with sweat. 'The air helps it heal. It's not really bleeding anymore. Mostly healed. Very common. Don't you remember?'

'Nicky was a formula baby,' Parker murmurs. Corinne's eyes widen in horror, and to allay another lecture on What's Best For Baby, I intervene.

'Okay. I'll try it on. Spanx, huh?' I ask. 'It looks evil.'

'Don't be a sissy,' Parker says. 'Honestly, you're such a weenie, Lucy.'

'I think you're perfect,' Corinne murmurs automatically.

'Help me get this on, then,' I say, bravely pulling the undergarment over one toe. My circulation is instantly impaired, and I wiggle my toes to make sure I still can. I tug. The Spanx doesn't budge. 'Jeez, Parker! It's like putting on a garden hose.'

Parker comes over and grabs, yanking so hard I stagger back. 'Work with me!' Parker laughs. We try again. The Spanx advances to my calf. Parker gives another savage tug, and I fall into the wall. Corinne laughs merrily, then gasps as Emma pops off.

'We need a couple of firemen, that's all,' Parker grunts, frowning at the evil Spanx.

'I'd rather set fire to my kitchen,' I say. 'This can't be right, Parker. It doesn't fit.'

'It does! Trust me, once it's on, you'll love

how you look. The men will be salivating. You'll definitely find someone tonight.'

My sister, both huge breasts now fully exposed, smiles. 'So where are you two heading?' she asks.

I can't answer, as Parker has managed to get the Spanx up to my midriff and all breathing is cut off. 'A singles thing,' my friend answers.

Corinne shoots me a wary glance. 'Singles thing? Oh, dear. Christopher might know someone. I'll ask.' Emma fusses, and my sister, looking as if she's about to be executed, shifts her to the other breast. Parker and I quickly avert our eyes as the baby, who apparently has razor blades in place of gums, latches on. Corinne whimpers, then assures the baby that she's deeply loved.

One more savage yank, and the Spanx is in place. My left leg is asleep, as I imagine the femoral artery was cut off when the Spanx grabbed onto my thigh like a furious pit bull.

'How's that?' Parker asks.

'Get it off me,' I wheeze. 'I'm serious, Parker.'

'Chris, hi, honey!' Corinne squeaks from behind us. 'How are you, hon?' She listens for a second, then shifts the phone away from her face. 'He's fine,' she informs us.

'I'll stop the prayer vigil, then,' Parker murmurs, yanking the Spanx back down.

I dig in the back of the closet and find some

jeans that aren't too painful and vow to limit my Twinkie consumption to two per day.

'Okay, we're off,' I say to my sister. 'Lock up when you're done.'

'Have a great time!' Corinne says, looking just a little lonely. 'I'm sure you'll have so much fun.'

If 'fun' means feeling somewhat like I'm a prisoner of war, then yes, I guess you could say I'm having fun. Not to be a bad sport or anything. Parker may have been having fun in the more traditional sense of the word, but personally, I'm wondering when the Coalition of the Willing plans to free me.

'Yes!' The man in front of me smiles. A man who smells like Aunt Iris's cellar, dank and moldering. His eye twitch doesn't advance the cause, either, I'm afraid. Neither does that belch he just barely suppressed. Gah!

'No,' I say as gently as possible. 'Thanks, though. I'm sure you're very nice. But . . . no. It's nothing personal. I'm a widow, see, it's just—'

'Change!' Lemminglike, I step left, my need to make everyone happy mercifully cut off. The next man is extremely thin with a desperate, hungry look about his red-rimmed eyes. 'Yes,' he says.

'No. Sorry. It's not you. It's me. I'm a widow. No one will ever measure up, you understand. Good luck, though.'

'Jesus Christ, Lucy,' Parker mutters next to
89

me, then eyeballs the guy in front of her. 'Yes.'

It cost seventy-five dollars to get into LoveLines tonight. Well, it cost Parker a hundred and fifty dollars to get in tonight, as she paid for my admission. For that sum, we stand in a line, shoulder to shoulder with about forty other women. Facing us is the men's line. Every ten seconds, we take a step left. The idea is to see if there's instant chemistry. Simply put, you look at each other and say only 'yes' or 'no.' If each of you says yes, you exchange cards and, in the next phase of LoveLines, meet for a ten-minute chat. If one or both of you says no, you simply move on.

I had no idea ten seconds could last so long. I quickly learn to hesitate as if torn, then drop my 'no' at the last possible second, so as to minimize the hurt feelings.

So far, Parker has seventeen cards. I have none. 'Stop saying no,' Parker hisses. 'You're standing there, arms crossed, big, sad eyes, looking like an orphan.'

'Prisoner of war, I was thinking.'

'I thought you wanted to find someone,' she says. 'You don't have to marry them, for God's sake. Just say yes. The next guy is pretty cute. Say yes to him.'

'Change!' bellows the moderator. Like members of a chain gang, we all shuffle sideways, advancing to the next man. Parker's right, I need to try. It just seems so . . .

impossible. So stupid, also. Is this what dating is like in your thirties? As always, I'm grateful for Jimmy, the adorable way we met, that long, heart-squeezing, life-changing moment in Gianni's kitchen. Good old Ethan, knowing I'd like his big brother.

I take a breath and smile gamely at the person in front of me. Average-looking, blond, brown eyes. *Be brave, angel,* I imagine Jimmy saying. What the heck. I smile, trying not to look like Oliver Twist.

'Yes,' I say.

'No,' he replies.

'Change!'

By the end of the Chain Gang Shuffle, I have collected four cards; Parker, twenty-one. We women go to our designated tables and sit, waiting for our suitors to visit.

My first Yes is just what the doctor ordered. He's rather bland but wears a nice suit. He has a serious, thoughtful face that bodes well for commitment and wise choices, unlike (for example) Ethan's devilish eyebrows and delicious smile. Even his tie bespeaks stability. Navy blue, no pattern, very unthreatening. The kind of tie an accountant might wear.

'Hello,' I say as he sits down. 'I'm Lucy Mirabelli.'

'Hi,' he replies. 'I'm Todd Smith.' Perfect. A nice boring name. Todd Smith simply could not be a dangerous man, not with a name and a tie like that.

91

'What do you do for a living, Todd?' I ask.

'I'm an accountant.'

My smiles grows more genuine. 'I'm a baker,' I say.

'Interesting.'

'Mmm,' I murmur. 'Yup.' We look at each other. My smile starts to feel a little stiff. I look at my hands, primly folded in front of me. Todd has a similarly wooden smile on his face. Or maybe it's his normal smile. I picture seeing that smile across the kitchen table for the next fifty years. Suppress a sigh.

Next to me, Parker is howling with laughter over something her guy said. She tosses her hair, and he leans forward, grinning. Across from me, Todd blinks and cocks his head. I'm reminded of a lizard. Blink, blink. Perhaps his tongue will shoot out and he'll catch a fly.

'So. An accountant,' I say.

'Yes. That's right.'

My toes curl in my shoes. Granted, I wanted boring. *Reliable*, my conscience corrects in a chastising voice. Yes, yes, reliable. Someone who didn't love me so much he tried to stay awake for twenty straight hours. Someone with the sense to pull over, no matter what his smitten wife might've said.

'Do you like movies?' I ask, searching my brain for something to talk about. 'I'm a big movie watcher. I watched *Star Wars* last night.' Surely everyone on earth has seen *Star Wars*.

92

'I don't watch movies, no,' Todd replies. His face is so impassive it could be carved from wood. 'I tend to watch CNN more than anything. Their financial reporting is top-notch.'

'And that Anderson Cooper sure is a hottie,' I add without thinking. Oopsy. Todd's face doesn't change. He doesn't seem to mind. Then again, he doesn't seem to be alive, either. I forge on, albeit with a creeping certainty that Todd is, in fact, an android. 'But you've seen *Star Wars*, right?'

'No.'

'But . . . I mean, it's part of Americana. NASA sent Luke Skywalker's light saber into space.'

'I haven't seen *Star Wars*.' He forces a smile and says nothing more.

'Do you like dessert?' I ask with a hint of desperation.

'I love Nilla Wafers,' he answers. 'Other than that, I really don't indulge. It's a sign of weakness, don't you agree?'

Okay, he's out. Mercifully our ten minutes are up. 'A pleasure,' Todd says, standing and melting back into the crowd.

'Bye,' I say, but he's already gone.

Parker's guy, who looks like Matt Damon, just for the record, smooches her on the cheek. 'Can't wait to read your books,' he says fondly.

'They're disgusting. Give them only to

children you hate.' She smiles and tosses her gorgeous hair back, then looks at me. 'So how was your guy?'

'He was a dud,' I answer.

'It's all good,' Parker says. 'There are bound to be duds. You're here. It's a big step. Hey, we should ask Ethan to come with us next time. He's probably looking, too, now that you cut him off.'

'I didn't cut him off!' I splutter. 'It was just time to end our . . . thing. And he was so fine with it, I wonder if he even noticed.'

Parker turns her attention to the guy in front of her. I wait for my own next Yes to show up, but apparently, he's morphed into a No, since he's over with a woman whose blouse is so low-cut I can see areola. I look away. After Corinne's little peep show in my room earlier, I've had all the nipple I can take.

Maybe I should work on Parker. Ethan asked her to marry him. Twice, actually. Once when she told him she was preggers, once a few weeks after Nicky was born. Granted, it was largely because of his Italian sense of family and honor, but still. He didn't have to.

I'm snapped out of my reverie by a tap on the shoulder. Ah, my third Yes. 'Hi,' I say.

'Hi,' he replies. 'I'm Kyle.'

'I'm Lucy,' I say. *I'm looking for a guy I don't love too much. Want to give it a shot?*

He smiles. It's a nice grin, but not too nice. Brown hair, hazel eyes. I imagine him coming

94

through the door every night. It's not horrible. Progress. Kyle takes a seat. 'So,' he says amiably. 'What's a nice girl like you doing in a place like this?'

I take a deep breath. 'Well, I'm a widow. And my friend thought this would be a good way to start getting out there, you know?'

He nods. 'A widow, huh? Awesome.'

I have to say, that's not the usual response. 'Excuse me?'

Kyle leans back in his chair and smiles contentedly. 'Well, you're not some skank nobody wants, you know what I'm saying? Like, some guy already thought you were pretty hot, popped the question, then ran into some bad luck, am I right?' My mouth opens, but no sound comes out. Kyle doesn't seem to notice. 'And you're not some trashy ho who plows through the dudes, either, I'm guessing, since you look all nice and clean and stuff. So you know . . . cool. You being a widow and all. You must be pretty horny, too, you know what I'm saying?'

Suddenly I feel the spirit of Attila the Hun, my ancestor, materialize at my shoulder. 'You're right. Being a widow *is* so cool. No one to mess up my stuff, you know what *I'm* saying? And you know what else, Kyle? Let me tell you a secret. One day, back when he was still alive, my husband took the last cup of coffee, okay? Didn't even tell me. So I said to myself, "Lucy, do you really want to live like

95

this?" And I didn't, so I killed him.' I flutter my eyelashes. 'You want to grab dinner sometime?'

Parker and I don't talk much on the way home. My last Yes turned out to be a firefighter, and though he was attractive, charming and polite, there was no way in hell I was going to marry a man who rushed into burning buildings with a rinky-dink little air pack strapped to his back. Parker took his card, though, and they have a date next week.

'You did good tonight, kid,' Parker says when we reach my place.

'And you did amazingly,' I say. 'How many dates do you have for next week?'

'Just three,' she answers.

'Are you really looking for someone, or are you just keeping me company?' I ask.

'Oh, I guess I'd like to find someone. Theoretically. It's different, though, having a kid. I already belong to someone, you know? It's just that he's four years old.'

I smile. 'You're so lucky, Parker.'

She reaches over and squeezes my hand. 'I know. Now get out of my car, you.'

'Thanks for driving,' I say. 'And thanks for taking me. Sorry you wasted your money.'

'It's nothing,' she answers. 'Talk to you tomorrow. And hey, Luce . . .' She turns to look at me, and as always, I'm struck by just how gorgeous she is.

'Yes?'

'Jimmy would be proud of you.'

There's a sudden lump in my throat. 'Thanks,' I say, my voice uneven. 'Kiss Nicky for me.'

'Will do.'

In the elevator, rather than pressing 4, I hit 5. Ethan's floor. Maybe he wants a little company. Maybe—I wince, feeling like a person on a diet standing in front of the freezer, knowing she's about to eat a pint of Ben & Jerry's—maybe Ethan wouldn't mind a friendly little tumble. One that means nothing . . . just a little nooky, a quick shag. Or a longer shag, maybe.

I knock at his door. If he's home, he's awake . . . it's only ten, and Ethan never goes to bed before 1:00 a.m. Or he didn't use to, anyway. Whatever the case, there's no answer. Feeling more deflated than I should, I go back down to my apartment, where Fat Mikey winds himself around my ankles in his traditional attempt to cause my death by tripping me. I pick him up, remind him that he loves me and I live to serve him, and kiss his large head.

Though I know I shouldn't, I find myself sitting in front of the TV, watching my wedding video once again, Fat Mikey's comforting bulk at my side. After attempting to find a date tonight, I just need to see Jimmy's face, see him in motion. Our time together was so brief—so many memories that

97

might've been were taken from me the night he died. We have no first anniversary, no birth of our children.

I hit Mute and watch the video in silence, undistracted by the sounds of the music, the laughter, other people talking. Instead I just drink in the sight of Jimmy, frozen in time at age twenty-seven, crazy in love with me.

CHAPTER SEVEN

The first time Ethan and I slept together was, um, well . . . it was memorable.

What brings a woman to sleep with her brother-in-law, after all? I'm going to have to go with honesty here. Sheer horniness.

See, it had been three and a half years. That's forty-two months of being alone. Things were better, they were. The darkest days were over, when I'd wake up and realize something was wrong but didn't know what . . . the desperate, terrifying realization that I'd *never* see Jimmy again, ever . . . somehow I'd gotten through that yawning, awful black time. Sure, I still had a few bad moments here and there. But I was trying.

Growing up around widows, I'd seen my mother and aunts embrace widowhood as a defining trait. Before all else, they were Widows, and God help me, I didn't want that to happen. I wanted to stay myself, the happy, optimistic person Jimmy had loved . . . not someone who waved the flag of widowhood wherever she went. Granted, I often felt that the best part of me died with Jimmy, but I tried to radiate the idea that yes, it was awful, but I'd be really okay someday. To try to keep positive, I did a little yoga, taught my pastry class, since baking soothed me even though I couldn't choke down the results, and listened to Bob Marley a lot. A line from 'No Woman, No Cry' would run through my head whenever I felt that backward pull toward blackness. *Everything's gonna be all right. Everything's gonna be all right. Everything's gonna be all right. Everything's gonna be all right.* I was managing. Everything *would* be all right, I was determined it would.

And then came my twenty-eighth birthday. And everything was not all right.

Because on that day, suddenly, I was older than my husband ever would be.

As my birthday dawned, I could feel myself sinking into the black hole that had been so hard to crawl out of. I was twenty-eight. Jimmy would never be. I was twenty-eight, widowed, childless, chubbier, paler. My life had been so wonderful with Jimmy and now— I couldn't avoid the fact today—my life sucked. I was baking bread instead of desserts. I wasn't featured on the cover of *Bon Appetit* or a guest judge on *Top Chef.* I was nobody in the world of pastry chefs, no one's wife, no one's mother, and none of that was likely to change anytime soon. While I was surviving, I was no fun. You get the idea.

When the Black Widows came into the bakery that morning, I told them I was leaving early. I'd never taken a day off from Bunny's, as the last thing I wanted was too much time on my hands. Iris peered anxiously in my mouth, looking for signs of 'the Lou Gehrig's.' Rose offered me one of her 'pep pills,' which I declined (not sure if they were Tic Tacs, cold medicine or Prozac). My own mother said nothing, probably knowing just why I wanted to hide.

The aunts clucked around me like worried hens. After much discussion, they accepted my assurance that the chances of me having ALS were probably not as high as feared. I told them I was fine . . . maybe I just needed a makeover, was just feeling blue. My mother gave me a rare hug, said we'd celebrate my birthday tomorrow, and Iris offered me her lipstick (Coral Glow, which she'd been wearing for fifty years and which bore more resemblance to a nuclear spill than anything that God made). I put a little on—it couldn't hurt, right?—and walked home.

My mood grew heavier as I skirted the park. In there was Jimmy's grave, incontrovertible evidence that he was not alive. When he first died, I went through all that magical thinking that widows do, coming up with possible scenarios to prove Jimmy's death was a mistake. That he *had* stopped, for example, at a motel. But someone had stolen his car, and it was that poor thief who died, not Jimmy. (The fact that I'd seen Jimmy's body at the funeral home was something I'd have been happy to overlook, should he come walking through the doors.) Or that Jimmy worked for the CIA and his death was staged, and any day I'd be getting a call from Zimbabwe or Moscow. Or if I just was brave and strong enough, that Jimmy would come back and tell me I'd done a great job and that he'd be alive again, sorry for the inconvenience, and I could just relax and go back to that sweet, happy life we'd once had.

Now, I forced myself to look in the general direction of my husband's grave, and a little more magical thinking occurred. 'Are you really going to let me be older than you?' I asked, aloud. 'Jimmy? You sure about this?'

The challenge went unanswered. With a lump in my throat, I continued on my way.

When I got home, my apartment was still dark, as I hadn't pulled up the shades. I decided to keep them down, too glum for sun. Then I tripped over Fat Mikey in the gloom, earning an outraged hiss. I heaved a sigh: 10:00 a.m. on the day when I'd officially be older than my poor dead husband. *Please, God, let this next year be better,* I prayed. *Let me have a little fun.* I hadn't had much fun since Jimmy died, as God well knew.

Yes. I straightened up. The next year—and all the years thereafter—*should* be fun. Wicked fun, in fact. Jimmy wasn't coming back, the selfish jerk. (That would be the anger part of grief—it reared its ugly head every once in a while.) I'd have fun, dang it all. I deserved a little fun, didn't I? 'I deserve some fun, Fat Mikey, don't you think?' I asked my cat. He twitched his tail in agreement, then yawned.

'You're right,' I said. 'No one deserves fun more than a tragic widow. You are one brilliant cat.'

Thus resolved, I opened my fridge, revealing coffee milk, the Rhode Island state drink, sour cream, lemons and a jar of pickles. My freezer contained six pints of Ben & Jerry's, a bag of peas and a bottle of Absolut vodka. 'Perfect,' I declared to my cat. Vodka and coffee milk . . . an Ocean State version of a White Russian, which, if analyzed, seemed almost to be a healthy breakfast . . . a little dairy, a little coffee, a little vodka. The drink went down so smoothly that I made myself another. Delicious. I took a few slugs, then poured a teaspoon of coffee milk into Fat Mikey's dish (no vodka . . . didn't want charges filed against me for getting a cat drunk), and he lapped it up. 'Only alcoholics drink alone,' I told him, stroking his silky fur.

He turned and gently bit my hand, then continued drinking.

Time to do a little inventory. I would greet my new age armed with a perky attitude, sure I would. Slightly dizzy, I decided to take a good hard look at myself, see what needed to change so I could have more fun. Tripping once more over the large mass of fur and fat that was my pet, I went into my bedroom, stripped naked and stood in front of the full-length mirror on the back of my door.

Gah!

My eyes looked bigger, courtesy of the bluish circles underneath them, which I'd acquired the night the state trooper had come to my door. The skin on my face was white, and a little flaky, especially around my chin. Oh, man! When was the last time I'd exfoliated? Bush's first term? And my hair! I'd had it cut here and there over the past few years, of course, but when was the last time? I couldn't remember. Just because it was in a ponytail at work didn't mean it had to be so flat and lifeless . . . I chugged the rest of my White Russian, needing a little liquid courage, then continued my self-perusal.

And what was this? Cellulite? I didn't have cellulite! Well, ten pounds ago, I hadn't had cellulite . . . How had this happened? And oh, crap, look at those legs. Had shaving been outlawed? Now, granted, I didn't go around wearing skirts or shorts, not when I was dealing with four hundred degree ovens, but there was no excuse for *this*. I needed to go to the beach and get a little sun, too, because my skin was so white that I could've modeled for med students studying the circulatory system. Bluish veins ran under my white skin like mold through a wheel of blue cheese. Those legs hadn't seen the sun for years. Years! How had that happened?

On to the feet . . . ew. Hey, if Howard Hughes didn't need to cut his toenails, apparently neither did I. And my God, those heels! So rough and dry! Gah!

In a sudden frenzy, I pulled on Jimmy's old robe, yanked open my bathroom cupboard and rummaged in the back. Scissors, terrific. Oh, great, a pumice stone. Forgot all about that thing. Hadn't used it since I was a newlywed. Here was some crusty old mud mask guaranteed to minimize my pores and give me 'the radiant glow of the Swiss.' I'd never been to Switzerland, but they couldn't look worse than I did.

The last thing I unearthed was an unopened bottle of spray-on sunless tanner. I checked the expiration date: 08/2004. Well. It probably wouldn't work, but it was worth a shot. I had to do something. I couldn't hit twenty-eight looking like something left in the basement for the past decade or so. Besides, what said fun more than a tan? Nothing.

'This calls for another drink, Fat Mikey,' I

said. 'And yes, you can have some more. But no vodka for you, my feline friend.' White Russians were fun. Girls who drank them . . . ditto. Fat Mikey watched me, his eyes slits of appreciation, I thought.

Yes. Things in the mirror were better when I studied myself a long while later, though that might've been because my eyes were having trouble focusing. I'd only intended to cut my bangs, but I'd done such a good job that I kept going. I looked cute in a ragged, Japanese animé kind of way, the bangs shorter on one side, falling in little points. Adorable. Elfin, really. My face was shiny clean, though I couldn't seem to get the dried mud off one ear. Even so, it was an improvement.

The tanner hadn't worked—I was still fish-belly white—but that was okay. At least my heels had a little color now, pink instead of gray . . . oops, one seemed to be bleeding a little, maybe got a little too energetic with that pumice stone. And the cherry-red nail polish I'd applied was kind of gummy, being that it was quite elderly, so my toes (and fingernails) were maybe a little smeary, but still and all, better. My legs bled in a few places, since my razor was a little dull, but I was smooth, at least. Much better.

Still wrapped in Jimmy's bathrobe, I meandered into the living room and flopped on the couch. Fat Mikey jumped up and kneaded my stomach—hopefully, he'd break up some of the cellulite—and then curled next to me. I felt better. I'd greet this new age o' mine smoother and cuter than I'd left it. All good. 'Don't I look nice?' I asked my cat. He purred in agreement. 'That was fun. We're going to have some fun, Fat Mikey. Look out, world, here comes the fun.'

Within seconds, I was asleep.

I was awakened by a knock on the door. The apartment, which had been dim to begin with, was now fully dark, and I stumbled to the door, hands outstretched, till I hit the light switch. Flipping it on, I squinted in the abrupt brightness, then peered through the peephole. Ethan. That's right, it was Friday, so Ethan was home. 'Hi,' I said, rubbing an eye as I opened the door.

'Hey, Luce, happy birth—' He broke off suddenly. 'Jesus, what happened?'

'Nothing,' I frowned. 'Why?' His face was slack with horror. 'Ethan. What is it?'

'Did you . . . do something? To your . . .'

'What?'

His eyes traveled up and down my form. 'Lucy . . .' He started to say something, then stopped. 'Oh, Lucy.' He covered his mouth with one hand.

'What?' I asked again.

'Uh . . . you . . . um . . .' He started laughing. Wheezing, really.

That was it. I fled to the bathroom, took a look in the mirror. And screamed.

106

My face was bright red, imprinted on the left side from the corduroy pillow on the couch. My right eye still had some grayish-green dried mud on the lid, which was preventing me from opening it all the way, sort of a stroke victim look going on there . . . Apparently, the aging mud mask had caused a rash, because my cheeks were red and bumpy. And my hair! Oh, Lord, my hair! Never cut your own hair while intoxicated . . . sure, *now* I remembered that particular rule. Seems so obvious, doesn't it? Yet I'd done it, and it looked as if I'd run face-first into a lawn mower, my bangs choppy and irregular, the hair on the left side significantly shorter than the hair on the right.

Then I saw my arms. And my legs.

'No!' I wailed.

Brown and orange streaks covered my formerly white, white skin, except for the patches where the spray tanner had missed. I looked filthy, as if I'd been picking crops in the dust bowl. 'No!' I moaned, slamming on the hot water and shoving a facecloth under the stream. I scrubbed the streaks violently, but no. Nothing changed, except my skin grew pinker under the fake tan.

That was it. I burst into tears. Pathetic, that's what I was. A pathetic, drunken, smeary widow with orange skin, insane asylum hair and a rash. Insult to injury. Not only had God taken my Jimmy . . . He'd let me go on a

White Russian bender while armed with scissors and tan-from-a-can! It was enough to make me an atheist.

'Come on, Lucy, it's not that bad,' Ethan said from the other side of the bathroom door, his voice carefully controlled. 'Seems like you just got a little . . .' He went silent, and I knew too well that he was laughing.

'Don't,' I said, yanking open the door. Ethan was bent over, wheezing. I smacked him in the shoulder. 'Look at me! This is ridiculous! This is what I get for trying to be fun!'

'Oh, I don't know. This is pretty fun,' he managed to say.

How could he laugh? 'You're so mean, Ethan,' I sniffled.

'It's just . . . you . . . your legs . . . and your hair . . .' He staggered back against the wall, rattling a picture, laughing so hard tears brightened his eyes.

'It's not funny,' I wailed. 'I'm older than Jimmy now, Ethan. I'm a widow, and I'm all alone and look at me! I should never have had those White Russians.'

'You think?' he asked, wiping his eyes.

I smacked him again, tears flooding my eyes, then turned away, hiccupping on a coffee-flavored sob. 'I hate you.'

'Okay, okay, I'm sorry,' he said. 'Come on, now, honey, don't cry.' He took my hand and led me to the living room, pulling me down next to him on the couch, where we'd logged so many hours together, watching movies or playing Extreme Racing USA. Fat Mikey jumped up, then, apparently horrified at how I looked, jumped back down and stalked into the kitchen, tail puffy with fear. Ethan patted my shoulder. 'I'll take you into Providence tomorrow for a good haircut. And the tan stuff will fade. Just, um, try a little Brillo. Maybe some Clorox.' That set him off again.

'You don't get it, Ethan,' I said in a smaller voice. 'I just feel so . . . I'm twenty-eight now. I'm older than Jimmy.' Swallowing, I looked down. For a second, I remembered Jimmy's blue-green eyes smiling at me, and my heart broke all over again. 'No one will ever love me like that again.' Dang, I was really crying now. So much for all fun, all the time.

'Oh, hey,' he said, his voice gentle. 'You'll be loved again, Lucy. The minute you're ready. You'll see.'

'I'm orange, Ethan,' I squeaked. 'And it looks like my hair got caught in a fan.'

He bit down on a smile. 'You're gorgeous,' he said. 'Even now, with all the, er, extras. You'd be gorgeous if you rolled in, I don't know, pig entrails. Cow manure.' He handed me a tissue from the box on the coffee table.

'That's so poetic. You should work for Hallmark,' I said, blowing my nose. Still, his words made my heart feel a little bit better.

'It's true. You're beautiful.' He smiled and

reached out to touch my cheek.

'Thanks, Ethan,' I said, blinking in alcoholic gratitude. 'You're the best.'

'I thought you hated me,' he said, one eyebrow raising in that elvish way, a grin curling the corners of his mouth.

'I don't. I was lying,' I answered.

'Just checking,' he said.

And then, quite out of the blue, he kissed me.

Ethan had kissed me before, of course. He'd been my friend since college, had been my brother-in-law, my protector and comforter, and he was Italian, and Italians kiss their relatives. So yes, Ethan had kissed me many times, on the cheek, as in *Okay, gotta run, see you next weekend.* But not like this.

This was just a gentle, warm press of lips. A sweet, almost innocent kiss after a long, long time of nothingness, and it was such a generous thing, that kiss, such an act of kindness, that my heart stopped in near-wonder. Then it was over, and Ethan pulled back an inch or two and looked at me. There were shards of gold in his brown eyes, and somehow I'd never noticed that. We stared at each other for a few heartbeats, barely breathing.

Without quite realizing it, I leaned forward, closing the distance between us. Ethan's lips were so soft and full and warm, achingly wonderful. There was the soft, bristly scrape

110

of his three-days beard against my face, the cool silkiness of his hair under my fingers.

The kiss deepened, a little less soft, a little more . . . meaningful. Ethan shifted, cupped my head in his hands. His tongue brushed mine, and that was it. I lurched against him, gripped a fistful of his shirt in one hand, his skin hot through the fabric. A little sound came from the back of my throat, and the way he tasted and felt made me feel dizzy, because it was so, *so* good to be touched, and held, and kissed again. God, I missed kissing.

And much to my surprise, I found that I liked kissing *Ethan*. Very much. It could be said, in fact, that (A) I was starving and (B) he was a buffet, because I'd (C) crawled on top of him, had his head clamped between my hands and was kissing the stuffing out him.

Of course, I'd imagined kissing someone since Jimmy died. Someone who was Not-Jimmy . . . imagined how I'd feel and how *difficult* and *sad* it would be. How I'd compare the two men, Jimmy and Not-Jimmy, and I'd find Jimmy so superior and then wallow in self-pity for my poor widowed self.

Somehow, I wasn't thinking those things now. Later, it would occur to me that I hadn't thought about Jimmy at all, not in the way I'd imagined I would. I hadn't forgotten about him, of course . . . he was part of me, and so thoughts like, *Jimmy's robe is slipping* flashed here and there. But they were interspersed with other thoughts . . . *Oh, God, that feels good, don't stop* . . . for example. As for a sense of Jimmy's ghost standing there, watching me in disapproval, no. Maybe it was the White Russians, maybe not, but all I could think of was how *good* it felt, how grateful I was to be wanted again. To have a man's hands on my skin, to feel the solid muscles of male shoulders, to inhale the dark, spicy scent of a man, to be kissed with that blend of soft and hard, tenderness and hunger.

Ethan was the one who pulled back, eyes dark and smoky, and took my hands in his, held them against his chest. I was straddling his lap, and my robe—Jimmy's robe—was half off, and while Ethan hadn't seen my boobs yet, it was pretty much a technicality. I could feel his heart thudding against me, and both of us were breathing hard. I may have been shaking. 'Lucy,' he said, and his voice contained a soft warning.

'Don't say anything,' I whispered, then I kissed him again, loving the fullness of his lips, the taste of his mouth. And when he didn't respond immediately, I took his hand and put it over my breast, holding it there as I kissed him.

'You sure about this?' he murmured against my mouth.

'Don't talk,' I repeated, and to make sure he wouldn't, I grabbed his shirt, it was one of my favorites, a black button-down, and I just ripped that thing open and oh, Ethan was pretty gorgeous, and he was so warm and solid and real. He was here, too, and alive. Couldn't overlook the little things.

'Take me to bed,' I commanded. And Ethan stood up, lifting me with him, my legs wrapped around his waist, and obeyed.

*　　*　　*

It wasn't until roughly fifty-three minutes later that common sense came roaring back with a brisk slap in the face.

I was lying under Ethan, still panting, my legs as weak as overcooked linguine, my skin damp with sweat. His face was against my neck, one arm around me, his hand in my newly shorn hair. I could feel his heart rate calming and suddenly, a cold river of dread flooded my heart. A horrible phrase sneaked into my mind. A phrase that implies one person is doing another person a favor by sleeping with her. That one person feels deep, deep sympathy, even pity, for the other, and it is only pity that motivates him to . . . Oh, God. Oh, no. Ethan had just given me a mercy f—

Oh, and one more thing. It was *Ethan!* I'd just had sex with Ethan! Horror clamped down on me like a thirty-foot python, and my eyes flooded with tears. I'd just done the *wild thing* with Ethan Mirabelli. My dead

113

husband's *brother*. I'd *cheated* on Jimmy (his death being a minor detail at this moment).

'I'm sorry,' I whispered as the tears spilled over. 'Um, Ethan, I need to . . . I should . . .' I wriggled out of bed, dragging a sheet over me, and on streaky, weak orange legs, I staggered into the bathroom, locking the door behind me. Pulling on my own bathrobe (as Jimmy's lay somewhere between the couch and the *bed*), I slid to the floor, a thousand recriminations bouncing around in my skull, grabbed a towel and buried my face in it to muffle the sound of my sobs. At least I wouldn't have to worry about (sob) pregnancy, as I'd been on the Pill for a while, due to irregular periods, something I'd managed to tell Ethan when he asked just how far we should go. And I knew that Ethan would never . . . but just the idea that I'd *done* it with Ethan *Mirabelli* . . . Oh, God.

'Lucy? You okay?' came Ethan's voice.

'Ehehehenngh,' I managed. I heard the rustle of clothes—he was pulling on his pants, I guessed. Because he was probably still *naked*. Because I'd made him *shag* me. Because he was too *nice* to say no.

Ethan tried the door. 'Open up, honey,' he said.

'Um, I need a minute,' I squeaked. The tears, hot and damning, slipped out of my eyes. *Oh, Jimmy,* I thought. He'd be so ashamed of me, mauling his brother, putting

114

Ethan in an impossible position like this.

The little lock on the door popped open, and Ethan came in, clad in jeans and nothing else.

'How'd you unlock the door?' I asked, not looking at his face.

'One of my many life skills,' he answered, sitting next to me. 'Lucy. Come on, honey. Don't cry.'

'I'm so sorry,' I hiccupped. 'Ethan, I'm so, so sorry.'

'What for?' he asked, taking my hand.

'I made you have sex with me,' I blubbered.

'Yes, guys hate that,' he murmured, tipping my chin up. 'If anyone's sorry, Lucy, it should be me. I'm the one who started it.'

'I was pretty much begging for it,' I said.

'And again, guys hate that.' He smiled.

'You're not just a guy. You're Jimmy's brother. I'm Jimmy's wife. We're related. And now you've seen me. Naked. Naked and orange.' A hitching sob stuttered out of me.

He rolled his eyes. 'We're not related, and you're not Jimmy's wife anymore, honey. You're his widow. And you look great naked, even if you're not the right color.'

This further kindness just caused my face to scrunch up in that awful expression of uncontrollable crying. 'I should probably move out,' I wept. 'Find another apartment. Leave Rhode Island. Become a nun.'

Ethan laughed. 'A nun, huh?'

115

'Don't laugh,' I said. 'I'm so ashamed, Ethan.'

'Okay, stop,' he said, his voice firm. 'Lucy. Stop crying.' He turned and grabbed the box of tissues from the back of the toilet. I noted there were scratch marks on his back. God, I was a complete slut! My face contorted again.

'Here,' he said. 'Blow your nose.'

I did, a couple of times. Wiped my eyes, finally getting off the last of the mud mask, it seemed. 'Ethan, really, I'm so sorry. We never should've done this. It was wrong, and it was all my fault.'

He took a deep breath. 'Lucy, listen.' He took both my hands in his and looked at me until I was able to look back. His dark eyes were serious for once. 'We both miss him. We're young, we're healthy, we're straight. And we spend a lot of time together. We just . . . comforted each other. That's all, honey.'

For a second, it looked like he was going to say something else, but then he must've changed his mind, because he didn't.

'Don't you feel guilty?' I asked. After all, I was Hungarian *and* Catholic. Of course I felt guilty. Ethan was also Catholic, and Italian. Surely he felt a few pangs, a little fear of hell—

'No. I don't feel at all guilty. Or bad in any way. My back's a little sore, maybe. How much do you weigh these days?'

I gave a surprised snort of laughter and

116

smacked his shoulder. His bare, rather perfect, nicely muscled shoulder. 'None of your business,' I answered.

'My chiropractor might say otherwise.' He winked, looking every inch the flirt he was.

His skin was so smooth. Which I could tell because apparently I was sort of caressing that shoulder. Ethan's torso was rather . . . gorgeous. The muscles in his arms moved and slid beautifully under his olive skin. Oh, look, he had six-pack abs. All that time outdoors, I guessed. And his hands . . . Manly, capable hands. The kind that knew what to do to a woman. Mmm.

Suddenly aware that I was ogling him, I jerked my hand away from that lovely shoulder and sneaked a look at Ethan's face. There it was again, that little crooked smile that changed his face from not bad to mischievous and adorable.

Ethan reached out and pinched my chin. 'Don't feel guilty, you crazy orange nut job,' he said. 'Okay?'

His hair was sticking up on one side. 'I'll try,' I said.

For a moment, we just looked at each other. Then, almost without meaning to, I reached out and put my hand against his lovely, warm neck and felt his pulse jump against my hand. A long, hot moment seemed to vibrate between us.

Then Ethan leaned in, slowly, slowly, and

kissed me again.

And we ended up doing it on the bathroom floor, Fat Mikey yowling outside the door.

When Ethan left on Sunday night, I promised him I'd never put him in this position again. Said promise was broken the next weekend, when I jumped him the second he came through my door, and then again a few hours later, when he said he should be going and kissed me goodbye.

After a few forbidden shags, we—well, I— decided we should be friends with privileges and nothing more. I made Ethan swear that this wouldn't change our friendship; that he'd dump me if he met someone else or wanted to get back with Parker; and that he'd never ever tell anyone about us, because the idea of my in-laws finding out that I was doing their younger son . . . Gah! No. As far as my mother and aunts went, God forbid they found out that I was *using Ethan for sex*. My family drew the line at the use of scarlet letters, but just barely. I remembered Cousin Ilona of the early menopause being labeled a hussy when, eighteen short years after her husband died, she let the postman carry in her groceries.

Breaking up—check that. *Ending the arrangement* between Ethan and me was a good idea. I wanted to move on, and Ethan was too dangerous a choice for a husband.

I just hadn't realized how much I'd miss

him.

CHAPTER EIGHT

'And this one? What would you call that, my dear?'

'That, Mr. Dombrowski, is our world famous chocolate chip cookie.' Famous perhaps for its utter blandness, and a far cry from the crispy, butter-soaked variety Iris bakes for family members. She says the recipe is not worth wasting on what she calls 'the great unwashed.'

'I see, I see.' He shuffles another inch alongside the case. 'And this one?'

I smile. 'That would be our legendary cheese danish. I believe you've tried those before.' Every day for the past twenty-three years, in fact.

'I think I may try that, then. You say I like it?'

'You do, Mr. D. You definitely do.' I take a danish out of the case and, because I like Mr. D. so much, put it in a little box and tie it with string. He deserves more than a bag. We had tea together once in his surprisingly bright and uncluttered house—and it took him about half an hour to set the table just so. I could relate . . . at the time, I'd been a new widow, and filling the hours was of utmost importance.

'I think I'll enjoy this,' Mr. Dombrowski says. He straightens his tie—he still wears one every day—and a wave of tenderness washes over me.

'Please come back soon,' I say, handing him the box. 'It's always so nice to see you.'

His creased old face splits in a smile. 'Thank you, my dear,' he says.

If Bunny's had tables and chairs and served coffee and tea, Mr. D. would have a place to sit every day. He might see more people than just the Black Widows and me.

'I think we should expand,' I announce as I return to the kitchen. The yeasty smell of Italian bread fills the air—Jorge just left with Gianni's Friday night order, and things are winding down at Bunny's. Iris and Rose are hunched over a newspaper, the pastry dough for tomorrow morning's danishes sitting in neglected lumps. When dough gets warm, it loses its flakiness. I glance at what they're poring over—it's the sports page, featuring a large picture of Josh Beckett of Red Sox fame. Aw. My aunts are cougars. How cute.

'Hello?' I say. 'Anyone baking back here? This dough's getting warm.'

Both aunts jump. Rose grabs a rolling pin and attacks the dough maniacally.

'Expand what?' Iris asks, her face taking on that bulldog look she gets whenever we discuss this.

'The bakery. It's silly that we don't have

120

seats or serve coffee. We're losing money hand over fist to Starbucks.'

'We're not some grunge hangout,' Rose says, and I have to say, I'm impressed she knows the term *grunge*. 'We're a bakery. We sell baked goods, not some overpriced coffee that tastes like you scraped it off the bottom of the pot. And a tall? What's a tall? What's a grand? They don't even say it right. GrahhhhnnnDAY. Please. Can't they just say small, medium, large?'

I arch an eyebrow at my aunt. 'You've been to Starbucks, Rose. How surprising.'

'What?' Iris barks. 'Explain yourself.'

Rose blinks like a frightened mouse, a strategy that's always worked well for her. 'I didn't mean to order a coffee,' she peeps in her little-girl voice. 'But those names are so confusing! I thought I was getting a hot chocolate.'

'We have hot chocolate at home!' Iris thunders.

'Not like the Starbucks,' Rose says, her face lighting up with something like religious adoration. She turns to me. 'Oh, Lucy, sweetheart, you have to try it! It's incredible! The whipped cream is—'

'You're a traitor to this family, Rose Black Thompson!' Iris barks. 'Mama would spin in her grave!'

My mother drifts in, navy pencil skirt, silk blouse printed in blue and green, bottle-green

121

suede Prada pumps that I'd nearly bought myself last week. 'I could hear you in front of Lenny's, Iris,' she says.

'Your sister has been to the Starbucks!' Iris says in the same tone as one might say, *Your sister strangled a puppy.*

'Stop being so domineering, Iris,' Rose dares, her face pink. 'I can buy a hot chocolate if I want to! You're not the boss of me!'

'Okay, stop, you two, or I'm turning a hose on you,' my mother says. 'Lucy, someone just came in. Take it, won't you?'

Gratefully, I scurry out of the kitchen. Charley Spirito is there, resplendent in Red Sox regalia—jacket, cap, sweatpants as well as a black eye and sheepish look. 'Hi, Luce,' he says hesitantly.

'Hey, Charley,' I answer. 'What can I get you?'

The bell over the door tinkles as Ethan comes in, insulated bag in hand. My heart does a little twist, which I try to ignore. He's not here to see me, of course. Tonight's Friday. Cocktail hour. 'Hi, Lucy. Hey, Charley,' Ethan says. 'Helluva black eye.'

'Your handiwork. How's it going, Eth?' Charley returns, shaking Ethan's hand. Apparently there are no hard feelings. Men.

The Black Widows trail out of the kitchen like Pavlov's dogs at the sound of Ethan's voice.

'Hello, you beautiful creatures,' Ethan

purrs in a low and very effective voice.

'Hello, Ethan,' they coo in unison. The man has a talent.

Tonight, after cocktail hour, Ethan and I are meeting his parents for dinner. They 'have something to tell,' so it's a command performance. I've barely seen Ethan since we, er, broke up, despite the fact that he's right upstairs every night now. I called him on Tuesday to see if he wanted to hang out—basically, to show him we were still friends, even though the benefits package had been canceled—but he had to work on a presentation for the West Coast sales reps. Even the mention of my cinnamon-raisin bread pudding with a Jack Daniels-browned butter glaze didn't sway him. I had, however, sneaked up and left a bowl in front of his door, sort of like the Tooth Fairy but with better stuff.

'What's he want?' Iris asks, jerking her chin at Charley. Ah, customer relations. The cornerstone of any good business.

'Charley, what can I get you? We're closing in a few minutes,' I say.

'Um, well . . .' Charley glances with rightful fear at Iris. 'Lucy, I was wondering if you'd like to have dinner with me. Sometime. Maybe. If you're not, uh, busy.'

I blink.

'On a date? Are you asking her out on a date?' Rose asks, her voice tremulous with

123

hope. 'Because she *is* dating, you know. She's looking to get married again and have some babies.'

Ethan smothers a grin. My mother sighs.

'Thank you, Rose,' I say, knowing there's no point in asking for discretion.

'The women in this family have always been brave in childbirth,' Iris muses. Then she slaps Charley with an intimidating gaze. 'So? You want to take her on a date, or is this a "just friends' situation?" Iris makes quote marks with her fingers. 'You're not gay, are you? My daughter's a lesbian doctor, so there's nothing wrong with that. Just want to see what you have in mind.'

Charley looks understandably confused. 'On a date, Charley?' I ask, just so we're all clear.

'Yeah. On a date.' He fiddles with the zipper of his Red Sox jacket and can't seem to look me in the eye.

Ethan is looking steadily at Charley. Maybe he put Charley up to this, to make up for the Black Widow crack at the game.

I don't know that I really want to go out with Charley Spirito, whom I've known since first grade, when he serenaded me the alphabet song in belch format. On the other hand, I have to give him credit for having the chutzpah to ask in front of the Black Widows. And Ethan.

'Sure,' I answer slowly. 'That would be

nice.'

He lets out a breath. 'Great. You busy tomorrow?'

I glance at Ethan. Most of my Saturday nights over the past few years have been spent, at least in some part and some form, with Ethan. He's pouring vodka into a martini shaker. Jeesh. Grey Goose, wasted on the Black Widows, who could drink gasoline and Hawaiian Punch and call it delicious. He doesn't look at me.

'Tomorrow's fine,' I say, turning back to Charley. 'Thanks.'

'I'll call you, then.' He nods at the Black Widows, slaps Ethan on the shoulder and leaves.

'Charley Spirito?' my mother asks. 'Isn't he the one who put gum in your hair when you were ten?'

'Yes,' I say. What the heck. At least I know him. Hopefully his belching/gum-in-the-hair days are in the past.

'So. She's got a date. And what are we drinking tonight, Ethan?' Iris booms.

'Sex on the Beach,' Ethan answers, grinning as he withdraws a bottle of peach schnapps from his little bag o' liquor. The Black Widows hoot in appreciation.

Friday night happy hour has never really been about me. Plus, I don't often drink hard alcohol (I did learn something from my run-in with the White Russians), so I grab my

125

backpack from behind the counter and heft it onto my shoulder. 'Have fun, guys.' I pause. 'See you at Gianni's later on, Eth?'

'I'll meet you there,' he says.

Three hours later, I'm seated at the family table at Gianni's Ristorante Italiano. Since Jimmy died, these family dinners have become more rare, but back in the day, it was one of the things that drew me to the Mirabellis—the kidding, the abundance of food, the menfolk. Jimmy, Gianni and Ethan . . . a husband, a father figure, a brother-in-law. It was all so reassuring, so safe and convivial.

Now, we sit, the four of us, Jimmy's absence still a gaping hole, never more so than when the Mirabellis are together. I sit next to Ethan, across from my in-laws. Slices of my own delicious bread sit in a basket on the table, a candle flickers, and all around us, Gianni's patrons swoon in delight. It really is a wonderful place, no matter how my father-in-law complains about the crappy help he gets in the kitchen, the dopey Russian sous chef he fired last week, the even dumber Sicilian he has now. I murmur in sympathy and eye the bowl of penne alla vodka that sits just out of my reach next to Marie. I'm starving.

Ethan's energy bristles off of him in waves, tense and still as an Olympic racer before the starting pistol. He's always like this with his parents . . . unlike Jimmy, who worked with

126

them with an ease and fondness that touched my heart every time I saw it.

If Jimmy had gotten old, he'd have looked like his dad—the Mediterranean Sea eyes, broad shoulders, maybe even the extra thirty pounds Gianni carries. Ethan, by contrast, looks like his mom's side of the family, dark hair and eyes, quick movements. He usually reminds me of an otter, rarely still, always up for fun . . . except in the presence of his family. It's as if when Jimmy died, he took all the laughter from his family. As if reading my thoughts, Marie sighs heavily, her eyes moist.

'Thank you for asking us to dinner,' I prompt gently, taking a sip of my wine and eyeing the chicken parmesan. We're eating family style, and neither Marie nor Gianni has started serving yet. My stomach growls.

Marie gives Gianni a look. 'We wanted you here because we love you like you're our own daughter, Lucy, honey. And Ethan, of course, you're like a son to us.'

'I hate to be overly technical here, Ma,' Ethan says, 'but in point of fact, I *am* your son.' His right eyebrow bounces up as he looks at me. The corner of his mouth curls, and I feel a wave of affection for him. Poor Ethan, always the second son. I give his knee a little pat.

'You know what I mean, Mr. Smart-Ass,' Marie replies, half fond, half irritated. 'Thirty-six hours of labor, okay? So shut up.'

'It gets longer every year,' Ethan murmurs, reaching for the penne and passing it to me. His father scowls, but Ethan ignores him. 'In the original story, I was born in a taxi on the way to the hospital. Now she's in labor for a day and a half.'

Marie reaches over and smacks Ethan's head. 'Hush, you, we're talking here. You know what I mean. She's like a daughter, you're our son, shut it.'

'Show your mother some respect,' Gianni says, more coolly than Marie's fond chastising. He's never gotten over Ethan's choice of profession.

'I respect my mother,' Ethan says, a hard edge in his voice. His small smile is gone. 'Mom. I respect you. Especially if it took me thirty-six hours to be born.'

'Your head was all squished when you finally came out.' She winces, a life skill if you're Italian, meant to instill guilt. 'And the stitches! Oh, Madonna!'

Gianni shifts uncomfortably. 'Do we have to discuss this at the table, Marie?'

'Oh, so my suffering, you don't want to know, is that it? Sorry to disturb you, your majesty.' My mother-in-law turns to me. 'Lucy, it was fourth-degree tear. Three inches long.' Gianni flinches, and I try not to smile.

'Sorry, Ma,' Ethan says. 'Didn't mean to be such trouble.' He smiles at his mother, but she's lost in thought.

'Of course, Jimmy was no picnic, either. He was bigger, you know, nine pounds, eight ounces. Those eyes even when he was first born, they were so special. Like the ocean, so amazing! The nurses, they couldn't believe it. Oh, he was the most beautiful baby I ever saw, Lucy.' Her mouth wobbles, and a spear of pain pierces my heart. Poor Marie.

I reach across the table and pat her hand, and at the same time, give Ethan's knee a squeeze. I'm sure Marie doesn't realize it, but she just told Ethan he *wasn't* the most beautiful baby she ever saw. Ethan removes my hand, giving it a quick pat. Still, the message is clear. Hands off.

Marie wipes her eyes and sighs again. Gianni growls at a passing waiter to check table fifteen, Ethan's leg jiggles with tension. All in all, a typical Mirabelli dinner.

'So what's the big news?' I ask, taking a large bite of the delicious penne.

'So we're moving,' Gianni announces. 'Arizona. Retirement.'

I drop my fork with a clatter, splattering the white tablecloth with the creamy vodka sauce, and swallow.

'Excuse me?' Ethan asks. His leg jiggling has gone still.

'Arizona,' Marie repeats. 'Valle de Muerte Community for Active Adults.'

'The Valley of Death?' Ethan asks.

'What Valley of the Death?' Marie asks.

129

'Valle de Muerte, I said.'

'It's not Valley of Death, smart-ass,' Gianni says to his son. 'Marie, you got it wrong. It's Puerte, not Muerte, okay? With a P. Valle de Puerte Active Adult Community. We're active, we're adults, we're moving.'

'When did you decide this?' Ethan asks.

'Last week,' Marie explains. 'Your father, his knees, his heart . . . and . . . well . . .' She glances at me, then down at her untouched plate.

'What, Marie?' I ask, the pebble already stuck in my throat.

'That goddamn Angelo,' Gianni explodes, shoving away from the table. He tends to leave at emotional times. I swear, he spent half of Jimmy's wake outside the funeral home, advising the valets on where to park cars.

'Ma. Why now?' Ethan asks.

'The restaurant is too much for your father,' she says, not looking at either of us. 'His blood pressure. And it's just . . . it's not the same without Jimmy. And now that you're moving on, Lucy, honey, and you're back to raise your son, Ethan, well . . . we're just not needed anymore.'

'You're needed!' Ethan barks. 'Nicky loves you! When are you planning on seeing him? Did you even think about your only grandson?'

'Ethan,' I interject in a low voice, but he

ignores me.

'We'll have him visit,' Marie says. 'You, too, Lucy, sweetheart. And we'll come back from time to time. It's just . . . we just don't want to stay around anymore.'

'Part of the reason I took this job in Providence was to be closer to you and Dad, Ma,' Ethan says.

'So? You don't need us. You're doing fine. We're very, uh, proud,' she says, tearing a piece of bread to bits. 'I'd better check on your father.' With that, she, too, hurtles away from the table, leaving me with Ethan.

I shift in my chair to look at him better. His jaw is tight, and a muscle jumps underneath his left eye. I reach out and give him a tentative pat on the leg.

'Would you please stop touching my leg?' he bites out.

My hand slinks back to my own lap. 'Sorry! Sorry, Eth,' I say. 'But listen, your parents deserve to retire. Why are you so mad, buddy?'

He gives me a look that could cut glass. 'Lucy, you're so obtuse sometimes,' he says.

'What? What am I missing?'

He continues to gaze at me dispassionately, like a teacher with a not-very-bright student. 'If Jimmy were alive, they'd never leave. They'd die in that kitchen.' He jerks his chin in the direction of his parents' escape.

'Well, Jimmy did die,' I murmur. My hand

131

wants to pat him again, but we know better.

'I'm aware of that, Lucy,' he says, his voice unfamiliar in its hardness.

'And they really should retire. They're in their seventies, aren't they?'

'Yes. And I don't begrudge them retirement. But why not Newport or the Cape or something? Why Arizona? It's a little far, don't you think? I just moved back here, and I was hoping . . .'

'Hoping to be closer with them?' I ask.

Ethan shrugs. 'I guess.' He pauses, pushing the food around on his plate. I sneak another mouthful, feeling somehow that I'm being unsympathetic by eating when my friend is distressed. Chewing without moving my mouth proves difficult, however, so I just go for it, letting Ethan brood next to me. It works.

'Did you know that Jimmy was named for our grandfathers?' he asks after a few minutes. 'They were both Giacomo.'

I smile. I did know that little fact, learning only when it was time to do our wedding invitation that Jimmy's name wasn't James, as I'd assumed. 'What's your point?' I ask gently.

Ethan straightens his fork. 'Do you know who I'm named for?' he asks.

'He's named for the doctor,' Marie announces loudly. Apparently, Angelo has been thoroughly chastised, because both my in-laws have returned to the table. They sit

132

now, Marie smiling, Gianni glowering. 'We were so sure you were a girl, honey,' Marie says to her younger son. 'Lucy, we didn't even have a boy's name picked out, we were so sure! You were supposed to be Francesca. Isn't that a lovely name?'

'It is,' I agree, grinning at Ethan.

'Even when the doctor said you were a boy, I didn't believe it. I was convinced you were a girl!'

'What every man wants to hear, Ma,' Ethan says, but Marie continues, undaunted.

'So then he shows me your tiny little parts—' Ethan closes his eyes and I giggle '—and we were just stumped! Then your father here—' Marie elbows Gianni '—your father says, "So what do we call the little bugger?" And my mind, it goes completely blank, so I look at Dr. Tavendish and I say, "What's your first name, Dr. T.?" And he says, "Ethan."' And that was that!' She and Gianni smile at each other fondly, warmed by the memory.

'And that's how this little *paesan* got a WASP name,' Ethan says. Then he gives his parents a smile that doesn't quite make it to his eyes. 'So tell us more about Valle de Muerte.'

*   *   *

After dinner, Ethan and I walk home. The street is quiet, as sidewalks tend to roll up

133

before nine after Labor Day. Ethan knows how I feel about the cemetery, and it's nice not to have someone trying to coax me through like they're cajoling a reluctant dog out of a crate. The stars gleam bright above, and salt flavors the air, putting me in mind of sourdough bread.

'Does it really bother you, being named after the doctor?' I ask.

'Not really. It's just . . . well, it doesn't matter,' Ethan says mildly. I suspect it does, but now that we're away from his parents, he's not going to reopen the subject.

'How's the new job going?' I ask.

'It's okay.'

'What do you do all day?'

He sighs. 'Meetings. Long-range planning, research on new markets.'

It's a far cry from what he used to do . . . schmoozing, basically. He was head of North American sales, rather astonishing, given that he's only twenty-seven. Instead of working at Gianni's during college, Ethan took a summer internship at International, and his employers so liked him that they offered him a job. I know from Parker that the new position is a promotion and Ethan's making even more money now, but I also know that long-range planning and research are not Ethan's thing. Certainly, though, it's safer than flying all around the country and doing all those adventure sports things.

'Do you like it?' I ask.

'Not especially.'

'Then why'd you take it?'

We've reached the bridge and stop for a minute, looking down at the Mackerly River, which flows from the ocean side of the island to the bay. The lights of the much more upscale Newport twinkle in the distance, but here on our little lump of land, it's quiet save for the murmuring rush of the tidal river and the occasional night bird. A breeze ruffles Ethan's perpetually rumpled hair.

He glances at me. 'Figured I should be around more for Nicky,' he says, dropping his gaze to the water.

'Right,' I answer. 'That's a good reason.'

'The best.' He smiles at the thought of his son, and, as always, my heart gives an almost painful twist. Ethan is such a good dad, and little is more appealing than a father who so obviously loves his child.

'So come on, tell me. What's the deal with being named after the obstetrician?' I ask, watching as the river rushes past the reedy banks.

'It's nothing. Just that Jimmy got the grandfathers' name, and they hadn't even bothered to pick one out for me.'

'Sure they did. You just decided to be difficult and come out a boy.'

'Right.'

'So?'

135

He turns to look at me. 'Well, a person could say that I disappointed my parents right from the get-go by being me. They already had a son. They wanted a daughter. They got me, and I wasn't as good as Jimmy.' He says it as if he's presenting a paper on the history of dirt— these are the facts, and while they're true, they're not all that interesting.

'Oh, Ethan, buddy, no one thinks that!' I protest.

His eyes crinkle in genuine amusement. 'Anyone ever told you, Lucy, that you're awfully naive?' I don't answer, and Ethan continues. 'I've pretty much spent my life being Not-Jimmy. He was the heir apparent. He was older, taller, funnier, better-looking, better in the kitchen. He got Dad's eyes, Mom's heart, the grandfathers' name. He got the restaurant, he got the family recipes, he got—well. Whatever I do in my life, it won't measure up to Jimmy.' He shoots me a sidelong glance. 'In my parents' eyes, anyway.'

My urge is to hug him, but I probably shouldn't. 'Does it bother you?' I ask quietly.

'Not so much anymore. I'm used to it. And my parents lost a child, so I try to cut them some slack. If anything ever happened to Nick, I don't know what I'd do, and I hope to God never to find out.'

I swallow, not willing to think such thoughts. 'You're just as good as Jimmy, Ethan,' I say sincerely. 'You're different, that's

136

all.'

He looks at me a beat, and I get the feeling there's something more he wants to say. But he doesn't. 'Come on, it's getting cold,' is all he offers, and we start walking once more, leaving the river behind, not talking until we reach the Boatworks. We stop at the entrance, which is one of the lovely touches of this building. Instead of an overhang, half a Herreshoff sailboat juts out from the brick. The building's front doors were taken from a shipwreck and restored. Obviously we each know the code to get into the building, but we just stand there a moment, sheltered by the old wooden boat.

'You want to come up?' I ask. 'I made profiteroles. And not just that . . . they're served with a warm hazelnut mocha sauce.' He doesn't answer. 'We could play Guitar Hero, maybe?' There's a desperate note to my voice, and I don't imagine Ethan misses it. 'Sound good, Eth?'

'Sounds great,' he replies with a considerable lack of enthusiasm. 'But I don't think I should come over, Lucy. Thanks, though.'

'Why? You don't like my desserts anymore?' I ask. 'Trying to drop a few, are you?' My joke falls flat . . . A) Ethan is as lean as a greyhound; and B) I know the real reason and don't want it to be true. 'You don't have to eat,' I add. 'We could watch a movie.' My

137

heart is fluttering like a sick bird in my chest, and I feel dangerously close to tears.

'Lucy,' Ethan begins, looking down the street. 'Look. You know I think you're great and all, but maybe we should put some distance between us.'

'Why?' I squeak.

'Well, you want a new husband. He's not going to appreciate you having an ex-lover hanging around, being your best friend forever.'

'But, you *are* my best friend, aren't you?' I say around the pebble in my throat.

He hesitates, and that hideous bird in my chest goes into death spasm. 'Sure. But I don't want to be a substitute for what's missing in your life, either.'

'You're not a substitute!' I protest.

'Whatever you say, Luce.'

'Eth,' I attempt, 'aren't we still friends?'

'Lucy, you asked for some distance. I'm giving it to you.' There's an edge to his voice now, and that little muscle under his eye ticks again.

'Well, forgive me, then,' I say, my voice brittle. 'I thought we were friends. I guess we could be friends when we were sleeping together, but not now, huh?'

'No, Lucy!' he snaps. 'You're moving on, good for you, you should and all that crap. But you can't have me filling in whenever you get lonely. Not if you're about to dump me for a husband one of these days.'

'Dump you? We didn't . . . we weren't . . .' My voice trails off.

'No. We didn't and we weren't. So fine. Go out with Charley Spirito. Find a new guy, but leave me out of this.'

'But—'

'Lucy,' he says tightly. 'You can't have everything, okay? So back off.'

'I'm not asking for everything! I just want you to . . . to be my friend. Like you were.' At his dark look, I hastily amend that statement. 'Well, without the sleeping together part. Just for us to be . . . buddies.'

'Buddies.' He raises an eyebrow. 'Okay, buddy. I'm tired and I have an early meeting, so let's call it a night.'

And with that, he punches in our code, holds the door open for me. When we get in the elevator, he pushes four for my floor, and five for his. Aside from 'Good night,' we don't say anything else.

CHAPTER NINE

'How was your date with Charley Spirito the other night?' Parker asks. 'Nicky, not so high, honey.'

I watch as Nicky pumps his little legs harder, trying to make the swing wrap around the bar from which the chains dangle. Seems like he inherited Ethan's thrill-seeker gene.

Corinne, wee Emma, Parker, Nicky and I are at Ellington Park, a safe two hundred yards from the cemetery entrance. It's one of those perfect September days, the sky so brilliantly blue it makes your heart ache. The yeasty, welcoming smell of Bunny's morning bread still flavors the air. I have forty-one minutes until the next batch is due out, but for now, I'm on my midday break. Emma smacks contentedly away at Corinne's breast. My sister wears the serene face of pain that I'm coming to recognize as 'nursing mother.' Or 'saint dying a martyr's death.' Same idea.

'You went out with Charley Spirito?' Corinne asks, snapping out of her haze to give me a dubious look. 'No sir!'

'Mmm,' I say. 'It was . . . well. Charley. You know.'

'Didn't he put gum in your hair once?' Corinne asks.

'Wow, good memory,' I comment. 'It was fine. I don't know.'

'Just a whole lot of nothing?' Parker guesses.

'That's about it,' I agree, tilting my face to the sunshine.

'Which is what you want,' my friend adds. 'Nick, no, don't jump. You're too high. Good boy. Thanks.' Nicky waves, then jumps. Parker sighs as her son comes running over. 'Nick, what would I tell Daddy if you snapped both your little ankles, huh? You want to go to the E.R.?'

'You shouldn't scare children with the thought of getting health care,' Corinne advises in the singsong voice she uses whenever lecturing those of us who don't have all of life's answers. Parker rolls her eyes.

'Can we go to the E.R., Mommy?' Nicky asks. 'I love the E.R.'

Parker tries to suppress a grin. 'You were hurt when we went there, remember? When they sewed your hand?'

'It was fun,' Nicky insists. 'I got a balloon, Wucy.'

'I remember,' I say, reaching out to tap his adorable nose with my index finger.

'Wucy, did you see me jump off the swing?'

'I sure did, honey,' I say, looking into his gorgeous brown eyes. Honestly, the boys always get the lashes, don't they? 'You looked like you were flying, but you know, Mommy's right. That could hurt, if you landed wrong.'

'I didn't land wrong. I landed up! Bye!' He canters over to the slide.

'He's so beautiful,' I say. Jimmy's nephew. Sad that Nicky is the closest thing to Jimmy's child I'll ever have. I think we would've made such gorgeous kids. The thought is a reflex by now, the pain worn to a nub with overuse.

'So, back to the date,' Corinne says. 'Is Charley a contender?'

141

I pause. In truth, Charley's not that bad. Just not the sharpest knife in the drawer. Honestly, he does match a lot of my requirements. Fairly recession-proof job. As a phys-ed teacher, he's in great shape, which is not only aesthetically pleasing but a huge plus with the Low Risk of Early Death requirement. Charley seems good-hearted, I guess. He obviously likes kids (though being a gym teacher, one could argue that in fact, he *hates* kids). It's just that the idea of sex with Charley . . .

Saturday night, Charley took me to Cuckoo's Grille in Kingstown. The waitress was the mother of a woman we'd been to school with, so it was a typical Rhode Island two-degrees-of-separation night. When the pleasantries and updates were completed and the order for stuffed clams, or stuffies, as we like to call them, had been placed, Charley and I stared awkwardly at each other across the table. Then he launched into a discussion of the Red Sox, passionately making the case that without Varitek's 'goddamn torn ligament,' there was no way in hell that those 'goddamn Yankees' would be in 'first goddamn place,' and furthermore, what was wrong with Boston's new shortstop, the guy was a 'goddamn zombie.'

At the word *Yankees*, I recalled my fond fantasy of Joe Torre as my stepfather. If such were the case, I wouldn't be on a date with

Charley . . . not when dear old Joe would fix up his beloved stepdaughter with a millionaire baseball player who was single, didn't do steroids, visit prostitutes, date Madonna, throw his helmet, chew tobacco, spit or scratch his groin in public, if such a creature indeed existed.

When our food came, Charley turned his attention to his steak and didn't lift his head until his plate was clean. It was this sort of thing that made me think I could probably sleep through sex with Charley without him noticing.

The last time Ethan and I, er, had relations, it was roughly ten minutes after he'd returned from a trip to Montreal, and I'd jumped him the second he walked through my door. We'd done it standing up in the hallway, me against the wall, legs wrapped around him and quite vocal, as I recall. A framed picture fell to the floor, the glass breaking, but we didn't stop until we, um, stopped.

No one slept through anything.

'Guess what?' Parker interrupts.

'What?' I yelp guiltily. Cripes, am I blushing?

'Ethan dropped by last night,' she says.

My cheeks burn hotter. 'So? He's the father of your child. He drops by a lot.' I look at my hands.

Parker gives me an odd look. 'Well, hush and let me finish.'

'Sorry,' I mumble. Corinne pats Emma on the back, eliciting a shockingly loud belch for so tiny a package.

'So he asked if I wanted to go out. On a date. He said that maybe we should try having a real relationship, rather than just be the two parents of our son. Nicky, get down, honey. That's too high. Good boy.'

'That's sweet,' Corinne says.

'Sweet,' I echo. My knees tingle with adrenaline, though I don't know why (the little hallway memory probably has a lot to do with it). *Sober up, Lucy,* I tell myself firmly. I've always thought there was more potential to Ethan and Parker than either of them did. 'So? Are you gonna try?' I ask.

She grimaces. 'I don't know. It seems good on paper. It's just not . . . I don't know.'

'You should. You should marry him,' I say. God knows I'd *love* to have someone I liked, respected, admired, would father adorable children and who didn't make my knees weak. And while my voice sounds normal, my heart is convulsing like a striper pulled out of the water.

Parker sighs. 'Maybe I should,' she agrees with a considerable lack of enthusiasm. 'But—'

At that moment, my sister's cell phone rings, and she jumps like it's the red phone in the Oval Office. 'Hello? Chris? Are you okay? Honey?' She's quiet a minute. 'Sure! I'm fine!
144

Oh, she's wonderful! Beautiful! Perfect! How are you, sweetheart? I love you so much.'

'For Christ's sake, they have medication for that,' Parker mumbles.

Glad for the change of subject, I feel my shoulders relax a little. 'My mother's last words to my dad were, and I quote here, Parker . . . "Get the hell out of the bathroom, Rob, I have my period and I'm bleeding like a stuck pig."' My friend snorts with horrified laughter, and I grin. 'So give poor Cory a break. She's just a screwball, as are we all.'

'You're too nice, Lucy.' Parker grins.

'True. More people should be like me. You, for instance.'

Nicky, who seems to have more energy than a herd of ferrets, dangles from the jungle gym by one hand. Corinne, finished assuring Chris that the world is a wonderful, *wonderful* place, hangs up and says, 'Parker, shouldn't you direct his play a little more?'

'I don't even know what that means,' Parker answers. 'He's a kid, Corinne! He's having fun.'

Corinne gives her a dubious look. 'Well, he's your son, I suppose. Lucy, I'm going to check Dad's grave. Want to come?'

It's my sister's habit to invite me on grave-weeding excursions. Someday, she's convinced, my little phobia will crack and I'll come along. She may be right, but today is not that day.

'Oh, no, thanks, Cory. Not today,' I say. 'How about if I take my little niece for a stroll while you do your thing over there?'

She hesitates, nervous about letting me, a know-nothing agent of death, hold her child without supervision. 'Please?' I beg. 'Pretty please?'

'Well, okay,' she says, unable to find a way out of it. 'Just make sure you keep a blanket over her head so she doesn't burn. She doesn't like to get sweaty, though, so make sure she can feel the breeze. Also, support her neck. And make sure she can breathe okay.'

'No smothering, Lucy, understand?' Parker quips.

'Got it.' I take the little bundle of love from my sister, who gives a reluctant grin.

'Sorry,' she says. 'I know she's safe with you.'

'Thank you,' I answer, breathing in the sweet and salty scent of infant.

'Nicky looks stuck,' Parker says. 'Back in a flash.' She trots over to her child, who is now upside down at the top of the crow's nest on the jungle gym.

'Want me to water Jimmy's grave?' my sister offers.

'That would be nice. Thank you.' I smile up at my sister. She's a sweetheart, despite her neuroses. And I'm in no position to cast stones.

Who will water Jimmy's grave after his

146

parents move? Ethan, I suppose. Or me. It could happen.

Emma turns her head so her face is tucked against my neck in the sweetest snuggle imaginable. Her slight weight is reassuring against my shoulder, her cheek so soft. I adjust her blanket, making sure she's protected from the bright sun. She sighs, and my heart swells with love.

Ellington Park's lovely wide paths are shaded by elm and maple trees. 'Isn't the shade nice?' I ask as we walk, dropping a kiss on her downy head. 'And there's a bird, a crow. They're pretty. And very smart.' Never too early to start teaching. That's what I've read, anyway. Talk to your baby. Read to them. That's what I'd do if I were a mommy.

Though I've been resisting it, I give in to the temptation, and just for a moment, I pretend that Emma is mine. My daughter. That this miracle of cells grew in me, that it was my tummy that grew round and taut, causing Jimmy and me to just about burst with pride. That I'd grown ripe and glowing, a happy, laughing mother-to-be, never complaining, never swollen, never exhausted. And when the time came, I'd heroically tolerate the pains of childbirth without any drugs. I'd push and push, and when the doctor said, 'It's a girl!' I'd turn to my husband, who'd be smiling down at me, his laughing brown eyes bright with—

147

Stop.

Jimmy's eyes were not brown.

Nor was it Jimmy's face I pictured.

My legs are suddenly weak with terror, watery and useless. Suddenly my teeth are chattering. Dear God, it's a panic attack, the likes of which I haven't had since the first year after Jimmy's death. I'm going to faint. I'm holding a baby and I'm going to faint. A bench waits nearby, and somehow I wobble toward it and sit heavily. *Don't faint, don't faint, don't faint,* I chant silently to myself. I take a deep breath and hold it, then release it slowly, as I was taught in grief group after Jimmy died. My heart shudders and flops.

'I won't drop you, Emma,' I whisper, and talking to her helps. I'm her auntie. I can't let anything bad happen. I love her too much. My racing heart slows, my teeth stop chattering.

'Auntie's okay,' I say, and my voice is stronger now. 'Auntie loves you, angel.' She makes a small sound, and my eyes fill with tears. I'm okay now. That image meant nothing. The face I pictured . . . okay, yes, yes, it was Ethan's face . . . that didn't mean anything. My breath jerks in and out, eventually calming.

I won't be having children with Ethan, God knows. Let's be honest. It's not Ethan's link to Parker—or Jimmy—that stops me from being with him.

It's the knowledge that I could really fall in

148

love with Ethan. That I could love him in a way that would rip me in half if anything happened to him. That losing Ethan as I lost Jimmy could ruin me, and that this time, I might not make it back.

And whatever I could maybe feel for Ethan, however much he's done for me— nothing is worth that kind of pain again.

'Auntie's fine,' I whisper again, stroking Emma's head with one hand. 'Auntie is just fine.'

CHAPTER TEN

'Ready to go in?' I ask as I stand in the parking lot.

Standing in the parking lot is a time-honored ritual whenever I go anywhere with the Black Widows. There's an order, you see, a hierarchy of who gets out first and how. First, tradition dictates that the youngest among us drives. That's me, and I'm grateful, as Iris and Rose's method is to point the vehicle in the desired direction and step on the gas. Getting out of the way is the responsibility of other drivers, pedestrians, deer, trees and buildings.

Upon arriving at our destination, tradition dictates that I hop out of the car and stand in attendance as Iris reapplies her Coral Glow, which was discontinued in 1978 but which she had the foresight to stockpile. She doesn't need a mirror to put on lipstick, a skill they must've taught back when Eisenhower was president, since I've never seen a woman under the age of sixty pull this off.

The next tradition, which we're living right now, is for Rose to gasp in horror, realizing she's lost her wallet, then rifle through her vast black purse, her lips moving in silent prayer. A moment later, St. Anthony, patron saint of lost things, miraculously restores the wallet, placing it right there next to the rubber-banded envelope containing Rose's medical insurance card, list of medications, several dozen coupons and her burial instructions.

After this bit of divine intervention, my mother must retie her scarf. She never goes anywhere without a scarf, winter or summer. Today's choice is a beautiful little orange and pink number, and despite the fact that we only left the bakery ten minutes ago, tradition must be honored.

'Does my neck look crepey to you?' Mom asks as I watch, my arms beginning to ache from holding the tray of apricot brioche I baked in class last night. My students, who range in age from seventeen to eighty-four, had raved about them.

'Not at all,' I answer. 'You're gorgeous, Mom.'

'Oh, I am not,' she says fondly. Another tradition—reject compliments. Then her gaze drops down to my faded jeans with the fraying hem, my utterly unremarkable brown wool sweater. 'Is that what you're wearing?' she asks.

'No. I'm wearing a ball gown, but it's invisible.' I twirl around, taking care not to spill the goodies. 'Do you like it?'

'It wouldn't kill you to dress up a little,' she says, adjusting her own skirt, a pretty, silky little number. She's right, of course— yesterday, I bought yet another cashmere sweater, my seventeenth (but really, this one could not be denied—it was a gorgeous peachy color with a wide neckline and the prettiest buttons). My closet appears in my mind, its doors opening in supplication. *Come on, Lucy,* the unworn clothes beg. *We're here for you.*

'Are we ready?' Iris asks, then, without waiting for an answer, strides ahead, leading the little parade of Hungarian widows inside.

High Hopes Convalescent Center is a poorly named nursing home, since most of its residents are dying. One of them is my Great-Aunt Boggy (her name is actually Boglarka, which means 'Buttercup' in Hungarian). Visiting is a regular gig for the Black Widows and me . . . we honor our elders, even those who don't know we're around. Such is the case with Great-Aunt Boggy, age one hundred and

151

four, nonverbal since my sophomore year in high school, a person who rouses only to eat, then slips back to the foggy place where she's been for so long.

'What's that?' Iris asks suspiciously, holding the door for me.

'Apricot brioche,' I say, lifting the cloth napkin that covers my tray. Boggy will eat one or two, and the grateful staff will eat the rest.

She squints, then pokes one in the side, where the flaky dough shatters obligingly. 'How'd you get them so light?'

'That's my secret, dear Iris,' I say sweetly. 'However, should you let me sell them at Bunny's, I'd be happy to share.'

'Unsalted butter?' she guesses.

'Well, of course, but that's hardly the secret,' I answer.

'Let me try one,' Rose says, breaking off a piece. Her palate is legendary. 'You used vinegar in the dough, didn't you, smart girl?'

'I absolutely did not,' I lie. Darn that palate.

'Come on, girls, we'll be late,' Mom calls from the second set of doors. She's armed with food, too . . . pureed chicken *paprikas*, which is basically chicken, butter, sour cream and paprika. Mom has also brought another Hungarian delicacy—*galuska* . . . salted, shredded cabbage fried in salted butter, mixed with salted, buttered noodles, topped with salted butter and then heavily salted. Horrifyingly delicious, nearly fatal in its fat

152

content. It's amazing that the women in my family live to be so old. You'd think our blood would've thickened to a lardlike sludge long ago.

'Oh, Boggy, don't you look pretty today!' Rose coos as we arrive in our shriveled relative's room. Iris agrees in her thunderous voice that Boggy does indeed look well, and the two of them adjust Boggy, who, as usual, stares into the distance, unresisting. Mom zips down the hall to heat up the food. I set my tray of baked goods down and sit on the little sofa in Boggy's room and listen to Iris and Rose argue over whether it's good or bad for Boggy's window to be opened.

I remember the glamour of Boggy coming to visit when I was a kid. She married a car dealer and was fairly wealthy. Great-Uncle Tony was rumored to be *connected*, though just about everyone in Rhode Island could claim some cousin or neighbor who was a made man. Boggy and Tony didn't have kids of their own and spoiled my mother and her older sisters when they were children, taking the girls on trips into Providence or down to the Connecticut shore for brunch, once even taking my mother to Paris for a week, which still causes flares of jealousy in Iris and Rose when mentioned. Long after she was widowed at age forty-eight (Tony was rumored to have been hit by a rival family, but the autopsy only showed that he had drowned), Boggy

153

continued the tradition of never marrying, never dating. She didn't lose her joie de vivre, however, and continued to dote on the Black Widows and her grand-nieces and -nephews. Once she took me to the Indian casino down Interstate 395, handed me five crisp Ben Franklins and told me to get busy. I was ten at the time.

But Boggy had a stroke when I was sixteen, and she's been at High Hopes ever since. Only her nieces (and I) visit, which we do with great devotion, mind you. But still. No grandchildren's loving pats, no great-grandchildren . . . just the four of us.

Will that happen to me? I suddenly wonder in a seize of panic. Will Emma be the only one to remember poor Aunt Lucy? Lord, I hope Corinne would have more babies if that's the case. Maybe she could have seven, and each one could take a day on my deathwatch . . . not that I would know, if I ended up like Boggy there.

I find that I'm sweating. My breathing is a little shallow. No. I won't end up alone. I'm going to get married again. I'll have a hubby soon, that nice, solid, slightly dull guy who will take really good care of me. I'll have funny, sweet little kids who will adore me. I won't have to borrow Emma or Nicky in order to have a child to love.

'How's the search for a husband going?' my mother asks, reading my mind. She sits gracefully next to me, a bowl of fragrant *paprikas* puree in her manicured hands, and takes on her Barbara Walters *Aren't we fascinating?* look.

'Oh, it's okay,' I answer, fiddling with the cuff of my sweater. 'Fine.'

'Have you gone out with Charley again?' she asks, stirring the sludge to cool it a little. Over by Boggy, Iris and Rose are still bickering over the health benefits/death threats of opening the window.

'Um, no. I don't think he's what I'm looking for,' I answer, breaking off a piece of brioche to test its texture. So flaky, the glaze gleaming sweetly. I bet it tastes great. My throat closes at the thought of actually eating it, and I swallow. Dang pebble.

'So what are you looking for? Another Jimmy?' Mom asks. 'Because you won't find one, sweetheart.'

'I know that, Mom.' I pause. 'Ethan and Parker might be going out,' I add. I wait, hoping she'll have something insightful and maternal to say about that.

'Oh, nice,' she murmurs, blowing on the *paprikas*.

'Ethan and Parker *should* go out,' Rose chirrups from Boggy's bedside. 'They should get married. Poor Nicky shouldn't have to grow up a bastard.'

'Rose!' I exclaim. 'Don't call him that! Half the kids in this country don't have parents

155

who are married to each other.'

'Which is why I wonder about you looking for another husband,' my mother says, meeting my eyes.

'I never wanted to remarry,' Iris states. 'My Pete was the Love of My Life. And what's this I hear about the Mirabellis moving? What do they have in Arizona that we don't have right here in Rhode Island?'

'Well, the desert, for one,' I say. 'And Jimmy was the love of my life, too, but I don't want to be alone for the rest of my life. I want kids.'

'So adopt,' Mom says.

'We got invited to Mirabellis' going-away party,' Rose says. 'I do love a party.'

'Boggy, lunch is ready!' Mom announces loudly. 'Chicken *paprikas*, extra sour cream, just the way you like it! And *galuska*, too!'

'Oh, I'm sorry, you really shouldn't give her that,' says a nurse, poking her head inside the door. 'The doctor just put her on a low-salt, low-fat diet.'

My mother and aunts recoil as if slapped. 'What doctor?' Iris demands. 'My daughter, she didn't say anything about low salt. And she's a lesbian doctor.'

'Poor Boggy!' Rose cries. 'Isn't it bad enough that she's—' Rose's voice drops to a melodramatic whisper '—in the coma?'

'She's not in a coma,' the nurse says. 'Not technically. Anyway, she needs to stick to her

156

diet.'

'Oh, gosh,' I say. 'Aunt Boggy's a hundred and four. She should get to eat a little *paprikas*, don't you think?' I smile, appealing to the nurse's sense of humanity. Depriving an ancient old lady of salty, butter-soaked food is the moral equivalent of water-boarding in the eyes of this family. A call to Amnesty International will be next.

'That's right,' Iris says. 'Lucy, you're right. So nuts to you, nurse!' She grabs the bowl from my mother's hands and marches over to Aunt Boggy, pushes the button on her bed to raise the old lady to a sitting position and begins spooning the chicken sludge into her mouth. The nurse sighs and walks away. I'm not sure, but I think Boggy smiles. And while it's a little disgusting to watch Boggy's droopy mouth open and close like a baby bird's, I have to say, it smells fantastic in here. Rose wipes Boggy's mouth, and Iris shovels in some more high-fat, salty, delicious food.

'Mom,' I say, turning back to my mother in the hope of resuming our earlier conversation, 'do you miss being married?'

She gives me a look of thinly veiled patience. 'Why? Did you see Joe Torre on TV?' Apparently Mom hasn't forgotten my timid suggestions way back when that she try to find someone like 'that nice Mr. Torre.'

'No,' I say. 'But—'

'Lucy, promise me you'll never wear that

157

sweater out in public again, okay, honey?' She gets up and spreads an afghan over the bottom of Boggy's bed, leaving me in the void where maternal advice is supposed to be.

Later that day and much to my surprise, my mother comes over as I'm packing up the afternoon bread. 'I just got off the phone with Gertie Myers,' she says, naming her hairdresser, who was also my Girl Scout troop leader. 'Her nephew Fred's divorced, and I told her you were looking.'

'Oh,' I say, my stomach clenching. 'Um. Okay. Thanks.' I pause. 'Is he nice? Have you met him?'

'Does he have his own teeth?' Rose adds with complete sincerity, coming out of the freezer, where she was stowing a tray of unwanted, unpurchased, unappetizing cookies for another day.

'I have no idea,' my mother says. 'But he's coming to your baseball game tonight. Good luck.'

*   *   *

'Hi, I'm Fred Busey.'

Gah! My mouth opens, but no sound emerges.

While Fred Busey may have his own teeth, the rest of the picture is not so pretty. He's roughly five feet three inches and somewhere around two hundred and fifty pounds. From

158

my lofty three-inch height difference, I am privy to a distressing view of his scalp. You know those infomercials where they're pitching what's basically a can of spray paint to cover some guy's bald spot? Yes. That. And the result is, sadly, quite, er . . . noticeable.

Granted, Number Four on my color-coded list is *Not Too Attractive* so as to discourage lust, which is part of chemistry of course, and can lead to infatuation and even love . . . but Fred is pushing the envelope here.

'Hi,' I say, remembering my manners. 'I'm Lucy Mirabelli. My mother gets her hair cut by your aunt.'

He grins. 'Nice to meet you, Lucy,' he says, shaking my hand. Oh, dang. He seems nice.

'Hello, all,' says my sister. Baby Emma is clutched to her chest, and I lean in to take a look. 'Not so close, Lucy, you're dirty,' my sister says, then sticks out an elbow to Fred. 'Hello, I'm Corinne, Lucy's sister, and I'd shake your hand, but as you can see, I'm holding my baby. She's eighteen and a half days old.'

'Congratulations,' Fred says, taking a peek at the baby. 'She's just beautiful. Looks like you.' He smiles at my sister, scoring thousands of points with Corinne. Charming, this guy, despite his outward resemblance to Jabba the Hutt. 'Does your husband play softball, too?' he asks my sister.

'Oh, God, no! Softball's way too

dangerous,' Corinne says, her eyes wide with horror. 'No, no. He's an umpire. Second base.' There's Christopher indeed, wearing the usual protective gear worn by umpires. And a Kevlar vest underneath. I'm not kidding. Corinne's certain a line drive could cause his death.

'Luce!' Charley Spirito galumphs over. 'Luce, you wanna get a beer after the game?' he says. At the sight of Fred Busey, Charley's dopey grin falls off his face. 'Who's dis?' he says, immediately adopting a Mobbed-up accent.

'Charley, meet Fred Busey. Fred, this is Charley, one of my teammates and an old friend.'

Charley gives me a look that conveys moral indignation and deep, deep hurt. 'And old friend, huh? So I guess last week meant squat?'

Fred, understanding that good-looking Charley feels I have thrown him over for Fred's own rotund self, beams. I close my eyes briefly. 'Charley and I had dinner last week,' I explain to Fred. Turning to Charley, I add, 'Those clams were great, Charley. I had a nice time.'

'Nice time, is dat right. I getcha. Fine. No prob, Luce.' He gives Fred a disgruntled look, then tromps off to right field, where we put all the guys who can't catch.

'So this is fun,' Fred says. 'I haven't been to
160

a game in a long time. Maybe we can grab a drink afterward?'

I swallow. 'Um . . . yeah,' I say. 'Let's see how, um, how long the game goes.'

'Sounds great. I'll be cheering for you.' He winks, then waddles off with Corinne over to the bleachers. Ah. Good. Parker and Nicky are there, too—we're playing Ethan's team again.

I don't see Ethan yet . . . he's been late a couple of times recently, driving in from Providence, but I start at seeing International's new pitcher. Doral-Anne Driscoll. Uh-oh.

In addition to being a loose-moraled, obscenity-spewing, nasty and not-always-clean bully, Doral-Anne was also the captain of Mackerly High's softball team. The year we won States. I wasn't on the team . . . my baseball talents were dormant till I started playing as an adult.

'Well, well, well,' Doral-Anne says, then spits. I square my shoulders. She can't scare me anymore. I'm a grown-up. A grown-up who bats .513.

'Hi, Doral-Anne. What are you doing here?' I ask.

'Ethan Mirabelli invited me to come,' she says. 'Saw him the other day. Said I wouldn't mind playing again, and he said his team could use a good pitcher, so here I am.' She pulls a face, daring me to protest.

161

'Welcome,' I say. My mind is racing. Why would Ethan invite Doral-Anne? Surely he can't be . . . *interested* . . . in her, of all people!

'Batter up!' calls Stuey Mitchell, our home plate ump. I take my bat, tap my cleats and go up to the plate.

Three pitches later, I'm out. Somewhat dazed, I slink back to the dugout.

'Way to go, D.A.' someone calls.

It's Ethan, walking toward the field from the parking lot, tucking his International Foods T-shirt into his pants. I can't help it, I know it's juvenile, but heck! Ethan's supposed to be my friend. He's not supposed to cheer when I humiliate myself at bat. He must see my disgruntled expression, because he smiles. 'Nice try, Lucy,' he adds.

Doral-Anne doesn't seem to have lost her stuff in the years since high school. She retires us in order, and I can't help but notice that Ethan and she have a laugh together back at the dugout.

Bemused, I get my glove and head for the mound.

Ethan's up first . . . the privileges of ownership, when he's around, anyway. Doral-Anne watches his ass quite intently as he walks to the batter's box. Super.

My first pitch is a bit inside. Okay, okay, it's a lot inside. Ethan jumps back, a swirl of dirt rising from his cleats. 'Ball one,' Stuey calls.

'Control yourself, Lang,' Doral-Anne

shouts, then spits in the dirt. God. Martha Stewart would just have to smother her with an eiderdown pillow, wouldn't she?

I try to ignore Doral-Anne and catch the ball Carly Espinosa, our catcher, throws back. She gives me the sign for an outside pitch. I shake my head. She gives me another sign—fast ball down the middle. I nod and, launching into the odd little windmill windup of softball, I let the ball fly.

The pitch is wild; Ethan jerks back, but the ball bounces off his helmet.

'Jesus, Lang!' shouts Doral-Anne. 'Is this how you always pitch?'

'Sorry, Ethan!' I call, ignoring Doral-Anne. 'You okay?'

'I'm fine,' he answers. He tosses his bat gently to Carly's son, who's eight and serves as batboy, and then jogs to first.

International Foods scores three runs that inning. Clearly I don't have my best stuff. Everyone hits me. Including the debutante princess, Doral-Anne, whose mother, legend has it, named her daughter after Dorals, her favorite brand of cigarette.

At some point later in the game, I manage to make it to first base on a weak little hit that's fumbled by International Foods' shortstop. Finally.

'Yay, Aunt Wucy!' calls my nephew. I glance over, then start. Fred Busey. Crikey, I'd forgotten all about him. I wave. He waves back, then smoothes his hand over his paint-enhanced hair. Parker says something, and they chuckle.

'Give 'em hell, Lucy!' my friend shouts.

'Go Bunny's!' Fred seconds.

Though I'm not one hundred percent sure I want it publicly known that the man with the inked-in scalp is with me, my battered ego is still somewhat soothed. I contemplate the distance to second base. Take a subtle step in that direction. Another inch. Another. After all, I've been known to steal a base or (ahem!) a hundred and twenty-two! League record, ladies and gentlemen! And besides, that would really piss off dear Doral-Anne, who's pitching far too well. If we're going to have a chance, I simply must get in scoring position.

Doral-Anne glances at me from underneath her too-long bangs, then decides I'm not worth watching. She goes into her windup, and I'm off. My helmet flies off as I sprint toward second, each step a joy, the thrill of stealing electrifying my legs. Ethan doesn't even see me, but I slide anyway, just as his glove comes down.

'Out!' says Christopher. 'Sorry, Luce.'

'Excuse me?' I pant, standing up, my foot securely on base.

'You're out,' he says.

'I am?' Openmouthed, I look at Ethan, who raises his eyebrows and grins that elvish smile. He holds up his glove, and sure enough, the

164

ball is right there.

'You weren't even close,' he says. 'Buddy.' He winks.

'Can we keep playing, or is the princess going to stay there forever?' Doral-Anne calls.

With no other option, still shocked that I was, for the first time *ever*, tagged out on a steal, I trudge back to the dugout.

Bunny's loses, 9-2. Worse, Ethan offers to buy drinks for both sides, so everyone will be heading to Lenny's for a postgame analysis.

'Tough loss,' Fred Busey says, panting a bit with the effort of walking the ten yards or so from the bleachers.

'You're telling me,' I say, forcing a smile. Truthfully I'm stunned at how badly I played. Three measly strikeouts. On base only once, and that because of an error. And caught stealing . . . jeepers.

Most of those heading for the bar do it logically . . . by cutting through Ellington Park. Which would mean also going through the cemetery. Which we all know I'm not willing to do.

'Shall we grab a drink?' asks Fred.

'Sure,' I say. I can have a drink with Fred. He's a nice guy. Besides, Ethan's just chitchattering away to Doral-Anne. And you know what else? I'm going to walk through the cemetery. Because it's time for me to stop being a dope when it comes to that. I should be able to take care of Jimmy's grave as a good widow should. The Mirabellis are moving—their goodbye party is just around the corner, and the very thought causes my heart to clench. So yes, I should get over this issue of mine. Should be able to walk through the cemetery. But that doesn't mean I have to walk fast, either.

Indeed, everyone else on the team trickles past us. Fred can't move too quickly, and that's fine with me, because I need a little time to shore up my courage. I try to follow Fred's tale of his recent divorce, his eight-year-old daughter, but the cemetery looms in front of me like the gaping maw of a shark. I make the appropriate noises, but my heart starts to clatter as we approach the end of the park . . . and the entrance to the cemetery.

We're getting closer. I'm a little out of breath. And why can't I hear Fred? Is he still talking? Lips are still moving . . . A buzz fills my ears, and my hands are slick with sweat. Up ahead, well into the cemetery, I can see Ethan's back, *Mirabelli* over a number 12. He's walking with Doral-Anne, laughing, unaware of my distress. If only he'd turn, see me, help me out . . . *Please, Ethan.* My psychic cry fails to hit its target. Ethan and Doral-Anne disappear around the bend.

'Um . . . Fred?' I say, and my voice cracks. We're just outside the stone pillars now.

'Yeah?' He looks up at me, his brows coming together.

'I . . . can we . . . um . . .' I'm having a hard time getting enough air, my chest bucking up and down erratically. Oh, jeepers, I'm going to faint.

'Are you okay? Want to sit down?' Fred, also panting though not for the same reasons, takes my elbow in his pudgy hand and leads me to a rock. I sit down with all the grace of a dying hippo. Dropping my head between my knees, I try to relax, try to let the breeze push air into my lungs. *Everything's gonna be all right . . . everything's gonna be all right.*

'Lucy? Should I call someone . . . 911?' Fred asks, patting my shoulder.

I shake my head. The panic subsides like the outgoing tide, bit by bit. I don't have to go in the cemetery. No one will know. Nice Fred won't mind, I can already tell.

'My husband's buried in there,' I whisper, and oh, it sounds so sad. Tears spring to my eyes, and I scrub them away, almost irritated. I should be able to say these things without crying by now.

'I'm so sorry,' Fred murmurs.

'Maybe we can just go around?' I ask. 'I'm sorry, I know it doesn't make sense—'

'It doesn't have to,' Fred says. 'Of course we can go around. Whenever you're ready.'

And so, feeling like an ass, I get up and take twenty minutes longer than necessary to get to Lenny's Pub.

'Hey, Luce!' a few of my Bunny's

167

teammates chorus. Ellen Ripling is sucking down a piña colada, flirting shamelessly with Leeland Huckabee. Tom Malloy, our first baseman, looks half plastered already, which is par for the course . . . the man just cannot hold his liquor, and I make a mental note to get his keys. Carly Espinosa, responsible for both our team's runs with a homer in the ninth, is on her cell phone. Roxanne, the surly waitress, growls at patrons to hurry up and order as she slaps down drinks.

And Ethan is yucking it up with Doral-Anne.

'What would you like to drink?' Fred asks.

'Oh, um . . . I'll have a . . . whatever you're having,' I say, my mind temporarily blank. I indulge in a guilty and relieved sigh when he turns his back.

'So what happened today, Lucy?' Tommy Malloy calls.

'Just having a bad day,' I answer. 'Don't worry. My mojo will be back when we play Nubey's.' We've never lost to Nubey's Hardware, after all.

Ah-ha! Ethan is coming my way. 'Hey, Luce.'

'Hi. Sorry I'm late getting here,' I say.

'Oh, were you late?' he asks, glancing at the bar.

'I just had a little . . . trouble. That's all.' I wait for him to inquire after my well-being. He doesn't. 'So. Taking steroids or something,

Eth?' I continue. 'Pretty aggressive there on second today. First time you tagged me out . . . ever, now that I think of it.' I offer a smile, and he grins back.

'It's not steroids, Lucy. Just treating you like my buddy. Why? Should I let you get on base next time?' His merry eyebrows rise, and his smile is full-fledged now.

'You don't *let* me do anything,' I object.

'Sure, Luce.'

'What are you saying?'

He laughs, not meanly but in genuine amusement. 'Lucy, Lucy. Do you really think you're that good?'

My mouth falls open. 'Yes! I'm great at softball! I bat .513!'

He nods. 'Yes, you do. Even higher than Tommy Malloy, who played for Arizona State. Amazing.' He winks.

My shoulders slump. 'So what do you mean? I'm *not* that good? People have been just being nice?'

'Yup.'

'No, sir!' *I'm not great?* 'Why would they do that?'

'Because you're Jimmy's widow, kid. Who's gonna strike out poor Lucy Mirabelli?'

My eyes narrow. 'Did you have something to do with this?'

He grins again. 'Well, I may have said to go easy on my sister-in-law. Back when you first started playing, anyway. I guess it got to be a

169

habit.' He pats my shoulder, and I catch a slight whiff of his cologne, such a comforting and familiar smell that I'm filled with longing. And jealousy, maybe, because he's . . . ah, dang it. *Snap out of it,* I tell myself harshly.

I glance around the bar. Fred, surrounded by taller patrons, waits patiently, unaware of the 'shove your way to the front' method of getting a drink at this fine establishment. I glance over to where Doral-Anne sits in a booth along the back wall. Where *I* usually sit. Often with Ethan, whenever he was around for a game, that is. Despite the fact that our more intimate relationship had always been a secret, Ethan was always quite protective of me. Quite solicitous, and everyone always gave him huge points for being such a good guy where his brother's widow was concerned. He'd get me a beer, praise my skill on the field (gah!) and usually walk me home. And often shag me.

Dang it, dang it, dang it.

Doral-Anne eyes me with all the warmth of a great white shark. 'You should probably get back to your date,' I say to Ethan, unable to completely hide the bitter note in my voice.

'Who? Doral-Anne? Oh, we're not on a date. Just talking.' He glances over to Doral-Anne, who jerks her glare off of me and pretends she was studying the menu.

'And what are you talking about?' I ask.

He considers me carefully. 'She's interested

in what International Foods does. Our new product line. Stuff like that.'

'Your product line?' I snort. 'Ethan, my dear boy, Doral-Anne's interested in *you*.'

'No, Lucy, she's interested in my company. We're both in the food service industry, in case you didn't notice. There's been talk about Starbucks closing the Mackerly store. She might send her résumé to International, that's all.'

'She's not good enough for you.' The statement falls out without my consent, but there it is. The truth.

Ethan's mouth tightens. 'So now you're an expert on who I should date, Lucy? Maybe you shouldn't go around judging people you barely know.'

I gulp. Great, he's defending her. 'Well, I just . . . whatever. Sorry I said anything. I'm sure she's perfectly wonderful.'

Luckily the door opens and Parker breezes in, smelling of J'Adore and not of sweat, like my own sticky self.

'Hey, guys!' she says, giving us both a fond squeeze of the shoulder, and some of the tension leaves the moment.

'How's our boy?' Ethan asks, his face taking on that dopey, adoring look he gets whenever he thinks of his son.

'Terrorizing the babysitter, like any good four-year-old.' She smiles at Ethan, he smiles back, and once again, I imagine them married.

171

Though Nicky was definitely unplanned, the result of failed birth control, neither of them ever regretted having the lad. They could have more Nickys . . . after all, it's not like they find each other repugnant, which is more than enough grounds for marriage in my eyes.

Parker snaps her fingers in front of my face, and I jump. 'Lucy, I just asked how the date was going. I hardly got to talk to him . . . your sister was telling him about Emma's poop and pee schedule, and I have to say, he took it like a man.'

'Did she show the cracked nipple?' I ask, grinning.

Ethan cocks his head. 'You're on a date?' he asks. 'Who is he?'

'It's not a date. Not really. We just . . . he's Gertie Myers's nephew. Fred Busey.'

'Fred!' Parker cries. Fred's enhanced head snaps around. 'Fred, be my best friend and grab me a Jägermeister, okay? Lenny, you old fart, pay attention! The man needs to be served!'

'So. I take it Charley Spirito didn't work out,' Ethan says. That little muscle under his eye twitches. 'On to Prospect Number Two, huh?'

'It's not exactly a date,' I repeat.

At that moment, Doral-Anne shoves her way into our little knot, right as Fred joins us, carefully holding a Jägermeister shot for Parker and two beers. He passes out the

172

drinks. 'Hello,' he says, offering his hand first to Doral-Anne, then to Ethan. 'I'm Fred Busey, a friend of Lucy here.'

'A *friend*, huh?' Doral-Anne says, making a mocking face. At some point after the game, she knotted her T-shirt to give the world a view of her tattoo (an orange and green snake, which curls around her pierced navel, forked tongue darting . . . adorable). 'Nice to meetcha. So, Ethan, if you wanna continue that conversation . . .'

'Doral-Anne, this is Parker Welles, my son's mother,' Ethan says, politely ignoring her rudeness.

'Hi, how are you? You work at Starbucks, right?' Parker asks.

'I'm the manager,' Doral-Anne says.

'I'm there all the time,' Parker murmurs, then shoots a guilty look at me. 'For coffee only, of course,' she adds.

'Well,' Fred says. 'Shall we get a table for five?'

'Oh, we don't want to interrupt your date,' Parker says. 'You guys have fun. Eth, mind if I join you two?'

And so I sit with Fred, who is perfectly nice, seems to be an adoring father and whose hair paint seems to be running, as a black streak is slowly but surely making its way down his forehead.

'She sounds like a real cutey,' I say at the appropriate interval in the story of Fred's daughter and her ballet recital.

We spend an endless hour chatting before I look at my watch, feign surprise at the hour and remind Fred that I have to get up at four and really need some sleep. Which is, of course, a lie. I'll be up for hours.

'Listen,' he says, and I mentally fumble for an excuse to turn him down on a second date. 'You're awfully cute, Lucy, but I just don't think there's chemistry here.'

Angels bless you, Fred, I think. 'You seem like a great guy,' I say honestly. 'But, well . . . yes.'

'Not over your husband, eh?' he says kindly.

I swallow. 'I think you're right,' I agree. 'Good luck with everything, Fred.'

I stop at the bar to remind Lenny to get Tommy Malloy's keys, then leave. The cheerful noise of the bar dies within a half block of my walk home. If I could just cut through the dang cemetery, I'd be home in ten minutes. As it is, it will take thirty-two.

The bugs of late September have left or died, and the only sound is one brave little cricket and the ever-present sound of the waves shushing against the rocky shore two blocks away. I trail my fingers along the cemetery wall. 'Hi, Dad,' I say at the appropriate spot. 'Hope everything's good in heaven.' The wind rustles the fading leaves above, and one or two drift down.

Maybe Fred's right. Maybe I'm not ready.

Maybe it's my destiny to be a Black Widow, have Grinelda do my whiskers and channel my dead husband. I do want more, I really do . . . I'm just not sure I can get it.

At home, Fat Mikey winds his hefty self around my ankles. Stumbling over him, I then reach down and pick him up, rubbing my face against his. 'Hello, you big brute,' I murmur. He tolerates me for a moment, honors me with a rusty purr, then jumps free.

With a sigh, I sit on the couch, which is directly in front of the rather fabulous plasma screen TV Ethan helped me pick out last year. I could play Guitar Hero, I guess, or challenge my computer to a game of Scrabble. I could go to bed . . . 4:00 a.m. comes early, of course.

I look at the wedding picture that hangs on the wall, a lovely eight-by-ten candid. Jimmy and me, laughing. Our faces are in profile, both of us turned to look at Ethan, who's not in the shot. His best man speech was funny as all get-out, and everyone had roared with laughter. Especially Jimmy. His laugh was one of the things I loved most about him, a low, dirty laugh that did things to my insides. He was larger than life, my Jimmy. The life of the party. The love of my life. Our marriage was more than just two people being together . . . it was everything I ever wanted.

I go into the kitchen and open my baking cabinet. Molten dark chocolate cake with a milk chocolate center? Or no, flip that . . .

milk chocolate cake with dark mocha chocolate goo for the center. Yes. A shot of espresso, some almond paste in the ganache. I'll call it Java Glory Cake.

The sounds of baking are the gentle music of my soul. I was born to be a baker. Bread has its own reward, but dessert is where I was meant to be. The clatter of the mixing bowls against the cool granite countertop, the crisp smack of the eggshells at the edge, the chirring of my whisk. And the colors! The lemony-yellow of well-beaten eggs, the seductive gloss of the bitter chocolate as it melts with the pale butter. The many shades of white . . . the matte of the flour, the purity of the baking powder, the cheerful gleam of the sugar. My vintage mixing bowls are also white, each one polka-dotted with a different color . . . green for the largest, then orange, then red, then robin's egg blue. Ethan gave them to me for Christmas a few years ago. One of the best presents I ever got.

As I measure out the ingredients, the sharp, pure smell of Mexican vanilla fills the air. I inhale, then rub a little on my wrist. Best perfume in the world, in my opinion.

By eleven, one of the prettiest cakes I've ever made sits in front of me. It's gorgeous . . . both layers came out perfectly, no tilting or sinking, no sir. The icing gleams, the brown so deep and lovely I wish I could live in it. Coffee and chocolate, butter and vanilla, the

176

inexpressibly comforting smell of cake fills my oven-warmed kitchen. Though it's probably just my imagination, it seems that on the shelf over the window, my little statue of St. Honore, patron saint of bakers, is smiling.

As rewarding as it might be, as good as my bread truly is, I really should be a pastry chef again.

I cut a slab of cake and gently transfer it to one of my pretty plates. Wrapping it in plastic, I tape a little note to the edge. 'Enjoy.' Then I slip out of my apartment and walk upstairs, leaving the cake in front of Ethan's door.

There is no sound from within. He might be at Parker's . . . he's been known to sleep over there from time to time; once when Nicky had strep and was having fever-induced nightmares, another time when the little guy got stitches after crashing his tricycle into a tree. Sometimes just to be there, and since there are seventeen bedrooms in Grayhurst, why not? Or he might be there for romantic reasons, and the image of Ethan kissing Parker, taking her hand and leading her to bed, causes my stomach to twist. I shouldn't be jealous—Ethan deserves every happiness, perhaps more than anyone I know. If he's with Parker, I should be glad.

The image of Ethan with Doral-Anne, however, is too horrible to contemplate.

With a sigh, I turn and retrace my weary steps back down to my place. I'm tired.

But rather than go to bed, I find myself casting another admiring glance at the remaining cake. Then I go to the pantry, grope around in the white cardboard box, take out a Twinkie and wait out the night.

CHAPTER ELEVEN

'Wanna see me light this on fire and drink it?'

Stevie, the poison-ivy eating, corpse-tipping cousin, stands before me, a glass of whiskey in one hand, a lighter in the other.

'No, Stevie. Do not light that on fire. Don't be an idiot.'

'God, you're no fun anymore,' Stevie says. 'Hey, heard you're looking for a new guy. I know someone, a buddy a' mine—'

'No, thanks, Stevie.'

'Come on, let me tell you about him! He's a good guy. Lotsa fun.'

'Stevie, sweetie, if he's your buddy and you think he's fun, then I'm under the impression that he likes to steal cars, get tattoos and shoot fish. Am I right?'

'Yeah. So?' Stevie looks injured. I pat his arm and wander off to mingle. I'm the daughter-in-law, after all, and this is the Mirabellis' farewell party as they depart for Valle de Muerte . . . er, Puerte.

Gianni's is mobbed . . . probably shouldn't

say that at an Italian restaurant in Rhode Island. Gianni's is packed to the gills, that's better. Half the town is here—the mayor, the town council, Father Adhyatman from St. Bonaventure, Reverend Covers from St. Andrew's, which is right across the street. (They often have attendance contests . . . the winner buys dinner at Lenny's, all very convivial. Beats a holy war.) Ash is here, dressed in the expected black and chains, and my mother is staring at her as one would stare at a particularly gruesome roadkill, not even noticing that Captain Bob is, in turn, staring at her. There's my excellent cousin Anne the lesbian doctor and her *special friend*, as Iris calls her. In fact, Iris is now trying to force-feed Laura, who has the willowy grace of a supermodel.

Gianni's Ristorante won't be closing—my father-in-law couldn't bring himself to go that far. Instead his cousin's husband's brother is going to take over, and they'll 'see how it goes' before putting anything up for sale. It was a relief, honestly . . . while losing a few restaurant accounts might make the Black Widows rethink Bunny's business plan, I'm not ready to lose the place where Jimmy and I met, where he worked so happily.

'Hi, Aunt Wucy!' My nephew hugs my legs, then wipes his mouth on my pants.

'Hi there, gorgeous,' I say, ruffling his hair. He smiles up at me, his lips curling in

179

identical fashion to his father's. I scoop the lad up and kiss his cheek. 'What's new, Superglue?'

He giggles. 'Nothing. I ate a squid.'

'Did you? Was it good?'

He nods, then reaches into the pocket of his little pink oxford shirt. 'Here. I brought you one.'

Sure enough, he holds a fried calamari in his grimy little hand. 'Thank you, angel!' I say, kissing him again. 'Can I save it for later?'

'Okay. Can I get down now? I wanna find Daddy. I have a squid for him, too.' I set him down, and off he runs.

'Hi, Lucy,' my sister says. Emma is, as ever, clutched to her bosom. Or I think it's Emma . . . it's a baby-size lump covered in a pink blanket.

'Can I peek at Emma?' I ask. 'I'd love to hold her. Can I?'

Corinne stiffens. 'Um . . . well, there's so many people.'

'Please? I haven't held her for a day and a half,' I plead.

'If you dropped her—'

'I won't drop her, Corinne. Can I please hold my niece? I won't kill her, I promise.'

My sister stares at me, wounded. As if summoned, Christopher materializes by her side. 'Hey, Luce,' he says affably. Ah. An ally.

'Hi, Chris. Think I could hold your beautiful daughter? I haven't had a chance

180

yet.'

'Sure,' he says, lifting his baby from Corinne, ignoring her Significant Look, and starts to pass her to me.

'Wait!' Corinne snarls. She fishes around in the diaper bag and withdraws a liter of Purell. When the requisite thirty seconds of hand-rubbing have been observed, I am allowed to hold Emma at last.

She's sleeping. I tuck the blanket under her chin. Corinne starts to advise me on how not to breathe on the baby, but then she spies Christopher snagging a mozzarella and tomato appetizer from a passing waiter. 'Chris! Do you know the cholesterol count on those?' she bleats, practically slapping it out of his hand.

I withdraw a few feet. The doors to the kitchen are shielded from the dining room by a small wall, and someone left a chair there. It's as good a place as any to sit and worship.

Emma's skin is amazing . . . poreless and porcelain, smooth as the inside of a tulip petal. Her tiny lips are the sweetest Cupid's bow, and her lashes are blonde and silken. She's so warm and cozy against me, her slight weight more precious than anything I could imagine. I trace a tiny eyebrow with my sterilized forefinger, and Emma sighs in her sleep.

A wave of love and longing pulls my heart in a painful, wonderful ache. My doubts about finding another husband seem trivial when the

181

prize could be this.

'You sure look good holding a baby,' comes a voice.

I look up abruptly. Ethan stands before me in the doorway of the kitchen. His eyes are soft, and the breath leaves my lungs. My heart slows in long, rolling beats, and Ethan's mouth tugs up. My knees go a little weak.

'Thanks,' I say, my voice husky. I clear my throat to cover and adjust Emma's blanket.

'Daddy! I found you!' Nick comes barreling around the corner and crashes into his father's legs. Ethan lifts him up and his face breaks into that amazing smile.

'Hey there, Nick the Tick!' he says, kissing his son loudly on the neck.

'I *am* a tick!' Nicky cries in delight, wrapping his arms and legs around his father. 'See? You can't get rid of me! I'm a tick! I'm stuck on you! I'm drinking your blood!'

'Disgusting!' Ethan pronounces, making his son convulse with laughter.

'I brought you a squid, Daddy! You have to eat it! Eat it, eat it!'

Ethan smiles. 'Squid, huh? Let me have it.' He opens his mouth, heedless of the grubby hand that feeds him. 'Delicious. Thank you, Tick Boy.'

'I love you, Daddy,' Nicky says with the absolute ease and sincerity only children possess. He lays his head on Ethan's shoulder, then, catching sight of me, asks, 'Is that your

182

baby, Wucy?'

'Oh, no, honey. It's Emma. Corinne's baby, remember?' I smile. 'She's my niece.'

'I'm your nephew,' he states, confirming his ownership.

'Yes, you are. My one and only.' I glance at Ethan. 'How are you, Eth?'

'Fine, Lucy,' he says. 'You holding up okay?'

At those words, I look down at Emma to hide the fact that actually, no, I'm not. All night long, I've been avoiding the reason we're here—I'm losing my in-laws, not to mention a huge link with Jimmy. My eyes sting, and I stroke Emma's little ear, touch her velvety cheek.

'Can I have my daughter back?' My sister's voice is sharp. 'I need to feed her. Sorry, Lucy.' Without any more ado, she slides Emma out of my arms, leaving a cold spot where the baby was nestled so sweetly.

'Hi, Corinne,' Ethan says.

'Hi, Corinne,' Nicky echoes.

'Oh, hello, boys,' Corinne says with a small smile. 'Sorry to interrupt. My breasts are so engorged they feel like they're about to crack open.'

'Ouch,' Ethan murmurs.

'Crack open?' Nicky asks.

'Ouch is right. You wouldn't believe the pain. It's agonizing.' Without further ado, Corinne canters off to nurse the baby.

183

Ethan sets his son back on the floor. 'Nicky,' he says, 'will you go find me another squid?'

'I will, Daddy! And then I'll come back and be your tick again, okay?'

'Okay, baby,' Ethan says, his face so gentle and loving it hurts my heart. Nicky bolts off once more, and then Ethan looks at me. The pebble in my throat cuts like a lump of quartz. 'Come here,' Ethan says, reaching for my hand. An electric jolt runs down my arm—I'd forgotten how warm and strong his hands are. Jimmy had hands like that. It's the one place where the brothers look alike.

Ethan leads me into the kitchen. The party is winding down, and the kitchen is miraculously empty for the moment, as all the food was served buffet-style in the dining room.

Ethan takes a long look at me, still holding my hand. His eyebrows come together in a frown. 'You okay, honey?' he whispers, and the endearment is like a nail in my heart. Oh, God, I miss him.

'Ethan,' I say, my voice cracking. I squeeze his hand hard, swallowing repeatedly. His mouth opens slightly, and in those brown and gold eyes is a question waiting to be answered. 'Ethan,' I try again, but my throat clenches.

Hot, helpless tears fill my eyes, and I look away, automatically locating Jimmy's shrine. Handsome, blue-eyed Jimmy Mirabelli, tall

184

and strong. And gone. Just a memory now.

I let go of Ethan and wipe my eyes with the heels of my palms.

'This is where you guys met,' Ethan murmurs. I nod, letting the moment where I might have said something pass. I can't have everything. Ethan was right.

The kitchen door opens, three servers come in with trays stacked with plates and glasses. Gianni follows.

'Hey, Dad,' Ethan says. 'How's everything going?'

'That idiot Carlo overcooked the chicken and it's like fucking rubber,' Gianni growls. 'Lucy, baby, sorry for the language. You okay? You get enough to eat?' Ethan's father steps between us, slings an arm around my shoulders. 'You'll come visit us, yeah? It's beautiful out there. Lotsa flowers. A golf course.' His eyes, like mine did just a moment ago, go to the picture of his son, and his face spasms.

'You bet,' I say, hugging my father-in-law. I feel the big man choke on a sob and hold him tighter, closing my eyes against the sorrow he has to carry for the rest of his life. Poor Gianni. Poor, poor man.

When I look up, Ethan's gone.

CHAPTER TWELVE

'The doctor will see you now,' the receptionist says, earning me the baleful glare of a roomful of women in varying degrees of ripeness.

'She's my cousin,' I explain. 'I'll only be a minute. I'm sorry.' No one deigns to answer.

I walk through the frosted glass door down the hall to my cousin's office.

'Hey, Anne,' I say, giving a little knock. 'Thanks for seeing me.'

'Sure, kid! How's it going?' Anne asks.

Cousin Anne ushers me into a seat. Her office is in Newport, and as Newport is the stylish city mouse to Mackerly's more humble offerings, so Anne is to me. She's ten years older, extremely gorgeous and wicked smart, as indicated by the diplomas from Harvard and Johns Hopkins that hang on her wall. Her graying hair is short and funky, and her skin is a testimony to sunscreen and good genetics. She dresses in comfortable, stylish clothes in soothing colors and wears great jewelry. Her office is likewise wicked cool . . . glass desk, green leather chairs, a gorgeous view of the graceful span that is the Newport Bridge. A bookcase holds dozens of medical books, a nice picture of Anne and Laura, and a beautiful glass sculpture of a baby in utero.

'I'm not pregnant,' I say, just to get that out

of the way. 'And I brought you blueberry cream scones as a bribe.' I set the string-wrapped white box on her desk

'I love bribes,' she says amiably, peeking under a flap. 'Yummy.'

'How's Laura?' I ask, stalling.

'Oh, she's great,' Anne answers. 'Busy with the new school year and all that. We're heading up to Bar Harbor for the weekend.'

'Sounds fun,' I say.

'It should be,' she agrees. Waits a little more. They must've taught that in med school. Sit silently till the patient can't stand it anymore and blurts it all out.

'So. Things good with the lesbian doctor practice?' I say, swallowing hard.

She laughs. 'Can you work on that? I'd really love to hear my mom say, "My daughter, the obstetrician" just once.'

I smile. 'Well, she's very proud. Drops your credentials whenever she can.'

I do have a regular doctor. It's just that I used to babysit Dr. Ianelli's kids. And Mrs. Farthing is the receptionist there, and she's the mother of my old high school classmate. The nurse, Michelle, is a bakery regular (two cheese danishes every Monday, Wednesday and Friday, and the pounds are starting to pile on, frankly). The physician's assistant, Caroline, was in Girl Scouts with Corinne. The usual.

Anne nods. 'So what brings you here,

Lucy?'

I hesitate. 'Doctor patient confidentiality?' I suggest.

'You bet,' she answers.

'I'm having anxiety attacks again.' Anne nods. 'I mean, I had a few after Jimmy died, of course, hyperventilating, heart pounding, stuff like that, but I haven't had any for a couple of years. Until a few weeks ago, actually.'

'Had anything changed in your life lately?' Anne asks.

'Well, my in-laws finally left yesterday,' I answer.

She nods and waits.

'And I'm . . . um, I'm starting to date again. Sort of.' I swallow sickly.

'That's pretty big, hon,' she says with a kind smile.

My sinuses prickle with tears. 'Mmm-hmm,' I murmur.

'How's it going?' she asks.

'Not awful, not great.' I sniffle, and Anne passes me a tissue box without comment.

'How are you sleeping?' she asks.

'I haven't slept that well since the accident,' I admit. 'A few hours at night, a few in the morning after I'm done at the bakery.'

'Sleep has a lot to do with your mental state, Goose,' she says, reverting to her childhood nickname for me. 'How about exercising? Any of that?'

'I ride my bike a lot. Around the island. I

188

rode here today. At my last check-up, the doctor said I was perfectly healthy.'

She nods, then opens her desk drawer and takes out a prescription pad. 'This is a scrip for a mild antianxiety medication,' she says, scribbling something down. 'Give it a try, see if it helps. It should help you sleep, too. The first time you take it, you should probably be home and not near hot ovens and all that, okay?' She rips off the paper and hands it to me, then stands up and comes round her desk.

'You hang in there, honey,' she says, folding me into a hug. 'Change sucks, and of course you're going to freak out a little, starting to date again after all this time. What's it been, five years?'

'And a half,' I say.

'Shit.' She sighs, then messes up my hair. 'You're normal, Lucy.' I give her a smile to show that I'm spunky and super-brave, and she smiles back. 'Listen, the lesbian doctor has to get back to her patients. These pregnant women get mighty testy if I keep them waiting. Call me if you need anything else. And hey, come for dinner one of these days. Maybe Laura and I can think of some guy for you.'

'Thanks, Anne,' I say sincerely. Good old Anne. She and Laura almost make me wish I were gay, too.

* * *

189

After I fill the prescription, I swing by High Hopes Convalescent Center to see Great-Aunt Boggy. I made a ton of scones last night, and the staff loves when I bring stuff in. Maybe Boggy will eat one, too. They're nice and soft . . . I'm guessing they don't need much tooth action, which is good, since Boggy doesn't have teeth anymore.

You have of course noticed that I don't eat my own desserts. It's a shame, since judging by the smell of them, they're fantastically stupendously wonderful. Not eating them probably keeps me from being an even better baker, because obviously, it'd help to know what things tasted like.

But the night Jimmy died, you see, I'd baked a beautiful dessert in my newlywed fervor. Jimmy and I hadn't spent a day apart since our wedding, and that whole day, I'd been missing him, the heat of young love throbbing most pleasantly. Despite the fact that I'd been at work at the fancy Newport hotel where I was slaving, I came home and decided to bake for Jimmy. Pictured him coming through the door late that night, weary but wired, full of stories about his day in New York. I'd present him the most beautiful dessert ever, smile and listen until he was sufficiently relaxed to go to bed, where my plan was to shag him senseless and make him unspeakably grateful that he had such a hot wife.

And so I pulled out all the stops to show him how much I'd missed him. To let him know how I adored him. To show off a little, too, because despite my mother-in-law being a wonderful dessert maker, I really wanted to be Gianni's pastry chef someday.

I spent the next few happy hours dipping golden peaches in a boiling water bath, slipping off the peels, slicing the succulent fruit wafer-thin. On a whim, I grilled them lightly, drizzling a sweet white wine over them as I did so. I toasted half a pound of pistachios, then ground them into rubble with some carmelized ginger, then cut that into unsalted butter for the crust. Rather than make one big tart, I made four little ones—baked the crusts, and when they were cool, added a generous layer of crème fraîche and lemon zest, topped with the thin-sliced peaches, their deep golden color darkening to a seductive red at the center. I arranged the slices to look like flower petals, then poached some blueberries in the wine and added them as the center of the flower. When I was finished, I had what was quite possibly the prettiest dessert ever made. And because I felt I couldn't possibly wait till Jimmy got home, I ate one. Right after Jimmy called to tell me he was just passing New Haven, I ate another, then saved the last two for my honey.

Well, obviously, Jimmy never got to try one, and ever since that horrible night, the desserts

I've baked have lost their taste for me. I still love to make them . . . I just can't seem to eat them. Whenever I take a bite of a cake or a tart or a pudding or even just a chocolate chip cookie, it tastes like dust—meaningless, empty and gray. If I try to swallow, I gag. It's pretty clear why.

And so I've resorted to the products of Hostess . . . Twinkies are my favorite, that slight tang of chemical preservative that gives the beloved icon its impressive shelf life, the spongy, sticky cake, the little tunnel of white through the middle. Hostess Cupcakes, too—the peel-away frosting with the cheery little swirl of white on top, the nondairy cream filling that I like to dig out with my tongue. Those pink Sno-Balls, like something from a science fiction movie. The Ho Hos, the Ding Dongs . . . sigh. My teachers from Johnson & Wales would have my name burned off the alumni register if they knew.

'Hello, dear,' says the receptionist at High Hopes as I walk through the door.

'Hello,' I answer, smiling as I set the second box of scones on the counter. 'How's my aunt doing today?'

'Oh, she's just as sweet as can be,' Alice lies kindly. What else is she going to say? *Well, she's been drooling really well today . . . dozing. A little napping here and there, between the bouts of deeper sleep . . .*

'Well, I brought a few treats,' I say. 'Let me

192

just grab one for Boggy, and you can divvy up the rest.'

'Thank you, dear!' Alice says. 'Aren't you nice to think of us.'

I really am, I acknowledge with a modest bow of the head. Then I snag the biggest scone for my aunty and head down the hall.

As usual, Boggy's in bed, sleeping.

'Hi, Boggy!' I say. 'I brought you a scone. Blueberry and cream. I think it's a winner, if I do say so myself.'

I press the button to raise the bed to an upright position—Boggy won't wake unless she's sitting up and she's hungry.

'Doesn't that smell great?' I ask, holding out the treat.

She opens her eyes. Good old Boggy. How nice that she never lost the urge to eat.

'Who are you?' she asks.

I jump about a mile into the air, dropping the scone on her lap. Her voice is creaky, the words running together, but my God! She spoke! I haven't heard her speak in fifteen years!

'I'm . . . uh . . . I'm your grand-niece. Lucy. Lucy Lang. Daisy's daughter.' My heart races, my hands are shaking. 'Your niece, Daisy Black.'

'Daisy?' The old lady squints, her face creasing into a thousand wrinkles.

'She's your sister's daughter.'

'My sister Margaret?'

193

'Yes!' I exclaim. 'Boggy! It's so . . . How are you feeling? Are you okay? You've been kind of . . . out of it for a while.' I dig in my pocket for my cell phone. 'I'm just gonna call my mom, okay? Let her know you're, um, awake.'

'Can I eat this?' Boggy asks, then coughs a little. She picks up the scone and gives it a suspicious sniff.

'Well, sure! It's a scone. Uh, go ahead.'

She takes a gummy bite, then smiles up at me, innocent and happy as a puppy.

'Bunny's,' my mother sighs into the phone.

'Mom! I'm at High Hopes. Boggy's awake and talking!'

'What?'

'Get over here right now! She's sitting up in bed, eating a scone, and she . . . well, just come! Hurry!'

Six minutes later (a new land-speed record), the Black Widows come into the room, their faces hopeful and suspicious at the same time. I'm shaking with excitement. 'Aunt Boggy,' I say, my voice thick with happy tears, 'do you remember Iris, Rose and Daisy?'

My mother and aunts approach cautiously. They are holding hands, which touches me more than I can say.

Boggy studies them carefully. 'Well,' she creaks. 'I hope you girls don't expect me to cook.'

And with that, the three nieces burst into

tears at the sights and sounds of Boggy, awake after so, so long. They swarm around her, petting her, taking her gnarled hands into theirs, kissing her, all talking at once to their beloved aunt, whom they have so faithfully visited all these years.

I take a hitching, happy breath, then step out into the hall to call Corinne. I only get her voice mail, though, and leave a message to come to High Hopes as soon as she can.

Then, peeking in once more at the four women, I call Ethan. He'll love this. He'll want to hear all about it, maybe even will leave work early. He doesn't know Aunt Boggy, but he sure loves the Black Widows.

He answers on the fourth ring. 'Ethan, you'll never guess what!' I exclaim.

'Hi, Lucy. Everything okay?'

'Aunt Boggy woke up! And she's talking!'

'One second, Luce.' His voice grows muffled. 'Sorry, this will only take a minute,' he says to someone. 'Lucy, I'm in a meeting, I'm really sorry. That's great about your aunt.'

'I know! I brought her a scone, and there she was—'

'Luce, I'm sorry. I can't talk now. I'll have to catch up later.'

'Oh,' I say, deflating like a popped balloon.

'Sorry,' he repeats. 'I'm really glad about your aunt. Talk to you soon.'

And with that, he clicks off.

Well. He's busy, of course. The new job is

all about meetings, from the little I've heard. Still. It seems to me that a month ago, he would've stepped out of whatever he was doing to hear more of this incredible news.

By now, the word has spread that Boggy is a chatterbox after nearly two decades in a partial coma. Three doctors and two nurses are in her room, checking vitals and asking questions.

'Are there any more scones?' she asks, craning her skinny neck, and with a big smile, I run down the hall to the reception desk to get her some more.

CHAPTER THIRTEEN

Later that evening, I'm back in the apartment, getting ready for a date, slapping on mascara as Fat Mikey watches from his perch on the back of the toilet. Actually I almost forgot the whole thing, given the excitement of the day. I would've bowed out, but I got home at six, and we were supposed to meet at seven. Didn't seem nice to cancel an hour before.

I'd spent most of the day at the nursing home, filling in my cousins and phoning my sister about the Miracle of the Scone, as I'm calling it. I should sell these at the bakery. Lazarus Scones.

Boggy's return really is quite a miracle. The

doctors are stumped and pleased, and other than a *these things happen sometimes* explanation, they had nothing to add. A local news crew dropped in, thanks to a call from Stevie, who figured he could get some free publicity (he's planning to use his skateboard to jump over five cows and feels the world should know). Grinelda the Gypsy dropped in, too, claiming that just last night, she'd received a message that the Black Widows would be visited by someone they thought was long gone.

Finally we were all herded out. Boggy was tired. I'd run back home and got her another six scones, since she'd eaten three that afternoon. With promises to make whatever she liked, I kissed her withered cheek and bid her goodbye. Not sure if she remembers me, but it hardly matters.

I check my purse to make sure I have my cell phone. My date sounded pretty nice, though we've only spoken via e-mail and once on the phone. Has a steady job. Never been married. Seems terrifyingly normal.

At the notion of sitting in Lenny's with yet another candidate for husband, the pebble in my throat seems to swell. And hey . . . Here's the bag from the pharmacy. My new prescription. Ah, yes. Anne said they were mild . . . maybe I should take one. Thinking of my recent panic attacks, I decide to give it a try. I read the instructions on the bottle, take

197

a pill, eat a Twinkie in order to obey the 'take with food' requirement. Then I check my upper lip for whiskers, blow my cat a kiss and promise to return soon, and leave.

As I wait for the elevator, I wonder how Ethan's doing. He didn't swing by High Hopes. Nor did he call me back. Nor have we seen each other since the Mirabellis' going-away party, as I'd bowed out of the actual physical departure of my in-laws. Gianni, Marie and I had a big tear fest the day before they left, and that was as much as we could handle.

Outside, it's a little chilly, a stiff breeze knifing off the water. October is just around the corner. It's my favorite month . . . the shorter days seem more forgiving, gentler somehow, encouraging people to go inside and eat something warm. The smell of ocean is thick in the air as I head down Park Street, skirting the cemetery, noting that the maples are red and gold, the beeches a cheery yellow.

As I pass the spot where my father's buried, I stop for a second and peek over the wall. Convenient, that he's so close to the edge . . . I don't have to suffer the same guilt I feel over not visiting Jimmy's grave. 'Hey, Dad,' I say. For a second, I pull my father's image to mind, trying to find a real memory and not just something from a home movie or photograph. Ah. Here we go. An old favorite, worn but not diminished from the many times

I've summoned it. Daddy pushing me on the swing, his big hands propelling me through the air, the giddy tickle in my stomach, the wind in my hair, my father's big laugh behind me.

A little melancholy descends like a damp fog. If only my Lazarus scones could bring back my dad. Just for a day. Just an hour, even. Ten minutes, hey. I'm not greedy. If I could ask him how I'm doing, or what I should be doing. If I could feel his arms around me, smell his comforting Dad smell, which I swear I can almost catch sometimes. If my father would just tell me everything would be okay, I'd have a much easier time believing it.

Ah, well. Enough maudlin self-pity for the day. Be- sides, maybe my pill is starting to take effect. I feel a little . . . light. Maybe I shouldn't have taken it before a date, but then again, what better time?

I get to Lenny's and wave. There's Tommy Malloy, shooting pool with Obie Chisholm. Carly Espinosa is here—she and her husband, Ted or Todd, I can never remember—have a standing date on Thursdays.

I look around the bar . . . hmm. That's odd. Seems like my head is still moving, even though it's not. What's my date's name again? Something weird. Oh, yes. Corbin, as in Corbin Dallas, the Bruce Willis character from *The Fifth Element*. I love that movie. 'Corbin Dallas,' I say aloud. Oops. Yes, it's fair to say the pill has definitely kicked in. Kind of a nice feeling, really, like I've just had a big glass of Chardonnay.

Well, he doesn't seem to be here. I take a seat at an empty booth, only to be joined immediately by Stevie.

'Can you fucking believe Aunt Boggy?' he asks. He holds a martini glass filled with purple liquid. A haze of smoke hovers over it, and I wince. God knows what's in there. Could be anything from dry ice to formaldehyde, knowing Stevie.

'It's pretty amazing,' I say.

'Hey, you're gonna come to my thing, right?' he asks. 'When I break the record?'

'Is there really a cow-jumping record to break, Stevie?' I ask.

'I dunno,' he grunts, taking another slug of whatever's in his glass. 'If not, I can set it.'

'Sure, I'll be there,' I answer. 'Sounds fun.'

'Watch this, Luce.' Stevie tips his head back and balances the martini glass on his forehead. 'Cool, huh?' he asks.

'Wicked cool, Stevie,' I agree.

'Okay, gotta run.' Stevie removes the martini, sloshing a little liquid into his hair. 'There's Craig Owens. See ya, cuz.' Stevie, never the most focused lad, wanders off to his oldest friend—the one who once dared him to eat poison ivy.

'Lucy?' I look up.

'Yes. Are you Corbin?' He nods, smiles and

sits down.

Corbin and I have not met face-to-face, though I saw his picture on eCommitment. A rather plain guy, classic New England face—light brown hair, small blue eyes, straight teeth, the short nose of the Boston Irish. He meets many of the criteria for my next husband: He is an executive at an insurance company and enjoys running and golf (the desk job and frequent physical exercise meeting the Low Risk of Early Death requirement). His job is with an old, well-established company (about as recession-proof as you can get in this day and age). He volunteers with troubled youths at a camp for two weeks each summer, so his Fatherhood Potential is high. And he's not making the blood thrill in my veins. Another plus.

Still, I fail to feel as pleased as perhaps I should. Also, my eyes feel cold. That's weird. 'So,' I say.

'Thanks for meeting me,' he says. 'Have you ordered yet?'

Lenny lumbers over to take our order. 'So, Luce, you playing the field again?'

'Not exactly, Len, not exactly. Lenny, this is Corbin . . . um, sorry, Corbin, I didn't get your last name.'

'Wojoczieski,' he answers.

'Huh. I thought you looked Irish,' I said.

'My mother's Irish,' he answers, seeming pleased.

201

Wojo-something. Now that's a name that will take a little studying. Wojo-et cetera. Hmm. Lucy Wojo . . . nah. Lucy Lang, that sounded the best. Even better than Lucy Mirabelli. Maybe I should go back to Lang. Maybe I could make up a new name, even. When I was a little girl, I wanted to change my last name to Ingalls Wilder, for obvious reasons. Maybe I can do that now.

'Luce? You want something?' Lenny asks, giving me a nudge.

'Chicken salad and seltzer, okay, Len?' I say. Even in my present state, I'm quite aware I shouldn't drink even one drop of alcohol tonight. Because it's clear that I'm a little . . . well, I hesitate to say *stoned*, since it implies illicit drug use, but *affected* by this medicine. However, and I have to give Anne credit here, I am not feeling anxious at all. Kind of floaty, kind of fun, really.

'The most amazing thing happened today,' I tell old Corbin as Lenny leaves. 'My great-aunt Boggy woke up from the dead. Well, almost dead. Woke up from the near dead. She's a hundred and four.'

'Isn't that incredible!' Corbin says with a beaming smile. 'My goodness! Amazing!'

'It was amazing, Corbin, it was indeed,' I agree. I wonder what would happen if my eyes froze like ice. Would I still be able to see? Move my eyes? Would they crack like an ice cube? 'Wojoczieski? Did I get it right?'

'Yes, you did! Well done,' he says, beaming proudly. It *is* quite an accomplishment, after all. 'So tell me more about this amazing woman.'

'Sure. Well, it was the scone or something.' I launch into the story, and Corbin is quite delighted.

'Isn't that a marvel,' he murmurs, pausing as Lenny sets down our drinks.

'It is. It really is. Hey, do your eyes ever feel cold?'

'I can't say that they do,' he answers amiably. 'Cheers.'

We clink glasses. Boy, the bubbles in my seltzer water are so pretty. So floaty and pretty and round.

'You're a baker, right?' Corbin says.

'That's correct, Corbin Dallas,' I say. 'I bake bread. Lots of kinds. Honey wheat, rye, marble, Italian, French, cinnamon raisin. It's really good bread.' I tilt my head and smile, but it feels like my head keeps moving. *Is* my head still moving? I reach up to check. Nope. *Head is stable, Houston. All systems go.* Hey, that's funny. Houston and Dallas in the same thought bubble. Cool.

'And I know you said you were a widow,' Corbin prompts. 'I'm so sorry for your loss.' He reaches across the table and squeezes my hand, his little piggy blue eyes filled with compassion. I squeeze back.

'That's nice of you, Corbin,' I answer. 'You

203

have nice manners.' I nod, and there goes that *head still moving* feeling. 'Um, listen, Corbin. I took some medicine before we came here,' I add. 'I'm feeling kind of strange.'

'Oh, dear,' he says. 'Are you okay? Can I do anything?'

'Nah. I'm sure I'll feel better once I eat something more than a Twinkie.'

Corbin smiles broadly, charmed. And why not? Am I not charming?

Speaking of not charming, the door opens, and in comes the surly Doral-Anne Driscoll. She catches sight of me and sneers. I just barely restrain myself from flipping her off. She heads over to a table, and dang it! There's Ethan. He stands up, kisses her cheek and they sit down.

Ethan's *here*. He didn't call. He didn't want to hear about Boggy or the Lazarus scones. Instead he's here with that nasty white trash Doral-Anne. I mean, fine, but still. Can't he do better than Doral-Anne? What about Parker?

'There's no accounting for taste,' I say aloud—oops—but apparently my response makes sense to Corbin. Whatever. Nice guy. He keeps talking, smiling away, but I'm having trouble hearing.

Roxanne stomps over to our table with our food, slapping the plates down on the table with her trademark clatter, scowling. 'Thank you!' I sing out, suddenly starving. I take a huge bite of sandwich . . . it's a little hard to get food to the right spot, but I do feel a bit better after scarfing the thing down. Tasty. Quite tasty. Lenny puts a little curry powder in the chicken, a few red grapes. Very nice touch.

'So, Lucy,' Corbin says. Crikey, I almost forgot he was there. 'Forgive me for asking, and you certainly don't have to discuss it, but . . . how did your husband die?'

'It was a car accident,' I say around a large mouthful of fries.

'Oh, no,' he murmurs.

'He fell asleep at the wheel. Six miles from home.' I swallow and take another bite of chicken salad.

'Oh, no. You poor thing.' Again with the hand grip. 'How old were you?'

'I was twenty-four, and Jimmy was twenty-seven. We'd only been married a little while. Not even a year.'

'So sad.' Those little blue eyes seem wet. I'm not sure if this makes me like or dislike Corbin.

'It really is,' I say, nodding. It sure is. It's sad. But there's something wrong with me, like I can't really compute or something. I look at my hands. The fingers seem very, very long. 'Do my hands look big to you, Corbin?' I flex my fingers. They look so odd. Like flippers. Like that Olympic kid who won all those medals—Michael Phelps? Yes, that's it! Like his feet. He has flipper feet or something, right? And my hands look just like that. Freaky. I look at Corbin to see if he shares my concern.

But Corbin is not looking. No, Corbin has one hand over his eyes. Corbin seems to be crying.

'You okay?' I ask. 'Corbin Dallas?'

He's crying, all right. He puts the napkin down and bridges his hands over his nose. 'I'm sorry,' he says, the tears dripping down his face. 'It's just . . . oh, Lucy, I didn't realize . . . I'm so sorry.' He takes a shuddering breath, tries to smile, fails. Lenny gives us an odd look, and heads at the bar are starting to turn. 'I'm sorry. I didn't mean to do this . . . See, my dog . . . I have a dog. Biffy. And he was recently . . . well, he needs surgery. For a cyst over his eye. And I'm worried, I guess, and when you said your husband fell asleep at the wheel, it just brought up all this . . . emotion. You know, if you love someone, the level of worry is the same. Biffy is so . . .'

His voice goes on. Surely he is not comparing his dog's cyst to my husband's death. But yes, he is. Wow. I'd react, but my fingers seem to be growing. Whoa. I think I should probably call Anne. Pronto. But my fingers seem too big to fit into my pocketbook. Are they? I fumble with my purse, unable to get the snap undone. Maybe my cold eyes are screwing up my depth perception. I have no idea, really. Meanwhile,

Corbin is working up quite a tear-storm.

'Everything okay over here?'

I look up, and there's Ethan. 'Are my fingers growing?' I ask, waving them around. I turn my hands over to see if they look weird from that side. They do. 'They're so big!'

Ethan looks down at Corbin, a slow fury filling his features. He looks . . . damn. Kind of hot, really, all scowly and protective. I do love that neat little beard on Ethan. Smokes him right up. Mmm-hmm. Too bad Doral-Anne has just joined our little group. I close one cold eye so I don't have to see her and just drink in the sight of Angry Ethan.

'What did you do?' he growls, reaching out to grab Corbin's shirt. 'What did you give her?'

My date's eyes are wide and wet. Ethan yanks him out of the booth, tipping the table a little. My seltzer water sloshes. 'Oh, no, the pretty bubbles!' I exclaim.

'What did you do to her?' Ethan yells, shaking Corbin like a rag. The bar is so quiet. It's like I can feel the silence. Like the silence is blue and warm. I wish I could wrap the silence around my cold eyes and— 'Answer me!' Silent except for Ethan, that is.

'Don't hit me! I didn't do anything! Lucy, tell him!' Corbin squeaks.

'Call the police,' Ethan barks over his shoulder. 'He slipped her something.' He grabs Corbin around the throat. 'You'd better tell me exactly what you gave her, or I'm going to rip you apart right here.'

Oops. I should probably speak up. 'Oh, Ethan. Hi, there, pal. Listen, what's-his-name here, he didn't give me anything. It's Anne. My cousin the lesbian doctor? She gave me some medicine.'

Ethan looks down at me. 'What medicine?'

I blink. My hands are still weird. 'A drug kind of medicine? Um . . . gosh, I can't remember the name. Something that rhymes with magazine? Listerine? I can't remember. It's for panic attacks.' Ethan's eyebrows lift in surprise. 'I think I'm having a bad reaction,' I continue. 'Do my fingers look big to you? Like I can swim really fast?'

Ethan releases Corbin Dallas in absolute disgust. 'She's tripping, and you didn't even notice? Jesus Christ.' Corbin huddles on his side of the booth, pale and shaken. 'Come on, Lucy,' Ethan says. 'I'm taking you to the hospital.'

'Aunt Boggy woke up from the dead today,' I tell him as he takes my arm and helps me stand. My legs buckle, and the next thing I know, Ethan's got me, holding me in his arms without so much as a grunt. His lovely smell, that warm, spicy man-smell, envelops me like a blanket. 'This is nice,' I tell him, my face against the smooth skin of his neck. 'Except I think I might throw up.'

'Call 911,' he says to someone.

208

'Idiot,' Doral-Anne mutters. She flips open her phone and does what she's told.

CHAPTER FOURTEEN

'Are you mad at me?'

'I'm not mad at you,' Ethan says wearily. It's one o'clock in the morning, and we're waiting for me to be discharged from the Emergency Room.

The good news is, I'm fine. Also, I've seen the inside of an ambulance, which was a learning experience. The bad news . . . I've also puked on the inside of an ambulance. And on Ethan. And on Mikey Devers, whom I once babysat and had to tie to a chair so he wouldn't bite me. He's a paramedic now. Oh, and half the town has now seen me on some bad, acidlike trip as I chatted merrily about my Phelps fingers and asked people to take off my shoes so I could see if my feet were webbed.

I'm not sure what happened to Corbin; Ethan rode in the ambulance with me as I puked on him and Mikey and told them all about Aunt Boggy between gags.

The E.R. doctors took my history, mostly from Ethan since apparently I tried to give out the recipe for my Lazarus scones, figuring the good doctors should know there's a new cure for comas. A nurse called Anne to get my prescription, and someone else had Ash go to my place and count the pills left in the bottle, as if I'd tried to overdose. This rankled, and I punished the slanderous staff by refusing to open my mouth for the thermometer until Ethan told me to stop being such an ass and do it. Which I did.

Since I'd already puked up whatever was left in my stomach, my only treatment was time and humiliation. My fingers returned to normal size, my eyes once again warmed to body temperature.

Which brings us to now.

'I'm really sorry about all this,' I say for perhaps the one hundred and forty-third time.

'Nothing to be sorry about,' Ethan says, not looking at me. His leg jiggles, his arms are folded over his chest.

'Okay!' the E.R. doc asks, breezing into the room. He looks to be about twelve and exudes all the loving sincerity of Paris Hilton. 'How's she feeling?'

'Much better,' I say. The doctor ignores me, as he seems to hate me—I believe I threw up on him also—and waits for Ethan's confirmation.

'Much better,' Ethan agrees.

'Does she have someone to stay with her overnight?' the doctor asks, scribbling on the chart. Clearly he doesn't think I can answer for myself.

Ethan glances at me. 'Yes,' he answers, dropping his gaze to check the time. The message is clear. *I'll do it because I have to, even though you completely screwed up my night.*

My throat grows tight. If Corinne weren't nursing her baby every twenty minutes, I'd ask her to stay with me. If Parker didn't have a four-year-old child with a tendency to wake up before dawn, I'd ask her. If it wasn't one in the morning, I'd ask my mom. Hell, I'll ask my mom anyway. Better than forcing Ethan to babysit me.

'I'll call my mom,' I say, smiling at the doctor. He doesn't deign to look at me.

'Don't be silly,' Ethan says. 'I'll stay with you.' He glances at me, his gaze bouncing almost immediately back to the doctor. He's not being mean—Ethan just doesn't do mean—but he's not being nice, either.

Now if Jimmy were here—which would negate my need for dating, antianxiety medications and a nursemaid—if Jimmy were here, we'd be laughing about this. We'd laugh our heads off. He'd make jokes and lie on the gurney with me and cuddle me and play with my hair, ignoring the fact that I smelled like vomit. There would be no guilt or feelings of being a burden or pain in the ass or anything. Times like this, I miss Jimmy so much my heart actually hurts.

'She's good to go, then. Here are her

instructions.' Dr. Hateswomen turns to me. 'Obviously, miss,' he says slowly, as if talking to a befuddled child, 'you need to throw away that medication. All of it. Don't keep any. Don't take it ever again. You're very allergic to this medication, and that should go into your medical file. Do you understand?'

'Yes, I—'

He interrupts, turning again to Ethan. 'Call me if you can't wake her or if she starts to hallucinate again.'

'Will do. Thank you.' They shake hands, then the good doctor turns and leaves without a glance at me.

'Let's go, then,' Ethan says, offering me a hand as I scootch off the gurney. I ignore the hand and stand, mostly steadily.

Out in the parking lot, Ethan walks me over to his Audi and opens the passenger door. Someone—Doral-Anne, maybe, or Tommy Malloy or Lenny himself—must have driven Ethan's car over to the hospital. He waits for me to get in, closes the door, then gets in the driver's side and starts up the car.

'Do you still have your motorcycle?' I ask, just to be chatty and friendly.

'Yep.' Then, realizing he's being less than kind to the poor patient, turns to look at me. 'How are you feeling?'

'Um, not bad,' I answer. 'Just tired.'

'Okay, well, let's get you home to bed, then.'

We drive through the quiet, darkened streets of our little town, and I'm grateful that Anne had advised Ethan to take me to the local hospital and not anything farther from home. It's only a few minutes to the Boatworks. Ethan parks in his spot, then hops out and slides over the hood of the car à la Starsky of *Starsky and Hutch* fame to open my door. A ghost of a grin appears on his face, and once again, my throat, raw from the evening's adventure, tightens. I miss that smile.

He walks a pace behind me, ready, I'm sure, to take my arm if I wobble. I don't.

We don't speak in the elevator, though he catches me looking and gives me a quick smile that doesn't reach his eyes.

Ethan's face has rather perfect and unremarkable features. His nose is straight, his eyes are evenly spaced and of average size. His mouth is well proportioned, his cheekbones symmetrical. Nothing special . . . not until he smiles, and those lips curve up in that unusual, unexpectedly charming grin. I've never seen a face that's so transformed by a smile. Or that's so carefully blank without one.

After a small eternity, we arrive on the fourth floor. Ethan precedes me down the hall and unlocks my door—he's had a key since I moved in. Ash pokes her head out.

'Hey! You okay?' she asks. She looks

213

shockingly young without her black makeup. 'I waited up to see you.'

'I'm fine, honey. Allergic reaction. Lots of puking.'

'Hi, Ash,' Ethan says, smiling at her. She blushes.

'I'll see you tomorrow,' I say.

'Okay,' she says. 'Feel better. Night, Ethan.'

'Good night, kiddo,' he says. He opens my door, then steps aside as Fat Mikey greets us.

'Are you hungry?' Ethan asks, following me in. He goes into the kitchen and opens the door to the fridge to assess the contents.

'No,' I say. Fat Mikey rubs himself against my calf and gives a rusty meow. I bend over and pick him up, grunting at the effort of it, and rub my cheek against his. He gives me a fond head butt and pricks his claws into my shoulder and as ever, I'm grateful for his curmudgeonly affection.

Ethan walks down the hall to my bedroom, opens the door as if to check something—I haven't made my bed today, since I usually save that task for after my nap, and today—an eternity ago—was the amazing recovery of Aunt Boggy. My head buzzes from fatigue and whatever leftover drug is still in my system. I close my eyes, ready to fall asleep right here.

'You want to wash up, then, Lucy?' Ethan asks. Opening my eyes, I see that his arms are folded over his chest, the fabric of his shirt taut at his biceps. I've known him long enough to see that he's itchy to be done with me. Can't say that I blame him.

'Good idea,' I answer, setting my cat down.

The bathroom mirror reveals that I look about as you'd expect a woman to look after she's been hallucinating and vomiting all night . . . that is to say, not my best. My face is pale, my hair matted on one side and my mascara is just a messy smudge under my eyes. Trashy pop star after a bender. With a sigh, I turn on the shower, pull off my clothes and get in.

When I'm done, I smell a lot better, but I'm so tired I can barely stand. I pull on the pjs that hang on the back of the door and brush my teeth.

As soon as I open the door, Ethan gets up from the couch, where Fat Mikey has him pinned, and comes down the hall. 'I changed your sheets,' he says, 'and I left a glass of water on the night table there. I'll have to wake you up a couple times, make sure you're all right. Okay?'

'Okay.' He'll be sleeping on the couch, of course. Or in the guest room. The truth is, I wouldn't mind him sleeping with me, arms around me, warm and reassuring, but I'm not so out of it that I actually request this.

He watches me climb into bed, not smiling, not even when Fat Mikey jumps up next to me and starts his kneading ritual, something that used to make Ethan laugh. Back when we were sleeping together, that is.

'Anything else you need, Lucy?' he asks.

'I'm sorry you had to take care of me tonight, Ethan,' I say, swallowing hard. I try to keep my voice casual, but my eyes sting with the warning of tears.

'It's no problem.'

'It sure seems to be.' I pause. 'Ethan, aren't we friends anymore?'

Ethan opens his mouth to say something, then reconsiders and looks down, pushing his hands into his pockets. 'Lucy,' he says, and his voice is tired, 'I don't know what you expect from me. You tell me you're ready to move on, but you leave treats outside my door. You ask me to hang out and watch movies. You warn me away from Doral-Anne—'

'She's so mean, Ethan!'

'—and all the while, you're scraping the bottom of the barrel of the dating world right in front of me. And now you're on medication for panic attacks and you wind up in the hospital.' He takes a deep breath and lets it out slowly. 'I just don't know what you're trying to do, Lucy.'

I scratch Fat Mikey's head so I won't have to look at Ethan, who stands next to my bed like a disappointed parent. 'I'm just . . . trying to put a life together, Ethan. The kind of life I can handle.' I swallow, then swallow again.

'What does that mean, a life you can handle?' His voice is soft.

'I don't know.' It comes out as a whisper. A

216

tear plops onto Fat Mikey's ragged ear, and he shakes his big head in response.

Ethan sighs. A second later, the bed sags under his weight as he sits. 'You must be whipped,' he says. I nod, still not looking at him.

'Go to sleep, then, honey,' he says, and I obey, closing my eyes so I won't have to see his face. He pulls up the covers to my chin and leans over to turn off the light. Then he kisses my forehead, just the gentle scrape of his beard and the soft press of his lips. 'I'll be in to check on you in a couple hours,' he says quietly. And with that, he stands up and walks out of the room, closing the door behind him.

Which is good, because another second, and I'd have begged him to stay.

CHAPTER FIFTEEN

When I wake in the morning, I know immediately something's wrong. Squinting, I sit up. My head is a little achy, but other than that, no apparent residue from my Michael Phelps flip-out.

Wait a sec . . . I'm squinting. It's sunny. Which means it's . . . 'Gah!' I squawk. The clock on the night table reads 8:04.

I leap out of bed and lurch down the hall. Ethan sits at the kitchen table, a newspaper in

217

front of him. 'Hey,' he says, standing up. 'How are you feeling?'

'I have to go! The bakery . . . My mom will—'

'Sit. Calm down.' He goes to the cupboard, takes down my favorite mug and pours me a cuppa joe. 'I called the bakery a while ago, told Iris you were sick last night and needed the day off.'

'Oh.' I pause. 'How many times have they called since then?'

'Four. Iris is wondering if you have Lou Gehrig's disease. Rose thinks it sounds more like cancer. Your mom said feel better, she'll see you tomorrow.' Ethan allows a small smile as he pours some half-and-half in my cup and hands it to me. 'Sleep okay?' he asks.

I realize, with no small degree of shock, that I did. 'Yes. Thanks.' I pause. 'Did you check on me? I don't remember.' And I find that I'd like a sleepy little memory of Ethan taking care of me. I'd like that very much.

'Yep,' he says, his face impassive. 'You seemed fine. Want me to make you breakfast?'

'Oh, no, that's fine. Thanks, though.' We look at each other for a minute.

Ethan and I have logged in a lot of hours in this kitchen. Many were the happy weekend nights that I'd bake him something while he told me stories of the people he met, the airports he loved, the thrill of bringing on a

218

new account or the crazy things he'd do in the name of selling *Instead*.

And we did a little more than talk and bake here, too. Once, we did it on the island, the granite cold, Ethan hot. Jeepers! I should *not* be thinking about that.

'I've got to run, Luce,' Ethan says, setting his own cup in the sink. 'You sure you're feeling okay? You're a little flushed.' He frowns.

'No, no, I'm fine. Thanks, Ethan. You were really great.' I pause. 'As usual.'

'No problem. I called Parker, by the way. She'll swing by after she drops Nicky at nursery school.'

'Okay. Thank you.'

And away he goes, stopping to say something to Fat Mikey, who answers in a throaty meow. There's something awfully endearing about a man who is loved by a grouchy cat. Then the door closes, and I'm alone again. Alone again, naturally, like that sappy song I'd discovered in my parents' tape collection. Oh, I'd loved that song! Many happy, maudlin hours were spent weeping and singing along to my cassette player until my mom burst in one day, snatched the tape from the machine and snapped it in half.

I take a sip of coffee and close my eyes in simultaneous appreciation and horror . . . the dark, almost burnt taste is unmistakably delicious. Starbucks. Not from my own

219

cabinet, of course, which means Ethan must have brought down some of his own. Which means, probably, that he gets it from Doral-Anne. God, I hope they're not dating. I chew on my lip, then take another sip, unable to resist the siren call of the coffee god.

The buzzer rings, and I trot into the living room and press the intercom. 'Hello?'

'It's Parker, you nasty, drugged-out ho! Let me in!'

With a smile, I press the button, and a minute later, Parker breezes into my apartment, all blonde and expensive-looking. She takes a hard look at me, then raises an eyebrow. 'Did we have fun?'

'If by fun, you mean puking on the father of your child, then yes. I had so much fun.'

'God! Ethan had me in stitches this morning! You poor thing! And you were on a date, too? The poor guy! What did he say?'

'I don't know,' I admit. 'Ethan scared him pretty good. I guess he thought the guy slipped me a mickey or something. Want some coffee?'

'Oh, yes, I do. Nicky's gotten into the horrifying habit of waking up at five and wanting to snuggle. The snuggles are great . . . the five o'clock I could do without.'

'By five in the morning, I've made dough for more than six dozen loaves of bread,' I tell her as I pour her a cup.

'So you're a freak of nature. We knew that.'

220

She accepts her cup and sits back, her catlike green eyes growing somber. 'So seriously, Lucy. Ethan said it was some medication gone wrong. Are you okay?'

'Sure. It was quite a trip, though. I thought my fingers were growing.'

She smiles. 'I meant, why are you taking medication? You're not sick, are you?'

I glance at her. 'Ethan didn't tell you?'

'No.'

I bite my lip. 'Well, I've been having panic attacks. I had a few after Jimmy died, and they're back, pretty much since I started looking for another husband. And last night, Ethan kindly pointed out what a mess I've become, so you can save the lecture.'

Parker sighs, heavy on the melodrama.

'What?' I ask.

'What do you think, dummy?'

'I think friends shouldn't call each other dummy, dummy.' Parker takes a long pull on her coffee, surveying me over the rim of the mug. 'What?' I ask again. 'Did Ethan say something? Do you guys talk about me?'

She contemplates me, sets her cup down. 'We don't,' she admits. 'But I just want to point out, my dear—' Parker's voice takes on its prep-school drawl '—that when you and Ethan had your extra-special arrangement, you both seemed happier.'

I fiddle with the hem of my pajama top. 'Well, what guy doesn't love no-strings sex?' I

221

mumble.

'I suppose that's true,' she agrees. 'But rubbing Ben-Gay into each other's achy joints fifty years from now has its own appeal, too.'

I chug the rest of my too-good coffee, then set the mug down. 'You're a fine one to talk,' I say, my voice mild. 'What about you two? I thought you were talking about getting back together.'

Parker tips her head back and smiles. 'Interesting that you should ask. He came over one night last week, right? We all had dinner together, then we got Nicky to bed.' She takes a sip of coffee, and my toes curl in hard, waiting for the rest of the story.

'Do go on,' I say.

'Mmm-hmm. So there we were, just Ethan and me, and I said, 'Okay, Eth, you ready? Let's give it a shot.' Then I kissed him. And he kissed me back.'

My stomach clenches. Gorgeous blonde Parker Harrington Welles, five-foot-eight inches, built like Heidi Klum. I can just see them kissing, Ethan's gorgeous hands cupping Parker's face, the gentle scrape of his beard against her skin, the heat from his body . . .

Realizing that Parker is waiting for me to rejoin the conversation, I ask, 'And? How was it?'

'Oh, Lucy, it was . . .' She pauses, lifting a silken eyebrow to torture me. 'It was gross. Like kissing my brother.'

The breath I wasn't aware I was holding whooshes out. 'Really?' My voice is incredulous.

She laughs. 'Yeah. I don't know.' She stares at her coffee cup. 'When we were together way back when, it was all fun and games, you know? And I have fond memories of those times, Lucy, fond memories.' She grows serious. 'But all these years of platonics and being grown-ups and sharing Nicky . . . I don't know. The chemistry's gone. We ended up playing Scrabble.'

A warm rush of satisfaction fills my stomach, much to my shame. 'What about Doral-Anne? I know she's interested in him.'

'The Starbucks chick?' Parker asks. I nod. 'Jeesh, I don't think so. He mentioned her once or twice . . . I think she wants a job with International or something.'

'Or something is right,' I say, staring out the window.

In the tradition of adoring the ones who hate them, my cat jumps up on Parker's lap, only to be forcibly ejected. Deeply wounded, Fat Mikey reacts in typical fashion, which is to say, he lifts his leg and begins licking his genitals.

'Lucy,' Parker says hesitantly, 'can I ask you something?'

'Sure,' I answer, not sure at all.

'Why not Ethan? Seriously.'

My stomach twists. Should've seen that one

223

coming. 'Well, here's the thing,' I say slowly. Fat Mikey leaves his grooming and rubs his head against my ankle, and I appreciate the comfort. 'Ethan's . . .' I swallow. 'He's Jimmy's brother. That matters.'

'But you could get past that, right? You got past it enough to sleep with him.'

I nod. 'Yes, I did.'

'So it's not just that.' Her beautiful eyes are kind.

'Right again,' I whisper, then clear my throat. 'Ethan . . . Ethan could do some serious damage, you know what I mean?'

'Why would he damage you? He cares about you, Lucy. You must know that.'

'He's been a prince, I know that. But, jeez louise, Parks,' I blurt. 'What if I fell for him? Really let myself just . . . love him? What if we did get together and I loved him and he left me?'

'Well, I just don't see—'

'What if he died?' I interrupt. 'What if I really am a Black Widow and I kill another Mirabelli boy, huh? What if one of those stupid things he does killed him? What if he got into a motorcycle accident? What if some idiot was driving over the Newport Bridge in a U-Haul and didn't see him and hit and crushed him? Or sent him right through the railing and over the edge and he broke every bone in his body and sank like a rock? What if he was out sailing and the boom swung around

224

and hit him in the head and sent him overboard and he drowned, or he was treading water, waiting for help, but a shark came up and ate him and we only found out because his leg washed up on shore?'

'Not that you've ever pictured any of this, of course,' Parker says dryly.

'Did you know he took some corporate idiot skydiving last year, Parker?' I demand, my voice rising. 'He jumped out of an airplane! What if his chute didn't open? What if the lines got tangled? And that stupid helicopter skiing, they drop you off at the top of a mountain that's so high you can't get to it another way, and what if—'

'Okay, okay, stop. Honey. Stop. You're getting hysterical.' She gets up, and in a rare gesture of affection, puts her hand on my shoulder, then moves to refill her mug with the traitorous coffee. 'First of all, Ethan's not doing those things so much anymore.'

I don't answer.

'And secondly, Jimmy didn't do any of those things, did he? And he still managed to die.'

My eyes fill. 'Good point.'

She sits back down and contemplates me. 'You haven't said the big one yet. The big what-if.'

'Well, since you know everything, you can just go ahead and say it for me,' I mumble.

She gives me a wry smile. 'Well, one could say that you *do* love Ethan already. The big

225

question must be, what if you didn't love him as much as Jimmy?'

Hearing it said out loud like that, right here in the kitchen with the sun shining in the windows, my African violets blooming on the windowsill . . . it's a slap in the heart. 'I really don't want to talk about this, Parker,' I whisper.

Parker sighs. 'Okay. I'm sorry.' She pauses, and I swallow against the pebble, knowing she's not finished. I'm correct. 'But Lucy, you're never going to know unless you give him a shot, are you? And if you don't, you'll end up with some loser who leaves you cold. Is that what you want?'

'What I want . . .' I stop. What I want is for Jimmy not to have died, for Ethan to meet someone wonderful and be happily married. I can just about hear the Fates laughing at me. 'Parker, there's got to be some happy medium. Someone I could love, just not too much.'

'Listen to you,' she says fondly as if talking to a not very bright child. 'Forgive me for saying this to the poor widow, but I think you're being kind of . . . obtuse.'

I stare out the window. 'It's a self-defense mechanism,' I acknowledge.

'Right. Well, listen. You're my friend, kid. So's Ethan. I love you both and just want you to be happy, that's all.'

'I appreciate it.' I take a sip of coffee and don't look her in the eye.

226

'All right. Well, I have revisions on those nasty little Holy Rollers.'

My shoulders relax. 'What's this one called?' I ask.

She grins. *'The Holy Rollers and the Poor Little Kitten.* Someone's cat gets squished by a tractor, and the smug little bastards get to explain heaven. So watch yourself, Fat Mikey.' With that, Parker gets up, pats my shoulder and leaves.

*   *   *

'Over here, we have the famous Dead Man's Shoal,' Captain Bob says over the mike on board the tour boat. Since I had a hooky day, I'd figured I'd help out my old pal, and luckily, there was a tour scheduled. The thought of a day spreading out before me with nothing on the schedule meant two things—blow some more money on clothes I don't wear, or help out Captain Bob.

'In 1722, Captain Cook of the West Indies fame brought his wife along on a trip, and as you know, ladies—' it's a church group from Maryland, on a brief recess from power gambling down at the casinos '—women are bad luck on a boat.' The ladies giggle appreciatively. 'The crew rebelled and set Mrs. Cook on that very shoal at low tide. She tried to swim to Mackerly's shore, but alas, the night was rough and the poor woman

227

drowned. You can still hear her ghost moaning on foggy nights.'

'Is that true?' one of the ladies asks me.

'No,' I whisper, steering gently back toward the dock.

'And that concludes our tour! Ladies, if you're looking for the finest pastries and goodies on the East Coast, I strongly urge you to stop in at Bunny's Bakery, just two blocks north of our dock,' Bob says, taking a slug of his Irish coffee. He winks at me—we're both quite aware of what Bunny's does and does not offer, and I smile back at him. 'In fact, I'd be happy to walk you up there myself. Thank you so much for choosing Captain Bob's Island Adventure!'

Bob takes the wheel and steers us the last few yards to the dock. 'Thanks, Lucy,' he says. 'Nice having you with me this morning.'

'You're welcome,' I say, standing aside so the passengers can disembark. 'My pleasure.'

'Think your mother's still at work?' he asks hopefully.

'There or at the nursing home,' I say. 'Did you hear about my great-aunt Boggy?'

'I did indeed,' Bob murmurs. 'Unbelievable.'

'I'll probably head over there now,' I say. At that moment, my cell phone rings, and I fish it out of my pocket and glance at the screen. 'Oh, here's Mom now. Hi, Mom,' I say.

'Lucy? Where are you? Are you still sick?

228

I've been trying everywhere.'

A cold sweat breaks out over my body. 'I'm two blocks from the bakery,' I tell her. 'What's wrong?'

My mom pauses. 'You're okay? You're not still throwing up?'

'I'm fine, Mom! What's wrong?'

'It's Boggy, sweetheart.' She sighs. 'Are you sitting down?' Without waiting for an answer, she drops the bomb. 'She died this morning.'

CHAPTER SIXTEEN

'I dunno. It was like she was fine one sec, then she just started coughing and the next thing I know, she's dead.' Stevie, unaccustomed to a tie, pulls at his collar as we stand next to the open casket at Werner's Funeral Home, gazing down on our tiny great-aunt. 'Maybe it was one of your scones.'

I look at him in horror, guilt punching my stomach with a cold fist. 'Was she eating a scone when she started coughing?' I whisper.

'No. But I was. Maybe she inhaled a crumb or something. It wasn't *my* fault, that's for sure.'

'Of course it wasn't, sweetie.' Aunt Rose sniffles, patting her son's arm, then blowing her nose with an astonishing honk. 'But those scones *were* awfully crumbly, Lucy. You should put in a little sour cream next time.'

'Boggy choked on a scone?' Iris asks, giving me a sharp look.

'No! She didn't choke on anything, right, Stevie? You were with her.'

Stevie shrugs, then scratches his ear. 'We were watching *Matlock.* She said that old dude was still handsome, I'm eating the scone, she starts coughing, and then—' Stevie widens his eyes and sticks out his tongue '—dead. I thought about giving her a scone. Brought her back the first time, right, Luce?'

'You didn't give her one, did you?' I ask, cringing at the idea of him stuffing a pastry into our ancient aunt's mouth as a bizarre form of resuscitation. Granted, his IQ is roughly the same as a chicken's, so it is possible.

'No, Luce, I'm not stupid,' my cousin protests. 'But you're the one who said they brought her back to life.'

'I was hallucinating at the time, Stevie.'

'Will you two stop your bickering?' Iris says. 'You're ruining this perfectly lovely wake.'

I close my eyes. The cloying scent of lilies makes my head throb, not to mention the saccharine organ music that simpers in the background. Personally I'd rather have the Brandenberg Concertos or the Smashing Pumpkins or something. Anything but 'On Eagle's Wings.'

My mother bustles up in her usual cloud of
230

Chanel No. 5, looking like Audrey Hepburn: a black silk dress with a large white bow at the waist, strappy, three-inch black Manolo Blahniks which make her feet look like they enjoy a little bondage. 'You look incredible,' she gushes, reaching out to touch my shoulder. Yes, I'm wearing a skirt, a sweater, some decent shoes (just some Nine West pumps . . . unlike Mom here, I thought it inappropriate to use Boggy's wake as a showcase for my slutty shoes). 'It's wonderful to see you all dressed up! That color is fantastic on you!'

'Mom, settle down. We're at a wake,' I say.

'Oh, you,' she says fondly. 'Those earrings are darling!'

Let me explain. The Black Widows love nothing more than a well-planned wake, the flowers, the people, the tears. They attend everyone's, and to be fair, they *know* everyone, being second-generation locals in a town of two thousand. There's a complex scoring process for such events—number of attendees, expense of the flower arrangements, classiness of the charity the deceased's family chose for the *in lieu of flowers* bit, who's catering the after-funeral reception. Iris booms out how beautiful the deceased looks, Rose chirps about how *thoughtful* were those who sent flowers, and Mom announces how *kind* so-and-so was to come.

I myself have a little less fun at funeral

homes, though they don't present the same degree of distress as the cemetery. But Stevie has seized the idea that an errant crumb was carried on a rogue draft of air into Boggy's esophagus, and this was in fact her cause of death. Furthermore, he is now relaying this fact to anyone who will listen. And lastly . . . well, lastly, none of us was prepared for little old Boggy to pass away so quickly.

'I was planning to visit her today,' my cousin Neddy, Iris's son, complains.

'Well, if you'd wanted to see her, you could've come any time over the past fifteen years, Ned,' Iris says in stentorian tones. 'This is what you get for waiting till the eleventh hour. Not that we *knew* it would be eleventh hour, that is. She was doing so well. A medical miracle. *Dateline* was going to pick up the story. Poor Boggy!'

'It's a tragedy!' Rose weeps. 'We should've had her for years more!'

Years more. How long was Aunt Boggy supposed to hang around, huh?

Good old Cousin Anne tries to be the voice of reason. 'Aunt Rose, Ma,' she says firmly. 'Boggy was a hundred and four. It was just her time. She had a very long life, and dying at a hundred and four is hardly a tragedy, now, is it?'

'It is!' Rose sobs. She does love to cry, that woman. 'How can you be so heartless, Anne! All those years, she just lay there like a dead dog, and when she finally woke up, Lucy just had to bring her something that she'd choke on. Lucy, why didn't you bring her ice cream instead? Why? Really, a little common sense . . .'

'She did *not* choke on a scone!' I protest loudly, forcing a smile to the next person in line.

'Reverend Covers!' my mother sings. 'Aren't you wonderful to come! How thoughtful!'

Iris and Rose discuss Boggy's tragic death to everyone who comes by, and that's the whole town, since news of the medical miracle and subsequent death has piqued everyone's curiosity. The line is long, and my feet are killing me.

There, in the back of the room, is Ethan, wearing a navy blue suit and red tie. His eyes catch mine, and my heart squeezes abruptly. I haven't seen him since the morning after my little Michael Phelps incident, and I'm not too sure how he's feeling toward me these days. I give a little wave, and he nods. No smile. My throat tightens. Ethan and I need a little sit-down. We need to talk. Something's got to give.

'Yo, Luce, so sorry for your loss.' Charley Spirito stands in front of me, Red Sox jacket over a shirt and tie.

'Thanks, Char—' My words are cut off as Charley engulfs me in his gym-teacher arms.

He buries his face against my neck, planting a wet kiss on my collarbone. 'Ick!' Crikey! He just copped a feel! 'Knock it off, Charley!' I snap.

'Can't blame a guy for trying,' he says. 'Plus, I was wondering if you might wanna go out again sometime? Since the fat dude didn't work out?'

'I am at my great-aunt's wake, Charley!' I say, straightening my sweater.

'Is that a yes?' He grins.

'It's a no! Get out of here! Shoo!'

'Lucy, are you dating that boy?' Rose trills.

'No. I'm not dating anyone.' My face is tight with heat as Charley saunters away, stupidly proud for getting away with a little groping. I catch Ethan looking at me, his face still blank, and look away abruptly.

I need a break. With a word to my mom, who's acting like she's Ryan Seacrest on the Red Carpet at the Academy Awards, I head for the back of the room. There's sure to be a blister on my heels tomorrow morning, and I sit gratefully and take a deep breath. My heart beats a little too fast. I almost wish I could take another floaty pill.

Jimmy's wake took place here, too. It was, of course, surreally awful . . . part of me kept saying, *This is not really happening. He'll show up any minute.* So many of our wedding guests were there that it was almost confusing. Everyone had been so happy just a few

234

months earlier. Could it really be possible that Jimmy was actually gone? Forever? It was like one of those dreams that start out happy, but bit by bit, you realize you're lost and someone's chasing you with a big knife, and there's nowhere to hide.

Speaking of wedding guests, Debbie Keating, my best friend from childhood, stands at the casket, chatting with Rose. She was one of my bridesmaids, but when Jimmy died, Debbie dropped me. She didn't come to his wake or funeral. She didn't send a card. Instead, her mother informed me, right there as I stood next to my husband's casket, shaking and stunned, that Debbie was taking Jimmy's death *really* hard and was *very* sad. I never heard from Debbie again. When she got married two years later, I wasn't invited.

It happens more than you'd like to know. People don't know what to say, so they say nothing, ignore you, pretend not to see you, and, when trapped, do what Debbie's doing now—smiling in my general direction to pretend that we're still friends, only to shift her eyes away just before we actually make eye contact.

Someone sits next to me. It's Grinelda, smelling of uncooked meat. 'Hi, Grinelda,' I say. 'How are you?'

'I'm not bad, kid. Yourself?'

'I'm okay.' I sneak a peek at her outfit— pink tulle ballerina skirt over purple corduroys, topped with a red velvet shirt and black down vest. 'So, did you foresee Boggy's death, Grinelda?' I can't help asking.

'Welp, I'll tell you. Sometimes wires get a little crossed. I might've seen it. Or not. Plus,' she adds, lowering her voice and remembering to sound like a gypsy, 'all is not for me to know.'

'And what is for you to know, exactly?' I murmur.

She sighs rustily. 'Whatever those who have passed want to tell me.' She cuts her hooded eyes my way. 'Did you check the toast?'

'Yup. Checked the toast. Haven't burned a single piece since you gave me the message.'

'Good, I guess. Now, I need a smoke,' she says, then bursts into a long bout of phlegmy coughing. I pat her back, trying not to cringe as she hacks and wheezes. Finally she grunts, then struggles to get out of the chair. I stand up and give her a hand.

'Take care, Grinelda,' I say.

'You, too, Lucy.' She shuffles off to Reverend Covers and hands him a purple business card.

'I'm sorry your aunt died, Wucy,' comes a voice from the region of my hip.

My heart swells with love. 'Oh, hey there, Nicky,' I say, picking him up for a smooch. 'Thanks, sweetheart. Did you come with your daddy?'

'No. I came with Mommy.' He drapes a

236

companionable arm around my neck, and I kiss him again. His cheek is velvet, and I see that he has a new freckle just below his ear. 'Wucy,' he says, toying with my necklace, 'will Aunt Boggy see Uncle Jimmy in heaven?'

The question hits me like a punch in the stomach. I sink down slowly, shifting Nick so he sits on my lap. 'I don't know, honey,' I whisper. 'Maybe. I don't see why not.'

'Maybe he can make her dinner. Daddy says he was a good cook.'

The image of my husband in the kitchen is so strong I can almost smell the tomato sauce—Jimmy, dirty blond curls secured under the red bandana, his big hands dexterously chopping parsley, the sizzle of chicken in hot olive oil.

'He sure was a good cook,' I murmur, noting my nephew's expectant eyes. 'He would've cooked all your favorites, I bet.'

'That's what Daddy says. Can I have a candy?' Nicky asks, wriggling off my lap. 'There's candy here. A big bowl of candy by the door.'

'Ask your mom,' I say.

'Bye!' Nicky dashes up to Parker, who absently strokes his dark hair as she talks to Ellen Ripling. The little boy clings to her leg, clearly trying not to interrupt. His eyes are just like Ethan's, brown and mischievous, always a hint of a smile waiting there.

Except I haven't seen Ethan smile lately.

Even now, he looks a bit tired as he waits in the receiving line to offer his condolences to my relatives. Rose's face lights up when she sees him, and he grins as he always does around the Black Widows, leaning in to kiss her cheek. He takes both her hands in his and says something that makes her smile. Such a way with the older women, that Ethan. Something moves in my chest as I remember the way he kissed my forehead the other night.

He moves on to Iris, whispers something into her ear . . . something naughty from the look of it, since she makes that delightedly outraged face and reaches up to smack the side of his head. Then he reaches my mom, who tucks her arm through his as she talks with her best friend, Carol. Ethan looks so . . . decent. He nods to Carol without interrupting my mom, looking like what he is, really. A good son. Too bad he lacks that easy grace with his own parents.

I look down, imagining Jimmy here, doing much what his brother is doing. Charming my mother, sweet-talking my relatives, then coming over to sit next to me for a kiss. He'd hold my hand, murmur a few words, then get up to herd our children—we were planning on four—when they got rowdy. If anyone implied that crumbs from my scones had killed Boggy, Jimmy would put that silly notion to rest in a heartbeat. His presence would cushion me

238

from the shallow Debbie Keatings and the dopey Cousin Stevies of the world.

It's the widow's burden and blessing, too. For the rest of my life, I'll picture Jimmy everywhere. He did love me so. And God knows I loved him, too.

'Hi, Lucy.'

I look up at Ethan, and for a heartbeat, it's almost as if *he's* the one I've been missing all these years. 'Hi,' I whisper through the fog of emotion that's enveloped me.

'I hear those were some killer scones,' he whispers, then dissolves into silent laughter, sinking into the chair next to me and covering his face with his hand.

The tenderness in my heart drops with a thud. It's the last straw. Hard to imagine I was just wanting to sort things out with him, to make him smile again. Without a word, I stand up and move past him.

'Lucy, I'm sorry,' he says, catching my hand. 'Don't be mad.'

I pull free. I am just not in the mood. Emotions churn in my heart, good, bad, ugly, and I need a little space.

In the back of the room is Stevie, acting out Boggy's last moments from the look of it, his hands on his throat, tongue extended as Father Adhyatman watches in horrified fascination. *There were no crumbs involved,* I mentally tell the priest, then weave my way past them. Veering down the hall toward the

239

bathroom, my throat is tight, my eyes sting.

Then, out of the bathroom comes Debbie who was once my friend. She gives me that vacuous smile she's perfected, shifts her eyes to the left of my head and tries to slither past.

'Hello, Debbie,' I say, blocking her way. My voice may be a little too loud.

'Oh! Um . . . Lucy!' she says as if she hadn't recognized me. Her eyes dart away, a deer caught in the headlights. No. A possum in the headlights. She always had a sneaky little face. 'Hi! How have you been?'

'Well, funny you should ask, Debbie. My husband died five years ago. I know you were quite sad. But guess what? So was I. It would've been nice if you called me *even once*. Since you were supposedly my friend and all.'

She stares at me, her face twitching in surprise. Her mouth opens wordlessly, but whatever she may or may not have to say, I don't want to hear it. Instead I step aside to let her scuttle past. My breath comes hard and fast, and I look around for a hiding place, knowing I'm irritatingly close to tears.

The coat room. Great. No one's in there. I step in and close the door behind me, take a deep breath and cross my arms over my chest. Three large racks of coats surround me, the empty metal hangers clanging softly in the wind current caused by my arrival.

'Lucy? You in there?' It's Ethan. Of course.

I don't answer. The coat room door doesn't

have a lock. Ethan comes in and shuts the door quietly behind him.

'First you make out with Charley Spirito, then you tell off Debbie Keating,' he muses. 'Busy night.'

'Please don't,' I whisper.

He nods and looks at the floor. 'I'm sorry,' he says. 'The scones comment was in poor taste. Forgive me?'

I nod, my throat too tight to speak.

'Come on back out, then. Your mom is looking for you.'

'Ethan,' I attempt, my voice cracking. My mouth wobbles and I clamp my lips together.

'Hey,' Ethan says, his eyebrows rising in surprise. He steps closer, erasing the small space between us, and takes my upper arms, his hands warm and strong. 'What's going on, sweetheart?'

Tears slop out of my eyes, and I find that my face is suddenly pressed against Ethan's shoulder, my arms around his lean waist, and I'm crying. Rather hard. 'I was so proud, Ethan,' I choke. 'To be the first face she saw after all this time. That maybe something I said, or those damn scones . . . maybe I triggered something. She was talking and smiling and everything, and it was like the old days, you know? The Black Widows were so happy, and it was like a party and everyone was so amazed, and then . . . it's so stupid, but why does everyone have to die?' I hiccup on another sob.

'Honey, she was a hundred and four,' Ethan says against my hair. His arms are around me, and one hand is rubbing between my shoulder blades, where there are knots the size of acorns. He feels so good. Smells so good. 'She just . . . wound down. That's all. And you had this incredible day with her, this one last day where she was back to her old self.' His voice is gentle. 'You should be happy, sweetheart. That was a gift. You got to talk to her one last time. I can't tell you what I'd give—'

His words stop abruptly. It doesn't matter. I know what he was about to say.

I pull back a little to look at him, and his eyes, those smiley eyes, are so sad.

In all my times with Ethan, I have never seen him cry, not at Jimmy's funeral, not in the horrible days immediately thereafter, not ever. I wonder now what warehouse of emotion he's got bottled up in his heart.

Ethan pulls back, too. Very gently, he runs his thumbs under my eyes, wiping away my tears. 'Don't cry, honey. I can't take it,' he whispers.

And then I kiss him. His lovely, full mouth is so warm, so familiar. For about three entire heartbeats, he doesn't move a millimeter. Then he kisses me back, just a little, his lips barely moving, and I slide my fingers through his hair and pull him a little closer, and oh, God, I've missed him. Missed this.

His arms tighten around me, and the hangers rattle again as we knock against them, and now his lips are on my neck, the gentle scrape of his beard contrasting with the warm silkiness of his mouth. My knees soften in an almost painful rush. Then his mouth finds mine again, and the kiss is not so gentle this time . . . desperate, hungry, hot and forbidden and utterly welcome. His tongue brushes mine, and molten heat leaps through my veins. My hands move to his chest, and his skin is hot, practically burning me through the cotton, and I can feel the hard thudding of his heart. Without thinking, I tug his shirt and slip my hands underneath.

'Lucy,' he mutters against my mouth. 'Honey, wait.' But I just kiss him again and slide my hands against the smooth skin of his back, his ribs, and pull him closer, wanting him against me. He shifts so we're closer, his mouth hot and hard. Waiting is forgotten.

Suddenly the door opens, and I release Ethan so fast that I stagger into the hangers once more. He catches my arm, and we turn to see who's there.

'Jesus, you guys, can't you do it in the backseat of a limo like everyone else?'

It's Parker. She grins and puts her hands on her slim hips, raising an eyebrow. My face is on fire, guilt fanning the flames of lust, and I nearly choke on the sudden clamping of my throat.

243

'Hello, Parker,' Ethan murmurs calmly, not letting go of my arm.

'Tsk, tsk,' Parker says. 'Making out at a wake? Shame on the both of you!' Glancing over her shoulder, she smiles. 'I found them, Mrs. Lang.' My stomach rises in abrupt horror, and I clap a hand over my mouth. Then Parker looks back at us. 'Just kidding, guys,' she says with a flashing smile. 'You're safe for the moment. But seriously, straighten up and get out of there, you wicked children, you.'

With that, she closes the coat room door and, I presume, leaves.

Which leaves me with Ethan. I take a wobbly step away from him. His hair is rumpled, his cheeks are flushed, his shirttails hanging out. I swallow convulsively. So classy, making out in a funeral home. Quite the aphrodisiac, apparently, to those of us pervs who enjoy shagging our brothers-in-law.

'Lucy.' Ethan hasn't moved. His voice is low.

'I'm sorry,' I whisper, looking at the carpet. My hands are clenched into fists.

'Look at me.'

I nod and force myself to obey.

Ethan's face is calm. He tips my chin up a little farther, and man, it's hard to look into those gentle brown eyes. But I do. 'Give me a chance,' he says quietly. A cold fist squeezes my heart. 'Give me a chance to be with you.

244

The right way this time.'

I open my mouth, then shut it, then try again. 'Ethan, you know I . . .'

'You have to.' His gaze is steady and sure.

My heart, which wasn't too regular a few minutes ago, knocks wildly around in my chest. I do have to. I know it. It's just . . .

'Okay,' I whisper.

He cups my face in his hands, and just looks at me. Then he smiles, and my dopey heart surges out to him, even as my stomach churns. 'It'll be all right. You'll see.'

My knees buzz painfully, and numbness seems to have gloved my hands. The pebble in my throat is more like a fist right now.

Ethan kisses my forehead, and I close my eyes and put my hand over his heart for a second, then step back and adjust his collar. He grins, tucks his shirt back in and then opens the door and peeks out. 'All clear,' he says, looking like his old mischievous self.

'See you around, cowboy,' I mutter, then totter down the hall on wooden legs to rejoin my family. For the rest of the night, I can barely hear. I feel slightly ill.

I believe I'm in deep trouble.

CHAPTER SEVENTEEN

I walk home after the wake, hoping to settle down. My stomach's been a wreck since Ethan kissed me—well, since I kissed him, to be fair.

I don't know what I'm doing. Ethan is not the type I want. He's much too . . . too . . . lovable. I swallow sickly and head off down the street. Past Nubey's Hardware, past Zippy's Sports Memorabilia. Haven't seen a customer go in there in months, and I wonder idly when Zippy will give up the ghost, if the Black Widows will be able to find another tenant. It's eight-thirty, and Mackerly is quiet, Aunt Boggy's wake being about the extent of socializing in this town tonight. And here's Bunny's. *See you in a little while,* I think, looking forward to the quiet balm that is bread baking, the sweet yeast smell of the dough, the warmth of the oven. Odd, to be so fond of a place, but I do love the bakery. I just wish it wasn't slowly dying.

I head around the park, trailing my hand along the brownstone wall, its rough surface scraping against my fingertips. The temperature is dropping, and the tips of my ears grow cold. A seabird cries, mournful and shrill, and the smell of low tide sharpens the air. The wind catches the hollow spot under the bridge, and a lonely, soft howl comes from below. Or maybe it's Captain Cook's wife, like Bob said.

I go straight to Ethan's. He answers on the first knock.

'Hey,' he says. His suit jacket is off, his shirt unbuttoned a couple. He smiles, then stands back to let me in. I don't move, as my head is in the emotional equivalent of a spin cycle. 'Come on in, Lucy. Want a glass of wine?'

'Sure,' I answer, obeying abruptly. 'Thanks.'

As Ethan goes to the kitchen to pour me a drink, I look around the living room. His apartment's layout is identical to mine, but being one story higher, his view is better. Now, though, there's nothing but a few lights sprinkling the town, the deep black of the ocean beyond that. A tiny glow flickers on the horizon—a fishing boat. Someone's out tonight, rocking on the sea, checking lines. It seems so cozy out there, far away from shore. A blue glow from the Aronsons' house indicates they're watching TV. Rose made a cake for their fiftieth anniversary party last month. Fifty years.

Turning away, I almost jump at the sight of Ethan, standing there with two glasses of wine in his hands. 'Here you go,' he says, offering me a glass. Our fingers brush, mine cold against the warmth of his skin. 'To Aunt Boggy,' he adds, clinking my glass.

'To Boggy,' I return, then chug the wine. It's red, a cabernet, I think, and it might have

247

a nice body and an intricate web of flavors, but I can't really tell, as I've glugged it all down. I let out a breath. Ethan's eyebrow raises.

'Liquid courage?' he suggests, the corner of his mouth rising.

'Maybe,' I agree, taking a seat on his couch. It's a nice couch. Brown leather. Ethan furnished his apartment in one mighty swoop at Restoration Hardware. Manly dark furniture, very nice, very solid. Aside from the many photos of Nicky (and a few of Nicky and Parker, and even one of the three of them), his place looks like a catalog. He takes a seat in the matching club chair adjacent to me.

'You don't have any pictures of Jimmy,' I observe. I've noticed it in the past, commented on it, even.

'I'll have to ask my mom for one. Now that I'm here full-time.'

'You must miss him.'

Ethan looks at me a beat or two. 'I do.' He sets his wineglass down on the coffee table and links his hands loosely in front of him. 'Do you want to talk about Jimmy? Or would you like to talk about you and me?'

My heart does a slow, sickening slide. 'They're kind of intertwined, aren't they?' I ask.

Ethan nods. 'I guess they are.'

'I'm your brother's wife, Ethan. Are you sure you want to be with me? There's a lot of baggage, obviously.'

'You're my brother's widow, Lucy,' he corrects, and his voice is a little sharp. 'We're not committing adultery here.'

'I *know*, Ethan,' I return, just as sharply. 'But this is not your normal situation, either.'

He doesn't move for a second, then comes to sit next to me, angling himself so he can see my face, though I can't look at him just right now. He slides his hand across my neck. 'How do you want this to be, this thing between us?' he asks, his voice gentle.

I don't want it to be at all, Ethan, I'm petrified. I risk a glance at him, those gentle brown eyes. 'You have to swear,' I whisper, 'that we'll still be friends, Ethan. No matter what happens. If we work out, great. But if we don't . . . I can't . . . I've missed you these past few weeks.' My eyes fill. It's an unreasonable demand, but I can't help it.

'Okay,' he says quietly. 'I've missed you, too.' He drops a kiss on my shoulder, and I swallow hard. 'What else?'

'I don't know,' I admit. His hand stays on my neck, and I'm not sure if I like it or if I want a little space. 'I don't want to tell your parents right away. Or my family, either. Not till there's something . . . definite. Okay?'

Something flickers in Ethan's eyes. 'Okay.'

'And maybe we should wait to . . . you know. Sleep together.'

He nods once. 'Okay. That's probably a

good idea.'

'That's it?' I ask, perversely irritated that he's so damn agreeable. 'Just 'okay' to everything? Anything you'd like to add?'

'Thank you,' he says, tilting his head, that damnably appealing smile curling on his lovely mouth.

I blink. 'What for?'

'For giving me a chance. I know you're scared, and I know you're not a hundred percent sure, and I'm grateful. That's all.'

'Dang it, Ethan,' I whisper. 'You're such a prince.'

I can't help it, I kiss him, soft and slow, and I feel like I'm falling, falling and the only solid thing to hang on to is Ethan. His arms slip around me, one hand cups the back of my head, and he feels so strong and safe, and he smells so good and tastes like wine. And just like before, I'm suddenly starving for him, a junkie getting her fix. I pull him down with me so that I'm half lying on the couch, and wrap my arms around him, bringing him closer, and God, he feels so good. His hand slides under my sweater, burning my skin, and I suck in a breath. The prickle of his beard, the softness of his lips, the heat of his mouth . . .

Then he breaks the kiss and pulls back, flushed, breathing hard, his eyes smoky and dark, and it's like I was drowning and didn't want to come to the surface.

250

He touches my cheek with one finger. 'No sleeping together,' he murmurs. 'So who's hungry?'

And with that, he rolls off me, leaving me limp and horny, and staggers into the kitchen.

CHAPTER EIGHTEEN

'So you're good, sweetheart? You're happy?'

'I'm doing pretty well, Mom,' I say into my cell phone, earning a glare from my own mother. She never liked it that I occasionally called Marie Mirabelli the same thing I called her. 'How is it out there?'

I can almost hear the shrug, perfected by generations of Italians, a sort of *who knows, what can you do, I'm suffering but I won't complain gesture.* 'It's hot,' she admits.

'It's Arizona,' I say, opening the oven door to check my beautiful loaves. Two and a half more minutes ought to do it, both with the bread and my mother-in-law. 'How's Gianni? Getting in some golf?'

'Oh, him,' Marie says. 'Golf. You'd think maybe he could relax, but instead he's at the grocery store all day, buying enough food to feed an army. People don't eat out here, Lucy. They *exercise.*' It's clearly a dirty word. 'It's shameless! They want me to go to a yoga class. Yoga! Me! Like I want to twist myself around

251

like a snake!'

'It sounds nice,' I answer, smiling. 'All the things you've been too busy to do.'

She sighs. 'Who said I wanted to do yoga?' She pauses. 'How's Nicky? You were an angel to send pictures. Has he grown?'

'He's great,' I answer. 'The sweetest boy in the world. And yes, he's sprouting up. Ask him to sing you the Halloween song when you call. So cute.'

'Oh, I miss that little guy.' She sighs again. 'And Ethan? How's he?'

I grimace, wishing Ethan called his parents more often, since I'm often left shoveling them information on their son. 'Ethan's good.'

'Do you think he's getting back with Parker? The two of them . . . I don't understand. A beautiful child together, but they won't get married. And now with Ethan living there all the time, what's stopping them?'

I glance at my mother, who continues to eavesdrop shamelessly. 'I . . . I'm not sure,' I fib. This would be the perfect moment to say something. *Actually Ethan and I have been seeing each other a bit . . .*

But I don't say anything. It's too soon. Instead I give Marie my love, ask her to hug Gianni for me and tell her how much I miss them both. Then I hang up, avoid my mother's eyes and check my bread.

Ethan and I had dinner the other night,

252

and it was an agony of discomfort. We'd gone to Lenny's, and I'm fairly sure no one realized we were on a date. Ethan and I have been out to eat many times before, after all. Less frequently in the past two years, granted, when smokin' sex was how we spent our time, but I'm sure this dinner didn't look any different to the untrained eye. But Ethan was practically levitating with energy, talked nonstop, trying—way too hard—to entertain me. I was so nervous I could barely eat. It was beyond tense. I couldn't think of anything to say—mentioning Jimmy seemed verboten, but avoiding the subject altogether felt unnatural, too. All the little customer stories I had from the bakery evaporated as I tried to think of something—anything—to talk about. We were reduced to talking about the weather and our food. Pathetic.

When we walked back to the Boatworks, Ethan escorted me to my door, then leaned against the wall, waiting for me to find my keys as Fat Mikey yowled from inside.

'Well, thanks, Eth,' I said, blushing. I didn't want him to kiss me. I just wanted to be inside, safe with my cat. Oh, I wanted him to kiss me, and if he did, then we all know what would happen . . . I'd maul him right here in the hallway. Fat Mikey began headbutting the door as if he could break it down. Ethan's eyes were steady, waiting. I looked at the floor.

'You're welcome,' he said, then kissed my

cheek. 'See you soon.'

Before he even disappeared around the corner to the stairs, I missed him.

I ended up knocking on Ash's door to see if she wanted to practice making pumpkin walnut cheesecake, which is what's on the menu for our next class, and lucky for me, she did. And the whole time, I couldn't get my mind off Ethan, and so it's been. When he's around, I feel like I'm going to jump out of my skin. When he's not, I miss him.

'So what's eating you, Lucy?' Iris asks now, cocking her head in a concerned manner.

'Oh, nothing. Preoccupied, I guess,' I say, smiling at my starchy aunt. Though Rose is the more affectionate aunt, Iris is a bit more perceptive, despite her bulldozer personality.

'Dating's not going too well?' she suggests.

'It's . . . I don't know. It's harder than I thought,' I say.

'I thought I might date a little, too,' Rose says, making me bobble the tray of bread I just took out.

'Oh, yes,' Iris confirms, the sarcasm dripping. 'All of a sudden, this one wants to see what's out there. You should've seen her at the senior center when we got our flu shots. Four men, fanning around her, ignoring me. Just like when we were young. Me the smart one, her the pretty one.'

'I'm smart, too!' Rose cheeps indignantly. 'And you're pretty, Iris. You just don't know how to flirt.'

Iris rolls her eyes. 'I'm seventy-six years old, Rose. And you're not much younger. Flirting. You should be swapping prescription lists and asking if they want the CPR when their hearts stop.'

I laugh as Rose clucks in disapproval, and Jorge, who's materialized from the back, grins. He and I begin bagging the still-warm bread with practiced efficiency.

'Lucy?' my mother calls from up front, her voice strained. 'Someone's here to see you.'

'Okay,' I call, then turn to Jorge. 'Can you get the rest of this?' He nods. 'So Jorge, what do you think of Rose? She's interested in dating again.'

'Oh, pish, Lucy,' Rose giggles. 'Jorge's just a good friend.'

Jorge flashes her a grin, his gold tooth winking.

I push through the swinging doors to the front of the bakery just as Mom comes into the kitchen. 'Lucy, honey, wait—'

I lurch to a stop at the sight of the man standing at the counter.

It's Jimmy.

*   *   *

My knees buckle, and Mom grabs me before I fall.

Of course, it's not Jimmy. But it's close, and

255

I'm not the only one who thinks so. Rose is dabbing tears, and Iris's hand is pressed against her heart.

Matt DeSalvo—he gave us his name at some point—is tall and broad-shouldered. His dirty blond hair is cut short. He has a wide, straight smile, and his face is angular and strong. Matt has a dimple, and Jimmy did not. Matt's eyes are blue—not the astonishing blue-green that Jimmy's were, but a more true blue. And he's wearing a suit, which Jimmy rarely did.

But still. The resemblance is shocking.

We sit across from each other at the table in the bakery kitchen. Mom fixes tea, clucking, and Rose repeatedly tells me I'm white as a sheet. Which is natural, since I feel like I've seen a ghost. My hands are trembling, and I feel a little sweaty.

Since Jimmy died, I've seen him around. I know from my aunts and mother, as well as from the widows' group I'd belonged to, that seeing your dead spouse was not uncommon. Once, when I was driving up from New London, a man crossed the street in front of me, looking so much like Jimmy that I'd done a U-turn and gone back to find him, searching for half an hour, my heart clacking in my throat, tears spurting out of my eyes. Another time, when I was leaving the hospital after Nicky was born, I'd heard Jimmy laugh clear as day . . . the low, dirty laugh so singular to

Jimmy that I was convinced his spirit had dropped down to earth to visit his newborn nephew.

But seeing a Jimmy lookalike across the table from me . . . it's overwhelming. At my near faint, Mom had explained the resemblance, and Matt had very nicely helped me into the kitchen, where I melted into a chair and put my head between my knees.

I wipe my eyes and blow my nose once more. 'I'm sorry,' I say again.

'It's completely understandable,' Matt answers kindly. His voice is not like Jimmy's at all, which helps. Close up, the resemblance isn't that shocking. Matt's nose is a little longer, and his chin is rounder than Jimmy's, which was square and ridiculously masculine. But still. He looks more like Jimmy than anyone I've seen. More like Jimmy's brother than Ethan does, for that matter.

'How long has it been?' he asks.

'Five and a half years,' I answer, stealing another look at his face.

'It was such a tragedy,' Iris announces.

'So tragic,' Rose cheeps at the same time.

'Why don't you girls go down to the Starbucks?' Mom suggests sharply. 'Lucy could use a coffee. One of those expensive, silly things. Go. Shoo.'

The aunts, looking wounded at being kicked out, do as they're told, and Matt stands up politely as they cluck and don their cardigans. I take the delay to get myself under control, though my hands are still trembling.

'So how did your husband die?' Matt asks. My mother, feeling that this is too personal a question, rattles the kettle loudly. Though she's gotten rid of the aunts, there's no way on God's green earth that she's going to leave.

'A car accident,' I say distantly.

'I'm so sorry.' He says it just the right way, looking right into my eyes without flinching. Sympathy, not pity. There's a huge difference, and we widows appreciate it, let me tell you. 'You must've been awfully young.'

'Twenty-four,' I murmur.

My mom sets down the tea tray with a clatter. 'So what brings you to Bunny's, Mr. DeSalvo?' she asks, sitting next to me. She tugs on her tailored, cropped jacket, crosses her legs, jiggling her foot so that her high-heeled shoe dangles precariously.

'Well, this may not be the time to discuss it, if you're still feeling shaky,' Matt answers. 'I can certainly come back.'

'I'd think she'd feel less shaky if you said your business,' Mom retorts. I give her a questioning look. Not like her to be so rude. That's more Iris's terrain.

Still, Matt pauses, looking at me, and I have to admit, I like that he's waiting for my approval. 'I'm fine, Matt. Go ahead.'

'I represent NatureMade,' he says, naming an organic chain grocery store that dots our

258

fair state. 'Are you familiar with us?'

'Too expensive for real people to shop at, but yes,' my mother says.

He gives a half nod. 'Well, yes, organic food is more expensive,' he acknowledges. 'We like to think that our customers understand the value of good health—' Mom snorts, and I give her a reprimanding nudge. Matt laughs. 'Okay, I'll save the sales pitch. I'm here because we think Bunny's bread is the best in the area, and we'd like to be the sole distributor in Rhode Island.'

My mouth drops open. 'Wow,' I murmur.

Matt gives me a nutshell idea of the details—NatureMade would sell four types of Bunny's bread in its baked goods department. We could still supply bread to the restaurants we use now, as long as it didn't interfere with NatureMade's quota. If the bread sold well, they'd ask for more varieties, then discuss the possibility of distributing Bunny's bread in the Connecticut and Massachusetts stores as well.

Matt smiles as he talks, a good salesman. His voice is low and confident, and he holds eye contact well. God, he reminds me of Jimmy! Not just how he looks, but the whole take-charge attitude. He has a plan, it's a good one, and he knows it.

'What about selling it here?' Mom asks suspiciously. 'We're not going to stop selling here, of course.'

'Well, we would ask that you'd limit the

259

number of loaves and types available here,' he said. 'And of course, we'd do an ad campaign in all the Rhode Island newspapers and some radio commercials, too, announcing that we carry Bunny's bread. I imagine you'd see a bump in customer traffic, thanks to the publicity.' Mom huffs but doesn't contradict him.

He fishes a card out of his breast pocket and places it on the table. 'I know you'll have a lot to talk about,' he says. 'Can I call you in a few days?'

'Sure,' I say. 'That would be great.'

He shakes Mom's hand first, winning points for good manners, then mine, holding on a bit too long. 'I'm sorry I startled you,' he says, a half smile on his mouth. My stomach flips, not unpleasantly.

'It's not your fault,' I answer. I may be blushing.

'Great to meet you both,' Matt says. 'And if it wouldn't be too much trouble, I'd love a few of those cheese danishes for the road.'

'I'll get them,' Mom grumbles, getting up from the table.

Bemused, I sit at the table, my tea cooling next to me, toying with Matt's card. Statewide bread distribution would be a huge shot in the arm for Bunny's. Huge.

But it's not really the bread I'm thinking of.

'I didn't like him,' Mom announces, bursting through the swinging doors a minute later.

'Why?' I ask.

'Too slick,' she says, brushing a speck of imaginary lint from her lapel. 'Did you see that suit? Armani, I'm thinking.'

'You're the one dressed like Michelle Obama, Mom,' I point out. She doesn't answer. 'He really looked like Jimmy, didn't he?' I add.

'Oh, not so much.'

'Mom. He looked like Jimmy's brother.'

'So?'

'So nothing, not really. He just did.' I'm quiet for a minute. 'It was kind of . . . comforting . . . seeing a face so much like Jimmy's. That's all.'

My mother's eyes fill with tears. She bends and gives me a rare hug. 'He did. He looked just like Jimmy.' She sits down and dabs her eyes.

'Was there anyone who ever reminded you of Daddy?' I ask.

She stares over my shoulder, lost in memories. 'You know that actor?'

'Which one, Mom?'

'The good-looking one? With brown eyes?'

'George Clooney?' I suggest. My father had lovely brown eyes, something I like to think I inherited.

'Is that him? The crinkly eyes?'

I nod. Only Mom wouldn't know George Clooney.

261

'Sometimes I rent movies that he's in, just to . . . well.' Mom blushes a little at the confession.

I smile and squeeze her hand, then take a sip of my lukewarm tea. 'So what do you think about the offer?'

Mom hesitates, then shrugs. 'I don't know. Mostly up to you, since you're in charge of bread.'

'I only own ten percent of the bakery,' I remind her.

She stares out the window. 'Lucy?'

'Yes?'

Mom sighs, then adjusts her wedding ring . . . she's never stopped wearing it. 'I know I'm not the best mother in the world,' she offers, still not looking at me.

'Oh, Mom, I wouldn't say that,' I say.

She gives me a smile, then looks back down. 'The thing is, when you lose someone like we have . . . it's like part of your heart is cut out. And you always worry about how much more you can afford to lose. It can make a person sort of . . . stunted.'

I don't say anything. She has, of course, just voiced my deepest fear. The pebble swells.

'I just . . . I just don't want you to be disappointed, honey. Maybe you can find someone . . . you're younger than I was, and without kids, maybe you'll have an easier time of it. But don't be surprised if it doesn't work the way you picture it.' She sighs gustily. 'Well.

Good talk. Let me know what you decide about the bread.'

Then she squeezes my hand and bustles off to the front.

When my work at the bakery is done, I decide to go for a bike ride and head north on Newport Road. The brisk wind stings, and my hair whips around my face. Salt is heavy in the air, as well as the smell of the autumn leaves, sharp and sad and lovely. I turn inland on Mickes Street. There's Doral-Anne's old house. It's still the hovel it was in grammar school, a seedy little ranch with three rusted-out cars in the yard. The grass is long and thick with weeds.

Doral-Anne and I were on the same school bus, her stop about ten minutes before mine. Once, when I was about seven, she'd trudged down the bus steps and turned to look back, something like loneliness on her thin face. Surprised, I waved to her. She flipped me the bird in response. I can still remember the way heat flared across my cheeks, how I wish I hadn't offered that stupid, naive wave that was so instantly and graphically rejected. It was the first time Doral-Anne had singled me out, though it wouldn't be the last.

Ah, well. A mist is starting to fall, and I need to pay attention to the road, since it's a little slick. After about a mile, I turn onto Grimley Farm Road, the wind in front of me now, slowing me, almost warning me off.

When I reach my destination, I lean my bike against the telephone pole and walk down toward number 73. The driveway is still unpaved, the sand softened by recent rains. My footsteps make a pleasant scraping sound as I approach the house where Jimmy and I never got to live.

It's painted white now, our little Cape. It was gray when Jimmy and I bought it, but the white looks nice. The shutters are still green. I'd painted them myself.

Jimmy had surprised me with this house. Told me we were going on a picnic, came up here, said he knew the owners. I wondered why we were going to eat in someone's yard; the house didn't have a view of the water, and the property was fairly unremarkable. But Jimmy wouldn't answer my questions. Instead he just grinned, took my hand and led me through the front door. The house was empty of furniture except for one small table in the living room. On the table was a jewelry box, and in the box was the key to the front door.

It might not have been the house I'd have picked out, but it was affordable, and the cost of real estate on Mackerly definitely limited our choices. While I'd felt a prickle of alarm that I now owned a house I'd had no part in choosing, Jimmy's pride and excitement had swept that away. It was a grand gesture, and he loved making those. This was the guy, after all, who'd sent four dozen roses to my dorm room the night after our first date. Who surprised me with a honeymoon to Hawaii when I thought we were going to Bar Harbor, Maine. Who couldn't spend one night away from me, even if it meant driving all the way home after a long day.

I'm not sure why I'm here now. I've visited a few times over the years, unable to ignore it completely, this little place that was going to be ours. It sold quickly enough . . . a family bought it, which was nice. A swing set adorns the backyard, and a little plastic car sits in the driveway.

I turn around and head back for home. The mist has turned to rain, and I'll be soaked by the time I get there. My pastry class starts at five, and I decide to bring Ethan home some of the amaretto zabaglione that we're scheduled to make, rather than letting the class eat it all, as I usually do. I guess I'm feeling a little guilty, mooning over Jimmy after nearly fainting at the sight of his doppelganger. Yes. Ethan more than deserves a little sweetness from me.

*　　　*　　　*

When class is over, I return to my apartment. Ethan's not home yet, even though it's eight-thirty. I try to quash the worry and click on my computer. When Google comes up, I type in 'NatureMade' and sit back to read.

265

NatureMade is a sound company, from all accounts. Expanding slowly, holding tight when the economy's been rough, good to its employees. Matt DeSalvo is mentioned a couple of times, in promotion announcements and as a contact person, stuff like that. After a moment's hesitation, I try an image search on him, wondering if he really did look that much like Jimmy, but nothing comes up.

I wander to the window and look out into the dark. Where's Ethan? It's still raining, and with leaves on the road, it could be slick out there. His car is new. That's good, but what if he's not used to it enough? What if he had an accident? I left a message on his home phone earlier, announcing that dessert awaited him, if he was so inclined. So far, I've resisted the urge to call him on his cell, since I don't want him to be talking while he's driving, which is another thing he does that drives me crazy, even if he does use a Bluetooth.

Finally a knock comes on the door, and I start, then vault for the door. Sure enough, it's Ethan.

'Where have you been?' I demand, my face burning at the sight of him.

'Hi,' he says, frowning. 'I had a meeting.'

'Well, isn't that nice to know,' I sputter. 'I thought you were dead.'

His face softens. 'Well, I seem to be alive,' he says, smiling just a little.

I almost kiss him. Almost hug him. Then

the moment passes when that would be natural, and we're left just looking at each other, Fat Mikey working on a hairball under the chair.

'I made zabaglione,' I mutter. 'Come on in.'

He follows me into the kitchen, taking his usual seat at the table. 'Thanks,' he says as I set a bowl in front of him. Then I sit down, too, and watch him eat.

'Want a bite?' he asks, holding out a spoonful.

'Wasted on me,' I answer. I'd tried some at class, actually . . . the smell of the eggs and cream, the vanilla and lemon zest was so tempting, and I'd tried a spoonful. As usual, it hadn't tasted like anything.

'How was your day?' Ethan asks, and I tell him about the offer from Matt DeSalvo and NatureMade. For some reason, I don't mention that Matt looks like Jimmy.

'That's really something,' Ethan says, scraping his dish. He gets up and helps himself to another one, then rejoins me. 'Think you'll take him up on it?'

I hesitate. 'I don't know. Probably,' I answer slowly. Fat Mikey butts his head against the leg of the table, on the prowl for pudding. Ethan obliges, putting his empty dish on the floor so Fat Mikey can lick it clean.

'Seems like a great way to increase business,' Ethan says.

'I know,' I agree. 'I'm just not sure I want

to be a bread baker for the rest of my life. Even a really successful bread baker.'

'Mmm-hmm,' Ethan says, still eating. He looks at me expectantly.

I shrug. 'I guess I still want to be a pastry chef.'

'And why aren't you?' He leans over, setting dish number two on the floor for my cat, who purrs in appreciation.

I frown. 'I can't just leave Bunny's, for one.'

'Why not? Didn't the Black Widows get by just fine before you?'

'Well, first of all, I'd miss them. I love Bunny's. And secondly, no. They were going out of business, inch by inch. Jimmy pretty much saved the day by getting the bread orders.'

'Ah, St. Jimmy,' Ethan says, smiling, his eyes slightly mocking. I frown, peevishly glad that I didn't bring up Jimmy earlier. 'But that was all before you started at the bakery, Lucy,' he continues. 'They could hire someone else to do the bread. Your recipes, of course. I'm not saying you don't make incredible bread.'

'So what are you saying?' I ask a bit crossly.

'I'm saying you should do what you want to do, that's all.'

'Right,' I murmur, still irked. It's just that . . . here it comes, the inevitable comparison. Jimmy would've sat down with a notepad and mapped out a plan. *Here's what you should do,* he'd say, and he'd outline the next ten steps

268

with utmost enthusiasm. Ethan . . . Ethan's not helping.

Instead he looks at me with a half smile. Then he stands, comes over to me and takes my hand. 'Come on,' he says. 'Give us a hug, grumpy.'

My cheeks flush as I do what I'm told. God help me, I love the way he smells. His hand plays in my hair, his heart thumping steadily against mine. I remember that earlier this evening, I wondered if he was hurt, or worse.

Without another thought, I kiss Ethan's warm neck, slide my hands up his back, the starched cotton of his shirt crisp under my palms, the heat of his skin radiating through the cloth. His beard scrapes gently against my cheek as he turns his head, and then the smooth, warm perfection of his mouth is on mine. Fat Mikey twines between our legs, and I feel Ethan smile, and there it is again, that painful, wonderful squeeze in my heart. He doesn't do more than kiss me back, letting me set the pace, cupping my face with gentle hands.

It's different this time—this isn't a warm-up to sex, and this isn't the hot, desperate kissing of two lonely people. We're just kissing, mouths gentle, hands tender and chaste, but his heart thumps harder against my chest, and my knees are weakening. The sheer pleasure of the way he feels outweighs that faint flare of alarm in the back of my heart. I deepen the

269

kiss, sliding my hands up his sides, feeling the lean muscles over his rib cage, tasting the faint combination of amaretto and Ethan, and the thought occurs to me that I'm already—

The phone rings, stopping my thoughts. Rings again, and a third time. I don't move away from Ethan's warmth, his mouth, the hint of the smile that always plays under the surface when we kiss. But then my sister's voice comes on the answering machine.

'Lucy! Please! Christopher had a heart attack! Come to the hospital right now!'

CHAPTER NINETEEN

Corinne's usually perfect hair is wild, and Emma wails in her arms.

'How is he?' I ask, but my sister is sobbing so hard she doesn't make sense.

'I'll find a doctor,' Ethan says, leaving the waiting room where we found Corinne.

I sit next to my sister, who's shaking wildly. 'I can't believe it,' she manages. 'After all this . . . I thought . . . he never . . .'

'Okay, okay, sweetie, calm down,' I murmur, rubbing her shoulder. 'Here, let me take Emma.' I pry the baby out of Corinne's arms and snuggle her against my shoulder. She stops crying instantly, snuffles around for a second and takes one of those shuddering breaths that indicates she's done. Corinne, however, continues.

'When did you guys get here?' I ask.

'Two hours ago,' she says.

'Oh, honey! You should've called me right away.'

'There were too many things to do,' she says, wiping her eyes on her sleeve. I rub her back with my free hand. Emma sighs against my neck, warm and heavy with sleep.

'Should I call Mom?' I ask, rather surprised she isn't here already.

'No!' Corinne wails. The baby jerks in her sleep. 'You're bad enough!'

I give her a quizzical look, then sigh. Right. I'm a harbinger of death. Forgot. 'Okay, honey, okay. That's fine. Now try to calm down and tell me what happened.'

Bit by bit, sob by sob, I get the story. Christopher and Corinne had been discussing the fact that Chris hadn't eaten any leafy greens that day, and she was urging him to finish his spinach. Chris rubbed his chest, said it felt a little tight and Corinne had screamed, made him lie flat '—so I could give him CPR, you know?—' and called 911, convinced he was breathing his last. It did seem to get worse while she was on the phone, and once he was in the E.R., the doctors just whisked him away.

'He could be dying!' Corinne squeaks. 'All alone, dying!' I hug her awkwardly around

Emma. My own eyes fill. Please, Daddy, I pray. Please, Jimmy. Don't let this happen to Corinne, too.

'He's really healthy, Cory,' I murmur, trying to sound calm and wise. 'I'm sure this is nothing.' Chris *is* healthy, my goodness. His cholesterol is 142, a number called 'unAmerican' by the doctor and proudly relayed to me just a few days ago when Corinne gave me the health update.

But, already, images of Christopher's funeral are knifing through my head. Emma growing up without her dad, as Corinne and I did, but without the cushion of memories that I, at least, have held like little diamonds all these years.

The door opens. 'Hey,' Ethan says, smiling at Corinne. 'He's fine.'

'Oh, thank you, God!' I blurt, patting my niece's back. *Your father's fine, sweetheart. Thank you, Jimmy, thank you, Daddy.*

Ethan sits next to Corinne and puts his arm around her shoulders. 'The doctor says you can come on down and he'll talk to you and Chris together. Okay? You need a drink of water first?'

She leans against Ethan for a second, struggling to stay under even moderate control, and shakes her head, then turns to me. 'Please come,' she says in a small voice, and my heart pulls.

'He's fine, did you hear, honey? He's fine.' I

kiss her cheek and stand, Emma still snoozing away. Ethan rises and offers Corinne his hand, which she grabs gratefully.

'You're sure he's fine?' she asks Ethan.

'That's what the nurse said,' he assures her.

We walk down the hall, back toward the busy E.R. 'Right here,' Ethan says, pointing to a curtain.

'Ethan, will you hold the baby?' Corinne asks. 'I don't want her near all these germs.'

'Sure. I'll take her up to the lobby, how's that?' Ethan offers, gently taking Emma from me. His hands are practiced and sure, and he drops a kiss on Emma's little head. Then he looks at me, and his mouth curls in a smile, causing my stomach to squeeze.

'Thanks, Ethan. Lucy, come on,' Corinne urges. She pushes back the curtain, then bursts into renewed sobs at the sight of her husband, who looks quite healthy to me, sitting up in bed in a johnny coat.

Corinne falls on him, sobbing. 'Christopher! Oh, baby! I thought you were dead!'

The words echo in my head. I'd said the same thing to Ethan this very night.

'Hi, there,' comes a voice. Great. It's Dr. Hateswomen. He frowns at the sight of me, then shakes Corinne's hand. 'I'm Dr. Porter. Your husband here is going to be just fine. His EKG is completely normal, and the first two rounds of blood work are fine.'

273

'He had chest pain!' Corinne objects. 'My father was only forty-two, and he died of a heart attack.'

'Right, right,' the doctor says condescendingly. 'Well, your husband is fine, as I just told you. It was just stress.'

'Stress? He doesn't have stress!' Corinne objects.

'Yes, I do, damn it!' Christopher barks, causing Corinne and me both to jump. 'You're killing me, Corinne! Every damn day, you're waiting for me to die! I eat a piece of cheese, and your face goes white. I'm five minutes late, and you've called the police! Everything in our house is so fucking perfect, I feel like a goddamn bull in a china shop! And the baby, my God! You make me feel like I'm going to drop her on her head, following me around every time I pick her up! It's gotten so I'm scared to touch my own child!'

Corinne looks like she's been clubbed. I can't say I've ever heard Christopher swear before. 'Chris—' I begin.

'No, Lucy. You don't understand. She's terrified she'll end up like you, and she's sucking the joy from our lives, and it's no wonder I landed in the E.R.'

'He has a point,' Dr. Hateswomen says. 'We certainly advocate a healthy diet and regular exercise, but he told me about how you time him on the elliptical and won't let him order for himself in restaurants, Mrs . . . .uh—' he

274

glances at his chart '—Mrs. Duvall. It's a bit much.'

'And I've had it. I can put cream in my goddamn coffee if I want to, Corinne,' Christopher bellows. 'That's right! Cream! Not even half-and-half!' He swings his legs over the side of the bed, jerks off the hospital gown and grabs his shirt. 'I'm staying with Jerry Mitchell tonight,' he informs Corinne, whose eyes look like they're going to pop out and roll across the floor. 'I'll call you tomorrow.'

With that he stands, then looks at the doctor. 'Can I go?' he demands.

'Sure,' Dr. Hateswomen says. 'Try to keep the stress level low.'

'Great advice,' I can't help saying. Corinne wrings her hands.

The good doctor turns an impassive gaze on me. 'Do I know you?'

'Um . . . I was in a while ago.' I feel my cheeks warming.

'Oh, yes. Hallucinations. Gotcha. *Ciao.*'

With that he leaves, his white coat flapping after him.

'Chris, honey, you can't . . . I didn't . . .' my sister attempts, tears streaking down her cheeks.

'Corinne, I need a little space. Okay? We'll talk soon.' My brother-in-law looks at me. 'Maybe she can stay with you tonight,' he says in a gentler voice.

'Sure,' I answer.

Then Christopher is gone, and Corinne falls apart for real.

* * *

A few hours later, Corinne is sleeping on my couch, wrapped in an afghan. She's zonked, thanks in large part to the Valium Dr. Hateswomen saw fit to give her upon hearing her wails after Chris left. Ethan made a run to Corinne's house to fetch the portable crib, diapers and thirty-six other things that Corinne listed as absolutely necessary for an overnight away from home.

I'm in the kitchen with Emma, who's taking her first bottle like a champ. Corinne keeps a can of formula in the diaper bag in case of her own death, and Emma is glugging away, eyes closed. Her skin is miraculously gorgeous . . . all shades of pink perfection, and her fingernails have completely charmed me. She holds my pinkie as she drinks, and it's fair to say I'm madly in love with my little niece.

'Hey.' Ethan's voice is soft. With some effort, I tear my eyes off of Emma and look up at him. 'I set up the portable crib in your room. Figured Corinne needed some sleep.'

'Great,' I answer. 'Thanks, Ethan.' I look back down at Emma and ease the nipple out of her mouth. Her lips purse, but her eyes stay closed.

'You'll make a great mom,' Ethan murmurs, and I don't look at his face. My heart twists painfully, afraid that he's about to say something more. It's just not something I can think about right now, not after imagining another husband dying tonight. Instead I look back down at Emma and adjust her blanket.

'I guess I'll head upstairs,' Ethan says.

'Okay,' I agree, then look back at him. 'Thank you, Ethan. You've been great.'

He gives a little smile. 'Sleep tight.'

Sighing, I ease out of the chair and carry Emma carefully into my room. Ethan made the little portable crib with a sheet and a pink blanket, which is folded neatly at the bottom. A stuffed pink giraffe is there, too. Nice touch. He really does have that fatherhood thing down.

I lay my niece in the crib and cover her, moving the giraffe well away from her face. She gives a little murmur, and again, my heart catches. I stay for a moment, resting my hand on her little shoulder to reassure her, then straighten up slowly, my back muscles protesting. It's been a long, long day.

Corinne is awake. 'Is she okay?' she asks as I come out of my bedroom.

'She's great,' I answer. 'Sleeping like a little angel.'

Corinne smiles a little at that. 'Did Christopher call?' she whispers.

I motion for her to sit on the couch, then

curl up in the chair opposite her. 'No, honey. Not yet.'

'We've never fought,' she says, two tears spilling out of her eyes.

I blink. 'And you've been married for three years?'

'Three years, six months and nine days,' she says, and that's what breaks my heart, because I, too, always knew exactly how long Jimmy and I were together.

'That's a long time to go without a fight,' I murmur.

'I just want everything to be perfect,' she says, wiping her eyes. 'What if we have a fight and then he dies? What if the last thing I say to him is "I hate your mother" or "Can't you ever remember to take out the trash?" What if I was like Mom, yelling at him to get out of the bathroom? I'd never forgive myself.' Corinne weeps. I get up and fetch a box of tissues and a glass of water.

'Thanks,' she mumbles, blowing her nose. We're both quiet for a minute or two. Outside, the wind gusts off the ocean, catching that particular hollow under the bridge in an unearthly, mournful howl.

'I'm so scared of ending up like you,' Corinne says softly. Her mouth wobbles. 'And I'm so sorry for you, Lucy.'

I sigh, feeling about a hundred years old. 'It was horrible,' I admit. 'But, Corinne, I . . . I lived, you know?' I look square at my sister.

'And you know what I miss the most?' She shakes her head and wipes her eyes. 'I miss . . . I miss the everyday stuff. The not-perfect stuff.'

My own eyes fill abruptly. 'We had this fight,' I say, my voice wobbling. 'It was over me doing the desserts at Gianni's. Marie did them all, you know?' Corinne nods. 'And I just wanted them to carry one thing of mine, this limoncello tart with raspberries . . . well, heck, it doesn't matter. But he took his mother's side, and we fought that night, and I was folding laundry and I threw a pair of socks at his head.'

I can still see the stunned look on Jimmy's face when the socks bounced off his forehead. Suddenly a hundred dopey, beloved memories slice through my heart like shrapnel . . . Jimmy's habit of just walking into the bathroom, no matter what I was doing in there. The way he'd do a hundred push-ups before bed, then admire his biceps and encourage me to do the same. His inability to start the day without cross-checking three weather forecasts as if he was a sailor dependent on the winds.

'I miss the everyday stuff,' I whisper. 'Don't smother those things trying to make every minute special, Cory. You can't keep it up. You're a wreck.'

She nods, tears still slipping silently down her cheeks. 'It's been so hard,' she admits.

'I'm so tired, Lucy. My boobs are killing me, and I have no idea what I'm doing with the baby, and I feel so guilty sometimes when she cries and I just think, "Oh, please, not again, Emma, I can't take it anymore." The other day, I was in the grocery store, and Emma was fussing, and I'd had about an hour's sleep the night before, and this old woman told me this was the happiest time of my life and I wanted to stab her with a knife!'

I burst out laughing at the vision of gentle Corinne killing a senior citizen in the produce aisle. After a minute, Corinne laughs, too.

'So . . . and I'm just suggesting here . . . maybe you have a few things bottled up,' I offer. 'You know what I think? I think Chris will love you even more, once you drop the Stepford wife thing.'

She looks at me, the circles under her eyes making her look like a scared little kid. 'Really?' she asks.

'Yes. Trust me. I'm your big sister,' I say, hugging her. 'Now you need to get some sleep. The bed's all made in the spare room. If Emma's hungry tonight, I'll feed her. She took the bottle just great. Okay?'

She starts to say something . . . advice, no doubt . . . then reconsiders. 'Okay. Thanks, Lucy.' She stands up and heads for the guest room. 'Luce?' she says, her voice tentative. 'I'm sorry I said I was afraid to be like you. You know what I meant, right?'

'Sure, honey,' I assure her. 'Now go to sleep.'

I check on Emma once more . . . she's sleeping, her eyelids twitching, her little mouth working as if she's blowing kisses in her sleep. I touch her head with one finger.

You'll make a great mom, Ethan said tonight. For a second, I imagine going upstairs to report on Corinne, to kiss him good-night before coming back down to watch over Emma. To thank him for once again coming to the rescue. Maybe even to tell him that I think he's a great father.

But I don't. Instead I give Emma one more kiss, then slip into the living room and watch my wedding DVD with the sound off.

CHAPTER TWENTY

'Maybe you'd like the cheese danish, Mr. Dombrowski?' I suggest.

It's been a long day. Corinne came in for lunch so Emma could be worshipped. Chris had said he wanted to go away for the weekend, do a little camping in the Adirondacks, and Corinne needed some reassurance on the odds of his being eaten by a bear or falling off a mountain. I complied dutifully, thinking his odds of a car accident were a lot greater than grizzly attack but knowing to keep my mouth shut.

Mr. Dombrowski weighs my words with considerable gravity, then nods thoughtfully. 'I think I'd enjoy that, dear,' he says. 'Thank you.'

I glance at the clock . . . it's three-thirty. 'I'd love to have a cup of tea if you have the time, Mr. D.,' I suggest.

His solemn face lights up. 'That would be lovely,' he says. 'Maybe we could take a little walk and get something at the place down the street.'

I wince. 'Starbucks?'

'Yes. It's quite the rage, I understand. The coffee culture.'

'Sure,' I concede. After all, this will be a big deal for Mr. Dombrowski . . . an outing with another human. Any petty feelings I have toward Doral-Anne hardly measure up against that.

'I'll be back in a while,' I call to my aunts. 'Mr. Dombrowski and I are going out for a coffee.'

'How sweet,' coos Rose. 'Have fun!' As I take off my apron, she darts to my side. 'See if he's interested in a date, Lucy. I wouldn't mind an older man.'

I smile. 'Okay, Rose. Want anything from Starbucks?'

'Oh, no,' she says, glancing at the clock. 'It's almost happy hour.'

Right. It's Friday. Taking Mr. D.'s arm, I

push open the door and remind myself to go slowly. We shuffle down the street, a few leaves drifting down around us. Mr. Dombrowski is dressed in a tweed jacket and a cap.

'You look rather dashing, Mr. D.' I smile.

'I bought this jacket when my son graduated from college,' he says, chuckling. 'And this hat . . . my wife bought it for me when we were in Ireland.'

'She had wonderful taste,' I say, pushing open the door to Starbucks. It's the same as they all are . . . muted colors, progressive rock drifting from speakers, a few plants here and there. Three teenagers sit at one table near the window . . . plenty of hair tossing and exclaiming going on over there and I smile, the wise older woman. *Of course we notice you,* I think. *You're beautiful and bright and young. Don't try so hard.*

'What are you doing here?'

Ah, my nemesis. 'Hi, Doral-Anne,' I say pleasantly. 'Mr. Dombrowski and I were in the mood for a little treat, right, Mr. D. ?'

She glances at the ancient man on my arm. 'Your new boyfriend, Lucy?' she sneers.

As ever, I'm stunned by her meanness. 'I should be so lucky,' I say clearly.

Mr. D. smiles and squints at the menu. 'What's in an Americano?' he asks.

'Espresso and water,' Doral-Anne grunts.

'I think I'll have the salted caramel hot
283

chocolate, Mr. D. What do you think?'

'Sounds mysterious and delicious,' Mr. Dombrowski agrees. 'I'll have the same.'

'Tall, grande, venti or short?' Doral-Anne asks.

'Small, please,' I answer for the sheer pleasure of rebelling against the ridiculous lingo.

'Small for me as well,' my little old buddy seconds.

'Nonfat, two percent, whole or soy?'

'What did she say?' Mr. D. asks.

'She asked what kind of milk we'd like,' I inform him, smiling. 'How about two percent?'

'I guess I don't really care,' he murmurs. 'I'm ninety-seven years old, after all.'

'Make that whole then, Doral-Anne,' I tell her, relishing the fact that she absolutely hates waiting on me. 'You only live once, right?'

'Whipped cream?' she bites out.

'Absolutely,' I answer. Mr. D. nods.

'This is gonna take a few minutes,' she mutters as we stand expectantly. 'You can wait over there.'

'Let's sit down instead, Mr. D.,' I suggest and am instantly rewarded with another scowl from Doral-Anne.

When we've taken a seat far away from the teenagers, Mr. D. looks around happily. 'This is a lovely place,' he pronounces. 'Very pleasant. Thank you, Lucy.'

284

'My pleasure,' I say sincerely.

'How are you these days?' he asks. 'Your aunts told me you're dating again.'

'Well, I guess I am,' I admit. From behind the counter comes the phlegmy sound of the cappuccino machine.

'Have you found someone nice?' Mr. D. asks.

'Um, yes. I have.' I hesitate. 'I'm just not sure it's going to work.' I bite my lip. What the heck? Mr. D. would understand. The cappuccino machine gurgles its last few breaths. 'I'm afraid I'll always compare him to my first husband and—'

'And God knows he was such a prince,' Doral-Anne says loudly.

Once again, I'm stunned by her rudeness, but my companion doesn't seem to have heard her. 'And what, dear?'

I lower my voice but try to enunciate so he can hear me. 'I'll never love him the way I loved Jimmy.'

Mr. Dombrowski nods sadly. 'I suppose that's a natural fear,' he says.

'Did you ever think about dating again, Mr. D. ?' I ask.

He smiles. 'I don't think there are a lot of women out there who'd like to date me, Lucy.'

'My aunt Rose would,' I say, grinning.

He gives a startled laugh. 'Is that right? How flattering. She's a lovely woman, that Rose.'

285

'She really is,' I agree.

'Your order is ready, Lang!' Doral-Anne barks.

'That girl is rather rude, isn't she?' Mr. D. comments, frowning over at our barista.

'She really is,' I say again.

*　　*　　*

I see Mr. D. to his door, my heart light. The knowledge that forty-five minutes of my time could make someone happy is heady stuff, and I'm humming as I go back to the bakery, rather buzzed with lack of sleep and a surplus of sugar. My God, that hot chocolate was unbelievable. No wonder people flock to the dang place.

A not-unpleasant nervousness shoots through my legs as I open the back door. Ethan's here, measuring out vodka. 'Hi,' I say.

'Hey, Luce,' Ethan says. 'Dirty martinis today. Want one?'

My face feels hot, and Ethan's mouth pulls up on one side in a knowing grin.

'Sure,' I say. 'Thank you.'

'My pleasure,' he says, and my stomach squeezes in that uncomfortable, wonderful way.

'Ethan,' Iris says, swirling her drink appreciatively before taking a sip, 'Lucy must've told you that she wants another husband. Do you know anyone?'

He looks up at me for a moment—*You haven't told them yet?*—then pours some olive brine into the martini shaker. 'Can't say that I do,' he murmurs.

'Iris,' I say. 'Can you please—'

'Ethan, dear,' Rose begins, her nose glowing with alcohol consumption. I'll have to make sure she's not driving. 'Does it bother you, Lucy leaving Jimmy's memory behind?'

'No,' Ethan says, shaking the metal cylinder, then pouring the martini into a waiting glass. 'I think Lucy should be happy. Jimmy would want her to move on.' He looks at me steadily. This would be an opportune time to tell my aunts and mother that Ethan and I are together . . .

'I don't know,' Iris says. 'I wonder what Pete would say if *I* decided to date again. He always was jealous. Rose, remember the Knights of Columbus dance, when Tom O'Reilly cut in, and Pete punched him in the nose? Oh, I have to admit, that made me feel like the most beautiful woman in the world!'

'Violence does that for some people,' I murmur, taking a slug of my drink, then wincing.

Rose tries to take another sip of her martini, then frowns as she finds her glass empty. Ethan pours her another. 'What about you, Daisy?' she asks. 'Do you think Robbie would've minded?'

Mom taps a perfectly manicured finger on

287

the wooden countertop. 'I don't care if he'd mind or not. He was the love of my life, and I'm just not interested in dating or getting married again. He was enough to last me a lifetime.' She glances at me. 'But everyone's different.'

I sneak a peek at Ethan, whose mouth is tight. Well. He knows how the Black Widows are. And he said he'd be patient. He sees me looking, and I give him a little smile. A muscle under his eye twitches, but he smiles back.

'I'd get married again if I didn't have to have sex,' Iris muses in her booming voice. 'I don't want to have sex with an old man.'

'And yet here I stand, young, healthy, heterosexual and ignored,' Ethan says, bouncing a devilish eyebrow, and as usual, he gets a round of hoots and giggles from his biggest fans.

Iris cuffs him fondly. 'Don't tempt me, young man,' she says.

'If only I were twenty years younger, Ethan,' Rose giggles.

'I love older women—you should know that by now.' He kisses her cheek, slings an arm around her shoulders—she's about a foot shorter than he is—then turns to me.

'Lucy, would you like to come up for dinner tonight?' Ethan asks, a tad abruptly, I think.

'Um . . . well, uh, sure,' I stammer. 'That sounds nice, Eth. I'll bring dessert.'

'Sounds great.' He packs up his bartending

kit, then kisses each of the Black Widows in turn. 'Good night, you Hungarian beauties,' he says.

'Good night, Ethan,' they chorus.

We all four watch him go out the back.

'Maybe you could marry Ethan, Lucy,' Rose suggests.

'Nonsense!' Iris immediately trumpets. 'It's against the law.'

'Excuse me?' I blurt. 'It's not against any law. But actually—'

'Well, God's law,' Iris interrupts. 'I was watching *The Tudors* on Showtime last night,' she adds, as if that explains everything.

'You get Showtime?' my mom asks. 'It's so dirty.'

'I know!' Iris agrees happily. 'They showed Anne Boleyn's *mellbimbók,* can you believe it?'

'I'm pretty sure it's not against the law, God's or anybody's,' I say mildly.

'Well, Henry VIII thought it was, Miss Smarty-Pants,' Iris says. 'That's why he divorced Catherine the Great.'

'He was a pig, for one, and two, it was Catherine of Aragon,' I correct.

'She's so grouchy these days, Daisy,' Rose chides, as if it's my mother's fault.

'I know,' Mom agrees, ignoring my sigh. 'What else do you watch on Showtime?'

'There's a show called *Dexter,*' Rose breathes. 'Iris made me watch it. Terrifying!'

Once again, I let the opportunity to say something about Ethan and me pass by, untouched. They barely notice as I pack up my stuff and head for home.

*　　　*　　　*

Dinner at Ethan's is fine. Delicious, really . . . eggplant parm, an old favorite of mine. Salad. Red wine. A loaf of Italian, made by my own two hands this very day, served with a gorgeous garlic- and pepper-infused olive oil that I'm tempted to drink. Ethan makes short work of the blueberry crisp I made . . . such a simple, pleasing dessert. From the looks of it, anyway, and the way the aroma filled the kitchen.

'What's the secret ingredient?' Ethan asks, scraping up the last bit of his second enormous helping. The boy can eat.

'I threw some cranberries in. And I ground the nutmeg myself,' I add, pleased that he noticed something special.

'Nice,' he says.

Ethan is trying hard to be normal, but like most liars or poker players, he has a tell, and the little muscle below his eye jumps with regularity. He tells me about a book Nicky and he wrote—well, Nicky dictated and Ethan typed—and I laugh as Ethan describes the many sword fights and severed limbs that inspire my nephew.

We manage to load the dishwasher under our *everything is fine* pretense. It's when we sit down in the living room that things get really itchy. Ethan pours us each a second glass of wine, which, on top of the few sips of martini that I could manage, has gone to my head . . . not a bad thing, considering how tense I am.

'So, Lucy,' he says, sitting in the chair adjacent to the couch, where I'm clutching a pillow to my stomach and trying to look relaxed.

'Yes, Ethan,' I answer.

He looks at his hands, which are loosely clasped in front of him, then up at me. 'Luce, I think we should try to move things forward a little.'

I swallow my mouthful of wine hard and fast, wincing at the slight burn. 'Um . . . do you mean sex?'

'Not necessarily,' he says, looking at his hands again. The muscle jumps, and I resist the urge to press my fingers to that spot and ease his worry. Instead I sit tight and listen as he continues. 'Obviously I noticed that you haven't told your aunts and mother about us. Or Corinne. Or my parents, given that they asked me again today when I'm going to make an honest woman out of Parker.' He looks at me, an eyebrow bouncing up. 'So.'

'Right,' I say, shifting on the leather sofa. 'Well, um, I guess I'm still . . . wary. That things won't work out.'

'I think we need to try something before we decide if things are going to work or not, honey.'

Ethan has called me honey for years and years, but tonight, the word lodges in my heart like an arrow. His eyes are gentle, his hands still.

'What do you want to try?' I whisper, then clear my throat.

He smiles, his face transforming from serious to wicked in a heartbeat. 'Well, I *am* a guy, so sex is always welcome.' His laugh is warm and naughty, and I feel it in my stomach. Blushing, I clutch the pillow a little tighter.

'But anything would be okay, Lucy. Just telling people we're together. Or going out in public together.'

'We did go out together in public,' I say. 'To Lenny's.'

'Right. But you didn't let me hold your hand or kiss you good-night, either.'

I take a deep breath, nodding. 'I'm sorry,' I say.

'You don't have to be sorry, Luce.' He gets up from his chair and sits next to me, putting his arm around my shoulders. I rest my head on his shoulder, grateful that I don't have to see his face, welcoming the physical comfort he's always given me. 'I know it's scary,' he murmurs, his breath warm against my hair. 'But if you didn't want anything from me,

Lucy, I don't think you'd kiss me the way you do.'

'Good point,' I say, swallowing. I wish I could tell him the truth—that if I didn't love him enough—the way I loved Jimmy—he'd end up hating me, and that's something I couldn't bear. 'I just don't know how to . . . I'm not sure how to be anymore, Ethan,' I whisper, a tear sneaking out of the corner of my eye. 'But you're right. I do . . . feel things for you. It's just that I'm a mess, too.'

He pulls back to smile down at me. 'I know,' he says gently, wiping the tear off my cheek. 'I do know.'

'That I'm a mess?'

'Absolutely,' he agrees.

Then he kisses me, and as always, his wonderful, smiling mouth makes me forget my worries. When his hand slips under my shirt, a little moan sneaks out of my throat. Ethan would never do anything that would hurt me. I know this. Of course I do.

So when he stands up and asks me to come to bed with him, I go.

But here's the thing.

Sex with Ethan has always been a guilty, delicious pleasure, sometimes urgent, always smokin'. My college roomie had diabetes, and once in a while, when her blood sugar was falling, she'd come crashing into our room, wrench open the emergency jar of Nutella and inhale a big spoonful, then collapse gratefully onto the bed. That's what Ethan was to me. My emergency Nutella.

But now things are different. The hedonistic pleasure is gone, dang it. It's not that I'm lying there like a Regency virgin, mind you . . . it's that Expectations Are High. And I can't seem to shut off my brain. *Ethan unbuttons Lucy's shirt, kissing the exposed skin. He really does have the best mouth, doesn't he, ladies and gentlemen? Nice effect, with the bristly tickle of his beard.*

'So do you have a special razor or something?' I ask aloud.

He pulls back to look at me. 'What?'

'Never mind. It's just . . . never mind.'

He raises an eyebrow, then kisses the corner of my mouth. I sigh, running my fingers through the cool silkiness of his hair. I wonder what kind of shampoo he uses, then roll my eyes, wishing I could just be quiet and enjoy.

Folks, isn't it nice that Ethan takes his time undressing Lucy, knowing that she's about ready to jump out of her skin and run screaming back to her cat?

'Relax,' Ethan mutters against the lace of my bra. Not one of the La Perla confections I blew a ridiculous amount of money on . . . just a little thing I got at Target, nothing special, though it does have cute stripes on the—oh, for God's sake! Listen to me!

'Eth, could you move just a little? You're on my hair.' It used to be that Ethan could take me against the wall, and I wouldn't have noticed a crowd of fifty thousand. At the memory of the wall, I sink a little more into the bed. Oh, yes, the wall. Now *that* was hot.

'Better?' Ethan asks, shifting his weight.

'Perfect,' I say.

He smiles, then kisses my neck as he unhooks my bra. He's good at this. *Ethan is an expert at undressing women. He's certainly undressed Lucy quite a few times, hasn't he, folks?* I imagine applause from our studio audience. From downstairs, I can hear Fat Mikey start to yowl. *Merrrrrooooow! Merrrooow!* Did I feed him? Can't he be quiet for, I don't know, twenty more minutes so I can get this done? And where's Corinne? She said she might spend another night with me, not wanting to be at her place without Christopher. Will she feed Fat Mikey? Is she nursing?

I remind myself that I'm partially naked— actually, yes, I'm feeling it now, and I slide my hand up Ethan's gorgeous back, relishing the smooth skin at his neck, the soft, fine hair that always sticks up in the back of his head.

'Ouch,' Ethan mutters. 'Honey, your bracelet's caught.'

'Sorry,' I say. Sure enough, the gold chain has tangled in Ethan's hair. Poor guy. I turn my wrist, and Ethan yelps as he loses a few strands. 'Sorry,' I say again, feeling the giggles coming on. I clamp my lips together, shoot, just when he's kissing me . . . okay, here it comes, sloshing over the edge, and I can't help it, I start laughing. Hard. Wheezing, my features contorting in helpless hilarity. Grabbing a pillow, I clamp it over my face. *Stop, Lucy, this is really inappropriate, how much can the guy take?* I snort like a pig, which makes me laugh harder and snort again. Tears leak out of my eyes as I shake with near hysteria and slap the mattress, trying to stop.

'I take it we're not quite ready for sex,' Ethan says dryly.

'Sorry,' I wheeze, another gale sending me into convulsions of laughter.

'You're not sorry,' he says, rolling off me. But there's a smile in his voice, and he grabs the pillow, looks at my laughing face, grins and shoves the pillow back with considerable force.

'I'm taking a cold shower, woman,' he says, getting off the bed. 'I hope you feel guilty as sin.'

CHAPTER TWENTY-ONE

'And there we have Grayhurst, the lovely home of the Welles family,' Captain Bob says, suppressing a belch. He's pinker than usual today, making me glad I'm the one steering past Parker's dock. 'The house was built in

1904 as a gift to Lancaster Welles's second wife, who found her husband in the sack with a maid. She would be the first in a long line of wives who got a home as a pay-off for Lancaster's infidelity,' Captain Bob continues, taking a pull from his doctored up coffee. This, at least, is the correct version of the past.

'It's gorgeous,' says a lady from Nebraska. Her sweatshirt sports a Siamese kitten with sequined green eyes. The rest of the charter is similarly dressed . . . one lady is clad all in pink sweats, looking like she fell into a vat of Pepto-Bismol. Another wears elastic-waisted clam diggers and a sweatshirt proclaiming her World's Best Gramma. My mother would die if she saw them. Or murder them as a group.

'Oh, look,' Pepto-Bismol cries. 'A rich person!'

Captain Bob, who has eyes sharper than an eagle's no matter how many ounces of alcohol he's consumed, nods. 'That would be Lancaster's great-granddaughter, the lovely Parker Welles,' Captain Bob comments.

Sure enough, Parker, Nicky and Ethan are out on the lawn for a picturesque family romp. The Nebraskans leap to the side of the boat to snap photos of the three against the impressive backdrop of the back patio, which is about as big as a football field and bordered with animal-shaped topiary bushes. I give three short blasts from the horn. Nicky runs to the edge of the patio and waves, as do

297

Parker and Ethan. I think, as I so often do, what a good-looking couple they make, Ethan's dark hair and nice way of dressing a good match for Parker's stylish looks and blond hair.

When this tour ends, I'm heading over to Grayhurst myself for a little family dinner. Ethan, Parker, their son and me. *One of these things is not like the other,* I mentally sing. *One of these things just doesn't belong.*

'Beautiful ladies, if you'll turn your attention to that cluster of rock out there,' Captain Bob says, 'you'll see the site of Mackerly's famed pirate attack of 1868. Many were the maids who lost their hearts—and their virtue—to Captain Jack Sparrow in the weeks that ensued.'

I roll my eyes, but apparently, the Nebraskan ladies haven't seen *Pirates of the Caribbean,* because they sigh with wide-eyed wonder. Bob gives me a wink, and I grin and shake my head.

An hour later, I'm standing in the wine cellar of Grayhurst, shivering.

'What looks good to you?' Parker asks.

'Anything not too expensive,' I answer, imagining her father discovering his prize bottle of Château Lafite (reportedly once owned by Thomas Jefferson) missing, swilled by the Hungarian baker who is his daughter's friend. From upstairs, we can hear the muffled thump of Ethan and Nick, who are engaged in

298

a rowdy game of *Star Wars*. 'Release your anger and feel the power of the Dark Side!' Ethan booms, causing Nicky to burst into peals of laughter.

'Fruity? Dry? Oaken undertones with a hint of vanilla and a peachy-mango finish?' Parker asks, grinning.

'Um, gosh,' I say.

My friend, well aware of my discomfort around such displays of her wealth, surveys the rows and rows of bottles, the dim light making them gleam. 'Well, here. This one only sells for about a hundred bucks a bottle,' she says, pretending to ignore my grimace, and studies the label. 'So? How are things going with Ethan?' she asks, not looking up.

'Oh, you know. Not . . . not bad.'

'That sounds discouraging,' she says. 'What's wrong?'

I glance over at the stairs. 'Nothing. We're trying. It's a little weird.'

She just looks at me, sighs with exaggerated patience. 'Are you guys sleeping together again?' she asks.

'Um . . . not exactly,' I mutter, darting a glance around the wine cellar. No one to rescue me from this conversation down here, unless there's a ghost or two.

'Why not?'

'I don't know,' I admit. 'It's like our mojo is gone or something.'

Following my giggle fest the other night, I'd

fled back to my apartment after an appropriate amount of apology time. Then last night, we'd gone to see the latest Matt Damon explosion flick in South Kingstown. When he walked me to my door, Ethan had kissed me. Nicely. Very nicely. So nicely, so wonderfully, that perfect mouth, the scrape of his beard, his body so warm and close, and I'd felt myself slipping into that vortex where all I could think of was what Ethan was doing and how it felt.

Then I'd heard Corinne inside, and I'd seized on the excuse. 'I'd better go,' I whispered against his mouth. 'Corinne . . . she and Chris still haven't worked things out.'

He hesitated for a second, and my toes clenched. 'Okay,' he finally said, but I could see the disappointment in his eyes.

'So why aren't things working?' Parker asks. I get the impression I don't get to leave the cellar until she's gotten her answers, and I glance around, half expecting to see Fortunato, the guy who was walled up in that creepy Edgar Allen Poe story. *Un*fortunato, if you ask me, left to die behind the bricks.

'It's just . . . a little awkward,' I answer. 'Can we go upstairs?'

Like Ethan, she has mastered the art of the disappointed gaze. They must teach it in parenting school. 'Sure,' she says, then turns on her heel and leads the way past the racks of red, the undiluted barrels of single malt scotch, the tasting room where Mr. Welles enjoys showing off to his friends on the rare occasions he returns to Rhode Island.

We head up the frigid stone stairs, almost in the clear, when Parker stops. 'You should give him a chance, Lucy,' she says.

'I *am* giving him a chance,' I return. 'I am, Parker.'

'A real chance. Not just a token.'

'Well, you know, I'm trying. But maybe I'm just not ready.'

'It's been almost six years, Lucy,' she reminds me. 'Don't you think you *should* be ready by now?'

My blood pressure surges. Folks, unless you've walked the walk, never tell a widow it's time she moved on. Never before has Parker crossed the line, but she sure did just now.

'I don't need you to tell me how long it's been since my husband died, okay?' I bite out. 'You've never been widowed, and I hope you never are, Parker, but given that you have no idea what it's like, you might want to keep your advice to yourself.'

She sighs. 'I'm just saying—'

'And it's ironic that you're so keen on me being with Ethan,' I say, a decided edge to my voice now, 'since you passed on him first. Maybe *you* should be the one sleeping with him.'

And because my luck just bites, that's when Ethan opens the door, his son on his shoulders. From the expression on his face, I know he heard me.

*　　　*　　　*

Thank goodness Ethan and I came separately, I think a couple of eons later, watching him get on his motorcycle. His helmet is on the back of the bike. He doesn't put it on.

'Your helmet!' I yell as he starts up the engine. Mercifully his motorcycle is a BMW with a quietly purring engine, not one of those deafening midlife crisis Harleys.

Ethan glances at me, then reaches back for the helmet and puts it on. He gently revs the engine and heads down the long gravel driveway to the road.

Dinner was—what's the word I'm looking for?—a nightmare. Ethan barely spoke to me, which was completely understandable. Parker, perhaps trying to apologize for forcing the conversation in the wine cellar, did her best to be *über*nice and funny, telling us about her latest manuscript (*The Holy Rollers and the Crippled Puppy*). Ethan didn't talk a lot. At least Nicky was there to distract his father, but as soon as the boy was tucked in, requesting a multiple kisses and songs from each of the three adults present, Ethan headed out.

'Really fucked that up, didn't you?' Parker says mildly from behind me.

I turn and look at her. 'See, I was thinking

302

this was your fault.'

She grins. 'Time to kiss and make up, I guess. Go. Get out of here. Rock his world. You hurt him, he's wounded, you love that crap. Go.'

'I don't love hurting Ethan!' I protest. 'Jeez, that's the last thing I want.'

'Mmm,' she murmurs. 'Yet you've been hurting him for years.'

'I have not! Crikey, Parker, you're a pain in the butt, you know that?' I take a huffy breath. 'Please thank your chef for dinner, thank your dad for the wine. And thank you, Parker, for your lovely hospitality.'

'*Ciao.*' She laughs.

With a sigh, I climb into my faithful little Mazda and head down the road. Ethan is not in sight, and as if by rote, I scan the side of the road for his twisted body every ten yards or so. His helmet cracked, unable to protect him. His unmoving, broken legs, pointing in impossible directions. Fun hobby, really.

Ethan's motorcycle is parked in its usual spot when I get home, and my shoulders lower a notch. He's not dead. Not hurt. Just *wounded*, as Parker said. I'll just drop in to feed Fat Mikey, then go upstairs and make things right with Ethan.

But when I open the door, I see my sister, sniffling as she nurses Emma. My TV is on—dang. Corinne's watching my wedding DVD. It's the part when Jimmy's dancing with his mom. Obviously I'd had to forego the father-daughter dance, but Jimmy danced with his mom to the tune of the sappy tear-fest that was Celine Dion's 'Because You Loved Me.' Not a dry eye in the house, ladies and gentlemen. Tall, strong Jimmy towered over the happily sobbing Marie. Despite her low center of gravity and rather rotund figure, Jimmy had dipped her at the end, making her scream a little, which nicely undercut the wonderfully saccharine lyrics.

'Hi,' I say to my sister.

'I don't know how you can even get out of bed,' she sobs.

'Um ... well. How are you?'

'Christopher hasn't called,' she says, tears raining down on Emma's soft head. She pops the baby off the left breast and shifts her into burp position.

'I'm sorry,' I say. 'Anything I can do?' Other than stare at her naked, enormous boob, that is. Gosh, is that nipple still cracked? Jeepers.

'No,' she answers. 'You've been great.' Fat Mikey puts his front paws against her knees, and she smiles. 'Animals sense when you're sad,' she says, and I opt not to correct her by saying that Fat Mikey is probably about to make a move on Emma's dinner if Corinne doesn't cover up soon. Instead I pick up my cat and pet him, earning a disgruntled meow for interrupting his plans to nurse. He startles as my niece barks out a burp that would put

304

the Fenway Faithful to shame.

My door opens. 'Corinne?'

We both turn away from the TV. Christopher stands uncertainly in the doorway, looking rather awful. Cory gets up, seemingly unaware that her right breast is still completely uncovered, bobbing there like the marker buoy at the head of the channel.

'Chris!' she breathes. 'How are you?' Emma makes a little grunting sound and starts rooting around on Corinne's neck, looking for her next round.

Christopher holds out a bouquet of red roses. A good sign, I think with a little smile. 'I'm an idiot,' he says. 'Oh, Corinne, I love you. I do, and I'm so sorry I never said anything about how I was feeling.'

'No, baby, I'm the one who's sorry,' my sister whispers, her eyes spilling tears. 'I just want you to be okay. I want to be with you for the rest of my life. I don't want to end up like Mom or Lucy.'

I roll my eyes. 'Why don't I take Emma and go into the kitchen?' I suggest, but they're already hugging, around both Emma and the breast.

'You're the love of my life, Corinne,' Chris whispers, and a voyeuristic lump rises in my throat. 'But, honey, you're going to have to back off and just trust in the universe that we're going to have a long, long time together.'

'I love you, too,' she weeps. 'I never meant to send you to the hospital.' Fat Mikey once again puts his paws against her leg, sniffing the air.

Ten minutes later, Corinne hugs me, her boob finally covered. 'Thank you for everything,' she whispers.

'Oh, sure,' I say, hugging her back. 'Let him eat bacon once in a while. It makes life happier.'

'I'll try,' she says.

'Thank you, Lucy,' Christopher says, adjusting his daughter's hat.

'No problem,' I say, and with that, they're gone, lugging about a thousand dollars' worth of baby gear down the hall. In another second, I hear the ding that marks the elevator's arrival, and then it's completely quiet, except for the wedding video, which now shows everyone about to sit down for dinner. There's Ethan, looking considerably younger without his beard, talking to the DJ as the guy apparently explains how to use the mic for the best man speech.

I turn it off. Sigh deeply. Wonder what to do about Ethan Mirabelli.

For one tiny second, I have the urge to call Jimmy, so strong that my hand twitches as I almost reach for the phone. For just that flash, I can't believe I haven't called him already, since he's the only one who would understand how terrifying it is to be where I am.

Fat Mikey butts his head against my shoe. I look down gratefully, and there, on the carpet, is a dime.

My breath catches. I haven't found a dime in a while. A couple of years, in fact. With fingers that shake just a little, I pick it up and examine it. A perfectly ordinary dime that could have, of course, dropped from a pocket or a purse or Corinne's gigantic diaper bag.

Or not.

Back when Jimmy first died, it took me a while to notice the strange phenomenon of the dimes, but once I caught on, I started keeping them in a jar in my bedroom. I go there now and lean on the bureau, looking at them.

I don't know if they're from Jimmy or not, but it seems a stretch to think that I formed a habit of dropping rogue dimes. Not nickels, not quarters, not pennies . . . just dimes. I have no idea what they might signify, but I know that I believe—and want to continue believing—that they're a sign that Jimmy's spirit is still involved in my life.

I give the dime a kiss, then drop it in the jar with its eleven brothers and sisters. A minute later, I'm knocking on Ethan's door, not quite sure what I plan to say.

He answers, not opening the door all the way or standing aside to let me in.

'Ethan, I'm so sorry for what I said,' I blurt.

He sighs, looks at the floor and folds his

307

arms, Italian sign language for *We got a situation here.*

'Take me sailing tomorrow,' I say, surprising myself completely. And Ethan, too, it appears, since his head jerks up and his eyebrows raise. 'Let's get out of town for the day.'

'Really?' he asks, his eyes questioning. And hopeful. You've been hurting him for years, Parker said. That can't be true, but my throat still tightens under the familiar clamp of tears.

'Really,' I answer thickly.

'Okay,' he says, as I knew he would.

Still, he doesn't exactly look overjoyed that I'm proposing this little venture, so I stand on tiptoe and give him a quick kiss on the cheek. 'I'm so sorry,' I whisper. 'I didn't mean it the way it sounded.'

'It's all right,' he says, making me feel worse.

'Ethan, it's not all right. If we're going to have a real relationship, you have to let yourself be mad at me,' I say. 'Especially when I'm a jerk.'

'I'm fairly helpless where you're concerned, Lucy,' he says quietly.

That one takes my breath away. 'Well, stand up for yourself, laddie,' I say after a minute, my voice squeaking a little.

He looks at me, his arms still folded. 'Fine. You're the one I want to be with, Lucy. Not Parker. Don't try to get us together anymore.'

308

'Okay, fine, I do understand, and I am sorry.' I hesitate, then continue. 'It's just that, you know, when you guys were—'

'Lucy. Shut up.'

I obey. 'Sorry.'

His smile starts at his eyes, like a candle being lit on a dark night, and sure enough, the corner of his mouth curls up. 'Ten o'clock at the marina?' he suggests.

'Sounds great. I'll bring lunch, okay?'

'Okay.'

We stand there another second or two, just looking at each other. 'Well, good night, then,' I say a trifle awkwardly.

'Good night,' he echoes. But he stays in the doorway, looking at the floor, until I turn the corner.

CHAPTER TWENTY-TWO

There's a brisk wind the next day, and the boats bob on their moorings, the sounds of creaking wood and slapping water mixing with the cries of gulls as I approach the *Marie*, a sixteen-foot wooden sloop, its dark green hull topped with a stripe of maroon, the deck a caramel gold. The sails are tightly rolled, and the wind sings through the lines.

Ethan's head pops out of the small cabin. 'Hi,' he says, grinning.

'Ahoy,' I answer, feeling oddly shy.

His smile grows, and he steps out and offers me a hand. 'Welcome aboard.'

I've never been on Ethan's boat. He bought it when Jimmy and I had been married a couple of months, and I now recall that there'd been a little fraternal envy going on. Jimmy, who didn't sail, had never sailed and didn't much like being on the water, had stated that he, too, would have a boat someday. Marie had been quite charmed when Ethan named the boat for her and talked of it constantly at the restaurant. It was one of the few times, I imagine, that Jimmy had ever been shown up by his younger brother.

But although Ethan has invited me to go out many times, I've never said yes, and stepping onto the boat, which tilts precariously, that decision seems like a wise one now. The *Marie* is much less sturdy than Captain Bob's forty-foot rock of stability, and sits quite low in the water.

'Here's our lunch,' I say, handing Ethan the little cooler. Inside are two giant sandwiches on my best pumpernickel rye . . . turkey, avocado, bacon and mayonnaise flavored with dill and chives. Two little bags of Cape Cod potato chips. Four packets of Del's Lemonade mix. And a slab of dark chocolate layer cake with a seemingly sinful hazelnut-cappuccino frosting half an inch thick, which I'd made last night.

'Thanks,' Ethan says.

'Can I peek inside?' I ask.

'Sure,' he says, and I do. The cabin is snug and adorable . . . porthole windows where the ceiling curves up, miniature cabinets closed with brass fasteners. There's a table, a sink and a small door leading, I assume, to the head. A couch lines one wall.

'Do you ever go out overnight on this thing?' I call as Ethan unties the straps around the rolled-up sails.

'I haven't lately, but I used to,' he says. 'The couch pulls out into a bed. But since Nicky's been in the world, no.'

'Good,' I say. Ethan indulges in far too many life-threatening hobbies. He raises an eyebrow but doesn't comment.

A minute later, we're heading away from the dock into the channel. Ethan tells me to sit and raises the first sail. The wind fills it immediately, and the boat leaps forward.

'Yikes,' I laugh.

He grins. 'She's a fast little boat,' he states proudly. He holds the tiller loosely, the wind ruffling his hair, looking like an ad for the idle rich in his thick Irish fisherman's sweater, faded jeans and Top-Siders.

Ethan waves as we pass other boaters, occasionally tacking to give way. White sails dot the horizon, and seagulls wheel and turn overhead.

'Where are we headed?' I ask, gripping a cleat as we bounce over the wake of a motorboat.

'Where would you like to go?' he asks.

'Nowhere,' I answer. 'I just like being out here with you.' My face grows hot. It's not easy saying those words, but I'm rewarded with a smile from my captain.

For a while, we just sail out toward Point Judith, not too far off the coast, the slapping waves and wind a happy melody. The sun grows warmer, and I take off my sweatshirt. My heart thumps erratically, which has nothing to do with being in open water—I'm giving Ethan a chance. A real chance, not a token. Giving myself one, too, and it terrifies me. My hands tingle from time to time, the pebble seems firmly lodged in my throat. I look over at Ethan, who smiles. I smile back, and after a second, it becomes genuine.

We don't talk much, and eventually, I stop envisioning his death (which, I imagine, would come from a rogue wave that tosses us from the boat into the cold Atlantic, where we'd bob helplessly until sharks came and feasted on Ethan's beautiful olive flesh as I screamed helplessly). Okay, so maybe I can't exactly stop, but my shoulders relax a little, and my heart rate seems to slow.

Somewhere off Point Judith, Ethan turns the boat into the wind and drops the sails, where they flap companionably. The boat

312

bobs gently on the waves. 'You hungry?' he asks. 'I'm starving.'

'Sure,' I say, getting up to retrieve our lunch.

There are plates and cups in the cupboard. I make up two glasses of Del's and unwrap the sandwiches. Ethan spreads a blanket on the deck. The wind has conveniently died down, and I pass the plates to him, then join him on deck, the shy feeling back.

'This is gorgeous,' he says, picking up a sandwich and surveying it.

'Thanks,' I say, flexing my hands.

'You okay?' he asks.

'Yup,' I answer, swallowing. Then I decide to be honest. 'I'm feeling a little nervous,' I admit.

'Afraid you'll fall in?' he says with a grin.

'No.' I don't say anymore, just look at him steadily, my hands buzzing.

He tilts his head, the wind stirring his hair. 'It's just me, Lucy,' he says gently.

'That's the point.' I smile. 'I'll get over it. Don't worry. This is great. Let's talk about something else.'

He grins. 'Sure.'

'How's your job these days?' I take a bite of the sandwich. It's awfully good, I have to admit.

'It's okay,' he says. 'I don't love it.' He pulls his sweater over his head, revealing a white cotton oxford, a sharp contrast to his tanned

313

skin.

'Why are you doing it, then?' I ask.

He doesn't answer right away, just takes another bite and looks off to the horizon. 'I want to be near Nicky,' he says eventually. 'And the money's really good. Which makes me a soulless corporate monster, according to my dad.' He grins. 'But it's nice to be able to give Nicky's savings account a big check each month.'

'He doesn't need it, you know,' I say, then bite my tongue. Parker once told me that upon his birth, Nicky automatically inherited ten million dollars from the family trust.

'I know,' Ethan says. 'But I want to give something anyway. Even if it's nothing compared to what Parker's family has.'

'Well, the best thing you give him is you,' I say, earning another smile. My stomach flips, and my cheeks warm yet again. 'And Ethan, you shouldn't be in a job you don't like.'

'Well, there is the torture-the-parents benefit. We can't rule that out,' he replies, his voice light.

'Torturing your parents can't feel good,' I say.

He takes a pull of his lemonade. 'It feels okay,' he says evenly. 'After all, they've tortured me a fair bit over the years, too.'

'How?' I ask.

He considers me before answering. 'Compared with St. Jimmy, I'll always be the

314

next best thing.'

I swallow hard. 'I'm sure that's not true, Ethan,' I say. 'You have to stop thinking that, because it's just not true.'

He takes another bite of sandwich. 'Well. You might be right. You talk to them more than I do.' He pauses. 'Have you said anything to them about us?'

Once again, my throat works against the tightness that always seems to be there these days. 'Um, no, I haven't. Have you?'

'No. You said you wanted to wait, so I'm waiting.'

I take a deep breath. 'Maybe I should be the one to say something. It might be easier, coming from me.'

'Sounds good.' A breeze ruffles his hair, and he says no more.

I realize I've finished my sandwich and start in on the chips. A seagull circles overhead, recognizing the label, apparently. I throw a chip into the water, where the bird instantly pounces.

'Now you've done it,' Ethan says. Sure enough, four more birds appear out of nowhere, circling and crying overhead. The boat rocks gently, and I lean against the mast.

'So what would you like to do for work?' I ask. 'Go back to traveling and jumping out of airplanes and schmoozing?'

Ethan laughs. 'Nah,' he answers. 'Been there, done that.' He's quiet a minute, tossing his own chips to the happy gulls, who wing in closer and closer circles to the boat. 'I wouldn't mind being a chef,' he says, so quietly I almost don't hear it.

'Really?' I ask.

'Sure,' he says. 'Don't forget where we met, Lucy.'

'Oh, I know,' I say. 'But you quit. You dropped out before you finished.'

He nods. 'Yes, I did,' he admits.

'So that would be great!' I exclaim. 'You should take over Gianni's. You know your dad thinks the cousin's husband's brother is a total screw-up.'

Ethan gives me a look. 'Better the cousin's husband's brother than me, Luce,' he says.

'But you're a fantastic cook! You'd be perfect! And it's the family—'

'I'll never be Jimmy,' Ethan interrupts. 'And that's what my parents really want.'

There's an uncomfortable silence. Our chips are gone, and the gulls grow disgusted and leave. Ethan unwraps the cake. He holds it up in an offer, but I shake my head and watch, bemused, as he takes a bite. His eyes close in pleasure for a second, and I smile.

'What about you?' Ethan asks. 'Any progress with the grocery store offer?' He takes another bite of cake.

'Not yet,' I admit. I'd spoken to Matt DeSalvo twice last week, rather disappointed when he didn't offer to meet face-to-face so I

316

could see if he really looked as much like Jimmy as I thought. 'There's still a lot to talk about. But I'll probably take it.'

'I thought you weren't sure you wanted to bake bread,' Ethan comments.

'I'm not. But it's better than going bankrupt.' There's a splotch of mustard on my jeans, and I scratch it idly. 'And,' I admit, 'it's a way of becoming someone, you know? It'd be nice to write into the Johnson & Wales alumni magazine and say my bread's distributed state-wide. And Matt said maybe we'd go into Connecticut and Massachusetts, too. So.' I look up at Ethan. 'A nice offer.'

He nods. 'This cake is fantastic,' he says. 'Try some.'

'I don't—' I begin, but he leans forward and pops a chunk into my mouth. The rich, velvety texture of the dark chocolate melts on my tongue, and the hazelnut frosting is like a bit of divine perfection. It was a great idea to roast . . . roast the . . .

'Well?' Ethan says, then notices my expression. 'Lucy?'

'It's . . . it's good,' I stammer. And it is. And I can *taste* it. I swallow. Yes, there's the hint of coffee, just the slightest murmur of cinnamon.

'Here,' Ethan says. He smiles as he feeds me the last piece, and I close my eyes and concentrate. The cake is so *good*, Ethan's right. I can't believe I can finally, finally enjoy my own baking again after such a long time.

317

Something that was gone has come back, something that was part of my daily life for a long, long time, something I've missed so much. But now, today . . . today, I can once again appreciate something I made with my own hands, that I made with attention and care for the man in front of me, and to be able to have that back . . .

My eyes are wet when I open them. Ethan's smile drops.

'Are you okay, honey?' he asks, and with that, I reach out and wrap my arms around his neck and kiss him, tasting chocolate and Ethan, his gentle, beautiful mouth, the heat of him. His arms go around me, one hand cupping the back of my head. And I kiss him and kiss him and kiss him, feeling his heart beat against mine.

I pull back and look into his eyes. His gaze drops to my mouth, and he pushes a piece of my hair off my face.

'Make love to me, Ethan,' I whisper, and he stands and gives me his hand.

The sunlight comes in patches through the little windows that line the cabin. Ethan pulls the couch out, then straightens, not saying anything. I sit down, and he kneels before me. I touch his cheek, then unbutton his shirt with shaking fingers. His skin is beautiful, olive and smooth, the muscles hard underneath. I press my palm over his heart, feel the reassuring beat there, steady and constant. Just like

318

Ethan. Then I look at him, into eyes made of gold and brown, like fallen leaves in a clear stream.

Then he leans in closer so that our foreheads touch. 'You sure, honey?' he asks

'Yes,' I whisper, and his mouth is on mine. His hand slides under my T-shirt and cups my breast, and my breath catches. He tastes so good, feels like heaven and I can't believe I've waited so long for this. His mouth moves to my neck, a hot jolt shudders through me, and I sink into the bed, the sun hot on my skin, and give myself away.

And I realize that despite my intentions, I've fallen in love after all.

CHAPTER TWENTY-THREE

It's much colder when we head back . . . the sky clouded up while we were in the cabin, the ocean turning slate and choppy. We don't talk much; Ethan is fairly busy negotiating the rough waves around Point Judith and adjusts the sail frequently. We keep a fast clip, bouncing over the waves, and I watch my captain warily as I grip a cleat, spray stinging my face, and worry that my grim fantasies of Ethan's death will come true as we whisk and smack through the water.

Everything's gonna be all right, everything's

gonna be all right . . . Everything's gonna be all right . . . It's not lost on me that this snippet of Bob Marley was my mantra after Jimmy died. But every time Ethan looks at me, so damn happy, fear strikes my heart. *Don't let me hurt him, Jimmy,* I pray. Abruptly the thought comes to me that maybe Jimmy isn't all that happy that my heart has opened to someone else. That maybe he wants to be the first, the best, the most. *Forsaking all others, all the days of my life,* that's how the marriage vows went. And being widowed . . . that's not like Jimmy betrayed me. He didn't ruin my love for him. He just died.

I try to imagine how it would be if my soul had to watch Jimmy struggle through life without me. Of course I'd want him to find someone wonderful. But, I admit, clutching my stomach as we bounce over the wake of a lobster boat, I'd also want to be the love of his life. To be the one by which all others were measured.

'Doing okay?' Ethan calls over the rush of wind.

'I'm great,' I answer, determined to make it true.

When we finally make it back to the marina, I can't wait to be on solid land again. Ethan looks at me as he wraps the line around a cleat. 'You look a little green,' he says, taking my hand as I rise. 'Want me to drive you home?'

'I'd kind of like to walk,' I say honestly.

'Okay,' he says, climbing off the boat and helping me disembark. We stand there on the wooden dock, which bobs unpleasantly. Rain clouds darken the sky in the west, and leaves shower down from the trees.

'Come over later,' I say.

'Okay,' he agrees instantly, and again my heart clutches at the smile in his eyes.

'See you later, alligator,' I say, turning to head for solid ground.

'Lucy?' I turn back. His face is serious now. 'Thank you,' he says.

My heart softens dangerously. 'Thank you, too, Ethan,' I answer unsteadily. Then, bowing my head against the sharp breeze, I head for home.

Ethan seems to know I need a little time alone—either that, or he has his own stuff to do. Whatever the reason, he doesn't come by until about nine. Fat Mikey, distressed that he's seen so little of his favorite person, yowls until Ethan picks him up and scratches his battered ears vigorously. 'How you doin', Fat Mikey?' Ethan asks, doing a fair impression of a mobster. 'How's our friend here?'

I've been in the kitchen, baking since I walked through the door to see if the cake was a fluke. It's not, thank God, and that has to be a sign that Ethan is good for me. My melancholy lifted as I started with crème brûlée . . . satiny and rich, the hard shell of

321

sugar burned to perfection. After that, a batch of *pots de crème au chocolat*, the dark chocolate giving the sweet creaminess the perfect bite. Then a quick batch of bananas Foster, so simple and fun and delicious. I laughed as I lit them on fire, though tasting it a few moments later, I admitted I put in a little too much nutmeg. I've since moved on to a carrot cake, which is baking right now as the mixer churns a batch of cream cheese icing on the counter.

'I see we've been busy,' Ethan says, raising an eyebrow at my kitchen. Every mixing bowl I own is on the counter, flour spatters the dark granite countertops, dishes are heaped in the sink and the place smells like heaven. Like a pastry shop.

'Are you hungry?' I ask.

'Sure,' he says. I give him a crème brûlée *and* a healthy serving of bananas Foster. I watch as he eats, and when he offers me a spoonful, I open my mouth obediently. 'Nice that you can eat your own desserts again,' he says, wiping a bit of cream off the corner of my mouth.

'More than nice,' I agree.

He doesn't ask when that changed. Maybe he doesn't need to. Maybe he knows what it means. 'This is incredible' is all he says, gesturing to his plate.

I smile. 'Thanks.'

Then I wash my hands and take off my

apron. I ruffle Ethan's hair as I pass his chair, and he grabs my hand and pulls me in for a kiss, and after the briefest hesitation, I kiss him back. It's just going to take a little getting used to, I assure myself.

We go into the living room and sit, looking at each other. I swallow, then smile. He smiles back. 'Want to play Scrabble?' I ask, lust and nervousness rolling through me in tingling waves.

'Sure,' he says with a knowing grin. 'Hey, what's this?'

Leaning against the couch is a rectangular package, still in brown paper. Shoot. Forgot about that thing. Ash had signed for it and left me a note. 'Um . . . actually, it's for you,' I say, nibbling my thumbnail.

Ethan's eyebrows bounce up. 'Really?'

I swallow. 'Yes. Uh, I didn't realize it would be done so soon. I thought it would take a little longer . . .'

'Can I open it?' he asks, smiling happily at me. It dawns on me that maybe today isn't the best time for this particular gift. Then again, maybe it is.

'Sure.'

Ethan sits in the easy chair and takes the present. He pulls the paper off, unwraps the tissue paper protecting the frame and turns it over to see the picture. His face freezes. I wait for his reaction. It doesn't come. He just sits in the chair, staring at the gift, frozen.

I got the top photo from Marie when they were packing up the house a few weeks ago—Jimmy and Ethan at the beach. Jimmy was twelve in the picture, Ethan seven. The two boys are standing in front of the surf, Jimmy's arm slung around his much smaller brother's shoulders. Already, you can see that Jimmy's going to be tall—his shoulders have started to broaden, and his face has that amiable, open appeal it held all his brief life. His hair is sun-streaked, and freckles dot his nose. Ethan, on the other hand, is a scrawny little guy, dark as a gypsy, thin enough that you can see his ribs. He's laughing in the picture, both his top front teeth missing. His hair is wet, his skin sandy.

The lower picture is also of Jimmy and Ethan. That one's from our wedding day, and once again, Jimmy has his arm around Ethan's shoulders. Jimmy beams; Ethan looks a bit more sardonic, his elvish eyebrows raised as if to say, *Get a load of the big dope here.* I love that picture. Jimmy had loved it, too.

Ethan still hasn't said anything.

'Ethan?' I whisper. He looks up, then clears his throat.

'Thank you,' he says in a rather perfunctory manner.

'I . . . you didn't have any. Pictures, that is. Of Jimmy.' Dismay sits heavily in my stomach, and I suddenly wish I hadn't eaten three desserts tonight.

'Right. Well. This is very nice of you, Lucy.' His voice is oddly formal. He looks back at the picture, then rubs his forehead.

The timer dings in the kitchen, and I excuse myself, glad for the interruption. The cake is done. Smells incredible. Can't wait to eat the stupid thing, stomachache be damned.

I don't realize tears are leaking out of my eyes until one hisses on the oven door. I dash a pot holder across my eyes and take the cake out, setting it gently on the cooling rack. Ethan comes up behind me and slips his arms around my waist.

'I'm sorry,' I squeak.

'No, honey.' He lowers his forehead to rest against my shoulder. 'Thank you.'

'Bad timing,' I acknowledge.

He turns me around and looks at me. Rain patters against the window, and the wind howls under the bridge a block away. I have plenty of time to hear the elements, since Ethan doesn't speak right away. 'You don't need to remind me that he was here first, Lucy.'

I swallow painfully. 'I *was* married to him. He *was* here first. That can't be erased, Eth. I wouldn't want it to be.'

Ethan nods. 'Maybe he doesn't have to be here all the time.'

He's asking the impossible. Jimmy *is* with me all the time. His memory is constantly with me, and I don't think that will ever change.

'The bread guy looks a lot like him,' I say abruptly.

'Which bread guy?'

'The one from NatureMade,' I say.

Ethan raises an eyebrow. 'Really.'

'Yes. Very much like Jimmy.'

'Thanks for the warning.' He slides his hands down my arms, then lets go of me.

I notice that Fat Mikey is crouched on the table, eating the last ramekin of crème brûlée, and decide to let my cat live a little. Another sheet of rain slaps the windows. The muscle jumps under Ethan's eye, and not for the first time, I wonder how much he's holding in.

'Ethan,' I say slowly, 'I wasn't trying to make a statement.' My throat grows tight. 'I just wanted you to have a picture of him, and it happened to come today. I should've held it a few days. I'm sorry.'

He nods and takes my hand, examining a smear of batter across the back. 'Thank you.'

'Want something else to eat?' I whisper.

His mouth tugs. 'No,' he says, not looking up from my hand.

'How about that Scrabble game?' I offer a bit desperately.

'Maybe later,' he answers, and then he kisses me, there amid the ravaged kitchen, the smell of fresh cake and cream in the air, and my heart sings with relief. And rather than counting out tiles and checking dubious spellings in the dictionary, we end up in bed,

Fat Mikey regarding us with disgust as we mess up his favorite place to sleep.

CHAPTER TWENTY-FOUR

A few days later, Ethan has to travel to Atlanta, where the International Food Products manufacturing plant is headquartered, so I have plenty of time to contemplate the state of my life. Things have been okay between Ethan and me, though we're still pretty careful with each other, especially about the subject of Jimmy.

The other day, I packed Nicky into his car seat and drove into Providence to surprise Ethan at work. As Nicky was spoiled by the staff, repeatedly summoned the elevator, photocopied his hands and took cup after cup from the dispenser by the water cooler, Ethan introduced me around—no title, just 'This is Lucy,' but I held his hand the whole time, hoping he'd see that as a sign that I was in this. He was so happy, so proud to show off his son, and I got more than a few speculative looks, which made me blush constantly.

'This meant a lot,' Ethan said to me when we were waiting for the elevator, Nicky pressing the button over and over. I smiled and kissed him goodbye full on the mouth, my hands buzzing.

327

We're getting there. Since he left for Georgia, we've been e-mailing a couple times a day, with long phone conversations at night. When I hear his voice, my heart jumps, and if it feels like a panic attack, maybe it's something else. And blessedly, I'm still gorging myself on my rather incredible baking.

And baking is on my mind, as next weekend is the Taste of Mackerly, which is a chance for the town to draw in a few tourists before the season is officially done. Lenny's, Bunny's, Catering by Eva, Cakes by Kim, and of course, Starbucks will be there along with contributions from the Lions Club, the Exchange Club and the Polish Ladies Auxiliary, who hawk their pierogies like the end of days is nigh.

In the past, Bunny's has trotted out the same tired, pumpkin-shaped cookies with frosting so hard that, three years ago, little Katie Rose Tinker chipped a tooth. Last year we had four dozen at the beginning of the evening. At the end, we had forty-six, and only because Ethan bought one for himself and one for Nicky. Nicky's little teeth weren't up for the task of gnawing through the icing, so Ethan had discreetly tossed it into the trash, but he'd soldiered on through his own, grinning at me as I offered sympathy for his culinary choice.

On Wednesday, the staff of Bunny's sits down for a rare meeting. Jorge lingers in the back, drinking the sludge he calls coffee, and runs his hand over his bald head, mentally preparing himself for the ordeal ahead.

'Okay,' I say. 'We have the Taste of Mackerly coming up on Columbus Day, so—'

'I have a skin tag,' Rose announces, leaning forward. 'Right under my bra line. Here.' She hefts up her right breast and points. 'Carmella Bronson said I could just snip it right off with toenail clippers, but I'm scared it won't stop bleeding.'

'Go to a plastic surgeon,' Mom says. 'I'm thinking of Botox, myself.'

'Okay, about the weekend,' I say. 'I think we should really go the whole hog this year. I've been baking these—'

'Botox? That's spider venom,' Iris says. 'You'd have to be an idiot to put spider venom in your face.'

'It's a bacteria. Botulism bacteria. It's not venom,' I say. 'Anyway, I thought we could—'

'I know what it is, Miss Smarty-Pants,' Iris says, waving her hand dismissively. 'My daughter is a lesbian doctor, after all.' She turns to my mother. 'Why would you stick a needle full of bacteria in your face, Daisy? Did you turn stupid overnight?'

'I want to look my best,' my mother says, adjusting her scarf.

'We also need to discuss that offer from NatureMade,' I try again. Jorge grins.

'Vanity is a sin,' Iris says, adjusting her shirt,

which, from the look of it, belonged to her long-dead Pete.

'What about my skin tag? Am I supposed to go around looking like a goat with wattles all over my body?' Rose asks querulously. 'Or get Ebola by cutting off my own skin?'

'That would be tetanus, Rose,' I say. 'Don't cut them off yourself. See a doctor, okay? Now, back to the—'

'Did you get your flu shots, speaking of injections?' Mom asks her older sisters.

With a sigh, I slump down in my chair and wait them out. After twenty minutes or so, I eventually manage to steer the conversation back to the Taste of Mackerly and am outvoted, as usual, on the burning issue of the pumpkin cookies, which, according to Iris, everyone loved.

Then I give them the details on NatureMade's official offer . . . number of loaves we'd be able to supply, how the schedule would change at Bunny's, a bit more oversight from the company to ensure that our bread was consistent.

'So what do you think?' I ask when I'm done.

Mom studies her manicure, as ever seeming detached from the bakery where she's worked most of her life. Iris and Rose, on the other hand, sit like disgruntled trolls, dour expressions on their faces, arms folded across their ample bosoms. Jorge, still lurking in the back, purely for entertainment purposes, laughs silently and pours himself more coffee.

'I don't like some out-of-towners telling us how to do things,' Iris eventually says.

'I have to agree with Iris,' Rose cheeps, plucking the fabric above her skin tag.

I nod. 'Well, we could do nothing, too, and continue to ignore the fact that we make less every month.' Iris harrumphs. 'And eventually, we'll just go broke and close the bakery and sell the property to McDonald's. How does that sound? Everyone on board?'

'Sarcasm causes wrinkles,' Rose says.

'Mom,' I attempt, 'you thought it was a good offer, right?'

But the bell over the front door tinkles, and Mom's head snaps around like a Labrador scenting a pheasant. 'Grinelda's here!' she announces in the same tone a five-year-old might say, *Santa came!* 'Lucy, do you want your mustache taken care of?'

'I don't have a mustache!' I protest, my fingers flying up to double-check. No whiskers. So there.

The Black Widows have already stampeded away from the table, practically trampling each other to get to the psychic. 'What about the offer?' I call after them.

Iris pokes her head back through the swinging door. 'If you want to be bossed around by some chain store, you go ahead. The bread's your responsibility.' Her head disappears, and I hear her booming voice welcome Grinelda to the bakery.

'Wasn't that fun?' I ask Jorge. He winks and starts stacking the trays from this morning's pastries.

I take a deep breath, then place a call to Matt DeSalvo at NatureMade. 'Hi, Matt, it's Lucy Mirabelli from Bunny's,' I say when he says hello.

'Hi, Lucy!' he answers warmly. 'I was just thinking about you. Have you had a chance to look at our offer?'

'Yes,' I say. 'We have a few questions—' well, *I* have a few questions, my relatives couldn't care less '—but things are looking pretty good to me.'

'Want to meet for dinner tonight?' he asks. 'I'd be happy to come back to Mackerly. It's such a pretty town.'

'Okay,' I agree tentatively. 'Sure. Um, there's a place right around the corner from the bakery called Lenny's.' For some reason, I don't want to go to Gianni's, even with my in-laws in Arizona. It doesn't seem right to take Matt there.

'Seven o'clock work for you?'

'Seven's great,' I answer.

'I can't wait,' he says, and he sounds sincere.

When I hang up, there's an uncomfortable feeling wriggling around in my gut, and it takes me a minute to put my finger on it.

Guilt, I realize. I feel guilty because I'm meeting Matt for dinner. Even if it's just business. I look over at Jorge to see if he's staring at me in dismay and disappointment. Nope. He's washing pans.

I glance at my watch: 2:00 p.m. Ethan's still in Atlanta, probably in a meeting right now, but he's flying home this evening. I decide to text him. *Am meeting the bread guy at Lenny's, 7:00 p.m. Drop by if you can, okay?* After a moment's hesitation, I add, *xox, Lucy,* and a sudden, sweet warmth causes my heart to expand in my chest. Ethan will appreciate that, the hugs and kisses.

In the front, Grinelda is powering through a day-old brownie and spraying the Black Widows with crumbs. 'I'm getting someone who's name starts with an L . . . Is it Larry?' She stuffs a neon pink cookie in her mouth. 'It's Larry.'

'Oh, Larry,' Rose breathes.

'Larry wants you to be happy. Go ahead and date someone, he says. Share your light with the world.'

I have to hand it to Grinelda. She knows her audience well, because Rose's eyes mist over, and her face turns pink with pleasure.

'What about me?' Iris demands. 'Does Pete want me to find someone else?'

Grinelda takes a drag on her little brown cigar. 'Hmm. Let me see. Give me a minute.' She exhales slowly, then slurps her coffee.

'Someone's coming through. A man. His name starts with . . . let's see now . . . his name starts with P. Does anyone know a man whose name starts with P?'

I sigh and, as usual, am ignored.

Grinelda takes another bite of brownie. 'Pete says do what you need to do. But don't do anything you *don't* need to do.'

'Huh,' Iris grunts. 'You know, that makes sense. The truth is, I don't really want to date anyone.'

I sigh again, more loudly, and throw in an eye roll for emphasis.

Iris spares me a glance. 'What else, Grinelda? Don't mind the youngster here.'

But Grinelda is looking at me through the acrid smoke of her cigar. 'You,' she says, frowning. 'Jimmy's telling you to check the toast.' She frowns, her face cracking into a hundred folds of age-spotted skin. My aunts frown as well, clearly displeased that I haven't heeded my otherworldly message.

'Can't I get something better than that, Grinelda? Something about true love never dying?' I ask.

Then Rose gasps. 'Check the toast . . . or check the bread!' she squeals. 'The bread *man!* The one who looks like Jimmy! Oh! My! God!'

'The bread man! Dear Lord!' Iris trumpets. 'That's what he meant! Check the bread, right, Grinelda?'

Even my mother looks flabbergasted.

Granted, my faith in Grinelda is wafer-thin, but ice seems to be flooding my stomach right now. The Black Widows are beside themselves . . . *the bread man, yes, yes, the bread man!* . . . and I have to admit, it's a little spooky. Matt DeSalvo does look like Jimmy . . . I'm not the only one who thinks so. And Matt does deal in toast. Sort of.

'It's a *sign*,' Rose coos. 'Jimmy wants you to marry the bread man.'

'I'm not marrying the bread man,' I say firmly, though my voice sounds a little distant.

'Why? You're the one who wanted a new husband,' Iris says in the same tone that she might say, *You're the one who wanted to pee in the street.*

'The bread man looks like her dead husband,' Rose informs Grinelda.

'Which she'd already know, being psychic and all,' I say automatically. Still, I can't help but wonder if there's really something here. If Jimmy's trying to tell me not to date his brother—

'So? What's the plan, then?' Iris asks. 'Are you going to ask him out?'

'You should, Lucy,' Rose seconds.

Then I give myself a mental shake. 'Let's drop it, okay?'

'But you are meeting the bread man later, aren't you?' Mom asks. 'I heard you on the phone.'

I bite my lip and swallow. It's time to acknowledge Ethan here, but the words are hard to get out of my throat. The pebble is back. 'The truth is,' I say, and my voice is shaky, 'I've actually been—'

'I'm getting an R,' Grinelda says in her scraping voice. 'Ronnie? No. Robbie.'

'It's your Robbie!' Iris and Rose chorus, their heads whipping to my mother.

Any interest in me is swept aside as my father reaches out from beyond the grave. 'Robbie's glad you still look so good,' Grinelda tells my mother, who preens noticeably and gives Iris a satisfied smirk.

'Does he think she should get spider venom shot in her face?' Iris asks.

I head back to the kitchen to start the afternoon bread order. 'I'm dating Ethan,' I tell Jorge.

He raises his eyebrows, then gives a nod.

'Did you know, Jorge?' I ask.

He shakes his head.

I drum my fingers on the countertop. 'What do you think? Me dating my dead husband's brother?' I ask. 'Weird? Maudlin? Gross? Or does it make complete sense to you?'

Jorge shrugs, smiles a little, giving me a flash of his gold tooth. For the millionth time, I wish he'd just write something down if he can't talk. Then again, he might not be able to write. Jorge's mysteries go quite deep.

'Well, thanks for your input,' I tell him. He

pats me on the shoulder and fires up the oven.

*   *   *

I arrive at Lenny's two minutes before seven. Matt DeSalvo is already there, standing in the doorway, being ignored by the staff, as is traditional.

'Hi, Lucy! Thank you so much for meeting me,' he says the minute he sees me. He bends and kisses my cheek, making me blush furiously. 'Sorry,' he says, grinning. 'Here.' He extends his hand and shakes mine firmly. 'Good to see you.'

I laugh. 'Good to see you, too. Let's grab a table.'

'The sign says Please Wait To Be Seated,' he observes.

'The sign lies. They'll just ignore us until we starve to death,' I tell him. I lead him to a table in the back, blushing again as he holds the chair for me.

Roxanne tosses some cutlery wrapped in a paper napkin as we take our seats. 'Whaddya want?' she asks.

'Hey there, how are you?' Matt asks, naive as a newborn kitten to the ways of Lenny's surly staff. When she fails to answer, he asks, 'Um, do you have a wine list we could take a look at?'

'No,' she growls. 'White, red, pink. Full bar. Whaddya want?'

'How about two dirty martinis?' I suggest, remembering Ethan's last happy hour with my aunts. It sounds sophisticated, and the truth is, I'm a little nervous. Also, I'm wearing one of my La Perla bra and panty sets (don't even ask what it cost, it's just too shameful). But it seemed about time I wore something nicer, even if the lace is a little itchy. And I do feel pretty . . . I even cut the tags off a beautiful pale pink cashmere cardigan with black buttons, which I've paired with a short, swirly black skirt, silver dangly earrings and yes, my Stuart Weitzman kitten heels. I wanted to look like someone with a little business savvy. That's what I told myself, anyway.

Not only is Matt DeSalvo an executive with a big grocery store, but he also represents a huge shift in my own status as a baker. NatureMade is a prestigious store, on par with Whole Foods, if much smaller. This deal could keep Bunny's alive for the foreseeable future, as well as bump up my own status.

And Matt DeSalvo's really cute. And he looks like Jimmy. And he's the bread man. And maybe my dead husband wants me to date him.

'Did you grow up in Mackerly?' Matt asks, and I tell him, yes, I sure did. We chat amiably about our families, sip our cocktails. The dirty martini tastes like something you'd drink if your airplane crashed in the Sahara and the only fluid available to you was leaking out of

338

the engine block, but it does go a long way in relaxing me. We order a few stuffies to start off with, earning us another disgusted look from Roxanne, since now she'll have to make an extra trip to our table. She doesn't approve of appetizers.

Despite Roxanne being Roxanne, Matt continues to try to ease himself into her good graces, not realizing she doesn't have any. Jimmy, too, was always a sweetheart to waitresses, both at Gianni's and anywhere else we might eat, always chatting them up and asking what they'd recommend, where they were from. Matt also seems to find *me* really charming. Just like Jimmy.

We're halfway through our main courses (steak for me, salmon for Matt) when I hear Ethan's voice. I look past Matt, and there he is, talking to Tommy Malloy. He looks up, smiles at me, and once again, guilt flashes its hot brand across my gut. I wave. 'Ethan just got here,' I say to Matt. I'd mentioned Ethan earlier in the conversation . . . as Jimmy's brother and a fellow food executive. Not as my boyfriend. *Say something, idiot!* my conscience orders in a shocked voice. I don't. 'I told him to join us.'

'Great!' says Matt, seeming sincere.

Then I look back at Ethan and feel something else . . . I *missed* him. Haven't seen him for four days now, and as he approaches, weaving through the crowded restaurant, I

339

recall the goodbye kiss he gave me the other day, the heat that flowed through me, the way I kissed him back, almost making him miss his flight.

'Hi,' I say, standing up and kissing him quickly on the cheek. I give him a hug, too. Matt DeSalvo can draw his own conclusions.

'Hi,' he says, and though it's just one word, his voice reverberates inside me. He touches my arm, and a wave of lust rises hot and fast, making my knees feel a little unreliable. Ethan's lips curl into that slight, knowing smile, and those knees turn to mush.

Then Ethan looks at Matt, and his smile falls. 'Jesus,' he breathes.

'Ethan, this is Matt DeSalvo. Matt, this is Ethan Mirabelli.' I bite my lip. Ethan stares, his face pale.

'Hi there,' Matt says, half rising and extending his hand. 'I'm told I look a lot like your brother. Sorry.'

'No, no,' Ethan says, recovering a bit. 'But . . . wow. At first glance, yes.' He clears his throat. 'Nice meeting you.'

'Have a seat,' Matt says. 'Lucy says you're in the food business as well.' I'm glad he mentions this, as now Ethan will see that I talked about him. It makes whatever lingering guilt I'm feeling dissipate almost entirely.

'That's right. I'm in marketing at International Food Products,' Ethan answers.

'Makers of *Instead?*' Matt asks.

'That's right.'

Matt's eyebrows rise. 'I've heard of your company, of course.' He glances at me with a little smile. 'So, Ethan, what do you think of Bunny's going big time?'

Ethan glances at me, then back at Matt. 'I think Lucy will make the right decision,' he says a trifle awkwardly.

'Ethan, sit,' I urge.

'Actually I'll let you two finish your dinner.' He can't seem to stop looking at Matt. 'I told Nicky I'd drop by.'

'Oh,' I say. 'Okay. Tell him hi for me.'

'Will do. Matt, nice to meet you.'

'Same here,' Matt says. They shake hands once more. Then Ethan gives my shoulder a quick squeeze and with that, he's gone.

'Nice guy,' Matt says, watching him go.

'Yes,' I answer. 'Very nice.' I pause. 'He's very close with his son.'

'As it should be,' Matt replies, smiling. 'I love kids myself. Would love to be a dad someday.'

*   *   *

Ethan is quiet when he comes by later that night. My head is swimming . . . not so much with details of a bread distribution contract, but with how much Matt reminds me of Jimmy. Maybe it's nostalgia, but the whole time, I'd felt an unnerving tingle with Matt

341

DeSalvo.

'When you said he looked like Jimmy . . .' Ethan says, running a hand through his hair. 'I guess I didn't really think about it.' He sits on my couch and stares at the rug.

'Kind of strange, wasn't it?' I ask.

'Kind of something,' Ethan answers.

'So,' I say. 'We talked about the bread. Seems like a good thing.' Ethan nods but says nothing. 'How was your trip?' I ask.

Fat Mikey jumps up next to Ethan and headbutts him fondly. 'It was fine,' Ethan says, petting my cat.

'You said the hotel was nice,' I remind him.

'It was. Very nice.'

He looks a little lonely sitting there, scratching Fat Mikey's ragged ears, and I try to imagine what it felt like, to see someone who looked so much like his brother . . . and how much he must miss Jimmy. Poor Ethan.

'I missed you,' I tell him, and he looks up fast, making my heart squeeze.

'Did you?' he asks, his lovely smile curling his lips.

'Yes, I did,' I say, trying for a sultry tone and blushing a little. Rising to my feet, I stand in front of him, glad I'm wearing a short skirt and pretty underwear (and trying to forget that I donned these because of my dinner with Matt). I slip the top button of my sweater from the hole. 'Very much,' I add, raising an eyebrow.

'Do tell,' Ethan murmurs, watching my hands as I slowly undo the next button. He swallows.

'Move that cat,' I say, going on to the next button. Ethan obeys without taking his eyes off the pink lace of my bra. Fat Mikey lifts a leg to start a little inappropriate social grooming, but Ethan gives him a gentle shove with his foot, and the cat seems to sigh in disgust, walking off with his tail twitching.

Grinning a little and hoping I don't look like a total ass, I sit on Ethan's lap. 'Glad to be back?' I ask, reaching to undo his tie.

'I suppose,' he says, smiling into my eyes.

'You suppose. Well, *I* suppose I'll have to try to make you really, really glad.' I tip his face up and kiss him, a slow, wet, soft kiss. He slides his hands up my leg and makes a little noise in the back of his throat. His mouth is hot and hungry, but, feeling he deserves a little show, I break the kiss, then take his hand and put it over my heart.

'Did you bring me a present?' I whisper.

His eyes are unfocused. 'What?'

'Do you have something for me?'

Ethan grins. 'I do,' he answers.

'Will I like it?'

'I hope so,' he says with that smile. His thumb slides over the lace of my bra, and my girl parts clench hard and hot.

'I have something for you, too,' I murmur, definitely getting into the role of sex kitten

343

now. I unbutton his shirt as slowly as I did my own, resting my hand over his heart for a second, gratified to find it pounding. Ethan's hand slides up my back and unhooks my bra.

'Clever,' I whisper. 'One-handed and all.'

'Thanks,' he grins, and whatever guilt I might've felt earlier that night is gone, and Ethan is all that matters.

This is new for us, this teasing little seduction. Being with Ethan has always been . . . well, fairly *urgent*. In the past, we'd pounce on each other. Clothes would be torn off, shoved aside, thrown around the room . . . not removed inch by inch. In the past, it was something more primal, less emotional. But this is more meaningful, more . . .

I want to tell him I love him, but the words stay firmly lodged in my heart. 'I missed you,' I whisper again. It's the best I can do for now.

His shirt is open now, and I turn my attention to his belt, trailing a series of biting little kisses down his neck while I unbuckle.

'I think I'll go away more oft—' he starts to say, but his words are cut off as I kiss him again, fierce and hot, and he actually laughs, then shifts me so I'm underneath him on the couch, his weight hard and heavy and wonderful on top of me. I sling a leg over his hips, getting a groan as a reward.

Ethan kisses a particularly sensitive spot just below my collarbone, his beard scraping, his lips velvet and hot, moving lower. I moan

344

and arch most wantonly against him. Smokin',
ladies and gentlemen. Smokin'.

Then I hear the sound, but hey. I'm horny.
Ethan's gifted at what he's doing, and my
brain fails to grasp the significance of the
sound. Dimly I think *Fat Mikey* and ignore it
in lieu of . . . oh, yes, Ethan's hand is under my
skirt, his fingers skimming, *don't stop that, big
boy*—

'Holy Mother of God! Marie, turn around!'

I convulse so hard that Ethan is bucked off
like a cowboy riding an enraged Brahma bull,
and instinctively, I roll onto the floor with him
before my brain registers what's actually
happening. My sweater gapes open, my
unhooked bra flopping ineffectively. My cat
crouches under the coffee table, hissing since
we almost squished him. Ethan's pants are
undone, his shirt half off, a red mark on his
neck (for God's sake, what was I thinking?). I
scramble to close my sweater (and legs, gah!)
and clutch a pillow to my chest.

My in-laws stand before me, horror-
stricken, Gianni shielding his eyes, Marie with
both hands over her heart.

'Ethan,' Marie wails, 'for the love of God,
what are you doing to Jimmy's wife?'

CHAPTER TWENTY-FIVE

Ethan zips and buckles, jerking his shirt closed. 'Give us a minute,' he barks over his shoulder at his parents.

They obey frantically, almost falling over each other in a stampede to the door. 'We'll be right out here!' Marie calls, as if reminding us that they'll be listening should Ethan and I decide to finish the deed. The door slams shut behind them.

'Forget to mention something?' Ethan bites out, buttoning his shirt with sharp, almost violent movements.

'No!' I snarl. 'I didn't know they were coming! They just moved!'

'Tell me about it,' Ethan growls. He won't look at me. 'I'm guessing you haven't told them about us.'

Dang it! 'No, I didn't,' I answer, wincing.

'Well, this is just great,' he snaps. 'Thanks, Luce. They weren't going to approve under the best of circumstances. Now they think I'm a rapist.'

'Oh, Ethan, they do not,' I say, feeling the dangerous wriggle of laughter flopping around in my stomach.

His shirt is buttoned wrong, and seeing Ethan disheveled, he who's usually so perfectly dressed, I feel a rush of tenderness.

'Don't worry, Eth. I'll handle this.'

'Will you? That would be great, Lucy. Thank you so much.'

'This is not my fault,' I whisper. 'I'm not your enemy here.' Ethan doesn't seem to agree. 'Now, are you ready? Can I let them in?' He glares in response.

Swallowing repeatedly, I open the door as if I'm letting in the Grim Reaper.

'Hi,' I say. My father-in-law, his expression as mad as Ethan's, rubs his chest and doesn't look at me. *Message received, Gianni. I'm killing you.* Fat tears drip from Marie's face. 'Come on in,' I say. Ah, jeepers. Their luggage is in the hall. A lot of luggage.

'Ethan, how could you?' Marie demands, pushing past me. 'Shame on you! Your brother's wife! And Lucy, I have to say, we're stunned! Stunned!'

'We never expected this of you, Lucy,' Gianni growls.

'But you expected it of me?' Ethan suggests tightly.

'Well, yes! You've always wanted what your brother had!' Gianni shouts.

'For Christ's sake, Dad!'

'It's just not decent,' Marie sniffles.

'Okay, settle down, everyone, settle down,' I say. 'Look. This is awkward for everyone, right?' Three sets of eyes glare at me, two brown, one Mediterranean blue. Even Jimmy seems to glare at me from our wedding

347

picture. Marie sees my glance.

'In front of Jimmy, even!' she sobs, fumbling through her giant black purse for a hankie. 'Ethan, we're so disappointed!'

Ethan presses his fingertips hard against his forehead. *My mother is giving me a brain tumor.*

'Why don't you sit down, Gianni, Marie?' I suggest. They obey, blatantly avoiding the couch where, moments before, Ethan had been defiling their dear little Lucy. 'Eth, could you make some coffee? Guys, would you like something else? Wine, maybe?' I ask. 'I have some almond pound cake I just made today.'

'I couldn't eat,' Marie lies staunchly, clutching her purse against her stomach.

'I'll cut a few slabs, just in case,' Ethan says, not very nicely. But he goes into the kitchen, and some of the tension leaves with him.

'I'm very sorry you had to walk in on that,' I say quietly, taking a seat on the, er, couch.

'Not as sorry as we are,' Gianni growls. From the kitchen comes the sound of a cupboard slamming.

I swallow again. 'Well, first tell me what happened. Why didn't you call and let me know you were coming for a visit?'

Gianni sighs. 'We're not visiting. We're back.'

I nearly choke. 'Back?' I squeak.

'Arizona . . . it was so hot. So dry,' Marie says, frowning.

348

'Um, yes, it does have a bit of a reputation,' I murmur. 'But by "back," what exactly do you mean?'

'We're back!' Gianni practically yells. 'That idiot Luciano, what does he know about anything? He's running my restaurant into the ground! So yesterday, the ditzy broad who runs Valle de Muerte, she just happens to mention the waiting list to buy into the place, and I says to Marie, I says, "Marie, what are we doing here? We don't belong out here with these dried-up cactus people!" And the woman, she says she could sell our condo for ten grand more than we paid for it, and I says, "Do it, lady. We're going home."' He pauses for a second. 'Besides, we missed the little guy.'

I hope Ethan heard that last little bit, but he's slamming around in the kitchen with a vengeance.

'You could've called,' I say with a little smile. 'Or knocked.'

'We thought you'd be sleeping, with the hours you keep!' Marie cries in her defense. 'You gave us a key! Aren't you happy to see us?' Her face oozes betrayal and a crushed heart.

'Well, uh, sure, I'm happy,' I stammer. 'I'm very happy to see you! It's just . . . well . . . you know. The circumstances.'

'We wanted to surprise you,' Marie says with a little pout.

'And you sure did!' I reply, forcing a smile.

Gianni closes his eyes and shakes his head. 'That Ethan. What did I do wrong? First, that *schifoso* milkshake. Now, he's *arrapato* for his brother's *moglie.*'

A crash comes from the kitchen.

'He's not a bad person,' Marie whispers, reaching over to pat her husband's arm.

'Okay, look. Um . . . you're right. Ethan's not a bad person,' I begin. Talk about damning with faint praise. 'He's a very *good* person. And you know, he's been so wonderful to me since Jimmy died—'

'And now we know why,' Gianni snarls.

'No! It's not like that. He . . .' I pause. 'Look. I love you both. And you knew I was, um . . . trying to find someone.' I resist the urge to look at my wedding picture. 'Is it such a stretch to think that Ethan would be—' *A contender,* I'm thinking, but Marie jumps in.

'The next best thing?' she suggests. Her face wrinkles with the onset of tears. 'When you put it that way, maybe it does make sense.'

'Well, no, Marie, I'm not looking for another—'

Gianni snorts. 'If you're looking for another Jimmy, you're not gonna find him in Ethan, that's for sure.'

'I'm not looking for another Jimmy,' I say slowly, blinking at my father-in-law. 'Ethan's nothing like Jimmy.'

350

'Tell me about it!' Gianni shouts. 'His whole job is to get people to stop eating! That's a slap in my face, an insult to my life's work.'

'Maybe people don't like your life's work as much as you think,' Ethan bites out from the kitchen doorway. He carries in a tray of coffee, cups and a plate of cake slices and slaps it down on the table. 'Maybe a milkshake is a welcome change to overcooked pasta and leathery veal.'

'You're an ungrateful little—'

'Okay! Stop!' I order. 'Ethan. Your parents are upset, okay? Settle down.' He glares at me. I turn to Gianni, who also glares at me. 'Gianni, please don't say things you'll regret later. Ethan's your son, too.'

'Just not nearly as good as St. Jimmy,' Ethan snipes.

'Stop it,' I whisper. Ethan, all bristling anger and misbuttoned shirt, sits next to me, deliberately close. I take a deep breath. 'So.' I glance at Marie for a little solidarity, but she's eyeing the pound cake. I push the plate closer to her, and she takes a piece. 'A few weeks ago, Ethan and I—'

'Lucy and I are together,' Ethan interrupts. 'You can have a problem with it—you already do, I gather—or you can accept it. Obviously, it would be easier if you thought I was good enough for her, but then again, that would negate your little Italian melodrama. Still, if

351

you want to stay on good terms with your one surviving son, who happens to be the father of your only grandchild, you might want to mind your manners.'

'Watch how you talk to your mother,' Gianni growls.

'Ethan, you can't blame us for being shocked,' Marie tuts. 'We just found you doing God knows what with Jimmy's wife.'

Ethan closes his eyes briefly, and I reach out without thinking and take his hand. He looks at me, his eyes unreadable.

'This is just . . . ah!' Gianni says, rubbing his chest with vigor. 'Isn't it against the law or something? A man can't just . . .' He pauses, giving his son a condemning stare. 'Can't just take his brother's wife.'

'She's not anyone's wife,' Ethan growls. 'She's a widow.'

'Your *brother's* widow,' Marie adds.

'Thanks, Ma. I forgot.'

'Always with the sarcasm, you,' Gianni snarls. The muscle under Ethan's eye ticks.

There's an uncomfortable silence. 'So let's change the subject a little,' I say, since it's clear no one is going to leave happy tonight. 'You've come back to Rhode Island. What's the plan?' I pause. 'I'm guessing from the suitcases in the hall, you'd like to stay here.'

'Not if we're not welcome,' Gianni grumbles.

'You're welcome. Of course you are,' I

352

assure them, my heart sinking even further.

'I'd be happy to put you up in a hotel,' Ethan offers.

'What would we do in a hotel?' Marie asks. 'Hotels are for rich people. You might be rich, Ethan. We're not rich. Hotels are for people with no family.'

'Then you'll stay at my place,' Ethan orders, and I mentally thank him with all my heart. I love my in-laws, but God in heaven, I don't want to live with them. And while Ethan probably feels that sentiment a million times more, they *are* his parents.

'You can stay here,' I whisper to him.

'Oh, so now you're living in sin?' Gianni asks. 'Nice, Ethan. At least Jimmy married her.'

*   *   *

A thousand years and five slices of pound cake later, the Mirabellis depart for Ethan's apartment. 'You guys go ahead,' Ethan says. 'I need to talk to Lucy.'

'Sleep well,' I call to their backs.

'You, too, sweetheart,' Marie answers. 'Thank you for the pound cake. It was just lovely.'

'We're glad you're back,' I say, knowing this will eventually be true.

'Leave the luggage, Dad,' Ethan says. 'I'll bring it up in ten minutes.'

Gianni gives him a baleful look and grabs the handle of the biggest bag and begins dragging it toward the elevator. *I'd rather have another coronary than let you help me, whippersnapper.*

The door finally closes behind them. Ethan picks up the cups and carries them into the kitchen, and I follow with the plate of pound cake (sneaking in a bite of the remaining piece, not wanting Ethan to know I'm starving, since it seems insensitive).

'Gosh, that was fun,' I say, hoping to get a smile from my buddy there. I don't. 'So,' I continue. 'What's it like to be *arrapato* for your brother's *moglie?*

'Not funny, Lucy.' Ethan folds his arms and stares at me.

'Sorry,' I mutter, my figurative tail dropping between my legs.

'You said you were going to tell them,' he reminds me.

'I didn't,' I answer.

'Yes. I got that.' His jaw looks like he's grinding diamonds between his molars.

'Well, Ethan, I certainly wish I had,' I say with undeniable sincerity.

'So why didn't you?' he asks, looking over my head to burn a hole in the wall.

'I . . . I don't know.' I sag against the cool granite of the counter at my back.

'Then I'll assume you didn't tell them because you're either a coward or you're not sure we'll work out,' he says evenly.

'Or both,' I suggest, wishing I had the kind of sense of humor that would disappear, rather than mushroom, during tense events.

He drags his eyes to mine. Funny how they can look as inviting as a warm cookie sometimes, as forbidding as granite at others. They're definitely on the stony side now. 'Have you told your family?' he asks.

'Well, I tried. Today, actually, at our meeting. But then Rose wanted to talk about her skin tags, and Mom brought up Botox... you know how it is.' He looks as if he *doesn't* know how it is. Not at all. 'I told Jorge, though,' I offer.

'You told your mute assistant. Anyone else?'

'Um...'

'I see.' His jaw is so tight I won't be surprised if he spits out chunks of his own teeth.

'Ethan, why don't we sit down and—'

'I'm fine standing, actually.'

'Okay.' I consider putting my hand on his arm, then reconsider. 'Ethan, here's the thing, and I know you don't like to talk about it, but here it is.' He lifts an eyebrow. 'I'm scared.'

'That's clear, Lucy. When do you think you'll get over that?' Then he seems to realize how harsh he sounds, because he looks down. 'I'm sorry,' he mutters.

I take a deep breath. 'Ethan, look. When

Jimmy died,' I say now, my voice near a whisper, 'it changed me. I loved who I was back then, this dopey, happy bride, half of a couple. I loved thinking about the rest of my life. And when he hit that tree . . .'

Something flickers through Ethan's eyes and he gives a half nod, asking me to continue.

'Ethan, you know—you know better than anyone—how hard it was to crawl back from that sloppy mess you used to scrape off the floor every weekend. I had to . . . I don't know. Grow scar tissue over my heart, just so I could get through the days. And there have been so many days, Ethan.' My voice grows rough with tears, and I clear my throat.

'Lucy, I do know all this,' Ethan says. His voice is quiet, but still tight. 'But you have to decide when you're going to . . . deem me worthy or whatever.'

I swallow. Again. 'You *are* worthy, Ethan. The thing is, when I lost Jimmy, I lost me, too.' I pause. 'I'm just not sure if I can do that again. It's not that I don't . . .'

It's not that I don't love you. The words are obvious, if unspoken. 'It's not that I don't care about you, Ethan. You know I do.'

He seems to know it's the best I can do for now. His gaze drops to the floor.

'You said you'd be patient,' I whisper.

'I'm trying,' he says. 'But I can't wait forever, either.'

'I'm trying, too!' I blurt. 'Can't you see that? The whole thing on the couch just now, and on the sailboat . . . I'm trying, Ethan!'

He jams his fists in his pockets. 'Well, thank you so much, Lucy. I'm sorry if it's such a trial for you.'

'It's not a trial! Please, Ethan. I'm doing this because I want to. But it's hard. And it's hard for your parents. Tonight they saw their dead son's wife with someone else. Even if it was their other son, Eth. Put yourself in their shoes.'

The muscle under his eye jumps. He looks at me, waiting for me to say something else. But since everything I've said tonight seems to be wrong, I just reach out and press my hand over his heart.

And after a few beats, he puts his own hand over mine. 'I'd better go upstairs,' he says finally. 'Make sure my dad's blood pressure has come down.'

'Okay,' I whisper. 'See you tomorrow.'

'More than likely,' he says. Then he lets go of my hand and walks out, leaving me feeling like I've let him down, when all I've done is told the truth.

CHAPTER TWENTY-SIX

'So you're *lefekszik* with Ethan?'

This is my greeting the next morning when Iris and Rose come into the bakery. I don't know why I'm surprised. Word does get around in this town.

'Hi, Iris. Hi, Rose.' I pause. 'If by that tangled up word, you mean am I—' I pause '—*dating* Ethan, then the answer is yes. How did you know?'

'Saw your mother-in-law at the Starbucks,' Iris says, gesturing with her cup. My mother enters now, also clutching the trademark earth-friendly cup.

'Should everyone be going to Starbucks?' I ask, trying to keep the edge from my voice. 'They're our competition, remember?'

'Have you had the hot chocolate there?' Rose says. 'I thought I died and went to heaven!'

'You're all traitors,' I mutter. 'If you'd let me set up a café, we could sell hot chocolate, too, and—'

'So how is it?' Iris wants to know. 'Do you compare them constantly?'

'No, as a matter of fact, I—'

'I thought that was against the law,' Rose muses in her singsong voice. 'Iris, you told me it was against the law.'

'So? How long has this been going on?' Iris demands, reapplying her Coral Glow with surgical precision.

'I'd rather not discuss it,' I say as the bell rings over the door. Thank God. Captain Bob. 'Hi, Bob! What can I get for you?'

'Captain Bob, is it against the law to marry your brother-in-law?' Rose asks him.

'I—um . . . hello, there, ladies.' His bloodshot eyes find my mother. 'Good morning, Daisy. You look lovely today.'

'Bob. Thank you.' My mother gives him an imperious look and goes into her office, closing the door behind her.

'Why do men love the women who abuse them?' I ask Captain Bob.

'Self-hatred,' he answers. 'What's this about the brother-in-law?'

'I'm dating Ethan.'

His bushy eyebrows raise in surprise. 'Jimmy's brother?'

'Yes.'

'Oh.' He studies the tray of gooey danishes Rose is shoving into the display case. 'Can I have a cherry danish? And how's that going? With Ethan, I mean.'

'Uh . . . fine. Just fine,' I answer. The bakery fills with our paltry assortment of morning regulars.

'I always thought Ethan was so decent,' Rose comments as she counts out Mr. Maxwell's hard roll allotment.

'He *is* decent, Rose. You know that,' I plead.

'He and Lucy,' my aunt explains to our customer. 'She's . . . er . . . *dating* . . . her dead husband's brother.'

'Wouldn't that be incest?' Mr. Maxwell says, frowning.

'It's not incest!' I yelp. 'He's not *my* brother. He's—'

'Lucy! Check the bread!' Iris calls.

I shove through the kitchen doors and yank open the oven. Jeepers! My internal timer has failed me for the first time ever, and the bread is nut brown, not golden. Dang it. Four dozen loaves, unsellable. Unbelievable. Jorge pats my shoulder as he comes in, shrugging out of his coat, and I sigh, then head for the proofer, hoping I have enough dough to make up for it.

Around ten, I prepare to go home for my nap. Iris and Rose are dying to interrogate me . . . little comments have been dropped all morning, and I could really use a little quiet time.

'See you in a few hours, Mom,' I say, glancing in the tiny office.

'Okay, sweetheart,' she says, barely looking up from her computer screen, where a game of solitaire is in progress. My mother is the only Black Widow who hasn't weighed in on the subject of my love life, and I'm suddenly hungry for some maternal advice.

'Have you got a sec?' I ask, leaning in her

doorway. I'm exhausted . . . didn't sleep well for obvious reasons. All night, I tossed and turned and irritated Fat Mikey.

'Sure,' she says, closing the lid of her laptop.

Mom's office is barely big enough for her desk, let alone the guest chair that's wedged into the corner. It takes a little wrestling, but I manage to close the door for a heart-to-heart.

'So. Ethan and I are, um . . . together,' I say.

'I gathered,' she answers.

'Did you see Marie this morning, too?'

'I did,' Mom says. 'She was quite upset.'

I cringe, hoping my mother-in-law wasn't compelled to detail all that she saw but knowing better.

'Caught you and Ethan on the couch, I understand.'

'Yep,' I say, feeling my face ignite. I take a breath. 'So what do you think?'

Mom cocks her head. 'About what?'

'About Ethan and me,' I say a little crossly.

She shrugs. 'Do what you feel you have to, honey.'

'I could really use some advice, Mom.'

She purses her lips and glances at a framed picture of Emma, a new addition to her desk. 'I know you must want a baby,' she offers.

'Sure. A family of my own, all that.' I nod, glad she's on the right track.

'You know, single women can adopt from Guatemala these days. I read an article—'

'Is that your way of saying you don't approve, Mom?' I interrupt.

'Well, no,' she hedges. 'I just . . . if you want to be with Ethan, do it. But if you're looking for a sperm donor—'

'Mom!'

'So? You asked, I answered. Do what you want, honey.' She gives me an assessing look. 'I can't believe you wear that in public,' she murmurs, taking in my yoga pants and sweatshirt.

'I'm a baker, Mom,' I answer, standing up stiffly. 'Even Coco Chanel would dress down for baking.'

'There's dressing down, and then there's hobo,' she murmurs.

I think of the cashmere sweaters in my closet. The secret shoes and expensive lingerie. The mahogany boots that cost me a week's pay. The credit card bill that shocked even me last month.

'See you later,' I say. Mom smiles sweetly and with that, I leave, mother-daughter bonding complete. Forget the nap. Time for a little trip to Nordstrom's.

*   *   *

'So you're with Ethan, huh?' Ash's black-painted lower lip wobbles, but she puts on a good front, jamming her nail-bitten hands into her pockets and raising those painfully

362

overplucked eyebrows as if she's really interested.

'Um . . . yeah.' I'm not sure what else to say.

'I guess that explains why he was always here. Shit, I'm so stupid. Should've guessed.' She tries to give a tough-girl smile, but her lips don't quite make it. Ash shifts, her sooty hair swinging listlessly against her pale face. 'So, like, how long has this been going on, anyway?'

'A while,' I admit.

'That's great. He's great. So are you. Good for you both.' A tear slips out and runs down her face, leaving a sooty smear.

'I'm sorry, honey,' I whisper. 'I know you—'

'Don't pity me, Lucy, for Christ's sake! You can be with . . . I'm not . . . I gotta run.' She turns and walks down to her door, her chains rattling, her enormous, heavy shoes thudding. I hear a little squeak, and my own eyes fill. She's crying. Dang it, dang it, dang it! If only kids weren't so cruel, if Ash had a nice boy who was brave enough to see under that black paint and chains . . .

I'm about to face more music—Bunny's has its last baseball game of the season. And guess who our opponent is? International Foods, of course, due to their freak win over Nugey's Hardware. Doral-Anne's pitching put them over the top, dang it all.

The urge to hide in my apartment has never been greater. Ethan and I are now common

363

knowledge. Parker heard it at nursery school and left a cheery message—'Hey, heard you and Ethan came out of the closet! Good for you, girlfriend!' Bill at the post office expressed the commonly held and quite erroneous idea that Ethan and I fell under the porno/incest umbrella. When I stopped by the library today, the entire four-person staff fell abruptly silent, smiling awkwardly as I returned my books and DVDs.

At the ball field, the Black Widows sit in a row in the exact center of the bleachers, a plaid blanket across their laps. They're right next to Parker and Nicky, who are there with the Mirabellis. Nicky's sitting on Gianni's lap, tickling his grandfather on the chin.

The Mirabellis catch sight of me. Marie gives an awkward wave, and Gianni gives me a stiff nod. Parker waves, too, and I hope she'll do something to ease things a bit. Tricky, though, since Gianni and Marie really want Ethan with her . . .

'Hi, Lucy.' It's my sister, holding Emma, who's bundled up in the cutest little fleece hoodie.

'Hi!' I say, giving her a hug. 'Hi, Emma! How are you, sweetie? I missed you.' I give my niece a kiss, breathing in the smell of her shampoo. She grasps my finger and smiles, then spits up a little. 'How are things, Cory?'

'Things are pretty good,' she says, wiping the baby's face. 'A little nerve-racking, but good. In fact, I was wondering if, um . . . if Christopher could play on Bunny's team. Next year.'

I glance at the sidelines, where Chris is pulling on his umpire's mask. 'Really, Corinne? You'd let him risk his life through baseball?'

She gives me an uncertain smile. 'Baby steps, you know?'

'He's not wearing the Kevlar vest, is he?'

'He's not.' She bites her lip.

'Good for you, Cory. And yes, of course he can play!' I kiss Emma's little fist. 'Maybe you and Chris would like to go out sometime. Leave the baby with me for a few hours.'

Corinne pales, but to her credit, nods her head. 'Sure. Thanks, Lucy. That would be . . . lovely.' She pauses. 'I heard about you and Ethan.'

I swallow. 'Yep.'

She hesitates. 'He's always been good to you. He's wonderful.'

'Yes,' I agree. 'That's definitely true.' I glance around for Ethan . . . he's not here yet. I can't tell if I'm relieved or anxious.

'Well, have a good game,' she says, making Emma wave to me. I wave back, then watch as Corrine stops to say something to Chris. He grins and kisses her, then waves to me.

'I hear you're doing Ethan Mirabelli,' Charley Spirito says glumly, tapping his bat against his cleats.

I turn to my right-fielder. 'Hello, Charley,' I say brightly. 'I sure hope we win today, don't you?'

'Fine, fine,' he grumbles. 'It's just that I thought there was something special between us, Luce.'

I try to remember what might have given him that impression, but mercifully, Chris calls for the game to start.

Today, I find that I'm eager for the season to be over. That the idea of the approaching winter, the shorter days and biting wind, seem cozy to me, with hours spent at my kitchen table, formulating and finalizing my bread recipes for NatureMade. Ethan and I will spend time together like a regular couple. I'll put on some of my beautiful clothes, and we'll go out for dinner somewhere nice in Federal Hill.

It's really time to move on.

'Batter up!'

That would be me. Unfortunately Doral-Anne Driscoll is pitching for International. And there's still no sign of Ethan.

Doral-Anne stretches so that her shoulders pop, and we are all treated to a glimpse of the snake tattoo on her belly, as she has hacked off the bottom four inches of her shirt. Looking down from the mound, Doral-Anne squints at me, sneers, then spits. I believe I hear my mother muffle a scream.

Knowing her fastball is deadly, I swing at

the first pitch a full second before I think I should, and am rewarded with a solid thud of bat against ball. The bleachers cheer—good to have all my relations here—and I take off for first. The ball drops into shallow right, and I'm safe.

'Nice hit, Lucy,' Tommy Malloy says.

'Thanks,' I pant.

'Hey, I hear you and Ethan are giving it a whirl.'

'Yep,' I say.

'Good luck with that,' Tommy says, leaning forward, his hands on his knees, as Charley takes a practice swing. 'Though I thought he and Parker were engaged.'

'Nope,' I answer.

'Ah, well. To each his own, I guess,' Tommy says dubiously. Then Charley gets hit by a pitch, so I'm off to second.

By the seventh inning Bunny's is ahead, 8-2, and I personally have been on base three times already and scored twice. Doral-Anne is definitely off her game. She looks savage as Katie Rose Tinker takes her Mr. Microphone from a plastic case and taps on it to ensure she'll be heard. Last year, I gave her fourth-grade class a tour of the bakery (any hard feelings about chipping her tooth on the pumpkin cookie gone in the face of eating cupcakes warm from the oven).

Katie Rose warbles her way through 'God Bless America,' with all the squealy

367

enthusiasm of Mariah Carey as we all stand, hats over our hearts, waiting for the torture to end. ' . . . God bless America . . . my home . . . swee-ee-eeet . . . ho-wo-wome!' Her youthful voice jumps almost an octave, and if she's a couple of notes short of being in key, the crowd gives her a standing ovation for her enthusiasm.

And that's when Ethan appears. The crowd grows immediately quiet, sits right back down and turns their attention to us.

'Hey, guys,' he calls to his team. 'Sorry I'm late.'

'Hey, Ethan,' a few voices chorus.

Well, this is it. I walk over to him, take his face in my hands and kiss him firmly on the mouth. There will be no wondering about if we're together anymore.

Silence falls over the ballpark.

'Hi,' I say when I'm done.

'Ouch,' he murmurs. Perhaps I was a little too emphatic. But his lovely mouth turns up in that mischievous, curling smile, and he kisses me quickly (and gently), then trots off to second base.

My face burns, but I feign normalcy and take care not to look over at the bleachers, where my in-laws may or may not be engaged in heart attacks. Carly Espinosa, our catcher, gives me a slap on the bottom. 'I always thought Ethan was hot.' She grins.

And in the ninth inning, when I decide to

steal second, what do you know?

'Safe!' Chris shouts.

'Was that for real?' I ask Ethan. 'Or was that the return of my incredible speed?'

'Oh, the incredible speed, definitely,' he grins.

The final score is Bunny's 11, International 4. My team is once again Mackerly champions.

'Nicely done,' Ethan says, giving me a brief hug. It's no more or less than anything he's done in the past, but it feels different, with the eyes of the town on us.

'Going to Lenny's, Lucy?' Carly calls.

'But of course,' I answer.

'See you there,' Ethan murmurs, then moves off.

As my teammates trickle off the field, I give a brief statement to Mick Onegin, who covers town sports for the tiny local paper, saying how we all had a great time this season and were grateful to win against such impressive opponents. I see Ethan holding Nicky over by his dugout, talking to my aunts. No doubt they're grilling him about the two of us. Well, he can hold his own with the Black Widows. More than hold his own, since they eat out of his hand.

I head back to my team's dugout to make sure everything's packed up. As usual, someone left a glove, a thermos containing gin, from the smell of it, and a cleat. Honestly, how does someone not notice their shoe is missing?

'Think you're so hot, don't you?' comes a voice.

I turn, unsurprised. 'Hey, Doral-Anne. How's it going?'

'I hurt my arm last week,' she states, eyeing me with disgust.

'Oh.' I pause. 'That's too bad. I noticed you didn't have your usual stuff.'

'Did you, Lucy? You noticed? How *honored* I am.'

That's it. I jam my fists into my hips and consider her. 'Doral-Anne, honestly, what is your problem? We barely spoke in school, and to the best of my knowledge, I never ran over your dog or kicked your kid in the head. So why are you so dang nasty to me all the time?'

'Oh, am I supposed to feel *sorry* for you like the rest of this town does, Lucy? Didn't I *worship* you enough?' Her voice pitches up in a nasty impression of an adult. 'Poor Lucy Lang's daddy died, so everyone be nice to her. Pick her for your team, make sure you ask her to sit next to you.' She makes a disgusted sound. 'Working at your little bakery, going off to your fancy school like you were some sort of princess.'

'I never acted liked that, Dor—'

'Then you waltz back into town and scoop up Jimmy Mirabelli. And I guess one Mirabelli boy wasn't good enough for you,

370

'cuz now you're fucking the other one.'

'You kiss your children with that mouth?' I ask, but my knees seem to be shaking.

'Don't you talk about my kids,' she snarls. 'And you wanna know something else, Princess?'

'Not really,' I answer.

'No, you like sticking your head in the sand, don't you? Well, too fucking bad.' She leans in close enough for me to smell her gum. 'Your St. Jimmy was sleeping with me when you first met him. He was gonna marry me.'

A hot wave of shock smashes into me so hard I can't even breathe. My hands flutter, then clench into fists. 'That is not true,' I choke out.

'Really? Why do you think I got fired? Jimmy didn't want his precious little princess to be upset by an old girlfriend hanging around.'

I can't seem to get any air into my lungs— my chest is paralyzed with shock. And hate. 'You got fired because you took money from the cash register,' I manage to answer, my voice like ground glass.

'Yeah, well, those arrogant assholes had that coming. And I'll tell you one more thing,' Doral-Anne says, wiping her hands on her pants. 'You really deserved that faithless shit you married, but you don't come close to deserving Ethan.'

I slap her so hard her head jerks back. My

hand stings, my arm buzzes, then falls limply to my side. Doral-Anne's face turns red, then white, my handprint clearly visible.

'Don't you ever speak about my husband that way again, Doral-Anne. Do you understand me?' My heart pounds so hard and fast I can barely hear myself. I almost hope she'll say something else so I can . . . I don't know. Beat her up. Though, despite the red haze that colors my vision at this moment, I realize she'd probably cream me. Stomp on my carcass. Scalp me.

Surprisingly she backs down. 'Truth hurts, doesn't it?' she says quietly. And with that, she turns and walks out of the dugout, across the infield and into center field. Toward the cemetery, and God help me, if she does anything to Jimmy's grave, I'll . . . I'll . . .

I'm hyperventilating. Sinking onto the bench, I can feel my heart flopping around like a convulsing tuna. My throat is tight, my vision graying . . . and images of the past flit before my eyes.

When Jimmy and I were first dating, I'd popped into the restaurant. Doral-Anne was there, all right, in the kitchen, talking to Jimmy. And Jimmy's face had been . . . guilty. When he'd seen me, his gaze jacked back to Doral-Anne, and there was this strange, awkward moment. Then he'd just about pounced on me, hustling me out of there as fast as he could.

Another time . . . oh, God. I remember when he told me Doral-Anne had been fired, and to show a little solidarity, I'd told him I'd never liked her. I wondered aloud why someone would steal from a family that had been so good to her. And Jimmy had looked so miserable at that moment that I playfully accused him of being a softy. 'If someone steals from you, sweetie, you have to fire them. Your dad did the right thing.'

Now I can see that Jimmy's misery might've been something else. He dumped Doral-Anne for me, and she lashed out by stealing, and Jimmy . . . he knew exactly why she did it.

That time I met Doral-Anne at the gas station, just after Jimmy died, her stunning cruelty as she taunted me because I'd never have Jimmy's baby . . . I wondered then, and many times since, what would make a person say something so hateful, so vicious, and suddenly, the answer is clear.

Revenge. Humiliation. A broken heart.

He was gonna marry me.

Oh, God. Oh, Jimmy.

My breath slams in and out of my chest, and if I don't do something about it, I'm going to faint. Which would be totally okay right now, because fainting would be preferable to the thoughts that are ricocheting through my head like a barrage of bullets. I lean forward, dangle my head between my knees, staring at the wads of gum and sunflower seeds littering

373

the cement floor of the dugout, my thoughts as ugly as the view.

'Lucy?'

My head jerks back, my vision swims, then clears. Ethan stands in the dimming light of the evening, frowning.

'Honey, what's wrong?' he asks, kneeling in front of me.

'You're getting gum on your pants,' I say distantly.

'Lucy.' He gives my shoulders a little shake. 'What's the matter, honey?'

I lean forward and rest my head on Ethan's shoulder for a minute, feel his hand stroke the back of my head. 'Lucy,' he whispers. 'What happened?'

I raise my head and look in his eyes. 'Did you know about Jimmy and Doral-Anne?' I ask.

He hesitates, and I have my answer. Rage gathers in a fireball.

'You knew?' I spit. 'You knew, didn't you?'

He sighs, looks down. And nods.

Something ugly and hot twists in my stomach. 'She's been gunning for me for years, and you never said *anything?*' My voice rises to a near shriek. 'I don't believe this! That woman hates me, has taken every chance she's had to kick me when I was down, and you never said a word? What the hell, Jimmy?'

Ethan's head jerks back, and his hands drop from my shoulders. 'Ethan,' he says, his voice hard.

'What?'

'Ethan. You just called me Jimmy.'

The pebble in my throat feels more like a tumor, malevolent and strangling. 'I'm a little upset right now, *Ethan*. Doral-Anne just informed me that she slept with Jimmy.'

'So?' His voice is oddly cool.

'*So?* So . . . so the Jimmy I knew would never have gone for someone like Doral-Anne.' My voice is breathy and furious.

'Why?'

'Because! Because she's meaner than acid, and he was wonderful. She was not his type.'

Ethan stands up. 'Right. You were his type. He dumped her and went for you. So what's the problem?'

I splutter wordlessly. The *problem?* The problem is, I don't want to picture Jimmy—*my* Jimmy—with a nasty little number like Doral-Anne of the snake tattoos. Picture him kissing her, or oh, God, undressing her! Gah! Could he honestly have mentioned *marriage* to her?

'Lucy,' Ethan says wearily, 'Jimmy fell for you the second he laid eyes on you. And you fell for him.' His hands rase in frustration. 'Why are you complaining? Doral-Anne's had it rough—'

'Right. Poor misunderstood Doral-Anne.' I stand up as well, my legs shaking. 'I'm going home. Tell the gang sorry I couldn't make it.'

'Lucy—'

'Ethan, I really want to be alone. Okay?' And with that, I sling my baseball bag over my shoulder and head out of the park on my ridiculous path. Out of the park, around the cemetery. My throat thickens as I pass the point closest to my father's grave. I could really use a dad at this moment. I wonder if Joe Torre would take a call from me.

He was gonna marry me.

How could I never have known that? Jimmy kept that from me. Gianni and Marie must've known, too.

And so did Ethan, all these years. He befriended Doral-Anne and he never bothered to tell me why. Well, I think fiercely, slashing my hand across my teary eyes, they say the wife is always the last to know.

*   *   *

An hour later, I'm sitting on my couch, Fat Mikey on one side, a box of Hostess Cupcakes on the other, three empty wrappers on the floor. I stare straight ahead, my mind empty except for memories. On the TV screen, Jimmy and I stare at each other, smiling, kissing, laughing. He chose 'Angel' by Dave Matthews for our first dance. *Wherever you are, I swear, you'll be my angel.* Of course, *I* was supposed to be the angel . . . in the romantic, I-can't-believe-you're-so-wonderful way. Jimmy was supposed to stay alive and adore me. He wasn't supposed to leave me. And even though he didn't know me then, he sure as hell wasn't supposed to find Doral-Anne attractive. To sleep with her. To talk about *marrying* her.

At this moment in real time, Fat Mikey decides a wad of hair must be expelled from the far reaches of his intestinal tract. He starts hacking, then squeaks as I heave him into my arms. 'Come on, buddy, out on the balcony,' I grunt, opening the slider with my elbow. There. Made it. Fat Mikey shoots me a disgruntled look, aggravated that I prevented him from gacking on the couch, then returns his attention to the business at hand. I sigh and lean in the doorway, waiting for my cat. The potted ferns I bought last spring have withered from the cold, their leaves yellow and straggling. The long, gray winter is coming.

Then I straighten, goose bumps rising on my arms. There, on the wide railing of the balcony, something gleams, catching the light from the street.

A dime.

Without daring to breathe, I tiptoe over to the railing and touch the dime with one finger. Heads up, FDR quite youthful and virile.

'Jimmy?' I whisper. 'Are you there?'

No voice speaks, no image shimmers in the corner. The night is still. A little breeze blows from the ocean, rustling the dead leaves of the

377

ferns. From my dead husband, I hear nothing.

'I sure miss you,' I say, my throat tightening. I think about everything I wish I could ask him . . . what to do about Ethan, how to comfort his parents. If he ever loved Doral-Anne. If that matters. 'I could really use some advice, Jim,' I add. 'Not that "Check the toast" wasn't helpful.'

My cat kills the moment with an enormous gag. I wince, look down at the hairball. 'You'll clean that up, of course,' I tell my cat, who decides I'm adorable and butts his head against my shin. With a sigh, I pocket the dime and turn to go inside, then start in fright.

Ethan stands in my living room, staring at my wedding video, arms folded across his chest.

'Hey,' I say, closing the slider behind me.

'Hey,' he returns without looking away from the TV. I wonder if he just heard me talking to Jimmy. 'Having a nice night, Lucy?'

I sigh. 'Ethan . . .' Finally he looks at me, his eyebrows raised expectantly. Judgmentally, one might say.

Grabbing the remote off the couch where I left it, I hit the Off button, and the image of Anne and Laura dancing is cut short. Ethan remains where he is, arms still folded. 'Ethan,' I state firmly, 'I have to clean up a hairball.'

'Okay,' he says. 'Don't let me keep you.' He turns to leave.

'Ethan!' I bark. He stops, turns around, his

face unreadable. 'Look, I'm sorry I took your head off,' I say in a softer voice. 'It's just . . . hard, learning something about Jimmy that I—' My voice breaks a little. 'That I didn't expect. And I'll be honest, Eth. I don't like it that you knew all this time and never said anything. I figured you'd tell me something as big as that.'

'Why would I tell you, Lucy? You'd just be hurt and upset. Like you are now.' He stares at me, waiting. Always waiting.

I take a deep breath and let it out slowly, wondering if Ethan has other little pockets of decay on Jimmy. No. That's not fair to Jimmy. He dated Doral-Anne, and as Ethan said, so what? It was before he met me. Doesn't mean Jimmy was some sort of man-slut.

'So how are things with your parents?' I ask, not really wanting to hear the answer.

'They're okay. Improving,' Ethan says. A vast distance seems to be spreading between us like a tar pit, eager to suck us down and mire us in the muck.

'And how are you doing, Ethan?' I ask, my voice horribly polite.

'I'm fine, Lucy,' he says gently.

I swallow, then swallow again around the pebble in my throat. 'That's good. Tell your folks I said hi.'

'Will do,' he says.

'I guess I'll see you tomorrow.'

'Good night, then.'

'Good night, Ethan.' The door closes softly behind him.

Then, feeling sick and too full of sugar and chocolate, I clean up the hairball.

When that lovely task is complete, I flop down on my couch. The night is still painfully young. I could watch more of my wedding video, but crap, there's no point in that, is there? I can't have Jimmy back, dimes or no dimes. I could call Ethan or go upstairs and try to smooth things over, but I just seem to be making things worse lately. Maybe we need a little space.

Too bad Grinelda's not really psychic. Too bad I couldn't talk to my dad, since Mom has abdicated the throne when it comes to parental guidance. I briefly consider jumping onto the online widows group I belonged to the first couple of years after Jimmy died and asking for advice, but I don't really know what to say. I've moved on . . . sort of . . . and I love the man I'm with. I just can't seem to make him very happy.

And so I find myself in the kitchen, baking until midnight. Bittersweet chocolate cake. Fittingly enough, it's Ethan's favorite.

CHAPTER TWENTY-SEVEN

The Taste of Mackerly is not only a fun evening, it also raises funds for the town's emergency services program. In addition to the food vendors, there's face painting, games and a tank where citizens will have the chance to dunk town notables, including the mayor, Father Adhyatman and Lenny. (Right now, Father A. is taunting Reverend Covers for throwing like a Protestant, whatever that means.) Kids get hair weaves and henna tattoos, and Grinelda usually does readings (twenty dollars for fifteen minutes; I don't know how she does it).

The town green, which makes up the northern edge of Ellington Park and borders Main Street, is dotted with tents—Lenny's, Gianni's, Starbucks, Bunny's, Eva's Catering, Cakes by Kim. A band plays on a little stage near the entrance to the cemetery. The trees glow with color—this weekend is really the last of our glorious foliage. Teenagers huddle in groups, giggling and texting and flipping their hair. I hope Ash will have a few friends here tonight, I think with a pang. I told her she could hang out with me, but I'm not really her favorite person these days. I don't seem to be anybody's favorite person, in fact.

The crowning glory of the evening is

Stuffie—an enormous, papier-mâché stuffed clam. Tradition dictates that Stuffie be driven slowly around the park three times—the streets are closed off to all but the pickup truck pulling our mascot. After the final pass, Stuffie will be towed to the center of the park and, for reasons unclear to many, will then be ignited as the townsfolk cheer. It's rather primal, but Stuffie is an undeniable hit.

I'd skipped the Taste of Mackerly after Jimmy died, fleeing to Provincetown for the weekend, leaving the Black Widows to run Bunny's paltry booth so I could avoid the well-meaning assurances that I'd meet someone else and the hit-and-run glances of the pitying. But I've come to love this event. After all, I love Mackerly, and this is one of her finest moments.

Our booth looks especially pretty this year. We're right on the edge of Main Street, a prime location. Our tent is a cute little yellow-and white-striped number, and underneath, I've covered a large table with a brightly embroidered Hungarian tablecloth. Earlier this afternoon, I wound flower lights around the tent poles and through the bars that support the tent ceiling. Two clumps of helium-filled balloons are tied in front—red, green and white, the colors of Hungary. I put out a few vases, arrange some zinnias and late roses, hung out a banner that says Bunny's Bakery—The Finest In Hungarian Pastries.

After I begged for the opportunity to bring some homemade goodies, Iris finally compromised and agreed to make some authentic pastries in addition to the pumpkin cookies. 'I'll do it,' she said. 'You have your hands full with those Mirabellis.'

She was right, of course. Yesterday, I drove Gianni to his cardiologist, took Marie to buy some new shoes and a coat. Haven't seen Ethan for a day or two, though.

'I didn't bother with pastries,' Iris announces as she and Rose pull up in the Crown Vic they share. 'And no one wants to admit they eat prune anymore, so I didn't make the *lekvar kifli*.'

'You didn't? But you made *mezeskalacs*, right?' I ask. *Mezeskalacs* are honey cakes, spiced with ginger and nutmeg, perfect for the fall, and something only a Hungarian bakery could supply. Hauling out a bakery box from Iris's backseat, I peer anxiously within.

Dang it! There's nothing except those awful tooth-chipping cookies. Knowing Iris, these may well be the same cookies from last year. 'Iris, I thought we agreed you'd make some other things, too!' Slightly panicked, I look in the back seat for another box. Nothing. 'We don't have anything else? Why didn't you call me, Iris? I would've made something!'

'I didn't have time,' Iris announces breezily, applying a coat of Coral Glow. 'I was very busy last night.'

'Busy doing what?' I ask.

'For your information, *The Tudors* was on, Miss Nosy-Pants. And stop worrying! Everyone loves these cookies.' She gives me a peck on the cheek, then says, 'Help your Aunt Rose with that cake.'

Rose is struggling to get a wedding cake out of the trunk of the car . . . well, a plastic cake model covered in spackle-type frosting. It's a display, meant to charm soon-to-be brides, but unfortunately, this one looks rather dated. It's not bad . . . just a little plain, a few easy roses on the top and nothing else. In this era of ornate weddings, we could've used a little pizzazz.

'Pretty cake,' I lie, grabbing the edge of the foil-covered tray.

'Oh, this old thing?' Rose answers, peeking around the cake at me. 'It's from a few years ago.' She pauses to blow on the top of the cake, causing a puff of dust to swirl up into my face. 'I thought about doing another one, but . . .'

'The Tudors?' I suggest, coughing a little.

She smiles. 'Yes! Do you watch it, too?'

'I don't, Rose,' I answer.

My mother pulls up in her MiniCooper, looking like Katharine Hepburn about to go out for martinis—wide-legged winter-white pants, a red boatneck sweater, double rope of pearls and patent leather red pumps. 'Hello!' she calls merrily, her cheeks pink, skin glowing.

'Hi, Mom. Did you bring the drinks?' I ask. The beverages are Mom's annual contribution, and I'm hoping for hot cocoa, even if it's from a mix.

'I thought we'd serve Hi-C,' Mom says, pointing to an industrial-size jug of the sugary drink. 'Get that, will you, sweetheart?'

'Great,' I mutter. We have Hi-C and inedible cookies. Starbucks will have cake and brownies, cookies and tarts, not to mention all those dang coffee varieties.

'I hope the Starbucks will be selling that hot chocolate,' Aunt Rose says merrily, echoing my thoughts. 'It's like heroin! I can't get enough! Oh, look, there are the Mirabellis! Hello!'

Gianni's Ristorante Italiano is back under previous management. It took Gianni about twelve hours to get things back the way they were, and the cousin's husband's brother is now working as a prep chef as Gianni growls and barks, as happy as he gets.

'Hi, guys,' I say, blushing. One doesn't quickly forget that one's in-laws caught one in the act.

'How youse girls doing?' Gianni asks the Black Widows, giving me a nod. It's something.

Marie, at least, is willing to hug me and pat my cheek. 'You look so beautiful, Lucy!'

My mother smiles smugly. It's true . . . I'm

wearing real clothes today. A long, chocolatey brown skirt that stops about three inches from those gorgeous mahogany boots, which are making their debut today. A dark red cashmere sweater. Gold necklace, hoop earrings, even a little eye shadow and lip gloss.

'What are you selling over there?' Rose peeps. 'It smells wonderful!'

Gianni's, Marie tells us, is serving bruschetta (with my bread, ironically, the one good thing that comes out of Bunny's), bowls of minestrone soup, which is nice, since it's cool this afternoon and getting colder as the sun sets. Gnocchi with vodka sauce (Jimmy's recipe . . . apparently, the cousin's husband's brother had changed it and Gianni near stroked out when he was informed). And yes, Marie's famous tiramisu. I can't imagine anyone wanting our concrete-textured, clove-saturated pumpkin cookies painted with that garish, tasteless orange frosting when Marie's tiramisu is available.

'So how is it, being back?' Iris asks Gianni. Both being the bossy type, they've always had a grudging respect for the other.

'Not bad. We're back in our house. Sold the condo in Arizona for ten grand more than we paid for it, our house was still on the market, I says to Marie, I says, "Why not? We know what we're getting!" So Ethan called the movers and we'll be back in our own house next week. Like we never left.'

386

'Is Ethan here?' my mother asks. Marie, who is chatting up my aunts, falls abruptly silent.

'Oh, he's here, all right,' Gianni grumbles. 'With that *del cazzo* milkshake.'

Right. International Foods is the biggest sponsor of the Taste of Mackerly. They pay for all the tent rentals, the lights, the liquor permit and the extra cops to control traffic. In addition, Ethan's listed in the big donors section of the program, and it's already been announced that we've raised enough for new air packs for the firefighters as well as a new radio system. But that kind of generosity doesn't matter to Gianni, who still views *Instead* as a personal fork stuck in his heart by that no-good second son of his.

'What do you think of him and Lucy?' Iris asks, never one for subtlety. Gianni's impressive eyebrows lower.

Marie darts a glance my way. 'Well . . . it's . . .'

'Nonny!'

Saved by a four-year-old! Nicky comes charging over, crashing into Marie's legs. 'Well, hello, little man!' she exclaims, trying to pick him up. Unfortunately Marie is five-foot-nothing, and Nicky had a recent growth spurt.

'Come here, you,' Gianni says, his face softening with adoration. He picks up his grandson and kisses him loudly on the cheek, then chuckles and ruffles Nicky's hair.

387

'I ate a worm,' Nicky announces, holding up a bag of gummy strings.

'That's disgusting,' Gianni says. 'Here, have a cookie. Want Poppy to buy you a cookie?'

Nicky looks at the pumpkin cookies spread out on our table. 'Do I have to?'

'No, baby, you don't,' I say with a sigh.

'Hi, guys,' Parker says, joining us. 'Anyone have anything good to eat yet?'

'Not yet,' Marie says. 'How about you?'

Parker's cheeks stain with pink. 'Um . . . not really.'

'You've been to Starbucks, haven't you?' I ask.

'Busted,' she murmurs. 'But only for that hot chocolate.'

'Isn't it to die for?' Rose exclaims. 'Marie, have you tried it yet?'

Indeed, a dozen people mingle in front of the Starbucks tent, despite the fact that the Taste of Mackerly doesn't officially start until four, ten minutes from now. Ash, who used to boycott the chain store as a sign of solidarity, is waiting in line as well. Ouch.

Just then Ethan walks past Starbucks' tent, a large box in his arms. He stops to say hi to Ash, and I watch as her face turns red. Ethan grins at something she says, and Ash smiles back, glowing. Ethan moves on, then pauses before crossing the street—Stuffie the Clam is making a practice run lap before his immolation. Ethan calls something to the driver of the pickup—Ed Langley of Ed's Egg Farm, just before the bridge—then crosses the street. He pauses in front of his parked car to say something to Roxanne the surly waitress, and she laughs and pats his shoulder before crossing the street toward the green. Only Ethan could get a smile from Roxanne.

He's so *nice* to everyone. That's not news to me, but it feels awfully good to see in action just the same. I hope he'll come by soon, so we can smooth out anything that needs smoothing. I miss him. I'll tell him that.

I pull my gaze off Ethan, then freeze. Doral-Anne glares at me from ten yards away, Kate on one side, Leo on the other, the usual poison shooting from her eyes. Her daughter tugs her hand, and Doral-Anne looks down, puts her hand on Kate's head and says something, her face softening into a smile. Well, well. A moment of maternal tenderness from the lady with the snake tattoo.

A bit flustered by the jealousy that's reared its ugly head, I busy myself trying to arrange the cookies on our pretty table so they don't look quite so hideous, but it's no good. They're just so . . . graceless. So tacky. If I ever had control of the bakery, I'd ban these for life.

'Can we have a bunch of these?' asks a boy of about twelve.

I look over my shoulder to see who he's talking to—no one there—then back at the lad. 'Are you talking to me, sweetie?'

'Yes. Could we have some cookies?'

'Really?' I ask, then give my head a little shake. 'I mean, sure. Of course you can. How many?'

'Maybe ten?' he says.

'Wow,' I say. 'You bet.' I bag ten cookies and hand them to the kid, who pays, thanks me and dashes off.

Iris gives me an arch look. 'Guess they're not as bad as you thought, are they?' she says, tutting.

'Can I have some, too?' another boy asks.

'Sure!' I tell him, then glance at Iris, who's preening like a cat over a dead mouse. 'Sorry, Iris. I underestimated their appeal.'

'Yes, you did,' she agrees.

'Lucy, we're going to look around a little,' Rose cheeps. 'If you don't mind, of course. Want anything?'

Which means they're off to visit their friends, probably get a hot chocolate from Starbucks. 'I'm fine,' I say. 'Take your time, enjoy yourselves.'

'See you around,' says Gianni, still holding Nick. 'Parker, all right if we take the little guy with us?'

'Of course,' Parker says. 'Bye, Nicky. Give Mommy a kiss.'

He obliges, then blows one to me. 'Here's yours, Aunt Wucy!'

'Charmer,' I call, pretending to catch his

kiss. I blow one back, and he catches it dramatically, then presses it against his cheek, grinning.

'That boy is the image of his father.' I smile.

'Makes you want one, doesn't it?' Parker asks. 'A little Ethan?'

My smile drops a notch. 'Mmm,' I say. Clearly the cookies need rearranging. Or the Hi-C needs, er, checking.

'What? Things aren't going well?'

'His parents caught us on the couch the other night,' I mutter, my face burning.

'Oh, crap!' Parker crows with undisguised glee. 'Were you doing it?'

'Close.'

She throws her head back, a melodic peal of laughter filling the air. 'What did you do?'

'Covered up,' I say. 'Quickly.'

'Holy shit,' Parker sighs happily. 'How awful.' Then she notices my expression. 'Everything else good, though? I thought you guys were doing okay.'

'Yeah, well. It's fine. We have things to work out,' I say.

'Hello, ladies' comes a voice.

My face floods with heat. 'Matt! Hi! How are you? Wow! Nice to see you. I didn't know you were coming!' I'm babbling, I realize, but the shock of seeing him affects me, and Grinelda's words come back to me in a rush. *Check the toast. Check the bread. Check the bread man?* 'Matt, this is my friend, Parker

391

Welles. Parker, Matt DeSalvo.'

'Great meeting you,' he says, shaking her hand so hard she winces. Jimmy had a crushing handshake, too.

'Nice to meet you, too,' she answers, cutting her eyes to me. 'How do you know Lucy here?'

'He's from NatureMade,' I explain hastily. 'The bread man.'

'Oh, sure,' Parker says, giving Matt an assessing look. I wait for him to notice her— she's rather incredibly beautiful, after all, but he just smiles and turns his eyes to me.

'How's the decision-making process coming along?' he asks. 'Any more questions about our offer?'

'Uh . . . I . . . I don't think so,' I stammer. His presence really flusters me . . . so much like Jimmy, but not quite there. Sort of like how coffeecake made with nonfat sour cream lacks the richness of the real thing. How Coldplay doesn't quite measure up to U2. Matt is rather like . . . Jimmy Lite.

'You know what?' Parker says. 'I think I'll catch up with my son. Nice meeting you, Matt. I'll catch up with you later, Luce.'

'Nice meeting you, too,' Matt says as she leaves.

'She's my friend,' I say rather stupidly.

'I see,' he replies. He really does have nice eyes. Not as nice as Jimmy's, but pretty nice nonetheless.

'Um, about the offer, uh, I don't have any questions. You answered them the other night.' *Stop babbling, Lucy.* 'I'm just taking my time. Making sure it's the right thing for me.'

'As you should,' Matt agrees. 'Well, if there's anything I can do, just say the word. I do need a decision by November First, though. I think I mentioned that.'

'Yes. You did,' I say. He smells good. 'And honestly, I can't think of a reason to say no. It's a great offer, and I'll give you a definite answer next week, how's that?'

'That would be fantastic. We think your bread is the best, and that's what NatureMade wants. The best.' He gives me a little wink, and a little buzz attraction wriggles in my stomach.

'Flatterer,' I say, unable to suppress a grin.

'So tell me about this Taste of Mackerly,' Matt says. 'I'm probably hallucinating, but I think I saw a giant clam a few minutes ago.'

'Show that clam some respect,' I return. 'We're going to burn him later. These are his final hours.'

'I see.' He grins. 'Anything else I should know?'

It's easy to talk to him—he seems so . . . level. So uncomplicated, really, since there's no sticky past or mishmash of feelings here. I point out Lenny's as the place for stuffed clams as well as my in-laws' booth for Italian, and he promises to check both out.

393

'Hello, hello, hello!' Rose coos from behind me. All three Black Widows hold Starbucks cups.

'Well, if it isn't the *toast* man,' Iris says, giving me a wink that contorts her entire face. 'And how are we all getting along today?'

'What a beautiful coat,' my mother murmurs, reaching out to touch the sleeve of Matt's suede bomber jacket. 'I always liked a man who knew how to dress.'

The Black Widows seem to have forgotten that I'm actually dating Ethan these days. My stomach starts to ache.

Matt accepts a cookie from Iris, who gives me yet another arch look.

'Careful with those,' I murmur to him. 'The government is thinking of using them in Afghanistan.'

'Some boys were playing street hockey with them earlier,' he says, his voice low, and I burst into laughter. Poor Iris! Matt smiles down at me. He's a hair shorter than Jimmy— well, maybe more than a hair. Taller than Ethan, though. Not that I'm comparing them.

'Lucy, that string of lights isn't working,' Rose says, pointing to the ceiling of our little tent. She's right—the cord's come unplugged from the other string.

'I'll get it,' Iris says, but the thought of my seventy-six-year-old aunt standing on a chair is not a happy one.

'No, no, I've got it, Iris. No problem.' I

394

wrestle the folding chair out of her strong hands and stand it beneath the strand of lights. The ground is soft from last night's rain, and the chair isn't exactly stable.

'Let me help,' Matt says. He offers his hand, and I take it, standing warily on the chair. It wobbles, and Matt reaches up and puts his hands around my waist.

'Thanks,' I say, a little breathlessly. His hands are big. And warm.

The light is replugged. Matt helps me down, and I find that it's a little hard to look at his face. Somewhere on the other side of the park, a police car gives a short blip.

'Nice to have a man around to help,' Rose sighs dreamily.

'Thank you,' I say again, glancing up at Matt.

'My pleasure,' Matt says. His voice is low and intimate.

My face flushes. I glance across the street, and guilt floods my heart.

Ethan is watching me, standing stock-still on the curb as people mill around behind him, getting ready for Stuffie's triumphant circumnavigation of the park.

He looks like the last kid picked for a team. Forlorn, trying not to show it, and something cracks in my heart. He doesn't look away, and neither do I. The police car blips again.

'Holy Mary' comes a voice behind me. Marie. 'Oh, God. Oh, God, I have to sit.'

Without turning around, I know what's happening. Marie and Gianni have returned and spotted Matt, and the resemblance to Jimmy has hit them hard. I glance back—yep, Gianni's helping Marie to a bench, my mother flutters around them like a brightly colored bird, Iris's hand is on Matt's arm, explaining who the Mirabellis are. Matt glances at me, an apologetic half smile on his face, looking more like Jimmy than ever.

'Lucy, get some water,' Rose says, turning to me. 'Your mother-in-law's had a shock.'

I don't move. The police siren chirps again, closer now. Turning back, I see that Ethan's not there. 'Ethan!' I shout. 'Ethan!' There he is, a few yards up the sidewalk. Tommy Malloy stops him to say something, and Ethan nods. 'Ethan!' I call again.

He hears me . . . the setting sun illuminates his face as he turns toward me. He's waiting, and I know I need to say the right thing.

'I need you over here, babe,' I call. Loudly. There. *Babe.* Not a term that can be misconstrued. *Babe* is someone you're sleeping with. You don't call someone *babe* without good reason.

Tommy Malloy nudges Ethan's arm and makes some comment, and Ethan, not taking his eyes off me, grins. Relief sings through me—I didn't blow it after all. I smile back, warmth rising in my heart as I look at the man I love. Because yes, I do love Ethan, and it's time he knew it.

Ethan waits a second—Ed's driving Stuffie past just now—then, when the clam passes, starts into the street, each step bringing him closer to me. His eyes are on me, that smile still in place, and my heart swells.

Then one of the boys who bought the pumpkin cookies slaps a shot into the street. Another boy darts out in front of Ed Langley's truck, hockey stick in hand, and smacks the makeshift puck into a storm drain. Ed stomps on the brakes—he's only going about ten miles an hour—and yells at the kid, who runs into the crowd and disappears. No harm done. But Stuffie, unsettled by the lurching stop, sways, then slowly, inevitably tips into the street with a crash, right in front of an oncoming state police car.

Lights flashing, the cruiser swerves around the fallen Stuffie, then jerks back to correct course.

And hits Ethan.

Ethan tumbles through the air like a rag doll. My hand reaches out helplessly as he lands on the pavement with a sickening thud, ten feet in front of the cruiser.

He doesn't move.

The images rain into my head like bullets. The cop car screeches to a halt, the officer already on his radio. Ethan is so still, but pandemonium explodes all around him. People are screaming, and Tommy Malloy races to Ethan's side. Parker, too, emerges from the crowd, running to Ethan, her long hair wild around her face. He still hasn't moved. Ed Langley's out of his truck, his hand covering his mouth in horror. Roxanne the waitress is on her cell phone. Ash joins the crowd at Ethan's side, her chains swinging as she crouches next to his body. His *body*. I look down the street and see Nicky's eyes wide with terror, his mouth open in a scream, but I can't hear him over the roaring in my ears. Doral-Anne picks him up. Ethan has not moved. There might be blood. I think there's blood. Christopher, who was required to take a paramedic course before Corinne would agree to have children, materializes as well and puts his hand to Ethan's head, then withdraws it. Yes. There's blood.

'Oh, my God, who is that? What happened?' my mother gasps.

I turn to her. 'Ethan got hit by a car,' I say, and then the grass is under my face, damp and cold, and welcome, because at least now I don't have to watch Ethan die.

CHAPTER TWENTY-EIGHT

Ethan is taken to the hospital. I, too, am transported, once again, to the Emergency Room, not at his side, as perhaps would be fitting, but in my mother's car. By the time I'd come to, Ethan had already been packed up into the ambulance, and though I was repeatedly assured that he was conscious and talking, I couldn't seem to stop screaming his name over and over in a voice so contorted by terror I didn't recognize it as my own. My memory of those moments isn't all that clear. I do recall Iris stepping in and slapping me rather hard, which stopped the screaming, at least.

I'm put in a cubicle, as I can't seem to answer the question as to whether or not I'm okay. Unsurprisingly Dr. Hateswomen is the doctor on call. He asks me if I'm taking any more drugs, drinking or smoking anything illegal. My mother stands at my side, awkwardly patting my shoulder.

'Where is Ethan?' I ask hoarsely, my throat raw, my earlier screams echoing in my mind. I'm shaking uncontrollably, tears streak down my face, and I've thrown up twice so far. 'Are you sure he's okay? Is he dead? Are you just afraid to tell me?'

'He's not dead, honey, but I'll go check on

him, okay?' my mother says. Her face is white but set.

'Have you taken any more of that medication I told you to throw out?' the doctor asks, bending down to peer into my eyes with a searing flash of penlight.

'Turn that light off or I'll stuff it up your ass,' I snarl, batting his hand away.

'Patient exhibits aggressive tendencies,' he murmurs to himself. 'Please control yourself, Miss, er—' he glances at my hospital bracelet '—Miss Mirabelli . . . or I'll have to call for restraints.'

'He's just a few doors down,' Mom says, bustling back into the room. 'He's got a bad cut on his head, but he's talking and asked about you.'

'Are you sure?' I ask. My stomach convulses again, but I manage not to puke this time.

'Honey, he's fine,' she murmurs, stroking my hair, such a foreign gesture of motherly love from her that I don't believe her. Ethan's dead, or horribly hurt, and no one's telling me.

Dr. Hateswomen takes out his stethoscope. 'If we could stop chatting and get on with this exam,' he says, rolling his eyes.

'Leave her alone, you ass,' my mother snaps. 'Her husband died in a car accident, she just watched her boyfriend get hit by a car and she fainted. She'll be fine. Doesn't take four years of medical school to figure that out.' She takes my arm in a firm grip. 'Come on, honey. Let's see Ethan. You'll feel better.'

Ignoring Dr. Hateswomen's outraged cry of 'Patient leaving against medical advice!' Mom leads me down the hall to another examination room. My legs are shaking wildly, and my head seems to be disconnected from my body. Mom would tell me if he was dead, wouldn't she? She wouldn't tell me he was okay and then bring me to his body, would she? The tears continue to pour out of my eyes almost without me noticing.

There he is, lying on a gurney, holding a wad of bloody gauze to his head. A woman is pressing on his abdomen. His shirt is open and streaked with blood. His *blood*. My knees threaten to give out, but I stay upright somehow. 'Ethan,' I say in a strangled whisper.

'Hey,' he says, making a move to sit up. The doctor tuts and pushes him gently back on the bed.

'Are you okay?' I ask.

'I just got banged up, honey,' he says. 'I'm fine.'

'Hi there,' says the woman. 'I'm Dr. Pierce. Your husband's going to be okay, from the looks of it.'

'We're not married,' I answer woodenly. There's blood all over the side of Ethan's face. The pebble is back, and I give a choking cough.

'Ethan, I'll go find your folks and tell them you're okay,' my mom says, patting his leg.

'Thanks, Daisy,' he says, sounding reassuringly normal. 'Lucy, I'm really sorry I scared you, honey.' His eyes are worried.

'I think you're one lucky bastard,' Dr. Pierce says cheerfully, 'but let's get you down to Radiology and make sure. We'll do a CAT scan, just in case we're missing any internal injuries.' My vision grays momentarily, then clears. Internal injuries. Jimmy's official cause of death was massive internal injuries. 'Sometimes shock camouflages the pain,' the doctor continues, 'so we'll take a look and make sure that spleen is okay.'

Ethan looks at me steadily. More than likely, he knows what I'm thinking. I can't take my eyes off his bloody face. My hands buzz, and my knees are water.

The doctor glances at me. 'Lucy, is it? Have a seat, hon. You're white as a ghost.' She gives me a squeeze on the shoulder, then leaves the room, calling someone named Karen to transport a patient.

Ethan reaches out the hand not holding the gauze to his head. 'You okay, honey?' he asks.

I teeter to the edge of his bed and take his hand. 'I'm fine,' I say around the stone. 'Are you really all right?'

He nods, then winces. 'I'm fine. I guess I'll need stitches,' he says. 'And I'll be pretty sore tomorrow.' He looks at me seriously. 'You

402

sure you're all right, Lucy? Your hand is ice-cold.'

'I'm fine,' I repeat. I'm fine, he's fine, everyone's fine.

'What about Nicky? Did he see me get hit?' Ethan asks.

'I think so,' I repeat, not wanting to tell him that I stood there like a lamppost and watched his son scream. That as half the town rushed to his side, I remained rooted where I was, watching him bleed on the asphalt. That I fainted when he needed me the most.

'Damn it,' Ethan mutters. 'Can you make sure he knows I'm okay? He must've been so scared.' I nod, and Ethan again looks into my eyes. 'Your mom said you fainted,' he says, his thumb rubbing the back of my hand.

'Ethan, I'm so sorry,' I whisper, my eyes filling.

'Oh, honey, don't say that,' he says, pulling me in for an awkward hug. 'Don't cry.'

I nod and swallow, and swallow again.

An orderly or tech comes in, and I pull back from Ethan and stand on my unsteady legs. She unclicks a few things on Ethan's gurney. 'Going for a little ride, my friend,' she chirrups. 'You're the one hit by the giant clam, right?'

'Police car,' Ethan says, raising an eyebrow mischievously. 'Imagine the lawsuit.'

'Yes, indeedy,' the tech agrees. 'Okay, big guy. Off we go. Wife, you can stay here or go

403

into the waiting room with everyone else, okay? Back in a bit.'

I float down the hall, my mind numb, to the waiting room. There are the Mirabellis, Gianni's heavy arm around Marie's plump shoulders, Marie's mascara smeared from crying. Mom perches on the arm of Gianni's chair, patting his back. Parker holds Nicky on her lap, and he's hiccupping, thumb in his mouth, though he gave that up last year. Christopher and Corinne are there, too, Emma asleep on Chris's shoulder. Everyone falls silent at the sight of me.

'He seems fine,' I report in a squeaky voice. 'They're doing a CAT scan just to make sure, but he's awake, talking, all that. He's sorry he scared everyone.' I crouch down in front of Nicky and stroke his head with a shaking hand. 'Daddy's fine, honey. He has a cut on his head, but he's okay.'

Nicky buries his face against Parker's neck. 'Did you hear that, sweetie?' Parker murmurs, kissing her boy. 'Daddy's fine. I bet we can go see him when he's cleaned up a little.'

She's right. Forty-five minutes later, Ethan has been cleared by the radiologist, and a PA has put seven stitches in his head, who declares this 'a beautiful concussion.' Ethan kisses his son repeatedly, is hugged by his mother, watches his father wipe tears from his eyes and reassures everyone that he's fine.

'Why did Stuffie fall on you, Daddy?' Nicky

asks, pressing a button. Ethan's bed rises a few inches.

'Stuffie and I have never gotten along,' Ethan says. 'He's a big meanie.'

Nicky giggles. 'Maybe Mommy can put you in a book.'

'The Holy Rollers and Stuffie the Big Meanie,' Parker says. 'I love it.' Ethan smiles at her, then kisses Nicky again.

I observe the whole scene as if I'm floating above it, oddly detached. My heart stutters and races, and my throat is so tight I'm surprised I can breathe, but outwardly, I'm calm.

A nurse pops her head into the exam room after about a half hour. 'As soon as the doctor signs your discharge papers, you can go home, Mr. Mirabelli.'

'We'll wait for you outside, son,' Gianni says. He grips Ethan's shoulder briefly.

'Thanks, Dad,' Ethan replies.

'Come on, Nicky. We'll see Daddy tomorrow,' Parker says. She leans down and kisses Ethan's cheek. 'I'm glad you're okay, idiot,' she murmurs. 'Next time, look both ways when you cross the street.'

'That's right. Blame the victim.' Ethan grins. 'Good night, Nick the Tick,' he says, hugging his son. He winces slightly—he's probably a mass of bruises, let alone the concussion and gash on the head. Hit by a car. My brain leaps away from the image of him

405

tumbling through the air, the dull *whump* sound his body made when he landed on the street . . . I choke out another cough, wave to Corinne, Chris and my mother as they make their way out, too.

And then it's just Ethan and me. I help him button up his bloodied shirt, my fingers shaking as they fumble to get the job done. I can smell the sharp scent of disinfectant, can see where blood has matted his hair.

We don't speak.

Finally, after what seems like ages, yet another doctor sticks his head into the room. He looks at Ethan's chart, then does a double-take when he sees me. 'Okay, Mr. Mirabelli. Tylenol for your headache, a nice hot shower. You're gonna feel like you were hit by a car tomorrow.' He smiles at his own joke. 'Got someone to stay with you?'

'Yes,' Ethan says.

'All right.' He hands Ethan a copy of instructions. 'You're one lucky bastard,' he says.

'That I am,' Ethan agrees.

The doctor starts to leave, then turns to me. 'You're Jimmy Mirabelli's widow, aren't you?'

I blink. 'Yes,' I answer.

He looks at Ethan. 'So you must be Jimmy's little brother.'

'That's right,' Ethan says smoothly.

'I'm Tony Aresco,' he says. 'I went to high school with Jimmy.' He gives that sad smile

I've seen so many times in the past five and a half years. 'Great guy. I'm so sorry for your loss.'

'Thanks,' I answer.

'Take care,' he says. He gives my shoulder a squeeze as he leaves.

I stand there for a second, then pick up Ethan's shoes and hand them to him. He doesn't put them on, just places them carefully on the bed, then looks up at me, his hair sticking up on the side where they put the stitches.

'Are you feeling okay?' I ask.

'I'm fine,' he says for probably the fiftieth time tonight. Those brown eyes are steady on me. Ethan knows me, after all, knows me better than anyone, really, and no one has ever accused him of being dumb. My eyes sting as they fill with tears.

Ethan sighs, the sigh of the defeated, and looks at the floor. He knows. 'You may as well say it,' he says quietly.

I bite my lip hard enough to taste blood. 'I'm so sorry, Ethan,' I whisper, because whispering is easier with the stone in my throat. 'I can't do this. I want to, but I can't.'

He doesn't answer for a second, still staring at the floor. Then he shakes his head slightly. 'Okay, Lucy,' he says, weariness weighing down his voice. 'If this is what you want, fine.'

And just like that, we're done.

CHAPTER TWENTY-NINE

For the first time in six years, I spend the night at my mother's. The last time I did such a thing was right after Jimmy died.

The house where I grew up is not a place I spend a lot of time. Since Christopher and Corinne have been married, holidays have been spent at their place. Mom's has changed a lot since I was a kid, as my mother exhibits the same delight in dressing the house as she does herself. I haven't yet seen the new color palate for the living room—celery-green, white and red. It looks like the waiting room of an upscale salon, which is to say, vaguely superior and not very welcoming.

'Here,' Mom says, nudging my arm with a glass of something. 'Looks like you need it.'

I take a sip. Whiskey. It burns down my throat, which surprises me a little, since I'm fairly numb.

'I take it you and Ethan broke up,' Mom says, sitting next to me and slipping off her red high heels. She takes a sip from her own glass.

'Yes,' I say.

She nods.

'I know why you never got married again, Mom,' I blurt. 'I'm sorry I bugged you about it all those times.'

'Not that Joe Torre isn't a nice man, mind

you,' she says with a smile. Then she sighs and slides her arm around me, pulling my head down so it rests against her shoulder, and I inhale the comforting smell of her Chanel No. 5. 'Ethan's a good boy,' she murmurs. 'And don't worry . . . he'll do fine. He'll find someone else. You haven't ruined his life, sweetie.'

I try to picture Ethan in the future, a wife, a couple more kids, but instead, I see Captain Bob, forever fixated on a hopeless cause, drowning his love in alcohol. It would be good to cry about now, but the pebble seems to be acting like a cork. 'I called him over, Mom,' I whisper. 'That's why he got hit by a car.'

She snorts. 'Well, I'd say he got hit because that idiot cop would rather run down a human than a papier-mâché clam. Honestly, I'm surprised those troopers don't kill more people.' She takes a pull of her own drink. 'And those uniforms are just ridiculous,' she adds, her mind ever on clothes.

'The night Jimmy died,' I say, my chest convulsing, 'I told him I missed him. I wanted him to come home, and I should've told him to stop, take a nap, get a room, something—'

'Honey, stop,' she says firmly. 'Stop. You're being ridiculous. You didn't cause Jimmy's death. If you'd known how tired he was, you would've said just those things. You didn't know because he didn't tell you. And you didn't cause Ethan to get hit tonight.'

I nod obediently.

'You're not going to work tomorrow,' she says. 'Jorge and I will take care of the bread. It won't be as good as yours, but it won't be horrible, either.'

'Thanks, Mom,' I say.

She stands up and hauls me off the couch. 'Lucy,' she says, pushing a lock of hair behind my ear.

'Yes, Mom?'

She sighs. 'Sweetie, I know you're hurting over Ethan. But look at it this way. Life's going to be a lot less complicated if you stay alone. It doesn't sound very exciting, but there's a lot to be said for playing it safe.'

I nod. She sure has a point. Ethan wasn't safe. Not for me, not from me, and we'll both be better off. I can't live life fearing that every time my husband leaves the house, I'll never see him again. Life will be clean and smooth—like this living room, maybe. Not really the place you'd choose to be, but not bad just the same.

'Finish that whiskey,' Mom commands. 'It's the good stuff. Then get into bed. You can wear some new pajamas I just bought from Nordstrom's. They're silk.'

*　　*　　*

I sleep horribly, the memory of Ethan's accident playing over and over in my brain,

410

the sound of the car hitting him, of his vulnerable, helpless body thudding onto the hard pavement. I didn't want to break up with him, not when he was hurt, but he knew. And I just can't be with him. I tried, but I can't.

I'm sitting at the kitchen table, staring at the cupboard door, when Mom comes home from the bakery that afternoon. 'Look what came to the bakery today,' she says, dropping her keys on the table. She's holding a bouquet of white roses in her arms. 'They're for you.'

Listlessly I open the card, feeling more tired than I have since those endless days just after Jimmy died. ' "Sorry such an awful thing happened," ' I read aloud. ' "If there's anything I can do, say the word. Matt DeSalvo." '

'How nice,' Mom says, bustling the flowers over to the sink, where she fills up a vase. 'He called this morning to see how Ethan was. And how you were, of course. Very kind of him.'

'And how is Ethan?' I whisper, my eyes stinging.

'Well, actually, he called, too. Said he's a little sore but otherwise fine.' Mom pauses. 'I told him you might stay with me a couple of days.' She fusses with the flowers, filling a vase with water.

'Thanks,' I say. I grab a napkin and wipe my eyes. I'd called Ethan to see how he was—I needed to know he was okay, no matter what the status of our relationship—but he was

sleeping, Marie said, and doing fine. After I
hung up, I spent an hour and a half on the
Internet, looking up 'concussion' and 'closed
brain injury,' then called Anne in a panic with
a dozen or so somewhat terrified questions
about the possible complications. She put my
mind to rest—sort of. You never knew what
might happen.

Mom slaps the vase down on the table,
making me jump. 'Are you going to do that
bread deal?' she asks. 'Have you signed
anything yet?'

'Nope,' I said. 'I mean no, nothing's signed,
and yes, I think so.'

She sits down next to me. 'Well. I think it's
a good idea. Now. Do you want me to cook
something for dinner?'

'I should run home and check on Fat
Mikey.' He'll need food—plus, he misses me if
left alone for too long, which I can tell by the
way he ignores me when I return. 'Can I bring
him here for a day or two?'

'He'll probably hate being moved, but sure,'
she answers. 'Okay, I'll make dinner. We'll eat
around, say, six? You'd better get going, then.
Jump in the shower, honey. You smell a little
funky.'

*   *   *

An hour later, I'm standing in front of the
Boatworks, wondering if Ethan's home. How

412

he's doing. If he's mad/sad/completely disgusted with me. I don't have to wonder for long. Parker comes bursting through the doors, Nicky in tow.

'You!' she says, and I resist the urge to dart behind the lamppost for protection.

'Hi.' I reach down and pick up Nicky, kiss him on the cheek. 'How's your daddy?' I ask.

'He's good. I beat him at CandyLand. He was only in the Peppermint Forest when I won. And Nonny made me pancakes for lunch.'

'Good for you, Nicky,' I say.

'Lucy, walk with us,' Parker says in a terrifyingly cheerful tone. 'Nicky and I are going to the playground, right, pal?'

'Yup! I'm gonna go on the slide,' Nick tells me. 'You can come, too. I'll teach you. It's not scary.'

'Actually I have to—'

Parker grabs my arm and goose-steps me across the street. 'Lucy and I will watch you, Nick. Have fun!' she orders merrily, shooing her son over to the jungle gym. 'We'll be right here!'

The second he's out of earshot, she whirls on me, two pink splotches burning on her cheeks. 'Are you out of your mind, Lucy?' she hisses.

'Look, I know—'

'You dump him in the hospital? When he's bleeding from the head and has just been hit

413

by a *car*?'

'It wasn't like that,' I say, swallowing. 'I wasn't going to say anything, but—'

'But what?' she demands.

'But . . . but . . .' I stop, swallow again, hard. 'But he knew.'

'Knew what?'

I close my eyes. 'He knew, Parker.'

'Knew that you're scared? That it was sickening, seeing him hit? That you love him? That you're afraid he'll die? Knew what, Lucy?'

Suddenly my temper flares. 'Don't judge me, Parker. Okay? I did my best, I really did, and I just can't do it. You don't know what it's like.'

'Oh, I'm sorry,' Parker says sharply. 'Did you want me to pity you? Because I thought you wanted to be a normal person.'

'Well, I'm *not* a normal person,' I blurt, my voice harsh and shrill. 'There's something wrong with me. There's a hole in me and Ethan can't fix it and neither can I, and you just don't understand, so don't lecture me about what I can and can't do, okay?' The thud of Ethan's body hitting the pavement echoes in my mind, and I clamp my hands over my mouth and bend over, the horror of the memory, the fear causing me to gag. Nicky pauses from the top of the slide, looking over at us.

'Looking good, Nicky!' Parker calls, and I

414

manage a wave. My nephew resumes his activity, and Parker takes a deep breath, then slides her arm around my shoulders and wait till I can straighten up. 'Lucy,' she says quietly, 'Ethan got a call today from work. They want him to transfer to the Atlanta branch and head up the international sales division.'

I swallow once, twice. 'Well, that would be . . . great. For him, you know. He could do all those wild things, travel again . . . And the weekend thing seemed to work for you guys, so . . .' I blink hard. Oh. I'm crying again. I didn't realize.

She looks at me and bites the inside of her cheek. 'Lucy, I have to wonder what's going to happen to you two if you don't make things right.' I don't answer, just flex my tingling hands. Eventually Parker sighs. 'I love you both, that's all. You're more my family than my family, and I just . . .' Her voice trails off. 'Make sure you're doing the right thing,' she finishes.

'I'm trying,' I whisper. Then I wave to Nick and go to my apartment to feed my cat.

*   *   *

To punish me for my overnight absence, Fat Mikey brings me a mole with its head missing, a clear warning that should I ever leave him again, this is what will happen to me. I clean up the mess, picturing Mrs. Mole as she

415

wonders what happened to her husband, who was ostensibly going out for a tulip bulb or something and never came home. Do moles have widow support groups? Does she have life insurance on Mr. Mole?

'Try not to kill anymore, okay, pretty kitty?' I implore my cat, picking him up for a nuzzle. He purrs loudly, and I scratch his neck as he closes his eyes in pleasure. 'We're staying at Grammy's house tonight,' I tell him. He opens his eyes, irritated at this pronouncement, then wriggles out of my grasp.

I toss some work clothes into a bag. I don't know how long I'll stay at Mom's . . . I don't really even see what I'm packing, but it doesn't really matter. It's not like I'm going to France or something.

When I finally manage to stuff my cat into the carrier, I grab my bag, pick up the carrier and turn for the door, only to yelp in surprise.

My mother-in-law stands in the doorway.

'I'm sorry, dear, I didn't mean to startle you,' she says.

'No, no, it's fine,' I lie. Honestly, she's like a fox. 'How's Ethan?'

'He's a little sore. Planning to go to work tomorrow, even though I said he should stay in bed and let me cook him some cavatelli and sausage.'

I can't help a little grin at the thought of Ethan in bed, his mother serving him lunch and stroking his battered brow. Her idea of heaven, his of hell. 'Well, it's probably a good sign that he wants to go back to work,' I say.

'Are you nuts? He needs at least a week in bed,' she says. Then she brushes a hair off my shoulder. 'Lucy, honey, he told us you and he broke up.'

My throat slams shut. 'Oh.' I set down the carrier, as Fat Mikey weighs a ton.

'Gianni and I . . . well, we think it's probably a smart move,' Marie says softly. 'With you and Jimmy and your past and all. So complicated.'

'Right,' I agree distantly. She gives me a sad smile—sad, but relieved.

I take a deep breath, knowing Ethan would kill me for what I'm about to say. 'Marie, I think sometimes Ethan feels a little . . . second best to you and Gianni. Compared to Jimmy, I mean.'

She pulls back, an indignant expression crossing her face. 'I don't love one of my sons more than the other, Lucy,' she says firmly.

'I know. Just . . . I know you don't approve of where he works, and—'

'What's not to approve of? He makes a good living! He's an executive! We're very proud.' Her eyes shift away in a silent acknowledgment that perhaps her statement isn't a hundred percent accurate.

'Make sure he knows. That's all,' I say softly. Marie shrugs, then gives a little nod. 'I have to run. Tell Ethan I'm glad he's feeling better.' I kiss Marie's cheek, then pause. 'Marie, do remember a girl named Doral-Anne who used to work at the restaurant? She played on Ethan's baseball team?'

My mother-in-law's face freezes. 'Her. I remember, all right. The one who stole. Miss Tattoo. I told her she had to cover that thing up. "We're a family restaurant," I say. "No one wants to see what you did on a bender." She didn't like that, but—'

'Did you know she went out with Jimmy for a while?' I interrupt.

Marie freezes, and once more, her eyes slide away. 'Yes. I knew. Let me tell you, we were awfully happy when you showed up, Lucy. Sure, you weren't Italian, but at least you were Catholic and a nice girl, you know what I mean? Not trash. That girl was trash.'

I look at my mother-in-law for a second. 'Last night when Ethan was hit, Doral-Anne took care of Nicky. Did you know that?'

Her mouth takes on that *So?* expression the Mirabellis do so well . . . the slightly defensive posture, the jutting chin, the lifted eyebrow. 'Took care of Nicky how?'

'Parker ran into the street to help Ethan, and Nicky was crying and scared, and she picked him up.' Reassured him, no doubt. Turned away so the little guy wouldn't have to see his daddy lying unconscious in the street.

Marie remains unimpressed.

'I've got to go,' I say again. We walk down

418

the hall together, Fat Mikey yowling at the indignity of being carried in such a fashion.

'Come for dinner at the restaurant one of these days, honey,' she calls as I press the button for the elevator. 'You know how Gianni likes to cook for you.'

'Will do,' I answer, smiling. The second the doors close, my smile drops like an anvil.

*   *   *

The strange, numb version of myself continues for the next few days. I return to the bakery, waking long before anyone else is around, and go through the motions—weighing the dough, shaping the loaves, letting them rise, scoring the tops with robotic precision. I've never been more efficient, actually, and Jorge gives me a significant look on my third day back, when I do all the washing before he even comes in. After two nights with Mom, I went back to my apartment, figuring I couldn't hide forever. Corinne and Emma came for a visit. Ash dropped by as well and stayed for a game of Extreme Racing USA.

I haven't seen Ethan. Not at all. Marie told me he's away on business. His absence is a hole in my heart.

On Friday afternoon, I find myself alone in the bakery. Without the promise of happy hour, the Black Widows left at three, and

Jorge took care of the evening deliveries. The cooler hums. The cases have been cleared, Rose's sad cookies refrozen for a more hopeful day. The kitchen is clean, though maybe I could find a few things to do. Empty the grease from the Frialator. 'What an exciting life you lead, Lucy Lang,' I say out loud. My voice echoes.

I go out the front door and lean against the lamppost, looking over at the town green. Yet another sunny October day, the sky a deep and aching blue, the last few leaves of the beech trees clinging precariously. Over the sounds of the wind and a distant soccer game comes the sound of Canada geese. I look up and sure enough, a ragged V formation flies right over the cemetery, the geese squawking and talking as they head south for the winter. *Good luck,* I think. *Be careful. Don't get shot. Mind the airplanes.*

A bright flash of color rounds the corner— yellow skirt, orange winter boots, purple coat, orange poncho.

'Grinelda!' I bark.

She shuffles to a halt. 'Hello,' she says, pulling down her blue-tinted, Bono-style sunglasses to peer at me.

'Hey, have you got a minute?' I ask. She doesn't answer immediately. 'I can pay,' I add.

'Sure,' she replies. 'Got any cookies?'

'They're all in the freezer, but come on in. I'll find something.'

420

Ten minutes later, Grinelda is drinking an overly sweetened cup of coffee and eating a Ding-Dong I had in my purse.

'So,' she says, a clot of chocolate dropping from her mouth. 'You want a reading?'

I hesitate, then plunge in. 'Yes, please.'

'You're a believer now?' she says, grinning like Fat Mikey when he's slain a rodent.

'Well,' I murmur, 'I was wondering if maybe Jimmy had more for me than toast advice.'

She shoves the last half of the Ding-Dong into her mouth, her cheeks bulging, then swallows like a cormorant trying to get down a particularly bony fish. 'Let's find out,' she says. She closes her eyes and lets out a low hum. 'Uuuunnnnnnhhhh. Uuuunnnnnnhhhh.' This is new. She must've seen it on TV or something. 'Uuuunnnnnnhhhh.'

I sigh. It's come to this. I'm an official Black Widow.

'Okay, I'm getting someone. Name starts with a J.'

'I'm guessing that would be Jimmy,' I say neutrally

'Don't speak.' She breathes again. 'Uuuunnnnnnhhhh. Yes. J. It's a man. Tall. He's holding a frying pan. Is it Jimmy? Yes! It's Jimmy.'

I roll my eyes. 'Hi, Jimmy.'

'Uuuunnnnnnhhhh. Uhn— What's this? He's surrounded by food. Tomatoes, garlic, chicken—'

421

'Okay, Grinelda, you know Jimmy was a chef. That's no secret—'

'Shush. I'm getting something.' She opens one eye a slit. 'Got any more of those Ding-Dongs?'

'You know what, Grinelda? Never mind. I'll just—'

'Shh! Okay. He's showing me something. Bread. No, toast. He says . . . yes. Toast.'

'Right,' I mutter, more disgusted with myself than Grinelda. 'Check the toast. Got it, Jimmy. Anything else?'

'He's showing me something else. A wedding? Yes. A wedding. Marriage.'

Ah. Now we have something, I think. Of course, we probably don't, given that it's Grinelda and all, but still. I'm desperate.

Grinelda peeks at me again. 'Does this mean anything to you?'

At that moment, my cell phone rings.

'Cell phone usage is strongly discouraged during communication from the other side,' Grinelda intones.

I hit Mute and glance at the screen. It's Matt DeSalvo.

Matt DeSalvo. The bread man. Who could get my bread to thousands of people, who could then make toast with it. My mother and aunts felt that Jimmy was pushing me to the bread man. Now there's a wedding in the picture. And Matt just happens to call.

'He's going,' Grinelda says, and though it's

422

been almost six years and though I don't have a lot of faith in Grinelda's special gifts, I feel a lump rise in my throat just the same.

'Bye, Jimmy,' I can't help saying. It's no use. I'll never stop missing him.

*   *   *

That night, I decide that I can't avoid Ethan forever. I go upstairs, empty-handed, no cake, no custard, no cookies, and knock firmly. There's no answer. Right. He's away. I just assumed he'd be back—

The elevator bell dings behind me, the doors slide open and there he is, towing his suitcase. His eyebrows bounce up at the sight of me.

'Hi,' I say. My stomach cramps with nervousness.

'Hi,' he says, taking out his keys. 'How are you?'

'I'm good!' I chirrup. 'I came to see how you were doing!' I sound like the amped-up host of a children's show, all cutesy and super-duper friendly. 'Feeling okay?'

'All better,' he lies. I can see a shadow of a bruise along his temple.

'Great!' I bleat, apparently unable to sound normal. 'Welp—' yes, I say *welp* '—I just wanted to say hi. Hey, is it true you're going international? International sales, I mean? With International Foods?' *Shut up, Lucy.*

423

He leans against the door frame. 'I'm not sure,' he says.

'I was thinking of trying to buy a house, you know?' I say. 'Time to be a grownup and all that.' *You don't have to leave, Ethan. I'll move.*

'Sounds good, Luce.' He waits for me to say something else.

'Right. Well, I just wanted to make sure you were okay, Ethan.' It's when I say his name that my voice cracks. My face grows hot.

'Thanks for checking in,' he says, putting the key in the lock.

'Good night,' I say. 'Have a great weekend.' Then, head aching, pebble swelling, I head for the stairs. The sound of his door closing is horribly final.

CHAPTER THIRTY

The next week, I once again get dressed up to meet Matt DeSalvo to sign the papers. It'll be good, I assure myself as I brush my hair. It'll save the bakery. I'll have a career as well as something for the alumni magazine. All good.

At last, the beautiful October weather has given way to November's bleak promise. Daylight saving time makes November the harbinger of darkness, of cold winds whipping off the water, October's golden light replaced by something harder and meaner. The sky is a thin, pale blue, the branches skeletal against the sky. Add to that the fact that my dad died in November, and the month just can't win. Halloween came and went—I went to Nicky's school for the Halloween parade—Ethan wasn't there—and had coffee with my nephew and Parker afterward. On Saturday, Ash came over and we watched the *Bourne* trilogy and ate Ben & Jerry's. I haven't wanted to bake anything for a while now.

As I come into Bunny's, Captain Bob is stealing looks at Mom, and Enid Crosby is pointing to hard rolls. 'That one, Rose. No, not that one. Move over one. Yes, that one.' You'd think she was choosing a child from an orphanage. 'I hear you're selling the bakery,' she says to me.

'No, we're not,' I correct gently. 'Our bread will be sold statewide, that's all. Bunny's will stay Bunny's.' Alas. I suppress a sigh, looking at the paltry array of goodies in the case. God knows how many times they've been in and out of the freezer. Some of them are probably older than I am. Mrs. Crosby hands me a five, and I make change.

'Hello, ladies,' Matt says, coming in the front door. 'What a great day this is for NatureMade.' He smiles broadly, a dimple showing in his cheek.

'Come in back,' my mother says grandly. 'We have champagne.'

'It's eleven o'clock, Mom,' I say.

'So?' She winks.

'Out you go, people,' Iris booms. 'Come back later. We have business to do here. Out with you.' She herds our two entire customers out the door, then flips the sign to Closed, and we all head to the kitchen. Jorge is there, too, and starts to head out the back door.

'Jorge, please stay, buddy,' I call. 'This affects you, too.'

Matt lays out the contract on the wooden counter. I've read the dang thing a hundred times . . . there's no downside. There just isn't.

'I need all four of you to sign, since you're all part owners,' Matt says, 'right here—' he points '—and here . . . initials there, and finally, here.' He fishes a Cross pen from the pocket of his suit. 'Iris, would you like to go first?' Nice, being that Iris is oldest and all that.

My aunts and mother sign, Rose giggling as she can't seem to find all the spots to sign without Matt standing very close to her and pointing. I think she's got a crush. Matt seems to read my mind and tosses me a wink.

Low Risk of Early Death. Matt seems healthy. He does have to travel, but it's all fairly local. Also, he has a Volvo, and we all know that Volvos are basically tanks with slightly better gas mileage. *Strong Fatherhood Potential.* He likes kids. He said so, anyway. *Good heart.* Seems to. *Not too good-looking.* Well, Matt *is* pretty attractive. Not quite as

426

gorgeous as Jimmy, and lacking Ethan's naughty appeal (my brain jumps away from the thought of that), but attractive nonetheless. *Steady, recession-proof job.* I guess so. He's been with the company for nine years. *Nice to my family.* Check. *Not-too-good sense of humor.* Seems like another check mark.

'Lucy? Your turn,' Mom says, jolting me out of my daze. I look up at their expectant faces, glance back at Jorge, who raises an eyebrow.

'Right.' I take the pen, look at the contract. Bunny's three majority owners have all signed their full names and the titles they gave themselves years ago. *Iris Black Sandor, Chief Executive Officer. Rose Black Thompson, President. Daisy Black Lang, Manager-at-Large.* All that's left is me.

Lucy Lang Mirabelli. Bread baker.

The image of a patisserie flashes across my mind like heat lightning . . . the tarts I'd like to bake, the cakes and pastries and pies. All the desserts I've taught in class or made for Ethan over the years—zabaglione, raisin bread pudding, crème brûlée. And in their place, bread. Loaves and loaves and years and years of bread.

'I'm sorry,' I say, putting the pen down. 'I . . . I don't want to do this.' Matt's usually genial expression turns to a frown. 'It's just that I'm supposed to be a pastry chef.' I look at the Black Widows. 'I want to do more,' I

427

say, my voice shaking. 'I want to own a café with the best pastries and cookies and cakes around. I don't want to be run out of business by Starbucks, and I don't want to bake bread for the rest of my life. I'll give you all my recipes, but I . . . I quit.'

*　　*　　*

After half an hour of frowning, rereading the contract and finally deciding that he has to run this by corporate, Matt DeSalvo leaves, disappointed and even a bit reproachful.

'Well, there goes the future!' Iris barks as the door closes behind him.

'I'll give you the recipes,' I repeat for the fifth time.

'Oh, hush, you! You can't quit! That's ridiculous!' she returns.

Rose is sobbing into a hankie, and my mother just stares at me like I'm a hair in her salad. 'I'm taking a walk,' I announce.

'Fine! Shoo! Out with you!' Iris says, waving her hands. 'What a mess. I don't believe this!'

I grab my coat and head out the back, then feel a tap on my shoulder. I turn.

'Hey, Jorge,' I say. 'Sorry.' The idea of not working with Jorge brings a lump to my throat.

He puts his hands on my shoulders and looks at me. Really looks. Wrinkles fan out from the corners of his eyes, and the light gleams off his bald head. His eyes are dark, almost black. I feel my own eyes sting. Then Jorge nods once, slowly and gravely, and gives my shoulders a hard squeeze.

I put my arms around him and hug him hard. 'Thank you,' I whisper, then go out into the brisk air.

Twenty minutes later I find myself at the playground. I sit on a swing, the kind with the rubber seat that squashes you in tight. I've really screwed the pooch, as the saying goes. I don't have a job. I won't have any structure to my days. I have no game plan. I won't be surrounded by the Black Widows, and however they may have driven me nuts over the years, I love them with all my heart.

I've done the right thing nonetheless. I can't bake bread anymore. I just can't.

When my hands are practically frozen to the metal chains of the swing, I pry them open, stand up and head back, all the way around the cemetery, to face the music.

The music is not what I think. 'Get in here, you,' Iris says, dragging me over to the table. 'Such a drama queen, flouncing out the door like that!'

'I didn't flounce,' I reply.

'Your hands are so cold!' Rose exclaims, patting me. 'Last week, seventy degrees. This week, winter.'

'Lucy, we completely respect your decision not to bake bread anymore,' Mom says

429

formally.

'Even if you're the best bread maker around,' Iris mutters.

'But here's the thing. You can't leave Bunny's,' Mom continues.

'Of course you can't,' Rose seconds.

'Well, actually, I—' I attempt.

'Hush, you! We're talking!' Iris says.

'Lucy, we'd like to compromise,' Mom says.

I open my mouth, shut it, then open it again. 'I didn't think we did that in this family,' I say.

'Oh, you. So fresh.' My mother rolls her eyes. 'We'll make a deal. Stay and train the bread person—we just asked Jorge if he wanted to do it, and he said no.'

'Jorge speaks now?' I ask, looking around. He waves to me and grins, in the background as ever.

'No, smart-ass,' my mother continues. 'He made himself clear anyway. So hire a bread baker, and we'll expand. You know we own Zippy's—' the failing sports memorabilia store adjacent to Bunny's '—and we can just kick him out in December when the lease is up. He'll be grateful. Then you can have your café over there.'

My body breaks into goose bumps. 'Are you serious?' I breathe.

'With your fancy-shmancy pastries,' Iris grumbles.

'You could sell hot chocolate,' Rose

430

suggests hopefully. 'We could steal Starbucks's recipe.'

'No, we can't,' I say. 'Really? Are you serious? You'll do this for me?'

'You're a part owner of this place,' Mom says, looking pointedly at her sisters. 'It's time for a change.'

*   *   *

Back at my apartment a few hours later, when the Black Widows and I have nailed down a tentative plan, I call Matt DeSalvo and apologize again. 'I'm so sorry about this,' I tell him. 'I'm not trying to drive you crazy, I promise.'

'Oh, I know,' he says. He pauses a minute or two. 'All right, I think we can work it out. I'm glad. Sounds like you're really happy with the decision, Lucy.'

'Thanks, Matt. I am,' I say. Fat Mikey begins clawing the back of my couch, signaling his displeasure with my lack of worshipfulness. I rub his nose with my index finger, and he forgives me, emitting his rusty, diesel engine purr. 'I hope I didn't completely screw up your day,' I tell Matt.

'Not at all. You're a challenge, that's all.' He seems to realize that sounds less than flattering. 'I meant, getting your bread is a challenge. Well worth it, though.'

My eyes find the wedding picture on the

431

wall: Jimmy and me, laughing. So happy. So long ago.

'Matt,' I say slowly. 'Would you like to go on a date with me?'

CHAPTER THIRTY-ONE

A few nights later, Matt picks me up at the Boatworks. I wait in the foyer, looking for his solid Volvo. It's pouring rain, the noise drumming the Herreshoff above the door. Great night to stay home with a movie. Like I used to do with Ethan. Speaking of Ethan, I haven't seen him lately—he had another business trip, apparently—but that's okay. That part of my heart seems to have turned to stone, which is a far cry better than the open, ragged gash it was in the hospital.

Then Matt's headlights flash as he turns around the corner, and I run out and jump into his car.

The date is everything I've hoped for. Very pleasant. We start with a movie, a political thriller with lots of explosions, just what I love. Then comes a somewhat mediocre dinner at a chain Italian restaurant—if my father-in-law knew I was eating here, he would've clutched his heart and died on the spot. I order lasagna, Matt gets spaghetti and meatballs.

'I have to say,' Matt says, 'I'm really glad

432

you asked me out.' He grins, and I feel a little tug. Not a big one, not a wave . . . but something. That's good. If I wanted nothing, I'd be married to Charley Spirito.

'Me, too,' I say.

'Is it strange, being with someone who looks like your husband?' he asks.

'No,' I answer. 'I mean, at first glance, sure, you do look like him. But don't worry, I can tell the difference.' *He was the real deal, you're Jimmy-Lite.*

'How did you meet him?'

I pause.

'I'm sorry,' Matt says instantly, covering my hand with his own. 'It's none of my business.'

'It's okay,' I answer, extricating my hand and taking a sip of water. 'Ethan set us up.'

Matt pauses. 'I guess things didn't work out there,' he says delicately.

A razor-thin slice of pain cuts across my heart. 'No, it didn't work out.'

'Is he doing okay? After the accident and all?'

'He's great,' I say smoothly, though I find I have to swallow twice. 'What about you? Ever been married?'

Matt tells me about his brief marriage when he was twenty-six, ending in an amicable divorce when he was twenty-eight. Talk turns to business, inevitably. 'Have you hired someone to take over the bread?' he asks.

'Not yet,' I say. 'I put an ad out this

433

morning, though. Craigslist, the newspaper.'

'Great,' he says. 'We want to get cracking on this.'

I cover a yawn. 'I should probably get back,' I tell him. 'Four a.m. comes pretty early.'

Matt pays the bill and we drive home in the rain, not talking much.

I sneak peeks at his profile . . . he does look like Jimmy, though the initial shock has faded. He's been awfully nice about the bread deal. I decide I feel fond of him. And hey, fond is underrated. Fond can last a lifetime. Fond doesn't leave scars.

My heart twists a little . . . for a second, that lovely coating of numbness that's been sheltering me these past few weeks lifts, and I miss Ethan so much I can barely breathe.

You can't have everything. Ethan himself told me that. He was right. It will hurt him to have me move on with someone else, but I was hurting him when we were together, too. And I can't be with Ethan. He deserves someone who can love him with her whole heart, and damn it all to hell, that's not me. I had my heart broken once . . . no. Shattered. Destroyed. Ground into a bloody smear on the sidewalk, and it hurt so much I wondered that I didn't die from it. I just can't do that again.

Reminding myself to breathe again, I unclench my fists and stare ahead through the rain-smeared windshield.

Matt pulls up in front of the Boatworks. 'Let me walk you to the door,' he says. I look at him. Matt here will take me or leave me. He didn't know me before Jimmy died. He won't know what he's missing. He won't want more.

'Sure,' I answer.

The rain blows in gusts, and we rush to the shelter of the doorway, the old Herreshoff providing a little shelter from the weather. I can't wait to be upstairs, safe and alone.

'I had a really nice time,' Matt says.

'Oh, me, too,' I answer. It's not *that* untrue. 'Thanks for a lovely evening.'

He grins. 'You're welcome. I hope we can see each other again.'

I hesitate. Remind myself that a couple of months ago I had a plan for the rest of my life, and it didn't seem like an illogical plan at all. *Find a husband you don't love too much. Have a baby.* And maybe Ethan can get over me faster if I'm dating someone else. If he sees there's really no possibility for us.

'I'd love to,' I answer, and without any further ado, he kisses me.

It's fine—a gentle, rather respectful kiss. His lips are smooth and cool. Pleasant. Then he pulls me closer and kisses me more deeply, which is also fine, because now I know he's attracted to me and not just being polite. It's not the white-hot jolt I'm used to feeling with Ethan, or the heart-melting sweetness of

435

Jimmy, but it's not devoid of appeal. It occurs to me that boy, my brain sure is active during this kiss, and maybe I could muzzle my internal panel of CNN analysts and just enjoy. But by then, Matt's done.

'I'll call you,' he says again with a Jimmy-ish smile. 'Are you free Friday?'

'Friday sounds good,' I answer automatically.

'Excellent,' he says, then turns, shields his eyes with one hand and dashes back into the rain to the car. Thunder rumbles in the distance.

'Bye,' I call, watching him pull away. Then I turn to go inside and nearly jump out of my skin.

Ethan is standing not twenty feet away, apparently on his way in from the parking lot. Even from here, I can feel the heat in his eyes. I swallow as he starts walking toward me, his movements somehow predatory. He stops a foot in front of me, ignoring the rain dripping off him. His eyes burn into mine, and my breath catches.

'You don't kiss him the way you kiss me,' he says, his voice low.

My heart convulses in my throat. 'I thought you were away,' I croak.

He ignores my comment. 'You're dating him, Lucy?'

I swallow. 'Um . . . this was the first time. But yes.'

436

A muscle under Ethan's eye twitches. 'Why?'

'He's . . . very nice.'

'He's my brother's goddamn twin.'

I bite my lip and don't answer.

Ethan grips my shoulders hard, his jaw tight, his eyes almost black. 'I can't lose you to Jimmy again.'

My throat slams shut. 'I . . . what?'

'Stop looking for Jimmy and see me,' he says. 'See *me*, Lucy.'

'Ethan, I tried with you. I did, but I just can't—'

'Yes, you can, damn it! Pick me this time, Lucy, and stop chasing Jimmy's ghost.' He gives me a little shake.

My breath whooshes out of me. 'I'm not chasing his ghost,' I say, tears burning in my eyes.

'I loved him, too. I miss him, too. But he wasn't perfect, Lucy, and you need—'

'Well, he was perfect for me!' I exclaim, my voice cracking. 'As you knew he would be, or you wouldn't have fixed us up in the first place!'

Ethan lets go of my shoulders and looks at me, almost sadly. 'Lucy,' he says quietly, 'how many college sophomores go around fixing up their older brothers with pretty girls from school?'

My knees wobble dangerously, buzzing with adrenaline. I can only look at Ethan. If I could get a word out of my clamped-up throat, I'd tell him to stop.

'I didn't think you'd be perfect for him, Lucy. I thought you were perfect for *me*.' Ethan pauses. 'And he knew it.'

'Knew what?' My words are a harsh whisper.

'Knew that I was crazy about you. You were all I talked about. I told him I was bringing a girl home from school, someone special, and—'

'Stop it! Stop, Ethan!' My hands fly up to halt his words. 'Jimmy wouldn't do that! He wouldn't . . . make a play for me if he knew you—'

'He did.'

'No.' Oh, God, I think I'm about to throw up that mediocre lasagna. The thunder rumbles again, louder this time, and the wind whips cold rain against my burning face.

'I love you, Lucy,' Ethan says quietly. 'I always have.'

No, no, no. A thousand memories stab into my brain. The drive back to Providence after that first time at Gianni's, how I thanked Ethan for introducing Jimmy and me . . . All those family dinners before Jimmy and I were married, Jimmy and me holding hands, Ethan alone on the other side of the table . . . The bachelor party when Ethan drove a drunken Jimmy to my house because my fiancé had felt a burning need to serenade me from the lawn

438

at 3:00 a.m. Our wedding! Jesus, Ethan had been the best man . . . had danced with me at the reception and I never, *never* . . . And Jimmy had known?

'That just can't be true,' I whisper, tears spilling over. 'Jimmy loved you. He never would've hurt you, Ethan.'

'Lucy—'

'No, Ethan! I can't just . . . just rethink everything because you . . . It's not true. It can't be. Jimmy wasn't like that!' A harsh, hitching sob twists out of me. 'Don't taint my memories, Ethan. Don't you dare. That's all I have left.'

He looks away abruptly, and I stare at him, defiant tears snaking down my face amid the cold rain. His jaw is tight, his shoulders set. For a second, he closes his eyes, and when he looks back at me, his face is carefully blank.

'That's all I have left,' I repeat loudly.

He looks at me another few beats, then bows his head. 'You'd better get inside before you catch pneumonia.'

'Screw that,' I say harshly, startling myself. 'I'm going for a walk.'

And with that, I storm off, across the street, into Ellington Park. I don't look back.

CHAPTER THIRTY-TWO

Everything's gonna be all right . . . Everything's gonna be all right . . . Everything's gonna be all right . . .

Just because Ethan said it, doesn't mean it's true, I tell myself as I careen along the gravel pathway. I'm already soaked, hardly noticing the puddles I slosh through. *He's upset that I'm moving on.* And I have to move on. The image of him being tossed through the air, so damn . . . fragile . . .

My crappy lasagna surges up, and I barely make it off the path, throwing up violently into the bushes. Shaking, I stagger over to the nearest bench. Only then do I notice how close I am to the cemetery. A brief sheet of lightning illuminates the night, the asphalt road like a scar cutting between the granite headstones.

Somewhere in there is Jimmy's grave. My husband's grave. His body, that big, beautiful form I loved so much, lies in there. Closing my eyes, I tip my head back and let the rain pellet my face. How many tears have I shed for Jimmy? Enough that I used to wake up with salt stains on my pillow. Enough that the skin under my eyes was raw for the better part of a year. Enough that my mother gave me her ultra-expensive eye cream because I looked older than she did.

I *know* Jimmy loved Ethan. He wouldn't have made a move on me if he'd known. Ethan had a crush, maybe. That's all. Jimmy never would've hurt him. I'd bet my life on it. He asked Ethan to be his best man, for God's sake. A half-formed thought darts through my brain at that . . . there's something there . . . but it's gone, like a fish in a fast-flowing river. It doesn't matter. Jimmy loved his little brother. Everyone could see that. He'd sling an arm around the shorter, younger Ethan and ruffle his hair. 'Hey, Little E.,' he'd say, then kiss his brother's head.

For the first time, it occurs to me that Ethan must've hated that nickname.

I'm so tired. For five and a half years, I haven't had a full night's sleep. Except one, now that I think of it. The night Ethan watched over me after I'd come home from the hospital.

Something hot and biting rises in my chest, and I shove it down. It's too hard. Love is just too frigging hard. Love someone, and they have the power to ruin your life. Jimmy took everything that night, the whole lovely, safe, normal future we were going to have, the person I used to be. I can't let stories from Ethan—or Doral-Anne, for that matter—erase the Jimmy I hold in my heart.

'Everything's gonna be all right . . . everything's gonna be all right. Everything's

441

gonna be all right. Everything's gonna be all right.' *Come on, St. Marley, help me,* I think, my voice cracking as I sing. Can't imagine that Iris and Rose would approve of me praying to a reggae singer for help, but hey, I never really figured out the rosary. A nearly hysterical laugh wrenches out of my throat. Singing in a thunderstorm outside the cemetery. Jimmy's widow has finally chugged around the bend.

I lurch to my feet and slog back to the Boatworks. My nose is running, my feet are like ice, and I can only imagine how I look, my hair hanging in sodden strands, my mascara puddled, no doubt, underneath my eyes. In other words, I probably look as good as I feel.

I make it up to my apartment, and wouldn't you know? Fat Mikey finally succeeds in tripping me, and I fall over the giant cat, smacking my knee on the hard corner of the table. 'Thanks, Mikey,' I say, another dangerous laugh rising in my chest like a storm surge. 'The perfect end to a perfect night.'

A dime winks at me from the carpet under the table.

Without another thought, I pick it up and whip it across the room.

*　　　*　　　*

'Did you ever find out something about your husbands after they died? Something that

442

surprised you?'

My aunts regard me with surprise. Mom looks up from her crossword puzzle, then looks back down to fill in another clue. It's 10:00 a.m., and I haven't slept in, oh, twenty-eight hours. I have eleven and a half minutes left on this last batch of bread, and I intend to put the time to good use. 'Well?' I demand.

'What bee's in your bonnet?' Iris asks, turning her attention back to the pastry dough she's rolling out.

'I found out a couple of things about Jimmy,' I say. My voice sounds overly loud to me, and the Black Widows exchange a glance, confirming the fact that I'm acting insane.

'What things?' Mom asks.

'It doesn't matter,' I say, shaking my head. 'Did you?'

'Well, about a month after Larry died, I found out that he had a secret bank account,' Rose says slowly. 'Fourteen thousand dollars in it. His name only.' She looks sheepishly at her sisters, whose mouths are hanging open. 'I never found out what he was planning to do with it. Leave me? Pay off some illegitimate child? Bribe a judge? I never found out.'

'Been watching *The Sopranos*?' Mom asks dryly.

'What did you do with the money?' Iris asks.

'I invested in the stock market,' Rose cheeps. 'Stevie never has to work in his life if he doesn't want to.'

'That was very *prescient* of you, Rose,' my mother says, hiding a grin. 'Five down. Nine letters, having foresight.'

'What about you, Iris?' I ask.

She cocks her head and looks thoughtfully over at the Hobart mixer. 'Well, sure. Everyone has secrets, right?' She turns her attention back to the sweet pastry dough, her hands deft and quick. 'Pete had that little room in the cellar, you know? His tool room?' Mom and Rose nod, and I seem to recall it, too, a tidy little room with an oiled worktable and tools hanging on a pegboard. 'So I'm going through it one day after he died, and I come across this locked box.'

'What was in it?' Rose asks.

'I'm getting to that,' Iris growls, glaring at her sister. 'So I say to myself, "Why would Pete lock something away?" Maybe it's flammable, I don't know. Some chemicals he used to strip furniture. Figure I better open it.' The baking sheet is now filled with empty pastries, and Rose slides over the container of chocolate filling. Iris takes out the scoop, and with the skill acquired from decades of repetition, fills each pastry with chocolate as she continues her story. 'Finally I find the key, taped to the underside of a drawer. Lucy, honey, shove these on the rack for me, and Rose, would you pass me the raspberry?'

Rose and I obey promptly, and Iris starts on

444

another batch of pastries. 'So I open the box. Guess what was in there?'

'A human skull,' Mom suggests, making me wonder what secrets she herself might have.

'Not a skull. It was about a hundred copies of *Penthouse*.' Iris jams her fists into her ample hips and snorts. 'He'd been getting the porno.'

'The porno!' Rose and Mom cluck in unison.

'That's right. Had a separate post office box in Kingstown, if you can believe it, so I wouldn't know about his dirty magazines.'

'How'd that make you feel?' I ask, rubbing my gritty eyes.

'Well, crappy, of course! It wasn't just the naked pictures. It was the secrecy. He spent hours down in the basement when I thought he was fixing things, and instead he was doing God knows what.' She pauses. 'Though he always was pretty, um . . . amorous when he came up.'

'I bet,' Mom mutters, filling in another clue.

'You always talk about them like they were perfect,' I say, swallowing. The pebble's bigger than ever.

'Well, what are we supposed to do? Spit on their graves?' Iris snorts, then reaches out and pats my shoulder. 'So you found something out about Jimmy. So what. Doesn't mean he didn't love you.'

'Of course not,' Rose murmurs, giving me a

445

hug.

'What about you, Mom?' I ask my mother. 'Did you ever find out something about Daddy?'

My mom doesn't even look up from her puzzle. 'No, honey. Your father was damn near perfect.'

I wonder if it's true. Then again, I only had eight years with him, and if Mom's hiding something, it's kind of wonderful of her not to tell me, to let me keep that little girl's adoration.

'What did you find out, Lucy?' Rose asks.

'It wasn't anything that big,' I lie.

And maybe it wasn't. Maybe Jimmy steamrolled Ethan a little, but it wasn't like Ethan and I were an item. We were pals, no more. Him saying he's been in love with me since we met . . . I wonder. He never acted that way. Not before I met Jimmy, not after. In fact, he couldn't have been more . . . enthusiastic about us getting married. And then after Jimmy died . . . no. I don't want to have to look back at all the years I've known Ethan and reinterpret everything. He *never* acted like a man in love . . . well, maybe a little, recently. But he never said a word. He'd always been simply a friend. My best friend. He loved me, sure. *In* love for years? No.

My eleven and a half minutes are up, so I take the bread rack out—sourdough boules on the bottom, Italian on the top—and slide

446

them off the pans to cool. On a whim, I stick a boule in a paper bag and tuck it under my arm, its warmth as comforting as a puppy.

'I'll be back in about half an hour,' I announce.

'Bye,' the Black Widows chorus. As I head out the back door, I glance at them—Iris, strong and broad, Rose, smaller and plump, my mother, elegant and cool. Rose says something I can't quite hear, and the other two laugh.

They're happy, the Black Widows. Life threw them sucker punches, and they got over it. Their hearts were shredded on the cheese grater of life, just like mine was, and look at them now. Laughing, happy, watching *Showtime* and bickering with each other. I can do that, too. Be happy, I mean.

The smell of coffee is rich and dark in Starbucks. A few mothers sit around one table, babies on their laps, strollers against one wall. From over the speakers come the mournful voices of Sting and Sheryl Crow in a bittersweet duet.

Perry Wheatley is behind the counter, wiping down the cappuccino machine. I used to babysit her when I was in high school. Her parents always left brownies for me, as well as a video. They lived in a sweet house on the water, and I'd pretend it was mine, that I was a famous pastry chef, that I'd just been featured on the cover of *Bon Appetit* . . .

'Hi, Lucy! What can I get you?' Perry asks, her face lighting up at the sight of me.

'Hi, sweetie,' I say, smiling. 'How are you?'

'I'm great!' she answers, and she does indeed look great. A cute kid turned beautiful, long hair, slender waist, the dewy skin of the blessed. I can remember us playing Adventure on Care Bear Island, a game I'd made up which involved piggyback rides and some happy screaming. Time flies.

'Is Doral-Anne here?' I ask.

Her smile drops, and she gives me a mock grimace. 'Um, sure. Hang on.' She goes into the storeroom, says something and scuttles back. 'She'll be right out, Lucy.'

'Thanks, Pretty Perry,' I say. She smiles sweetly, making my heart tug.

Then Doral-Anne emerges. At the sight of me, her *Isn't Starbucks just the best thing to happen to Planet Earth* expression drops.

'How's Ethan feeling?' she asks, and I have to say, that's not what I expected her to say. *Fuck you,* maybe, or *Get out.* Not something polite.

'He's doing okay, Doral-Anne,' I say. 'Do you have a second?'

She scowls at Perry, who's obviously listening. 'Why?'

'I'd like to talk to you.'

With a grunt of disgust and a matching eye roll, she gestures toward the storeroom. 'Fine. Come on out back.'

448

Visions of fifth grade dance in my head, Doral-Anne tripping me at least once each recess, causing my knees to be constantly covered in scabs. Nonetheless, I follow her through the back, past the bags of coffee and mountains of cups, until we emerge into the parking lot.

'So what do you want?' she asks, her expression once again the familiar sneer.

'I just wanted to say thanks for looking after Nicky Mirabelli when Ethan was hit,' I say. 'That was great of you.'

Doral-Anne's head jerks back in surprise.

'You were a lot more help than I was,' I acknowledge. 'I just stood there like a fern. Until I fainted, that is.'

'And started screaming,' she adds, apparently unable to resist the dig.

My face flushes. 'Yup.'

She stares at me a minute longer. 'Did you want something else?'

I take a deep breath and look at her steadily. 'I also wanted to say I was sorry about slapping you. That wasn't real mature of me. I apologize.'

She looks down. 'Yeah, well, you had reason.' She glances at me from beneath her too-long bangs. 'I guess it freaked you out hearing about Jimmy and me being an item, huh?'

'It did,' I admit.

She sucks in her left cheek and makes a

slurping noise. 'Well. Thanks for stopping by. I was wondering how Ethan was. Glad he's okay.'

I remember the bag under my arm. 'Here. A peace offering.' I hand her the bread.

'It's still warm,' she says, looking down at it with a little smile. The healing power of bread.

A thought occurs to me, so freakish and wrong that I can't believe I came up with it. Even beyond that, I can't believe what I say next. 'Doral-Anne, Bunny's is looking for a baker to take over the bread for me. Ethan mentioned that this Starbucks might close. Whether it does or not, Bunny's is expanding, doing the whole coffee and pastry thing. But we're also selling bread to NatureMade. The hours are early, but you'd have more time with your kids after school.'

Her mouth falls open. With one hand, she pushes her bangs off her face. 'Lang, are you offering me a job?'

'I guess I am. If you're interested, give me a call. Or drop by Bunny's. The sooner you could start, the better.'

CHAPTER THIRTY-THREE

On Friday evening, I'm staring into my cupboard, realizing I have to make dinner, when my phone rings.

'Sweetheart, it's Marie,' says my mother-in-law.

'Hi!' I say. 'How are you?'

'Well, honey, we're having a little party here tonight. At the restaurant, and of course we want you here.'

I open my mouth to respond, but she keeps talking.

'It's our anniversary, see? Forty years, we haven't killed each other, that's worth celebrating, right? So Gianni, he says to me, "Call the kids, we'll have a party. Call everyone." So I've been on the phone all day, and your mother and aunts are coming, and that nice sister of yours, too, and Ethan of course, it would be good to see him before he starts gallivanting all over the world, and of course Parker and Nicky will be there, the more the merrier. Of course, I tried you before, but you were out, and machines, who knows if you'd get the message or not, so—'

'Marie,' I interrupt. 'I'm so sorry. I'd love to come, but I . . . I just can't tonight.' *I just don't want to see Ethan.* And God knows, he probably doesn't want to see me.

451

Marie is silent for a beat or two. 'Oh, sweetheart, I'm so sorry. I should've thought . . . Of course you don't want to come to the party. I'm so insensitive.'

'No, no,' I say, a guilty heat in my face. 'I just . . . I have plans.'

Her voice rises to operatic levels. 'I ask my son's widow to a party celebrating a long marriage. So stupid! Oh, I hate myself!'

'Marie, please! No, seriously, I would come . . . I just have plans.' *And it wasn't your first son I was thinking of, by the way.*

'Are you . . . seeing someone?' Marie asks, a suspiciously hopeful note in her voice.

I take a slow, long breath. 'Um . . . I might be. It's a little early.' My nails dig into my palm. 'Um, remember that man who looked a little bit like Jimmy? The one who works for the supermarket chain?'

'Him? Oh, he seemed so nice, honey! And a *little* like Jimmy! I thought I was seeing things!' She pauses, and there's a sniff at the other end of the line. 'It was good to see him. I know he's not Jimmy, but it felt good, anyway.'

I swallow. 'I know what you mean.'

Five minutes later I manage to end the conversation and hang up gently. There's the pebble. I try relaxing my throat muscles, let my jaw hang open and stick out my tongue. No improvement.

So it's true. Ethan's taking that other job.

452

Good. That's good. I clamp down on the part of my soul that wants to scream in protest. *Can't have everything. Let him go, Lucy.*

With a sigh I pull a jar of store-bought spaghetti sauce from the cupboard. Tonight is my second date with Jimmy Lite—really should drop that nickname—and though I'm the one who suggested we stay in for dinner, I regret that now. Inviting a man to your place . . . there's a certain expectation in that type of date, an expectation I have no intention of honoring. But the idea of going out to a restaurant was a little . . . tiring. Matt asked me to his place, but I preferred to stay on my own turf and reversed the invitation. I can handle Matt, and being involved with someone will help me get over Ethan. Again my heart protests, and again I shut it up. Can't have everything.

So here I am, in yoga pants and a sweatshirt, not pulling out any stops whatsoever. *Stop acting so pathetic,* I urge my lazy-ass self. *Matt's perfectly nice. This is what you wanted.* And so, obedient to a fault, I obey my orders, empty the sauce into a pan and pull out some breaded chicken patties to thaw. Not my best effort, but hey. Matt took me to a chain restaurant called the Olive Grove. He's not a true Italian. Not like the Mirabellis.

An hour later I'm showered, changed and waiting. When the knock comes, I take a deep breath and go open the front door.

'Hi,' Jimmy Li—Matt says. He holds a bouquet of flowers and a bottle of wine.

'Hi,' I say, and to show that I'm completely normal, I stand on tiptoe and kiss his cheek. 'Pretty flowers.'

'What a great place!' he exclaims, stepping in. 'Wow. Have you lived here long?'

It dawns on me that with Matt—or any other guy I meet—I'm going to have to tell them everything. Every scab, every bump.

'About five years. Right after Jimmy died,' I say. 'My brother-in-law found it for me. Jimmy and I had just bought a house, and . . . well. Would you like some wine?' I head for the kitchen without waiting for an answer.

'Sure,' he says. 'Lucy?'

I turn around and look at him. 'Yeah?'

'I think you're really brave.' He smiles.

I suppress a sigh . . . so brave, that's me. 'Thank you.'

As I uncork a bottle, I picture myself with Matt DeSalvo. Maybe we wouldn't live in Mackerly, but somewhere close. He's polite and charming. I could even come to love him in that nice, arranged-marriage way. I take a slug of wine to try to loosen the tightness in my throat, then tell him about my sister and Emma, even whip out a couple pictures.

'Listen, Matt,' I say carefully, putting Emma's picture back on the fridge. 'Um . . . about our date. I didn't want you to think, um . . . well, that because I invited you here, it

454

meant . . .' I pull a face, hoping that a grimace will express *there's no way in hell you're sleeping with me.*

'Oh, no! No, that's fine,' Matt says. 'No, it's nice. Taking things slow. Sure, Lucy. I'm on the same page.'

I've always hated that expression.

I serve dinner (cloth napkins and everything, I'm really trying).

'How is everything?' I ask after I've swallowed a few bites of the unremarkable meal.

'It's excellent,' Matt say, grinning. 'You're a wonderful cook.'

'Thanks,' I answer.

After dinner, Matt helps clear. 'Want dessert?' I ask, glancing in the fridge. Pear tarts with fresh nutmeg and lemon rind, whiskey reduction with a cranberry and ginger confit in the middle, pretty as rubies. Last night was our final pastry class. I didn't make these especially for Matt—they were just available.

'Um, maybe in a little while?' Matt suggests, patting his stomach. 'I'm a little full. Can't eat like I used to.'

'Right,' I say, closing the door. 'Well, come in the living room. Have a seat.'

Matt takes our wineglasses and brings them in. He hands me my glass, which I drain, then wanders over to the TV, glancing at my movie collection. The Bourne trilogy. *Die Hard. The*

Hunt for Red October. Body of Lies. 'You like guy movies,' he comments, sounding happily surprised.

'Yes, I do,' I agree.

Then he sets his wineglass down and looks at another case. 'Your wedding?' he says, holding it up.

I jolt upright. 'Yes.' God, hadn't I put that away? Rather daunting, dating a woman who's recently been watching movies of her wedding ...

Matt looks at it carefully. 'May 17, Lucy and Jimmy.' He looks over at me. 'Can we watch it? I'd love to see what he was like.'

My mouth drops open. 'Um ...'

'You know, if we're going to be, ah, closer, it'd be good to ... know him a little.'

My breath is a little shaky. 'Sure.' I stand up, walk over to the DVD player and put the disk in. Matt sits on the couch and pats the seat next to him. A little hesitantly, I sit next to him. He slings his arm around my shoulders and kisses my cheek.

'Thank you for letting me see this,' he murmurs.

I look up at his nice face, and his eyes are kind and smiling. 'You seem like a good guy, Matt DeSalvo,' I say, resisting the urge to wipe my cheek.

'I am,' he answers with a wink.

The DVD starts. And there I am, awfully young. Twenty-four years old, an age burned

456

into my soul as the last year I was the old me. Corinne, in college at the time, flutters around me, pulling my hair back and twisting it, chattering about how nervous she was.

I look so happy. I *was* so happy, after all. There's Mom, ageless and beautiful, her apricot-colored, floor-length dress sleek and lovely.

'She's still so gorgeous,' Matt says.

'You're right,' I murmur.

On screen, I get into the car, waving at the camera guy, and the scene fades to black. And then there's Jimmy, standing at the altar with Ethan, both laughing. Ethan . . . God. He looks like a teenager, skinny and cute as anything. He *doesn't* look like a man about to watch the woman he loves marry someone else. My shoulders relax a little.

And I see something else . . . Matt and Jimmy only have a superficial resemblance. Jimmy had a spark, a life force that just flowed out from his big heart. Matt doesn't have that. I'm sure he has other qualities, but he's . . . well, he's no Jimmy.

'Let's fast-forward,' I suggest and hit the appropriate button. 'Wedding ceremonies are all the same, after all.' The DVD skips ahead jerkily, and I hit Stop when I see the tent.

'Ah, here we go. My cousin Stevie. Very entertaining, this.'

During the cocktail hour, Stevie had done a pretty fair impression of John Travolta gyrating to 'You Should Be Dancing' from *Saturday Night Fever.* Right up until he accidentally smacked a waiter carrying a tray of champagne.

'Oops,' Matt laughs. He starts playing with my hair, his eyes on the screen.

There are Anne and Laura, the classiest relatives, kissing me, patting Jimmy's cheek. Iris, Rose and Mom . . . Gianni and Marie, my father-in-law looking proud and handsome, more hair and less fat than he now has. Marie dieted for months to get into the dress she bought, a pale green chiffon nightmare.

Matt's fingers are now caressing my neck. It feels . . . okay. Nice, I guess. I try not to tense. On screen, oh. Here we are, one of my favorite parts. Ethan's speech.

'He's a great-looking guy,' Matt says.

'Ethan?' I say, not taking my eyes off the TV.

'I meant Jimmy.'

I look up at Matt. 'Right. Yes, he was.' I turn my attention back to the screen. The DJ taps the mic and says, 'Ladies and gentlemen, if we could have your attention, the brother of the groom, Ethan Mirabelli, would like to say a few words.'

Something flips in my stomach, and I lean forward a little.

'You okay?' Matt asks.

'Oh, sure.'

On screen, Ethan takes the mic. 'I'm a little

458

nervous,' he says sheepishly. 'I want to do a really good job here, because Jimmy says if I do, I can be best man at his next wedding, too.' The camera pans to the laughing crowd, me smacking Jimmy on the shoulder, Jimmy grinning. 'Seriously, I've always looked up to my big brother—usually because he had me pinned . . .'

We'd loved it. Ethan was perfect that day, full of mirth and mischief. 'Jimmy, you're a lucky, lucky man . . . you leave here with a wife who's gorgeous and funny, someone who radiates warmth and love wherever she goes. And Lucy, you leave here today with . . . well . . . at least you can keep the pretty dress.'

'Funny,' Matt murmurs. I barely hear him.

I've watched this video hundreds of times. And always in the past, I'd stared at Jimmy's beautiful face, the love he had for me so evident on that happy, happy day.

But today—for the first time—I'm watching Ethan, not Jimmy. *Staring* at Ethan. Twenty-two years old when we got married. A consummate best man, charming, funny, kind. He describes how Jimmy used to hook a fish, then hand the pole to Ethan and let him reel in the catch. How Jimmy would make him hamburgers when their parents went out, because Marie viewed hamburgers as pig food. And then he tells how Jimmy and I met.

'I was there the first time these two laid eyes on each other,' he says, turning to Jimmy and me. You can't see our faces, as the camera stays on Ethan, but we were snuggled together, loving every word. 'One look, and that was that,' Ethan says gently. 'They fell in love, they've stayed in love, and today they promised to love each other for the rest of their lives.'

An audible sigh rises from the wedding guests.

'Ladies and gentlemen, boys and girls, please stand and raise your glasses. Enduring love, healthy children, long, happy life together. To Lucy and Jimmy.'

'To Lucy and Jimmy,' the crowd echoes.

'Sweet,' Matt says.

But I'm frozen. Unable to breathe or speak. Because there it is.

As Ethan finishes, the camera cuts to Jimmy and me . . . we kiss, and then Jimmy gets up and hugs Ethan, who thumps him on the back and grins.

I fumble for the remote and hit Rewind.

'What's the matter?' Matt asks.

'Shh!' I hiss. I rewind too far, then fast forward. There. There it is again. Then Jimmy and I are kissing . . .

I rewind again, more slowly this time, and watch again.

Ethan, who gave that beautiful, funny, touching speech, raises his glass, and toasts us. And for one second, just before the camera cuts over to us, I see it.

460

His job was done. He'd made the toast, and all the attention was back on Jimmy and me, and for one second, the mask dropped, and there it was. The love. The loneliness of watching the one you love choose someone else.

And I see something else, too. As Jimmy looks up at his brother, his face has a momentary flash of apology. Of guilt. And then gratitude.

Ethan loved me. And Jimmy knew it.

Check the toast.

Oh, my God. My body breaks into gooseflesh.

'Lucy?' Matt says.

'Um . . .' I breathe, still not looking away from the screen, 'Matt, you need to go.'

'Are you okay?' he asks, leaning forward.

'I'm . . . I'm in love with him,' I say, jerking my chin toward the screen.

'Jimmy?'

'Ethan,' I say. My breath rattles in my throat. 'I have to go. So you need to leave. I'm really sorry. I can't . . . it's just . . . I need to go.'

'You—you don't want to go out with me?' Matt asks slowly.

'Um . . . I'm sorry. No. I really have to go now.' I leap off the couch, grab his coat from the closet and shove it into his hands. 'Okay. Bye. Really sorry.' I jerk open the door and usher him out.

'Well. I don't know what to say.' Matt frowns, stepping slowly into the hall and turning to face me. 'This is quite a surprise. I thought—'

'Sorry. Bye,' I say, closing the door in his face.

Once more, I stand in front of the TV and watch Ethan's face fall. It only lasts maybe a second and a half, but it says everything.

Three things are clear. One, Jimmy wasn't perfect. He knew how Ethan felt, and it didn't stop him.

And, two, Jimmy had loved me with all his heart.

And three . . . oh, number three. Ethan loved me, too. He still does. Or he did, before I ground it out of him.

Fat Mikey is crouched on the kitchen counter, eating the remains of the crappy chicken. 'I have to go,' I call to him. *Check the toast.* My hands are shaking so hard I can barely open my closet, but I manage, shove my feet in some shoes and race out the door. I pound upstairs, but God, it takes so long, my feet feel like they're made of lead. I explode onto the fifth floor and run down the hall to Ethan's, bang on his door. 'Eth! Ethan, open up!' I yell. 'Ethan, it's me!'

And my God, I love him, too. The idea of living without him suddenly seems breathtakingly stupid and absolutely unbearable. Ethan Mirabelli is, simply put, the best person I know. The only one I want.

Oh, dang it, the party, the Mirabellis' anniversary party. Down the stairs I run, swinging around each landing, jumping the last few steps. Then I burst into the foyer and onto the street. The air is sharp and cold, and my breath fogs the air.

Without another thought, I run across the street, into Ellington Park.

Toward the cemetery.

It's time.

CHAPTER THIRTY-FOUR

There are a lot of ways to lose someone.

As I run down the path, my mind is in the past, on Ethan's steady friendship, the comfort of his company in those dark days . . . months . . . years after Jimmy died, when all my other friends felt I should really have moved on by now. When we started sleeping together, his irreverence toward the two of us . . . it was the only way I could handle being with him. Even when I pulled away and started to look for someone else, he let me. Ethan has always done . . . and been . . . exactly what I needed at the time. And he asked for nothing in return.

I can't lose him.

My feet pound on the gravel in a steady

beat. I remember when I told him a couple of months ago that I wanted to get married, have kids, that look on his face . . . he thought, for one second there, that I'd meant him. Instead I told him we needed to break up . . . ah, damn it. Damn *me,* for being so cruel and blind. In the hospital, when he was bleeding and bruised, I did it again. And then just two days ago, he told me everything, and all I did was cling to my image of St. Jimmy.

There's the cemetery, the stone pillars that flank the entrance offering a perpetual and somehow sinister welcome. Almost against my will, I slow to a walk, my breath coming in gasps. My hands are blocks of ice.

The trees are bare, the branches jagged black fingers scraping the November sky. Thin clouds hide the moon, but it's there somewhere, offering a feeble, diffuse light that makes the headstones seem to glow.

I'm surprised at how familiar the cemetery is to me. Over there, under the big beech tree with the wide spread of branches, lies my uncle Pete, who rolled out of his coffin twenty-six years ago. Not far away, right in the middle of one of these rows, is Uncle Larry, Rose's husband. My mother's parents . . . I can see their headstone from here.

Instead of racing, my heart seems to slow as I approach Jimmy's grave. Despite having been to it only once, I know exactly where it is. My knees are weak, but they haven't buckled.

464

My steps grow slower, my eyes skimming over the other names without really seeing them. I'm only here for one tonight.

There it is.

I stop.

Giacomo 'Jimmy' Mirabelli, age 27.
Beloved husband, son and brother.

And you were, Jimmy. You were beloved. By all of us, but maybe especially by Ethan. Ethan, who forgave you.

My legs are shaking badly, but I force myself to take a step. And another. Another. Then I crouch down and put my hand on the cold granite of Jimmy's headstone.

'Hi, honey,' I whisper, and my eyes flood with hot tears. For a few minutes, I just let them slip down my cold cheeks. The wind rustles the branches as I stare at my husband's grave.

'I'm here, Jimmy,' I say, my face scrunching. 'I'm sorry it took so long.'

Memories flood my heart—Jimmy's amazing eyes, his huge laugh, the strength of his arms. He was my world, and my future. He was the love of my life. My old life.

'Guess what?' I whisper. 'I checked the toast, Jimmy. I saw his face. And yours, too, honey. I know everything.'

I smooth my hand over the cold granite of his gravestone, trace the 'J' of his name. Far

465

away, an owl calls, and the fallen leaves rustle in the breeze.

It's so hard to say goodbye to someone you love, even if he's already gone. Even if he left you first. For so long, I've been Jimmy's widow. Maybe being widowed again wasn't the thing I so feared. Maybe it was being *more* than a widow. Maybe it was this exact moment.

'I'll always love you, Jimmy,' I whisper. 'But I need to leave you now.'

Those words burn like a brand pressed to my heart. I bow my head and let the wave of sorrow wash over me . . . and recede. And after a minute, the pain in my heart fades, too.

I press a kiss to my fingers and hold them against his name. I'll come back, I know I will, but it will be different. Tonight is the goodbye that has been so long in coming. I whisper one more thing, the last thing I need to say to my dead husband.

'Thank you, Jimmy. I loved every minute of my life with you.'

Then I stand up and wipe my eyes. I take a breath of the cold, clean, salty air, and another.

It's time to go now, to a new life. To Ethan, the man who has loved me with absolute selflessness for all this time. Who loved me enough to watch me marry someone else, who stood at my side through the darkest moments of my life, who has been waiting for me for so long. The man I've loved for years, though I've never admitted it till now.

I take one more look at Jimmy's grave. My breath catches.

At the base of the headstone, something glints in the faint light of the hidden moon.

A dime.

With a shaky laugh, I pick it up and kiss it. Despite the cold November night, the dime is warm, and I know, somehow, that this is the last one I'll ever find. 'Thank you, Jimmy,' I whisper. The pebble in my throat is gone. At last, it's gone.

Then I tuck the dime in my pocket and start running, my legs strong now, the air pure and cold. Five rows, six, nine. There's my father's grave, but tonight, I can't stop. 'Wish me luck, Daddy!' I call. *Good luck, Princess,* I imagine him saying.

And then I'm out of the cemetery, onto the town green, onto Main Street where Ethan was hit. I'm flying now, my feet hardly seeming to touch the ground as they carry me farther away from Jimmy, from my past, and closer to the one I hope will be my future, and I run faster still.

*   *   *

Gianni's is mobbed. Clearly the Mirabellis' anniversary party has mushroomed into a huge event. Every table is occupied, and more people stand near the bar, drinks in hands, laughing, talking as Tony Bennett's mellow voice drifts out from the speakers. Waiters buzz around with trays of food, bottles of wine, baskets of bread. There's my mom at a table with Corinne and Chris. Mom holds Emma and tilts her head up to say something to Captain Bob, who stands there, clearly waiting to be asked to join them.

I don't see Ethan anywhere. I'm still panting from the run, adrenaline zinging through my joints.

'Hi, Wucy!'

I look down 'Nicky! Hi, sweetie,' I say. 'Where's your daddy?'

'Guess what?'

'Can I guess later? I need your daddy.'

'I can burp whenever I want to,' my nephew informs me, then demonstrates his new talent.

'Is Daddy here?' I ask a little more loudly.

'Lucy? What are you doing here? I thought you weren't coming.' It's Parker, emerging from the ladies' room.

'Is Ethan here? I need to . . . I have to see him.' I stand on tiptoe to see the far side of the restaurant, but I can't find Ethan.

'Why?' she says, her eyes narrowing.

'Is he here? Please, Parker.'

Something in her expression softens. 'Is everything okay?' she asks, putting her hand on my arm. I nod. 'He's in the kitchen. Gianni hired some bozo to cook tonight, and he

468

didn't show, so Ethan took over.'

'Really?' I say. To the best of my knowledge, Ethan has never cooked for his folks . . . for me, sure. Yet another sign I'd so willfully ignored these many years.

Wishing I'd come in through the kitchen door—sure would've made life easier—I twist my way through the sea of tables, waving, saying hi, trying not to look like a desperate animal. It is, after all, the Mirabellis' anniversary dinner.

'Yo, Luce,' says Stevie. 'You look like something the cat dragged in.'

'Hi, Stevie,' I say distantly, not stopping. I'm almost to the kitchen, then nearly get run over by a waiter. As I lurch out of the way, I bump into Marie.

'Oh, hello, sweetheart!' she exclaims. 'You came after all! Did you hear the news?' My mother-in-law puts a plump hand on my arm.

'Hi, Marie, I just need to find Ethan and—'

'He's taking over the restaurant! Isn't it wonderful? He's in the kitchen now, and he told Gianni he wants to buy the restaurant!'

My mouth falls open. 'Ethan wants to work here?'

'Yes!'

'Are you serious?' I ask. 'What about Atlanta? You said—'

'He wants to be near the little guy,' Gianni says, joining us. 'Hi, sweetheart.'

'Hi, Gianni,' I say. 'So Ethan's staying? I—'

'Told me he doesn't want a partner, either—he wants to own it outright, the little bastard,' Gianni growls, though he seems rather proud, too. 'Already he's telling me it won't be the same. Says he'll change it from the name on down, if you can believe it.'

'Oh, hush, you old fart,' Marie says. 'Your son is buying you out. Stop complaining.'

'He's buying the restaurant?' I ask.

'Are you all right, honey? Where's that nice young man you're seeing?' Marie seems to notice my disheveled state for the first time. 'Your shoes don't match, dear.'

'I have to talk to Ethan,' I say.

'He's awfully busy,' Gianni grumbles. 'Not doing too badly in there, but still. Service is a little behind.'

I dodge a busboy, then shove my way through the swinging doors of the kitchen.

'Service for table ten,' calls Micki, one of the long-time sous chefs, sliding a dish onto the heating rack. 'Hurry up, Louie!'

'I need two bisques and a mozz special,' the waiter answers, grabbing the plates and placing them on a tray. 'Chef, any more veal?'

'I got three more,' Ethan says. His back is to me as he stands at the stove. He flips something, gives another frying pan a shake, adds some liquid, causing flames to leap up. The smells of garlic and meat are rich in the air.

It's like an amped-up circus in here. Two

people are on salads and prep, someone's checking something in the oven, and Ethan is stirring, flipping, banging. The dishwasher's up to his elbows in suds, the cousin's husband's brother is pulling something out of the freezer, and there are about ten things cooking on the stove at once. Servers buzz in and out, calling out orders, barely noticing me, just milling around me like I'm a sack of potatoes.

Not the best time, in other words.

But.

I can't exactly stop now.

'Ethan?' I say. He doesn't hear me.

'Get me two crème brûlées and two tiramisus,' barks Kelly, the waitress who went to school with me. She does a double-take when she sees me. 'Hi, Lucy.'

'Table four wants to know if you can do a chicken marsala without the wine,' Louie says.

'Sure. It won't be marsala, but sure,' Ethan says, tossing some chicken into a frying pan.

'Ethan?' I say again.

He hears me this time, and his head snaps around. 'Lucy. What's up?'

'Do you have a minute?'

An eyebrow raises. 'Not really.'

'Chef, table five says their meat's not cooked enough,' a waiter says, shoving a plate across the warming area. Ethan looks at it. 'It's medium rare,' he says to the server.

'Tell me about it. He wants it darker,' the

471

waiter grunts in disgust. Ethan nods and shoves the plate back under the broiler.

'Ethan, I really need to talk to you,' I say loudly. Micki gives me a look and continues chopping parsley.

'Lucy, there are fifty people out there who want to eat, and my dad's chef didn't show,' he says, sliding some vegetables from a frying pan onto two plates. He adds a veal chop onto one, chicken onto another, then grabs a bowl and fills it with ravioli, covering the pasta with sauce. Micki grabs the plates, sprinkles them with parsley, adds the garnish and puts the plates on the warmer. 'Service for table eight!' she yells.

Ethan's back at the stove, and more flames flare briefly. 'Carlo, can you get some more filet from the cooler?' he calls.

'You betcha, Chef,' Carlo calls.

I sigh. Okay, it's a bad time. Whatever momentum carried me here is gone, I guess. I turn to leave, shoving my hands in my pockets.

There's the dime.

I look back at Ethan. Since he's working at the twelve-burner stove, he's standing right in front of Jimmy's shrine. As ever, the candles are lit, Jimmy's bandana neatly folded, his picture smiling out at me.

It's time. I don't care how busy the restaurant is. It's time, damn it. 'Ethan?' I say again. He doesn't answer. 'Eth?' Nothing. 'Ethan, I need to talk to you now!' I yell.

472

Ethan gives me a quick glare, then says, 'Micki, can you take over for one minute? The steak and eggplant are together, and the chicken parm and ravioli go to six.'

'Got it, Chef,' she says, grabbing a pan.

Ethan maneuvers past the young man ladling soup into bowls and the girl who's on salads.

'What, Lucy?' he demands.

'Can we go outside for a second?' I ask.

'No!' he barks, running a hand through his hair. He takes a breath, then folds his arms in front of him. 'Tell what's so important it can't wait.'

I swallow—still no pebble, just nerves this time, and it occurs to me I haven't planned what to say. 'I—um, I went to the cemetery today. Tonight. To see Jimmy's grave.' I bite my lip.

'That's great, Lucy,' Ethan says, glancing over to the soup boy.

'Chef, we got a shellfish allergy on that eggplant parm, so be extra careful,' Kelly calls, grabbing a plate from the warmer.

Then Marie comes into the kitchen. 'Ethan, sweetheart, Mrs. Gianelli wants to know if you can make her that pasta with the—'

'Excuse me, I'm talking here!' I say sharply, looking at my mother-in-law. My breath is coming fast and hard, and suddenly, Ethan's attention is laser sharp.

'So talk,' Marie says, clearly wounded.

473

'Pretend I'm not here. I'm just the mother.'

I look back at Ethan, who's grown very still. 'Ethan . . . on the wedding video . . . when you gave your speech. Um . . . I saw it, Ethan.'

He blinks. 'Saw what?' His voice is very low.

Another waiter bursts into the kitchen. 'Chef, we need two more filets and one tilapia special,' he says.

Ethan doesn't answer. Doesn't even turn. 'Saw what, Lucy?'

It's beginning to dawn on the kitchen staff that Something's Happening. Though the food still cooks and the knives still cut, it's suddenly much quieter in here.

'I saw that . . .' My voice drops to a whisper. 'Jimmy knew.'

Something flickers in Ethan's eyes.

'I'm sorry,' I say. 'Ethan, I'm so sorry for everything I put you through. Tonight when I was watching the toast—'

Gianni bursts through kitchen door. 'Where the hell's the veal, Ethan?' he barks. 'Table four's been waiting for fifteen—'

'Quiet!' Marie orders. 'She's talking here.'

'Was that Lucy I saw?' My own mother's head pops in, and when she sees that yes, it is indeed her offspring, she comes in, still holding Emma. 'I thought you had a date. Honey, you're a mess! Your shoes don't even match.'

'I need to say something to Ethan,' I say loudly. 'If I could have a minute.'

The staff stops pretending to work. All activity ceases, and all eyes are on Ethan and me.

Ethan is watching. And waiting. I decide he doesn't have to wait anymore.

'I checked the toast, Ethan,' I say, and my breath catches in a half sob.

'The toast?' he asks. Clearly it wasn't what he was looking for.

'Forget the toast,' I babble, my mouth wobbling. 'Ethan, I love you. And I'm so sorry it took me so long to figure it out, but I've loved you for a long, long time, and I'm sorry about Jimmy and Jimmy Lite and when you were in the hospital and I said I couldn't . . .' I force myself to stop the projectile words that are flying out of me and just look at him.

His mouth is open the slightest bit. Other than that, he hasn't moved a muscle.

'You're my best friend, Ethan,' I say in a wobbling voice. 'I love you, and I'm sorry. Please give me another chance. Please say you will.'

He doesn't say a word. Emma coos. The party noises are a dull roar in the background, but Ethan doesn't say anything.

I'm too late. I put him through too much for too long, and he's done with me, and honestly, I can't blame him, but my heart closes in on itself like a hard fist.

Then Ethan opens his arms, and before I realize I've moved, I'm in them, my face

475

against his neck, my arms around him, holding on as hard as I can.

'Jesus,' Gianni grumbles.

'Shush, idiot,' Marie says, but I barely hear. Ethan's heart thuds against mine, and his arms are shaking, his head bent, his beard scratchy against my neck, and this is it, the place I belong.

'Well, if we were running behind an hour ago, we're totally fucked now,' someone says, and everyone laughs.

But Ethan's breath isn't quite steady, and it takes me a second to realize why.

He's crying.

'Thank you for waiting for me,' I whisper, and he nods.

'Chef, this is a beautiful moment and all,' Micki says, 'but I have no idea what to do with this salmon.'

'Shut up, you,' Gianni tells her. 'Here. I'll fix it. Can't you see he's busy?'

Ethan kisses my neck, then lifts his head to kiss me on the mouth, and God, it feels so right and so perfect that my heart nearly bursts with joy. And then the kitchen staff starts clapping, and Ethan smiles against my lips, pulls back and wipes his eyes with the heels of his hands.

'I love you so much,' I say, my own tears slipping down my cheeks.

'Took you long enough to figure out,' he says with a little laugh. He kisses me again, then hugs me against him, and I've missed him so much, love him so much that I think I might levitate from happiness.

I see that my mother is crying, beautifully of course. 'Good for you, Lucy,' she says, patting Emma's back. 'Good for you, honey.'

Marie sobs a bit more emphatically, and at the stove, Gianni smiles as he cooks.

Then I look back at Ethan. 'You will marry me, won't you?' I whisper.

His eyes fill again. 'I will,' he says, grinning that curling smile that always got to me. The smile that lit up those lonely, sad times, that reminded me there was still something left to laugh about, that brought me happiness when I thought happiness was gone.

The smile of the man I love.

EPILOGUE

Like so many times in the past, I struggle through the kitchen door of Gianni's, a large bakery box in my hands. Oops. It's not Gianni's anymore. I have to get used to the new name. Instead of bread, however, my box today holds five dozen cannoli, and not just any cannoli, let me tell you. The shells are light as air, crisp to the point of shattering, the creamy filling a smooth, dense vanilla with just a hint of lemon and almond. Classic, but stunning nonetheless. Cannoli weren't originally on the dessert menu, but Gianni nearly had a coronary, so Ethan conceded.

Ethan has indeed changed just about everything here. Tonight the restaurant reopens, and for the past few months workers and decorators and suppliers have made the place look like Grand Central. The staff is due in at four-thirty, and it's only three now. Ethan will be here soon . . . he just called me a few minutes ago and said he was on his way back from Providence, where he was buying some last-minute ingredients. For now, I'm the only one here.

I set the box down on the counter and go into the main part of the restaurant. Gone are the frescoes of gondoliers and the Colosseum, gone is the rough stucco that coated the walls.

479

Instead, the whole restaurant is painted a pale peach. Bright watercolor abstracts hang on the walls. There's a glassed-in fireplace in the middle of the restaurant, cheerful red gerbera daisies on each table, candles waiting to be lit. The whole effect is lovely . . . upscale, welcoming and happy.

Ah-ha! On the front desk is a stack of menus. Ethan's been working on them for months, but he wouldn't let me see the final draft. I pick up an embossed leather menu and trace the new name. It was the one thing that really bothered Gianni, the name change, but even he couldn't object to what Ethan picked out.

I open the menu and study the selections and their little descriptions, recognizing many as dishes Ethan cooked for me over the years . . . veal scaloppini, eggplant rolatini, chicken Luciano. Under 'Pasta,' I see something that brings a lump to my throat. *Penne Giacomo, featuring tender, homemade pasta with Jimmy's famous sauce, a perfect blend of tomatoes, cream and vodka.*

I hear the sound of the kitchen door opening and go back into the kitchen. Ethan's here, two brown grocery bags in his arms. 'Hey there, Chef,' I say. 'You nervous?'

My husband looks up, and his face breaks into a smile. 'Hey,' he says, setting the groceries down. 'How about a kiss, gorgeous?'

'You don't have to ask twice,' I answer,

complying with pleasure. I doubt the thrill of kissing Ethan will ever fade.

We got married on Valentine's Day—just a little ceremony at St. Bonaventure's, where I became Lucy Mirabelli once again. Nicky and Gianni were the best men, Corinne and Parker were my attendants. The Black Widows and Marie wept copiously, Stevie behaved himself for the most part, Emma gurgled and cooed throughout the ceremony, which was family only. Well, a few other folks came, too. Jorge. Captain Bob. Mr. Dombrowski. Grinelda.

Bunny's is thriving with the new bread arrangement, and Doral-Anne seems to be working out. We might not ever be best buddies, but she's a good worker, and the Black Widows respect that. Next door, my little café is doing pretty well. Of course, I supply desserts to the restaurant, which did mean I had to hire Marie as my part-time assistant, and if working with my mother-in-law makes me feel like a martyred saint sometimes, it's fine. Besides, I'll need help when the baby comes. We're having a girl . . . thinking about Francesca, which was supposed to have been Ethan's name, or maybe Violet to renew the tradition of flower names in my family.

'Oh, look at the two of them!' comes Rose's sweet voice as the Black Widows traipse through the back door. 'They're kissing! How nice!'

Iris tugs her shirt. 'My Pete and I were like that,' she announces. 'Always with the affection. It makes for a happy marriage.'

'Hello, dear. Should you be standing?' Mom says, eyeing my belly suspiciously. I've just begun to show, but since the moment my mother found out I was pregnant, she's been quite the overprotective nursemaid.

'I'll ask Anne,' Iris says. 'In my day, we were treated like queens when we were expecting. None of this working till the water breaks.' She frowns, looking me up and down. 'If you need bed rest, you need bed rest, Lucy. No point in having—' she pauses for dramatic effect '—the premature labor.'

'Go sit down, you beautiful creatures.' Ethan grins, holding open the door to the dining room. Friday-night cocktail hour has moved to the new place, and if it's a little early in the afternoon, I assure you the Black Widows don't care. 'I'll be right in. Make yourselves comfortable at the bar.'

'Oh, Ethan, it's so stylish!' Rose chirps. 'I feel like I'm on *Sex in the City*!'

With the Black Widows chattering away at the bar, it's just Ethan and me again. I take his hand and look around the kitchen. Though the main part of the restaurant has changed, the kitchen remains mostly the same. I squeeze my husband's hand, then slide my arms around his lean waist.

'I think Jimmy would be really proud of you, Ethan,' I tell him.

His eyes get a little wet. 'Thank you.' He clears his throat, then looks over toward the big stove. My gaze follows.

The shrine is gone—Ethan came home one night and without a word gave me the red bandanna, kissed me and left me alone. After holding the red cloth for a while, I placed a gentle kiss on it, then folded it carefully, put it in a box and tucked it in the back of my closet. I haven't opened the box since. But it's nice to know it's there.

In place of the shrine, several pictures are now showcased—the two I gave Ethan of him and Jimmy on the beach and on our wedding day. But there's another one, too, one I'd found only when packing up my apartment to move in with Ethan, one I hadn't seen in years.

It's a picture of Jimmy, Ethan and me, taken at my graduation from college. I wore a pink dress, Ethan had on sunglasses, and the sun shone on Jimmy's blond hair. We were all laughing as we stood three in a row, me in the middle, my arms around the handsome Mirabelli boys.

'I love that picture,' Ethan says, and his voice is a little husky.

'And I love you,' I say with my whole heart.

He kisses me then, one hand going to my tummy where our baby grows, his mouth perfect on mine.

There's so much love in the world. Sadness, too, and heartbreak, but more than those, there are love and happiness and miracles of joy. My father may have died when I was only eight years old, but his love has followed me my whole life. Jimmy died far too young, but the love we had for each other is like a pearl in my soul, untainted and pure and now, at last, tucked away to make room for Ethan.

And Ethan . . . Ethan is my gift. My present and my future and the man I'll love till the day I die.

Before my emotions—and hormones—get the best of me, I break off the kiss and wipe my eyes. 'Get in there,' I say, fixing his collar. 'You know the Black Widows don't like to wait for their drinks.'

'After you,' he says, going over to open the door. I precede him into the beautiful dining room and smile at my elders.

'There you are, Ethan,' Rose coos.

'Thought you got lost back there,' grumbles Iris.

'Leave them alone,' Mom clucks, adjusting her short skirt. 'They're in love.'

Ethan smiles at me, then looks at his first three customers. 'Ladies,' he says, raising an eyebrow. 'Mirabelli's is now open for business.'